W9-DJE-889

BLOODSTREAM

Books by P. M. Carlson

*Published by POCKET BOOKS

BLOODSTREAM

P. M. Carlson

POCKET BOOKS

New York   London   Toronto   Sydney   Tokyo   Singapore

This book is a work of fiction. Names, characters, places and incidents are products of the author's imagination or are used fictitiously. Any resemblance to actual events or locales or persons, living or dead, is entirely coincidental.

POCKET BOOKS, a division of Simon & Schuster Inc.
1230 Avenue of the Americas, New York, NY 10020

Library of Congress Cataloging-in-Publication Data
Carlson, P. M.
    Bloodstream / P. M. Carlson.
        p.   cm.
    ISBN 0-671-76977-4
    I. Title.
PS3553.A7328B57   1995
813'.54—dc20   94-45899
                                                          CIP

First Pocket Books hardcover printing June 1995

10 9 8 7 6 5 4 3 2 1

POCKET and colophon are registered trademarks of
Simon & Schuster Inc.

Printed in the U.S.A.

For Marvin

I want to thank Robert Knightly, David Linzee, Kay Williams, Joanna Wolper, the ghoulishly delightful Arsenic and Oolong Society, and especially Major David W. Toumey—Chief Deputy, Monroe County Sheriff's Department—for sharing their insight and expertise. Errors remaining are mine and not theirs.

Five miles meandering with a mazy motion
Through wood and dale the sacred river ran,
Then reached the caverns measureless to man,
And sank in tumult to a lifeless ocean:
And 'mid this tumult Kubla heard from far
Ancestral voices prophesying war!
—Samuel Taylor Coleridge, "Kubla Khan"

Attending to myth also means remembering that a myth is first of all a story, and that stories are told in order to be retold.
—Christine Downing, *The Long Journey Home*

THE FIRST SATURDAY IN JULY

1

IT WAS THE RIVER THAT UNCOVERED THE BONES.
Like most rivers in Indiana, the East Fork of the White
River begins quietly in the glacier-smoothed eastern uplands
that drain into small, slow creeks and rivulets. The stream-
lets crawl south and west, joining other gurgly young creeks,
turning frisky as they hit the rough, eroded limestone country of southern Indiana. They play hide-and-seek, dancing
into underground caverns and out again as springs, jitter-
bugging down limestone waterfalls, linking themselves into
a rambunctious conga line that bounces into Nichols County
as a full-fledged river. Now it swings around bends in a
switchy-hipped hula, slows to a sultry bump-and-grind in
the wider valleys downstream, and joins the West Fork to
head out for the Wabash, the Ohio, the Mississippi, and
the sea.

But in a wet July the river is not so kindly. Drunk and
swollen with rain, it is no longer smooth and pale, but
brown as old blood and wild as a bull. It thrashes wide in
its bed, roars at its banks, rips down trees and bridges, and
churns up dark and hidden things to the shivering light
of day.

*   *   *

3

"Nichols County Sheriff," said Deputy Foley, answering the phone.

Across the room, Deputy Marty Hopkins pushed a brown curl from her forehead. Rainy weather always frizzed her hair. Depressed her too. Though the depression might have come from a number of things. Maybe it was her upcoming vacation. She and her daughter Chrissie were going to drive to Memphis to see Chrissie's dad, and maybe he and Marty could figure out if there was any future to their so-called marriage. Or maybe it was that the man she'd had to shoot last year was back in her nightmares, still reaching out his dead, accusing hand.

Or maybe it was this sorry case. She moved the cursor to the next slot on the form she was filling out. Fourth of July—okay, you expected some brawls, some domestic calls, some auto mishaps involving patriots too full of whiskey. But it was sad to get a call from Dawn Arnold, on her way to work at the Unisex Salon early on the fifth, saying she'd glimpsed something laying down out in the middle of Milo Road. Marty had taken the call and sure enough, there had been a small, limp body right where the center line would be if Milo Road had a center line. She'd stopped the cruiser across both lanes, radioed in her position, turned on the flashing light, and gotten out to check. It was a boy, younger than her daughter, maybe eight or so. Skinny, brown hair. Breathing, all right—she could smell alcohol. And then there'd been a whisper of a sound, a footstep, and she looked to see another boy rushing her, a bottle upraised. She rolled aside and he struck the pavement with it. "Stop!" she shouted, scrambling to her feet.

But the boy was in a fury. "Leave him alone! You horseturd! You cunt!" He was about twelve. He still held the broken bottle by the neck. Marty focused on it, caught his arm, twisted it behind him, and brought him down. She was trying to pry the bottle from his fingers when she saw the third and largest boy climbing toward her from the roadside ditch. He held a stick. Shit. She hung on to the hand that held the broken bottle, kept her knee in the kid's back, and drew her gun on the big one. "Todd Seifert! You're on probation! One more step and you're back in the lockup!"

Todd stopped. Didn't have a lot of smarts but at seventeen he knew she meant it. Besides, a pickup was coming around the bend, slowing at the sight of her cruiser. Todd said, "Hey, Damon don't mean nothing. He's just trying to help his brother."

Damon was still yelling, "Cunt! Turd!" He smelled of alcohol too.

Marty gambled on Todd's desire for self-preservation and holstered her gun. She handcuffed Damon and said, "Todd, your little brother should go to the hospital. Why didn't you take him?"

"Car's busted. They don't have parts."

"Okay, I'll take him." She took her knee from Damon's back and shoved him into the backseat. "Damon, I'm taking you too. You're drunk." She closed the door and turned to Todd. "Where the hell's your mama?"

Todd waved a dismissive hand up the road. The Seiferts' run-down farm was somewhere along there, she remembered. "She passed out just like the squirt there."

"Well, when she wakes up tell her where they are." Marty heaved the youngest boy into the front seat and took off for the hospital, siren wailing. Damon cursed and kicked on the barricade behind her the whole trip. She'd be mad at the world too if her life was as rotten as Damon's.

All the same, she thought now as she filled in the next line of the report, he could've killed her.

Across the office, Foley cupped his hand over the receiver. "Lady out on State Eight-sixty wants to talk to you, babe. Sounds like she comes from back East."

"Back East?" Marty shrugged her ignorance and picked up her phone. "Deputy Hopkins," she said into it.

"Deputy Hopkins, this is Karen Brewster. I live at Rivendell Farm, remember? You talked to me last year, when you were looking for that missing girl."

"Oh, yeah." Karen Brewster's voice was back-East, all right, and an image formed around it in Marty's memory: a sturdy, boyish woman, brown braids, work boots, ear-

nestly explaining organic farming while she picked cater-
pillars off her plants. "So what can I do for you today,
Mrs. Brewster?"

"Well, you seemed to be an understanding person," said
the voice. "We have a sort of problem here. I'm sure it will
turn out to be nothing, but of course the mother and sister
are quite upset."

Marty had scribbled "Karen Brewster" and drawn a fuzzy
caterpillar in her notebook. Shouldn't doodle, she thought
guiltily—sometimes they looked at her notes in court. She
flipped to a clean page and asked, "Whose mother and sister, Mrs. Brewster?"

"Johnny Donato's. They live in New Concord, just up the
river from us. Some teenagers from an Arizona church
school have been camping here this summer, and Johnny
and Rosie come over sometimes to see the other kids. Well,
Johnny didn't come home last night. His sister is shaken up,
and Mrs. Donato is very worried too. I'm sure he'll turn up
soon, but I said I'd call you."

"How old is Johnny?"

"Fourteen."

"Mrs. Donato is with you now?" Marty guessed.

"Yes. She came to ask if I'd seen him, and now she's too
upset to talk, so I called."

"Tell her it's okay if she cries. I just want to ask her a
couple things."

She heard Karen Brewster explaining, and then a choked,
snuffly voice came on. "Yes?"

"Mrs. Donato? You're Johnny's mother?"

"He's a good boy! He doesn't run off!" There was a sob.

"Yes, ma'am." Across the room Foley stood, stretched, and
limped across to the supply cabinet. When Marty had first
come to work he'd had a pinup of some Playmate on the
supply cabinet door. Sheriff Cochran had made him move it,
but Foley had taped it to the inside of the same door. Now,
as he always did when the sheriff was out of the office, he
cocked the door carefully to give Marty a full view of the rosy
object of his lust. Marty couldn't decide if he was trying to
prove he outranked her somehow, or if he was trying to shock

her, or if he was afraid she'd think he was less than a man if he didn't flaunt it. Guys were afraid of the darnedest things. She ignored the cabinet door by concentrating on her notepad and said into the receiver, "When did you see him last?"

"At lunch yesterday. But Rosie—that's his sister—she came here to Miz Brewster's with him." She snuffled again. "They wanted to visit the kids at the church school camp."

"So when did Rosie see him last?"

"She doesn't remember exactly. About two-fifteen."

"Okay. Can you describe Johnny?"

"He's a good boy! Tall for his age, handsome."

Should have asked Karen Brewster, or anybody more objective than his mom. Marty, who thought her own daughter was darn good-looking, asked patiently, "What color hair?"

"Black hair, just like his dad's. And nice brown eyes."

"What was he wearing?"

"Wearing? Blue jeans, T-shirt. One of those Lily Pistols T-shirts. That rock group, you know?"

"Yeah. I've seen those shirts around. Black, with a white skull and flower design front and back, right?"

"That's it, yes!"

Marty looked out the window. It was raining again, just like yesterday. "Did he have a slicker or anything?"

"No, he won't wear it in the summer. I tell him to but he won't."

"Yes, ma'am. Can I talk to Rosie?"

But Rosie, after a timid hello, burst into sobs when asked about her brother.

Marty was suddenly tired of the Seifert boys' hopeless problems, of Foley's pinup, of the musty air in this office. Even rain was better. And this little Rosie needed help. She sounded about ten, the age of Marty's daughter. Chrissie had been crying some this summer too, not for a missing brother but for her long-gone dad. "Tell you what," Marty said, breaking into Mrs. Donato's apologies for Rosie and reaching for her Stetson. Already she felt less depressed. Helping people was why she'd taken this job. "Stay there at Mrs. Brewster's, okay? I'll be right out to take a look."

* * *

Sheriff Wes Cochran was out politicking.

The campaign didn't start officially until Labor Day, and his opponent, Chuck Pierce, a disgruntled deputy from old Sheriff Cowgill's day, was running mostly because he'd been laid off from the carpet cleaner's where he'd been working and hadn't found another job yet. Even so, when a member of the County Council asked you to talk about crime fighting at the Kiwanis lunch, you damn well went and talked about crime fighting.

Wes sat beaming benevolently at his meat loaf and gravy—scarcely touched, Doc Hendricks's orders, damn him—while Chuck Pierce gave his version of crime fighting in the county. Chuck was a sandy-haired guy in his fifties who rambled on about his long-ago experiences in a monotone. He was answering questions now, and his audience was beginning to fidget.

"One more question, folks," announced Dub Walters, emceeing for the Kiwanis. He was a vigorous, pink-faced man with a beer belly. Wes considered it a personal insult from fate that he and not Walters had been the first to be hospitalized with a heart attack. Well, he'd outlast him yet. Walters spent most of his time in cars, running Dub Walters Ford-Plymouth and moonlighting in real estate, and didn't get much exercise. Unless you counted toting money to the bank.

Dub was also on the County Council. Wes didn't report to the Council officially, but since it appropriated his salary and funds for the jail, it was only good sense to stay on the right side of Council members. He and Dub managed to work together without too many glitches.

"Thanks, Chuck," Walters said as the ex-deputy ran down. "Now we'll hear from another expert on local crime. Most of you know Sheriff Wes Cochran."

Wes shoved himself to his feet and took the podium. It took a minute to adjust the mike, because at six-four he was a good six inches taller than Dub Walters or Chuck Pierce. He hitched up his trousers and began, "Chuck gave you some background on crime hereabouts. I'll just bring you up to date. Shouldn't take us long."

Someone shouted "Hurray!" and there was a general

chuckle. Wes joined in and then went on, "Okay. Now, we just heard some stories about the good old days. But we all know those days are gone. Today we've got all those problems and a bunch more. You all use computers in your businesses, right? So do we. Here's a f'r instance. Suppose you get a call at six A.M. from a friend who says, 'The plate-glass window in your business got broken last night!' "

Rapt silence. That got 'em where they lived. Wes figured he'd already won this little campaign skirmish.

2

ROSIE DONATO WAS NO LONGER WAILING, BUT STOOD tense as a stretched rubber band next to her mother. Marty took off her Stetson and dropped to one knee to try to put the girl more at ease. "Rosie, honey, what was Johnny doing the last time you saw him yesterday?"

"Running. Toward the barn. It was raining." Rosie had dark eyes and hair, like Chrissie's but straighter. She was Chrissie's age, ten, and everything about her said scared.

"Do you remember what time it was, honey?"

Rosie gave a taut little shrug. Mrs. Donato had long, light blond hair, an ample, sagging bust, and worry lines around her tired, dark eyes. She stroked her daughter's dark hair. "She and Johnny left after lunch, and Rosie was home by three, soaking wet from the rain. Johnny's bike is broken, so they walked."

Karen Brewster, wearing a white camp shirt with an un-buttoned dark vest, her brown braids pulled back from her long, pale face, was sitting at a square oak table with fat turned legs. The Brewster kitchen had plain pine cabinets, a huge black woodburning stove with a shiny pipe that disappeared through the ceiling, a Hoosier cabinet with enameled work surface and roll-up door, bunches of herbs hanging from the rafters. Marty had seen old Nichols County hardscrabble farm kitchens that were similar, except this one was well-repaired and polished. These people were a lot better off than most farmers in these parts. Karen said, "Sometimes Johnny tags along when the church school group meets for choir practice about four, but he wasn't there yesterday."

Marty turned back to Rosie. "Was anybody in the barn? Maybe he was meeting somebody."

A swift shake of the dark hair. Too swift? But Marty didn't want to press a terrified child until there was real evidence that Johnny was in trouble. She asked, "Well, right before he started for the barn, was he talking to anyone?"

"Russ."

"He's one of the campers from the Arizona church?"

Rosie nodded. Then her eyes shifted to something behind Marty. Marty turned to see a man coming in the kitchen door, a big overweight man, jowly, with a small dark mustache. His hair was plastered down by the rain. He wore a bow tie, a dark open raincoat, and a white shirt that stretched tight over his belly, and carried a battered briefcase and a long black umbrella with a steel tip. Karen Brewster jumped up from the kitchen table, greeted him with a kiss, and introduced him as her husband, Drew Brewster. Marty wondered why they looked so familiar, Drew's round mustached face next to Karen's long one, until suddenly she realized that it was old movies. Give the Brewsters bowler hats and they'd look just like Laurel and Hardy.

Marty stood up, holding her Stetson. "Pleased to meet you."

"Same here." He waggled his plump fingers at her across the room. "You're sheriff's department, right? What's going on?"

Karen said, "Mrs. Donato's son didn't come home last night, and she came over to ask if I'd seen him. Well, I hadn't, so I called Deputy Hopkins to help."

"Mrs. Donato's son?" Drew put his briefcase and um-

brella under the coats that hung on a row of wooden pegs
by the door and unclipped his tie. "Why are you asking
about him here?"

Marty said, "His sister last saw him here. I'd like to talk
to the people who were around here yesterday afternoon."

Drew Brewster's dark eyes peered at her sharply from his
pudgy face. "Will this be in the papers?"

A strange question. Marty said, "Up to the paper. They
probably won't make much of it if he turns up soon."

"Yes, of course. Well, let's go look for him." He retrieved
his steel-tipped umbrella and opened the door briskly.

Marty said, "Mrs. Donato, I want you and Rosie to go on
home now in case Johnny calls or shows up. Call the sheriff's department at this number if he does, okay? And try
to find a photo of him. I'll stop by your place for it in half
an hour or so."

"Yeah. Okay." Mrs. Donato nodded, tied a plastic rain
bonnet over her pale hair, and took Rosie's hooded slicker
from a peg by the door.

Marty said to Rosie, "If you remember anything else, ask
your mama to call that same number. Okay?"

Rosie nodded, big-eyed and silent.

"Okay, let's go," said Drew Brewster impatiently, holding
the door.

They went out. Marty was glad to see that the rain had
stopped. Mrs. Donato and her daughter headed for a six-
year-old Chevy. Marty called, "Rosie, is that the barn Johnny
was headed for?"

Rosie looked at the big old-fashioned red barn and gave
a curt nod before slamming the Chevy door.

Karen was speaking quietly to Drew. When Marty approached the Brewsters, Drew tugged on his ear and said,
"I guess that sounded a little funny, when I asked about
the newspapers. Maybe I should tell you what we're doing
here at Rivendell Farm."

"I'd sure appreciate that, Mr. Brewster."

Drew said, "I teach English at Indiana University. But
Karen and I have had another dream for a long time, of a
community living here in harmony with nature and with all

humankind. Great books, great music, history, environmental science, all taught by people who are living the lives they are praising." He swept his furled umbrella in a half-circle, taking in the rainwashed landscape: the red barn, the rambling gray-painted house, the meadow that rolled down to a tangle of cottonwoods and maples along the riverbank, the flourishing vegetable garden. A few chickens pecked in the barnyard, a few small red-and-white cows grazed in the far corner of the meadow, and two brown goats watched the humans with bright, curious eyes. Drew continued, "This farm by the river is the ideal place. Have you noticed how many poets speak of rivers as holy places? Coleridge writes of the sacred river in which one hears ancestral voices. Dylan Thomas speaks of the sabbath ringing in the holy streams. And Eliot says the river is a god, a sullen god that makes us remember what we'd rather forget."

His wife gazed at him adoringly, and Marty realized that Karen wasn't seeing a middle-aged, overweight professor, but a romantic, poetic soul. Marty said, "I don't see the connection with Johnny Donato."

"Well, we've had a real stroke of luck this year," the big professor explained. "We've found an investor with some capital, and we're going to become a historic farm and village. It's exactly what people around here need, educational and good for the economy. So we don't want our investor to get nervous about the project just because a local kid runs away from home."

"Who's the investor?" Marty asked.

"A man named Bob Rueger owns some old houses in New Concord. He lives in Arizona now but he got his start here in Nichols County."

"His name is familiar," Marty said. "What does he do?"

"Well, he's a developer. Malls and things." Drew sounded almost embarrassed.

"Oh, yeah." The name clicked into place. "Rockland Mall, right?"

"That's right. He's worked in Illinois too, and of course in Arizona. But he has a special interest in this place. Seems his great-great-grandfather was Father Johann Rueger, who founded the New Concord community. You know the history of New Concord?"

"I heard those old buildings were built by some German religious nuts."

Drew laughed. "One way to put it. They were a splinter group from the Harmonists, the group that settled over on the Wabash. Father Rueger tried to set up the same kind of community here. They were hard workers, and their community was more than self-sufficient."

The three of them were walking toward the barn, the rust-colored mud underfoot sucking at their shoes. Karen said, "This place used to be one of the New Concord community farms. Our buildings are all later, of course, because the New Concord folks didn't build many farmhouses. They generally lived in town and walked out to tend the fields. Our neighbor Nysa Strand is one of Father Rueger's descendants, and she wrote a little history I can send you. It's interesting."

"Okay," said Marty. "So this Bob Rueger's great-great-grandfather built New Concord, and now Rueger wants to restore it."

"Right," said Drew. "You know, like the pioneer village in Spring Mill Park."

"Oh, yeah." Marty remembered visiting the pioneer village three or four years ago with Chrissie and Brad, Brad acting out the pioneer for them, casting them as farmhands, wealthy capitalists, oxen, whatever he needed. "Now, Chrissie, you're a bag of grist on the way to the grist mill!" he'd said, swinging a delighted seven-year-old Chrissie to his shoulder. "What's grist, Daddy?" she asked. "It's what goes to the grist mill! Now hush. Bags of grist can't talk." They could sure giggle, though, Marty remembered.

Drew was still talking, his Ollie Hardy mustache twitching. "Rueger approached us in January to buy a section of the farm to add to his historic restoration. Of course we didn't want to sell, but Karen and I realized immediately that this could be the perfect addition to our community. So we told Rueger we wouldn't sell, but we'd work with him."

"That's right!" Karen broke in, her long face bright with

enthusiasm. "We'd have the historic farm here, and New Concord right next door."

They'd paused outside the barn door. Drew said, "Rueger was very receptive to the idea. He said that his daughter's church group was looking for a summer project this year, and we could let them camp on our farm while they worked on restoring a couple of the houses he owned in New Concord."

Karen shook her head sadly. "It's really a shame, what people have done to those fine old buildings. So full of history, but they've reroofed them with asphalt shingles, or even tin. And aluminum siding—they've got no taste! The lovely old windows replaced by modern storm windows . . ."

Taste wasn't the problem; money was. Marty knew, because she'd put asphalt shingles on her own old house after she'd seen the price of the alternatives. She said only, "I guess Mr. Rueger is rich enough to do things the old way."

"Yes. Though he's a good businessman too." Drew seemed to be lecturing them. "How do we know? First, he talked down our price for the campground. Second, aside from our neighbor Nysa Strand as local historian, and her sister as livestock manager, he's got free help. Professor Stewart from Ball State volunteered to be technical advisor for the restoration, because he'll get publications from it. The Arizona church pays the youth minister who supervises the campers. And the kids who do the work actually pay their own way."

"Okay. So these campers on your farm work on Rueger's projects. And Johnny Donato came to see them?"

Karen nodded. "Yes. Some of the local New Concord families are suspicious of this kind of project, so we take every opportunity to explain the benefits, and we welcome their kids. Johnny and some of his friends are fascinated by the project, or maybe just by the fact that a lot of the campers are very well-off. New Concord is not a wealthy community."

Not wealthy? Shoot, there was an understatement. A rich kid from out of state might look very glamorous to New

Concord kids. Might be one reason their parents were suspicious of this project.

Drew said, "Anyway, you can see why we don't want negative publicity."

"I understand. Let's look at the barn."

The big door was cracked open. They stepped into a dusty darkness slashed by silvery blades of light from a high shuttered window. The barn smelled of sweet hay and fresh manure. The only sounds were the buzz of flies and a thin, irregular beeping. Marty's eyes struggled with the gloom and at last found the source of the beeps: a laptop computer set on a bench between two blond kids in their mid-teens, a boy and a girl.

Karen Brewster said, "Deputy Hopkins, this is Melissa Rueger and Kenny Ettinger. They're here from Arizona."

There were hi's all around. Kenny had an easy grin and wire-rimmed aviators and asked, "Are you a sheriff?"

"A deputy, yeah. We're looking for a New Concord kid named Johnny Donato."

"Johnny! What's he done?"

"Nothing. Just didn't go home last night. Have you seen him?"

Melissa shook her head. "Not today," Kenny said. "He wasn't around the dig this morning."

Drew asked, "Aren't you two supposed to be there today?"

"Yeah. But Justin—I mean Reverend Jeffries—sent a couple of us back to help Vicki with the animals. Naturally Melissa volunteered."

The girl was thin, wearing jeans and a cantaloupe-colored T-shirt. An expensive watch was all that indicated she was Bob Rueger's daughter. She said, "Well, I like animals."

"Better than people," Kenny teased, and Melissa giggled self-consciously. He indicated the laptop on the bench. "I was trying to teach her how to run that. But she won't concentrate. I think she'd rather pet the cows."

Melissa giggled again. "C'mon, they're special cows."

"How are they special?" Marty asked.

Kenny said, "They're mutts."

"C'mon, Kenny!" Melissa exclaimed. "They're mixed breed, just like the pioneer cows. They got them from that historic farm. And they're tougher than modern breeds. Vicki can explain. She'll be back any minute."

"Uh, hi, I am back," said a woman's shy voice. Marty turned to see a tall, slope-shouldered silhouette stepping through the door from the daylight outside. The long-legged young woman was in jeans, work shoes, and navy-blue camp shirt. Marty couldn't see her shadowed features well, but the brightness behind her made a halo of her golden blond curls. She noticed Marty's uniform and bobbed her head timidly. "Sorry, am I interrupting?" She stepped back.

"No, no, you can help." From her basketball days Marty recognized in Vicki the slouch of a girl who'd grown too tall, the embarrassed rounding of shoulders and ducking of head in constant apology to the world for reaching such an unattractive height. Basketball had been the salvation of some of those girls, the one place their height was an advantage and source of pride, the one place they could feel comfortable in their own bodies. Marty, a mere five-seven and on her freshman team for her quickness and grit, had seen some of her tall friends transformed by the game. This shy young woman could use a dose of basketball, she thought. But right now there was Johnny Donato to find. Marty said, "I'm Deputy Hopkins."

"I'm Vicki Strand. Uh, is it about the cattle? Ours are supposed to be the kind that the New Concord settlers had." She seemed to gain confidence as she spoke. Maybe cattle could be a salvation just like basketball. "See, the modern beef and dairy breeds die if you don't feed them in the winter. These don't give as much meat or milk, but they can survive on very skimpy rations. And food was scarce in pioneer days."

Marty nodded. "Actually I'm here because there's a boy missing, a New Concord boy named Johnny Donato. He was last seen around three-thirty yesterday, heading for this barn. Did you see him?"

"I wasn't around the barn then," Vicki said slowly.

"Did any of you see him yesterday?"

Kenny said, "Yeah. I didn't talk to him yesterday, but I think he was around. I was showing my computer to some people, and later we had choir practice."

"Wasn't he talking to Russ?" Melissa asked. "When it started raining?"

"Yeah. Yeah, I think he was."

"Where can I find Russ?" Marty asked.

Kenny said, "He's probably over at the dig with Justin—with Reverend Jeffries, if you want to talk to him."

"I will, thanks. Miz Strand? Can you add anything?"

"No, but—no." The golden head ducked apologetically. "We have a sick cow. Yesterday I had to track her down and give her medicine before the songs."

Why had she hesitated? "Did you see anyone else?" Marty asked sharply.

Too sharply. Vicki Strand stammered, "No. Only people going to the songs. Not close enough to really see."

"Well, if you think of anything, let me know." Marty made a mental note to come back to her if Johnny didn't show up. "Is it okay if I look around the barn?"

Vicki showed her the stalls and even took her up the ladder into the hot, sweet-scented hayloft. There was no sign of Johnny. They rejoined the others below. Marty asked, "Now, you say New Concord is walking distance?"

Drew Brewster, his paunch protruding, was sitting on the little bench. "About twenty minutes by the river path," he said, and Kenny nodded.

"I think I'll hike over there and talk to Russ. Okay if I leave the cruiser here?"

"Sure. But it's only a five-minute drive," Drew said.

"Yeah. But Johnny would have walked along the river, right?"

Drew heaved himself to his feet. "I'll show you the path."

17

3

THE REVEREND JUSTIN JEFFRIES PUSHED THE BLADE of his shovel into the sticky New Concord turf.

Justin was thirty-four years old, with a chin that reminded his wife Bonnie of Paul Newman, thinning brown hair, a dimple when he smiled, and a no-holds-barred volleyball game that kept his body trim and his teenaged charges full of admiration. His son JayJay was not so impressed, but at five JayJay was only beginning to understand the rules. He hadn't yet developed the killer instinct he'd need to be a top volleyball player. Bonnie, who was quiet but not humorless, teased Justin that it wasn't really Christian to want to win so much. "Hey, c'mon, gotta keep in shape in case they decide to launch another Crusade," he told her. Secretly he believed Jesus Himself would have enjoyed a good game of volleyball against, say, the moneylenders. So he continued to shout at the referee and spike the ball viciously whenever he could, emerging from the games feeling triumphant, a little guilty, and very sweaty.

He was sweaty right now, but it wasn't the volleyball, it was the humidity. After Arizona's desert air, it was hard to get used to the moistness of this place. If he had to do archeology, the nice dry Holy Land would have suited him better. But this was where God had sent him, and he knew he should trust that God had good reasons.

Justin lifted his shovelful of turf. This section of the yard had probably held the back wall of a vanished lean-to shed from old Father Rueger's day. You could still see nail holes where the shed roof had been attached to the old house on this lot, one of the properties Melissa Rueger's father owned.

He turned the sod over as he laid it aside. Nothing exciting. So far today he'd found three buttons and two coins. Inspection had shown them to be fairly recent, from the 1920s, but they still had to be recorded on Professor Stewart's forms. Justin had two of the kids working on the forms and the rest searching a measured, previously excavated pit with small tools.

"Hey, Justin, there's nothing in this muck," complained Russ, who was working in the pit with a trowel.

Justin straightened, glad for an excuse to rest his back. "That's information too. When we're done Professor Stewart will have a three-dimensional record of what's on this site."

"Who wants a three-dimensional record of muck?" Russ grumbled.

"Tell you what," said Justin, realizing that reason would not prevail just now. "If you guys finish that layer of muck today, I'll climb up on that shed roof, right over there, and sing 'Michael Row the Boat Ashore.' "

"From the roof?" sparkle-eyed Ellie exclaimed, scandalized.

"From the roof."

"All the verses?" Russ challenged him.

"All I know," Justin hedged, and the group got back to work, arguing about how many verses there were.

They were soon interrupted again. A woman in a sheriff's uniform was hiking toward them from the riverside path. She stopped on the wet grass and said, "Hi. I'm Deputy Hopkins."

All work halted as the teenagers gawked at the uniform. Justin brushed off his hand and held it out. "I'm Justin Jeffries. More or less in charge of this zoo."

Under the hat brim her gray eyes were direct and intelligent. She shook his hand warmly. "Glad to meet you, Reverend Jeffries."

"So what can we do for you today?"

"Well, I'm looking for a kid who lives right here in New Concord. His name is Johnny Donato. Have any of you seen him today?"

All of them shook their heads. Justin tried to remember

when he'd last seen Johnny, a dark-haired youth of fourteen who tried to hide his hero worship of the older teens by bragging, teasing the cows, and showing off his cassette collection. He did hang around, here at the dig and at the farm projects. The kids tolerated him usually.

Ellie said, "I saw Johnny hanging around yesterday afternoon while we were working in the Brewsters' garden."

"Did any of you talk to him?" asked Deputy Hopkins.

"Just a few words," Ellie said.

"I said hello," Justin remembered. "Just when they arrived. Johnny and his kid sister."

"I talked to him about his new cassette just before he left." Russ stood up in the pit, looking up at Deputy Hopkins with lively interest. "Did Johnny, like, do something wrong?"

There was a murmur of speculation from the others. Deputy Hopkins said, "Okay, let me talk to all three of you. You first," she said to Russ. "What's your name?"

"Russ Pratt."

"Okay, Russ, I'll borrow you for a couple of minutes, if that's okay." The gray eyes turned to Justin.

"Sure. Of course," Justin said as Russ hopped eagerly from the pit. Deputy Hopkins walked him a few steps away to the corner of the house and began to write notes in her pad as they spoke in low voices. She interviewed Ellie next, then turned to Justin.

"Reverend Jeffries? Could I talk to you next?"

"Sure." Justin took the shovel with him and leaned it against the corner of the house, then turned to the deputy. She was about thirty, he decided. Tanned skin and laugh lines, together with the uniform, gave her a tough, outdoorsy look that was softened by a gentle mouth, brown curls under the Stetson, and tiny silver studs in her earlobes. He wondered if she liked to play volleyball.

He also wondered why God had sent a deputy sheriff into his life.

"I'm trying to find out if Johnny told anyone where he was going yesterday," Deputy Hopkins said.

"Not me. He and his sister came by while we were weeding the Brewsters' garden. The sister—what's her name,

Rose?—anyway, she helped weed for a while until she got tired. Johnny never came into the garden, just hung on the fence and talked to Russ."

"Russ told me Johnny was just bragging about being the first to get a new rock cassette." She had read this from her notes, and now the sharp gray eyes met his again. "Russ said it was by Lily Pistols, and he couldn't remember any more. Do you have any ideas, sir?"

"No, but the bragging sounds like Johnny. He's always trying to impress the kids here. But he's younger than they are, and, well, it's hard to impress this group with materialistic things."

"You mean they're all spiritual?" she asked with a skeptical glance at his charges. "Or you mean they have plenty of cassettes themselves?"

"Cassettes, CDs, video games—you name it." Justin grinned ruefully. "Except for the ministers, our church in Arizona is wealthy. The pastor and I try to get them to focus on the spiritual, of course."

"Of course, sir. So you're saying Johnny is younger and poorer and can't win any points?"

"Oh, they tolerate him. They're good kids, really, and right after we arrived we had a focus session on the people who live here, how to love our neighbors, and so forth. Drew Brewster tells us there's some suspicion of this project by the locals, so we try to be friendly."

"So Professor Brewster represents the locals?" A twinkle of amusement in her intelligent eyes made him realize how different from most Hoosiers the big professor was. "Does anyone in your Arizona group seem to be a special friend of Johnny's?"

"Not really. The kids aren't rude, but they don't invite him to join in. Not that we're set up to include others, really. But you're asking about friends—he does have local friends too. There's a kid named George." Justin remembered tall, dark-haired Johnny showing up a couple of times with a shorter, tanned boy. "George had this flame-red mountain bike."

"Yeah, Russ mentioned George Muller. Do you know of others?"

"No, he's the only one I've seen with Johnny."

"I'll ask his family. Do you have any ideas about where he might have gone after he left your group?"

"No, I'm afraid not."

"A couple of people said he was running toward the barn."

"Could be he was getting out of the rain. That's also the way to the riverside path to New Concord."

"Yeah, the way I just came. Was anyone in the barn yesterday?"

"I don't think so. Vicki Strand usually does the morning milking and cleans it, then brings back the cattle for the evening milking about five-thirty, after choir practice. None of my guys were in there yesterday afternoon—I kind of keep track."

"Must be a job and a half," she said. "One other thing. Can you tell me what this digging is for? Professor Brewster said it was historic, about the first New Concord people."

"Sure, I can give you a general idea. It was a religious community, you probably know, and we're trying to find out more about how they lived. So we're looking for remnants of their way of life. We've found pieces of old wagons, birchbark canoes, flat-bottom boats. Here we're hunting smaller things, tools and so forth. This is a good area, around a shed that used to be attached to this house. People will kick broken tools next to a wall, maybe expect to fix them, and never get back to them—you know."

She grinned suddenly. "Yeah. Back of my garage is the same way."

"And over the years dust and leaves cover them, and soon they're buried in what the kids call muck. We're uncovering things, slowly and carefully."

"Anything interesting?"

"Yeah. Professor Stewart from Ball State has already taken a few things to his department for safekeeping. But—come on, I'll show you." He indicated the back door, and she followed him into the dark, barren back room. Justin opened the shutters. Gray light illuminated the once-whitewashed walls, the plank floor, the trestle table where they'd arranged the artifacts.

"Funny old tools," she said. "And rusty."

"Yeah, but effective in their day. Here's a saw we found this morning. A corn cutter. A broken apple parer. Lots of nails."

"Nasty-looking scythe."

"Yeah. There's a hand axe around somewhere. Blade on one side, hammer on the other." He looked around. "Maybe Professor Stewart took it. Here's a regular hammer. Over there, that tangled stuff is a horse harness, what's left of it. That thing used to be a wooden milking pail. Here's a cook pot."

"You can get a real feel for how they lived." Deputy Hopkins touched the milking pail. "Interesting. What's in the cardboard box?"

"Modern things we found. Nails, coins, a Mickey Mouse toy."

"You keep this place locked?"

"When we leave, yes. And Professor Stewart removes anything that might be of real value and takes it to the university. An old rifle—things like that."

"I see. Well, please let us know if you or any of the kids think of anything more. Chances are Johnny will turn up soon on his own, but until he does, we want to keep our ears open."

4

THE DONATOS' HOUSE WAS HARD TO RECOGNIZE AS one of the old ones because someone had added a solid 1920s porch, a flimsy 1950s carport, and peach-pink paint with white trim. It was one of the better-kept homes in New Concord, with flourishing flower beds of marigolds and nasturtiums, bright even on this cloudy day. The paint job was much more recent than the one on Marty's own house. It was so damn hard to save enough for a paint job, what with Brad's little financial emergencies and the hot water heater giving up the ghost. She'd been trying to save ever since that short vacation trip to New York last July, a whole year ago, and so far she only had two hundred and eight dollars. Shoot—another reason to feel depressed.

She pressed the Donatos' buzzer. A yapping little brown terrier with a kinky tail came leaping to the screen door, followed by Mrs. Donato. Her tired face was lined with anxiety, her eyes red-rimmed, her blond hair droopy. "Did you find him?" she asked even before turning the knob.

"I'm sorry, not yet," Marty said.

"Oh, I'm so worried he fell in a sinkhole somewhere! Or even in the river!"

Marty had spent some nasty hours in a sinkhole herself. But Johnny knew the area. He'd be careful. Wouldn't he? She said gently, "I came to get a photo of him."

"Yes, yes, I have one for you. Come in, please. Chuckles, get down!"

The dog subsided and Marty followed Mrs. Donato into a dim living room filled with provincial-style furniture, antique white with strawberry-colored upholstery. Matching drapes on the south-facing windows shut out the daylight.

"You want some coffee? It's made already."

"No, that's okay, Mrs. Donato." She could smell the coffee, heavy in the humid air. "Thanks anyway. Where's the photo?"

"Here." Mrs. Donato handed her a five-by-seven color portrait of a youngster with curly black hair and a stiff smile, wearing a blue blazer and necktie. A school portrait, probably retouched. In real life the kid was wearing a T-shirt, no doubt dirty by now, and instead of the airbrushed bloom on this portrait's cheeks he probably had zits. Still, it would be useful if it came time to widen the investigation.

"Thanks," Marty said. "Is Mr. Donato at work?"

"He'll be back soon. He only works half days on Saturday. He's real mad at Johnny." Mrs. Donato's eyes filled. "He thinks he stayed the night with one of his friends. But I called them all last night, Miz Hopkins. He's not there!"

Marty pulled out her pad. "Okay. I wonder if you could give me their names and addresses?"

Marty wrote them down and closed her book. Mrs. Donato blurted, "Do you want to see his room?"

The boy hadn't been missing very long, Marty told herself, and she should get on to other cases. But she knew how she'd feel if Chrissie went missing, and said, "Sure, let's take a look."

Johnny's room was neater than Chrissie's. There was an NFL bedspread and matching curtains, royal blue with the various team insignias scattered brightly across them. The walls were lighter blue, and Johnny had taped up two big posters, one of Madonna and the other of Lily Pistols, four young men in black with long hair, hostile expressions, bone necklaces, and earrings. An old chest of drawers painted royal blue to match the bedspread contained T-shirts, jeans, underwear, and comics and motorcycle magazines on top. A metal stand held a boom-box radio and tape player, and an array of cassettes were stored underneath.

In the closet a Sunday suit on a hanger shared space with plastic baskets of well-worn sports equipment—basketball, football, helmet, hockey stick, fishing rods, BB gun. A couple of cardboard boxes in the corner held a collection of little warrior toys and autos, and one old teddy bear, its tan plush pilled and threadbare. Little-boy toys, not yet thrown away.

The terrier Chuckles had come along to watch from the doorway, and as Marty closed the closet door she became aware of a pair of dark eyes peering at her from behind him. It was Rosie, still stiff and quiet, clinging to the dog. Marty wished she could help Rosie, wished she could find Rosie's much-loved bragging brother. She asked, "Does he have some of his things with him?"

Mrs. Donato shook her head. "No. Just what he was wearing."

That was a bad sign. Marty asked, "Now, did Johnny have a fight with anyone? One of his friends, maybe you or his dad?"

"No! He's a good boy!" Mrs. Donato declared indignantly. "He doesn't fight!"

Chrissie fought sometimes—with her friends, with Marty. Maybe Mrs. Donato was glossing things over. Or maybe she was a better mother than Marty. Marty asked, "Have you and Rosie thought of anything that might help us find him?"

"No. No, nothing more. I've racked my brains, but I told you everything."

"Rosie?" Marty looked at the little girl.

"Uhwiches," whispered Rosie, then buried her face in the terrier's neck.

"What?" Marty leaned down and coaxed, "Honey, can you say it again?"

"Oh, Rosie, baby!" Mrs. Donato transferred her anxiety to her daughter. "Johnny teases her because she's afraid of big animals. He said the cow witches would get her. But there's no such thing, Rosie, I told you."

"Cow witches?" Marty repeated, and was dismayed to see Rosie's thin shoulders begin to tremble. She wondered if a boy who teased his sister like this could really be as good as Mrs. Donato claimed. "Honey, it's okay. Your mom is right, there's no such thing. Your brother was teasing.

26

Don't worry." But something about the little girl's fear
frightened Marty too. Again she felt that urgency, that sense
that she must help now, soon. She thought a moment as
Mrs. Donato went to her daughter and hugged her. "Maybe
the barn," Marty said. "Rosie, did something frighten you
in the barn?"

Rosie shook her head, then jerked around as a door
slammed in the front of the house and a man's voice yelled,
"Sue? What's going on?"

Chuckles, yapping, ran toward the new voice. "It's my
husband," Mrs. Donato said, hurrying after the little dog.
Marty followed and Rosie lagged behind.

A muscular man with receding dark hair and a handsome
olive-skinned face was setting down a toolbox. He moved
stiffly, as though his back hurt. He wore a sage-green Helton
Gas coverall with "Carl" stitched over the breast pocket in
red script. As Marty entered he straightened slowly, staring
at her and scowling. "What's going on?" he repeated.

"I'm Deputy Hopkins, sir," Marty said. "You're Carl
Donato?"

"Yeah."

"Your wife here was telling me that your boy didn't come
back last night, and—"

"Doesn't mean anything's wrong!" Carl exclaimed. His
knuckles were red and scraped. "Sue always gets hysterical.
He just stayed with a friend. He'll be back."

"Which friend, sir?"

"Hell, I don't know! He's sure as hell going to be in trouble when he gets back, for scaring his mother like this. But
he can handle himself. He's a tough kid. Sue, I told you to
check with his friends—not call the sheriff!"

Sue Donato looked up timidly. "Carl, I did! I checked
with his friends, and he wasn't with any of them. And Rosie
and I went to look for him at the Brewsters'."

"The Brewsters!" Carl snorted, but Marty thought she
glimpsed fear in his eyes. "That stupid history thing! God,
those pansies from IU come down here, digging up people's
yards. And all those la-di-da kids from Arizona, showing
off their cassettes and CDs and their computers."

"Was there a problem with them?" Marty asked.

"Why can't they dig up their own backyards?" Carl grumbled.

"Yes sir." The Brewsters had been right. Their history project didn't seem to be very popular with Carl Donato. "Do you have any ideas about where Johnny might go, if he's not with his friends?"

"You trying to say he ran away? Look, if he's not with his friends—" He stopped, glancing at his wife. Sue Donato was sobbing. "Look, a kid gets in a scrape, he doesn't want his old man to find out, right? So his friends won't tell us what he's up to. But he'll show up. Don't worry, honey." He threw an arm around his wife's shoulders. "Don't worry."

"Sir, did your son have any quarrels with anyone recently?"

Carl stepped toward her, his dark face frowning. "Quarrels? You trying to say my son was mad at me?"

"No sir," Marty said. "Just asking."

"Look, I don't like what you're implying!" He glared at Marty.

Sue Donato was standing with her knuckles in her mouth. No help from that quarter. Marty closed her notebook and said, "Yes sir. Let us know if you want us to look for him." She went to the door to let herself out.

Sue Donato cried, "Yes, please, look for him!"

"Sue, shut up!" said Carl. But there wasn't much conviction in his voice.

Marty closed the door and started back down East Street. Carl was probably right—the kid would turn up soon. But she was uneasy all the same. She waved at Reverend Jeffries and his sixteen-year-old charges as she passed, heading for the Brewster farm to pick up her cruiser.

East Street ended in a graveled turnaround circle in front of a cement boat ramp. The narrow trail led east through a gate onto Rivendell Farm land and roughly followed the river, sometimes near the edge, sometimes separated by fifty feet of wooded bottomland. Near town the bank was steeper than behind the Rivendell buildings, the west-flowing river bending south toward New Concord and then swooping north and away again, disappearing under the state highway bridge on the other side of town. The river was high, tawny with all the mud it was carrying, and some of the hackberries and maples stood in a foot of water, their branches nodding over the hurrying current as though pondering a journey themselves. The river slapped at their trunks and roots, a far-off cow lowed, cicadas droned. It sure was warm today. The rain hadn't cooled things off much. Marty was out of sight of the town now, and a hill, frothy with Queen Anne's lace, still hid the Rivendell barn. She could see a couple of tents in the distance. The Arizona church school camp. She looked down at the riverbank. This morning's rain would have dissolved clear tracks, but there might still be signs if a kid had fallen into the river—broken branches, crushed vines, muddy grooves in the bank.

She didn't know why she was so sure Johnny was in trouble. Logically, his father was right. The likely thing was that he and one of his friends had gotten in a scrape and he didn't want to face his parents—or, at worst, that he had suddenly decided he was mad at them for some reason and had impulsively hitchhiked to Bloomington or Louisville. Probably he'd head right back after he'd been on his own a day or two. But Marty couldn't convince herself he was okay. Maybe because he'd taken no extra clothes, and because his bike couldn't be used. Maybe it was Rosie's fear; maybe the knowledge that if Chrissie ever disappeared, Marty would have fits too. Maybe the weather.

Maybe it was just her own depression, the sense of loss she couldn't seem to shake this week.

There was no special reason to be depressed. Her husband had been gone, except for short visits, for a year and a half now. First New York City, then the short-lived trip to Alaska, now Memphis. "My specialty is Elvis," he'd explained. "I can do great background on him. I'll be the best deejay in the business once they give me a break!"

"Brad, it's true, you're the best," she'd said—and shoot, it was true. Brad Hopkins's humor and enthusiasm and warm voice and eyes had kept her enraptured for years. "But I bet they already have fifty thousand Elvis experts in Memphis!"

The downside of his enthusiasm was that he always had to see for himself. At least from Memphis he was phoning regularly—in Alaska he'd quit calling for a while.

Was that a footprint? No, a bike tire track. It hadn't been rained on much. It veered off the path and right back on again. Not Johnny. His bike was broken.

The miracle was, Brad had found work. Not his usual job as bartender or housepainter's assistant, but an announcing job. The station was fifty miles from Memphis in Attica, Tennessee. Just last week he'd sent a tape, and there was the familiar voice, the familiar warmth, the familiar jokes, introducing songs by Elvis and other greats from the past. Chrissie was aglow. She'd brought all her friends over to hear her daddy's tape, and listened to it every night.

There in the mud was a set of fresh cow hoofprints. Down to the water, back up again. A lot of traffic here, looked like, though most of the prints were obliterated by the rain until you couldn't tell if they were animal or human. She removed her Stetson, wiped her brow, and replaced the hat.

What was more, Brad hadn't needed bailing out for weeks. He hadn't sent money yet, but at least he seemed to be paying his own rent and phone bills. Didn't even call collect.

So Marty should be delighted, right? Not depressed. Not convinced in her core that her marriage was dead and gone.

She squatted to peer at a track in the mud, but it was only a set of paw prints, from a very large dog.

"Can I help you find something?"

The woman tying off a small boat at the river's edge looked to be a couple of years older than Marty, almost as tall but fair and freckled, with high cheekbones and full lips. She wore jeans and her wavy blond hair was tied back casually with a star-spangled blue bandanna. She was lovely, and moved so gracefully and regally that to Marty she looked like a dancer. Or maybe a model in an ad for something "natural," spring water or breakfast granola. A pale aqua crocheted sweater was knotted around her waist, its sunburst design beautiful against the dark blue denim jeans.

Marty said, "I'm Deputy Hopkins. We're looking for a boy who lives in New Concord named Johnny Donato."

"No, I haven't seen Johnny for a couple of days. He does come by sometimes to ask about the old days in New Concord, or to listen to the singing." The woman's eyes were large, blue, and sorrowful as they checked Marty's badge. "It must be a serious problem to bring the sheriff's office."

"We hope not. You know him pretty well, then?"

A graceful shrug. "Not well, but you can't help knowing people in New Concord. I own the farm on the other side of town. We've got a good fishing rock there, and the folks from town use it sometimes. Johnny's done that. But this summer he's been hovering around the Brewster place instead, full of questions about the historic New Concord project. The Brewsters encourage us to explain the project to the local kids, and Johnny seems really interested." She smiled. "Actually, I think it's the teenagers from Arizona that attract him. You know about them?"

"Yeah, I've talked to some of them already." Marty took out her notebook. "What's your name, ma'am?"

"Nysa Strand. Spelled N-Y-S-A."

"Strand. Where—oh. You're a relative of Vicki Strand?"

"I'm Vicki's sister."

"I see." If you looked hard there was a family resemblance—the set of the sad eyes, the wavy blond hair. Vicki's hair was just as pretty, but in every other way Nysa was far more beautiful. Must have been hard for big, gawky Vicki to grow up next to a princess like this one. Marty got back to business. "You're working on the Brewsters' project too, right?"

"Yes, both of us," Nysa said. "Vicki's a genius with animals, and we hope to re-create the herds with the same breeds of cattle the settlers had. Later we'll restore the old springhouse where they kept the milk cool. As for me, I teach music at the junior college, and I'm something of a family historian. And it's a joy!" Her expression gleamed with intensity, and she touched Marty's arm. "Some of the German music came down in the family. Beautiful old music."

31

"Yeah, the Brewsters told me that you were descendants of old Father Rueger. Must seem like a family reunion, with Bob Rueger involved, and his daughter here for the summer."

"That's what Bob Rueger said too. Family reunion." Now there was coolness in Nysa's voice. "We never met them before, of course, so 'reunion' may not be the exact word."

So her newfound connection to Bob Rueger didn't thrill Nysa. Marty, on the other hand, would love to discover a rich relative. She'd figure out a way to get him to pay for a paint job. Marty said, "You told me Johnny's interested in the music and the old days. Anything in particular?"

"Well, he says the old hymns make him feel more peaceful. Lutheran hymns, mostly, seventeenth and eighteenth century."

"I thought Johnny's taste runs more to Lily Pistols."

Nysa laughed. "Yes, it does! But he loves the hymns too. Most kids enjoy them once they know what to listen for. But Johnny is mostly interested in the history. He's interested in the first Donato in the county."

"Who was the first Donato?"

"A skilled stone carver from Italy, Giancarlo Donato. Brought his family here early in this century. I remember Johnny trying to add up how long ago Giancarlo came. It's marvelous to see young people begin to grasp history!" Nysa touched her arm again, and Marty realized that part of her beauty was an intensity of caring that others might feel but that few people could communicate. "And Johnny wants to know all about Father Rueger. I think he realizes that these long-ago stories are the reason his Arizona friends came to this county. So he wants to hear the stories too."

This was an unexpected side of Johnny, Marty thought. Rock music, yes. Bravado, hero worship of older, richer kids, teasing a kid sister—all that was almost predictable. But interest in the history and people of the area was not usual. Marty had never investigated her own folks, the LaFortes. She knew they'd descended from a French trapper, but not much else. Maybe Johnny's interest was tied into the hero worship, as Nysa suggested. It probably had nothing to do with his disappearance. Still . . . "Are there any special stories he seems interested in?"

"Mostly how Father Rueger and his followers lived. They believed that the Second Coming was just around the corner, and that the last days of the world should be lived as Christ decreed. Their religion called for self-effacement, for egalitarianism, for self-control. Strange ideals to a modern kid who's used to ideas like individuality and competition and self-expression. Johnny likes for me to tell him what it was like to live in those days."

"What do you tell him?"

"Well, married couples lived in homes like his, singles in the men's or women's dormitory. Dress was very modest. Men wore dark suits and women wore gray high-neck dresses. It must have been uncomfortable in weather like this, but people wore them all their lives, even were buried in them. There's a little cemetery somewhere, this side of the river, but we haven't found it yet." She smiled at Marty. "Okay, on a typical day, they'd start with a church service. Father Rueger would inspire them—he really would. He had a lot of charisma, like most good politicians and preachers." Nysa brushed back a wisp of blond hair with a tense hand. "My own father was a preacher, and he truly admired his great-great-grandpa. Of course these days not many people believe the end is coming soon, but except for things like that my father found Father Rueger very inspiring. Used to talk about getting a group of followers and starting a community like New Concord." She shrugged. "Never did. Okay, after the service, Father Rueger's people would all march out to work in the fields, in their dark suits and gray dresses, singing hymns. They even had a small instrumental band to accompany them. Johnny likes that. Told me he'd want to be a member of the band."

Marty liked that too. She could almost see the people marching from town, those old hoes and scythes over their prim shoulders, led by trumpets and tuba. Pulling weeds and harvesting hay would go a lot easier with music. "What else interests Johnny?"

"He asked why there was no school. There were few children in New Concord back then. Father Rueger and his followers believed that the line in the Bible about becoming 'eunuchs for the kingdom of heaven's sake' meant total abstinence from sex." She glanced sorrowfully toward the decaying town. "A few late joiners brought children with them, but even married couples living together were supposed to remain celibate, and the community punished them severely if they didn't."

"Wait a minute. If they were celibate, where did you and your sister come from? And Bob Rueger?"

"Old Father Rueger had a son and three daughters—one my great-great-great-grandmother—before the angel told him to become celibate. The New Concord community lasted about fifteen years, but when he died it broke up and some of his children married."

"So it was too strict for his own children."

"Terribly, terribly strict." Nysa's mournful eyes met Marty's. "Though I think—I have to think he was sincere in believing in his angel voices."

"Yeah. Anything else that interests Johnny?"

"Mm. Those are the main things I remember." She touched Marty's arm again, concerned. "I don't know if any of this has helped you, really."

"Sure it has." Marty closed her notebook. "It's real useful to get a better idea of Johnny. You may have helped more than anybody."

5

"WES!"

Sheriff Wes Cochran had just shoved the key into the door of his cruiser. Over the past two hours he thought he'd discussed pretty well everything with the Kiwanis fellas. But here came Dub Walters chugging across the hot parking lot, leading with his belly, bringing some new problem or other. Wes pulled out the key and turned around. "What can I do for you, Dub?"

Walters pushed his hands into the pockets of his light blue suit. He was one of the seven County Council members, so maybe he thought that his high office demanded a jacket even in this humid July weather, though Wes saw that he'd loosened his tie a notch. "Off the record," Walters said.

"Sure."

"You know our little shopping center southwest of town at the intersection of the Bloomington road?"

"Yeah." Wes knew it well, a cinder-block building with a few stores sharing a covered sidewalk, the store names lined up on the turquoise steel awning: Buddy's Quick-Mart, Adorable Pets, Mary Ann's Fashions. His wife Shirley shopped at Mary Ann's sometimes. Dub Walters had put up the building back in the fifties.

"Well, that damn Corrigan from Bloomington opened up a video game arcade right across the highway."

"Yeah, I've seen it," said Wes cautiously. He could see what was coming.

"Well, Mary Ann tells me when school's out all the high schoolers come screaming up in their old cars. Place turns into a zoo until Corrigan's closes at midnight."

"Yeah, Mary Ann called us about that a week ago. We've been checking every day, but there's never anything but a bunch of kids playing the games and hanging out."

"Hanging out, yeah. Yelling, running across the highway to get snacks at Buddy's. Or they park in our parking places. Mary Ann says they spook her customers."

Wes propped an elbow on top of his cruiser and leaned back. "Trouble is, Dub, like I was saying inside, we can't arrest anybody unless we think they've broken a law. I'll keep sending my people by, but that's all I can do unless they do something illegal."

The county councilman smiled and answered a wave from one of the cars pulling out of the lot before looking back at Wes. "Well, now, Wes, I've been a good friend to you all these years. Bringing you here to talk to my friends, helping you crack down on crime. But see, Chuck Pierce says if he was sheriff, he'd post someone there, three till midnight."

"He said that, did he?" Even Chuck Pierce was smart enough to know a sheriff couldn't spare anybody for a whole shift. It was hard enough patrolling this county without taking a guy off to serve as Dub Walters's private security guard. The voters would know that too if they thought about it half a minute. Wes wondered if Chuck Pierce was running around promising guards for every block. Easy to point out the folly if you had campaign money. But the Committee to Re-elect Sheriff Wes Cochran, consisting at the moment of Mr. and Mrs. Wes Cochran, hadn't really taken Chuck Pierce's candidacy seriously, and had about two cents to its name.

Walters's high forehead was glistening, and Wes was sweaty too. He wished he could climb into the cruiser and get cooler. But Walters ignored the heat and smiled genially. "C'mon, it wouldn't be for long. Kids don't much like uniforms. Most of them will stay away when they see we mean business."

Business, right. Walters was probably jealous of the customers Corrigan's videos had attracted. Jealous that he hadn't thought of it first. Could be his plan was to have Wes drive away the young customers, so when Corrigan went bankrupt Walters could pick up the business cheap and reopen it himself for the same youngsters. Walters would probably describe them as the bright hope of the nation once those shiny quarters were going into his own pockets. Wes said, "Yeah, look, Dub, I'll send somebody past as often as I can. But you know we don't have enough people to keep someone there a long time. There's a lot of corners in this county to patrol."

"Yeah, I know—I'm in real estate, remember? But you gotta see the big picture, Wes. We don't want these Bloomington types bringing their crime and drugs down here. Corrigan's not the only one. Professor Brewster has another harebrained project up at New Concord. He's the one used to have those hippies on his farm. Now he's applied for one of those damn historic grants! You know what that means? Communism. They write a bunch of federal rules that say you can't fix up your own property—and he's got a bunch of teenagers camping on his land and digging up backyards in New Concord."

"I'll check into it, Dub."

"Needs more than checking, Wes."

The two men locked eyes for a moment. Wes was taller, tougher, popular with the voters. Dub Walters was richer, controlled the money for Wes's salaries and jail funds, and got his share of votes too. They'd never been buddies, but had always worked together well enough. Why was Dub testing him now? Wes owed him a favor, sure, but not one that would disrupt his whole department.

Dub smiled suddenly and gripped Wes's hand. "Hey, I didn't want to bring this up inside, but is your heart treating you all right?"

"No problems. Doc Hendricks has me eating right. Says I'm five years younger than last year."

"Glad to hear it. It's a tough job, being sheriff. The voters need someone who can take the stress. Well, we both have work to do. I'm sure you'll do the right thing, Wes. See you around."

"Yeah, see you."

Wes stood a moment, the car keys dangling, and watched

Dub Walters's broad retreating back. Walters was an operator, all right. Chuck Pierce hadn't been smart enough to mention it yet, but Walters had zeroed right in on the only issue Chuck had going for him in the race for sheriff: the fact that he'd never had a heart attack. If Pierce got enough campaign money to push the issue, he could sow doubts about Wes's health. Wes would need campaign money to fight back.

Last time around Walters had contributed to Wes's campaign.

Generously.

"Son of a bitch," Wes muttered, and unlocked the cruiser door.

Marty Hopkins got back to headquarters half an hour after Wes did. He could see the little furrow between her eyes that meant she was worried about something. Even at ten, when she'd been on the kids' basketball team he used to coach, that little furrow meant trouble. "What's up?" Wes asked.

"A boy's disappeared, sir," she said, tossing her Stetson onto a peg. The guys grumbled about having a woman deputy—not a job for girls, Foley said, maybe because his gimpy leg had relegated him to dispatch. But Wes knew Marty was quick and smart, and by now even Foley knew better than to say that she couldn't do the job. The bellyaching now was more along the lines that a guy couldn't relax and be himself if there was a woman around.

"How old a boy?" Wes asked.

"Fourteen. No one's seen him since yesterday afternoon."

"No big deal. Lot of places a fourteen-year-old could be."

"Yes sir."

"You checked his family and friends." It was a statement, not a question. If she hadn't she'd still be checking, not talking to him.

"Yes sir. This kid—Johnny Donato is his name—he was last seen on a farm near his house, going toward the barn. If he walked home from there he probably went along a trail that runs by the White River. I walked the trail but didn't see any problems. Still . . ."

"Yeah." Wes frowned. "Fourteen. He knew the area?"

"Yes sir, raised there."

"He'd know the river, then. The sinkholes too. But sometimes when a guy's fourteen he wants to prove he's a man. Impress people. Takes chances—"

"This summer he's been trying to impress a group of church school campers, teenagers, on that farm."

Wes looked at her sharply. "Up near New Concord? Who owns that farm?"

"IU professor named Brewster."

"Shit." He unfolded himself from his chair and walked to the county map on the wall. "Show me."

She pointed to a southward bend in the White River. "Here, south bank of the river. The Brewster farm is here. Johnny lives in New Concord, west of the Brewster place."

Wes said slowly, "I seem to recollect that Dub Walters owns one of those farms."

"Here, farther west, other side of the state highway."

"Shit," Wes said again, squinting at the map. "Lot of sinkholes around. What's a church school camp doing there?"

"It's a work project. They're helping with a historic restoration the Brewsters are doing with the Rockland Mall developer, Bob Rueger. Spring Mill Village type thing. Some of the neighbors are grumbling, including Johnny Donato's father."

"Also including Mr. W. W. Walters," Wes informed her. "Any of the neighbors in favor?"

"The Strand sisters on the next farm are working on the project. Otherwise it's the usual—the educated rich folks telling the working folks how things oughta be, and the working folks suspicious. But they're not making their kids stay away or anything."

That was the usual, all right, the pointy-heads versus the working stiffs, with the big money coming down on whichever side looked best and always winning. Money on both sides here, Dub's versus Rueger's. That was interesting. But it didn't help find a missing kid. Wes said, "You're not happy about this kid's disappearance, Hopkins."

"Sir, Johnny didn't pack anything. His bike is broken, so

he didn't go far alone. His friends seem really puzzled, and his little sister is terrified about something he told her. He was probably just teasing, but still . . ."

Wes frowned. "Family problems, maybe?"

"The father has a short fuse, but so do a lot of guys."

"Yeah," said Wes. "You working on anything else?"

"Have to get back to Child Protective Services about the Seifert kids. See what they worked out with the mother. Probably nothing."

"Yeah. Sad case." He pushed his wastebasket with his toe. "Okay. If the Donato kid hasn't shown up by four o'clock, get the neighbors out in search parties to check the sinkholes. And if that doesn't do it, we'll send out a bulletin."

"Okay, good."

"And Hopkins." Her gray eyes met his, and he knew that she'd heard the warning in his tone. "We're being extra considerate of Mr. W. W. Walters these days."

He could see her curiosity flare, but she didn't push. "Yes sir, considerate it is," she said.

6

THE REVEREND JUSTIN JEFFRIES FOLLOWED THE youngsters in the search party up the hill. He wiped the back of his hand across his damp brow as he climbed. It was so humid here, sweating didn't do much good. But they had to hurry because the sun would set soon, and they were all worried about the Donato boy.

He could see Melissa and Kenny ahead, hands touching as they climbed the rough slope, sidestepping the clumps of wild rose, bull thistle, and raggedy blue chicory, skipping across easy places where the soil had worn off to reveal pale stone. He could remember being fifteen, feeling the tingle Melissa and Kenny were feeling. And later too, of course, when Bonnie had come into his life. He'd loved Bonnie. Still loved her, he corrected himself sternly. Loved her, and loved little JayJay.

George pointed to the right. "This way," he called. George was a local boy, Johnny Donato's friend, a sturdy, tanned youngster of thirteen with sun-bleached brown hair. Justin shifted the coil of rope to his other shoulder and followed him.

A few minutes later they were all peering into a natural steep-walled pit twenty feet across and maybe fifteen feet at its deepest. "Hey, Johnny!" George yelled without much conviction. "Johnny, you down there?"

The long shadows already darkened half of the sinkhole, but there was enough light to catch motion, if there was any. There wasn't. Justin said, "I think we should check this one."

"I'm his friend," said George. He was speaking as gruffly as he could. His importance as the local expert among the older teens seemed to have matured him despite his youthful voice and short stature. "I go."

"Okay. We have to use the rope."

They tied it around George's chest and he climbed down the rocky pit wall cautiously, jumping only the last five feet. It took only a moment of exploring before his voice announced, "Naw, nothing here but some old rabbit bones."

"Yuck," said Melissa.

"Shall we pull you out?" Justin called.

George squinted up at the rim. "Just hitch it around that rock."

Justin did, and George used the rope and projecting rocks to scramble monkeylike up the steep side. He said hopefully, "There's another sinkhole half a mile south of here."

"Yeah, nobody's in this one. Let's go," said Russ. The little troop turned south.

Kenny began to sing "Michael Row the Boat Ashore" as he walked. Melissa joined in, and Russ. It was the same

41

song Justin had sung for them from the shed roof, paying off his promise to the kids. They loved seeing him make a fool of himself and he'd played up the difficulty of balancing on the roof ridge, waving his arms like a tightrope walker as he sang. They kept feeding him new verses. "River Jordan's deep and cold, something something," Kenny yelled, and then unexpectedly came Nysa's laughing voice, "Cools the body but not the soul." It was like a blow. He managed to croak out the verses, and finally it was over. How unfair of the Lord to send her here, where he was working, of all places in the world!

No, not unfair of the Lord. Hard to understand, perhaps, but the Lord's ways were not always clear to His people. Justin believed that the Lord challenged people, asked them to think things through, to grow spiritually.

He wondered if Nysa agreed that his chin looked like Paul Newman's.

George had reached the rim of another sinkhole. This one was in a depression, the meadow grasses growing down the slope to the edge, a puddle shining among the shadowy rocks at the bottom of the pit. It was clear that no one was there. His young face lined with disappointment, George said, "I think there's another sinkhole about half a mile southeast. Not very deep, though," he added doubtfully.

"There's not enough light left," Justin said gently. "We'd better go back and see if any of the other search parties had any luck."

"Yes sir," Marty Hopkins said to Dub Walters. "We'll be real careful of your fences."

"You see, honey, the thing is, I don't like the idea of kids running around on my land. I keep telling them to stay off."

They were standing on the white-columned porch of Dub Walters's grand two-story brick house. He was in a maroon polo shirt that stretched tight across his big belly. He reminded Marty of a big blunt-nosed truck cab without its trailer. She said politely, "Yes sir, I can understand that."

"Why isn't Sheriff Cochran here? He should clear this kind of thing with me officially."

"Yes sir." Marty felt a twinge of annoyance. Why was she standing here in this damn uniform, sweat trickling down between her breasts, gun belt heavy on her hips, if she wasn't official? But that wasn't the point of this discussion. She kept her voice polite and explained, "Problem is, an Illinois man totaled his feed truck on the Seymour road, other side of the county. Caught fire, the whole works. Sheriff Cochran had to go there. But we didn't want to wait too long to hunt for this missing boy, because the light won't be very good in another hour. He might be injured somewhere."

"Now, honey, you know I'm not trying to hold you up. You're interested in that sinkhole in the east pasture, you say?"

"Yes sir, and if you know of other dangerous sinkholes around here we want to check them too."

"No, there's only the one deep sinkhole. Pain in the neck; doesn't even hold water for the cattle. Kids shouldn't play there anyway. I tell them all the time. But they come over here, teasing the cows, chasing chickens—"

"Yes sir," Marty broke in, fearing a sermon. If he'd let them go, they'd leave by the river path that led under the highway bridge to the Strands' farm, and they wouldn't have to talk to him again. "Probably he's not here, but if he is, we'll get him out of here quick as we can."

Dub Walters frowned at the small troop of sixteen-year-olds from Arizona that waited for Marty on the broad asphalt driveway. "They all have to go?"

"We'll need the manpower if we have to help him out of a pit."

"Yeah. Well, all right, seeing it's you, honey," Dub Walters said grandly. "But make it as quick as you can."

"Yes sir. Thank you, sir." Marty turned away with a worried glance at the sinking sun. Not much daylight left today. "Let's move," she urged her helpers, herding them at a half-trot toward the east pasture.

But her search proved as fruitless as Justin's. It was Drew Brewster's group, returning along the Rivendell driveway after exploring a culvert under the highway, that found the little plastic case. "Karen saw it first," Drew told Marty later, stroking his small mustache with a plump finger. "She picked it up and said, 'Did anyone lose a cassette?' "

Karen nodded. Her arms were folded tightly across her vest, her face even longer than usual. "And Russ said it was Johnny's new Lily Pistols cassette. So we called you people."

Marty slid the cassette into an evidence bag. "We may need your fingerprints for elimination, Mrs. Brewster. We'll let you know. Can you show me exactly where it was?"

Karen pointed out a spot in the shaggy grass that bordered the long driveway, about four feet from the edge. It was about fifty feet to the highway. Marty turned and squinted in the other direction. Much farther to the Brewster house and barn, farther still to the distant river.

Drew's small eyes blinked. "I've been thinking. Maybe Johnny waited in the barn for it to stop raining, and fell asleep, and came out later to walk home along the highway. It's drier than the river path."

But not necessarily safer. Worry chewing at her mind, Marty nodded neutrally at the Brewsters and carried the new evidence to her cruiser.

7

"HARD DAY, CHAMP?" ASKED SHIRLEY COCHRAN, ON tiptoes to welcome Wes home with a kiss.

"Yeah." He sat down heavily at the kitchen table and wiped a hand across his face, then noticed how blackened it was. "Shit, look at that soot. Guy wrapped his truck around a tree and it caught fire. Full of poultry feed. Messy business."

Shirley was small, a little plumper than she used to be

but still blond with a little assist from Dawn at the Unisex Salon on the square. "Oh, dear. Was he killed?" She opened a diet Coke and put it with a bowl of unbuttered popcorn in front of him.

"He was still breathing. But it'll be touch and go." He took a handful of popcorn. Poultry feed.

She squeezed his shoulders. "Chin up, kid. It always reminds you of Rusty, doesn't it?"

"Yeah." Rusty LaForte, one of his best friends, had wrapped his pickup around a tree too. Peeling a guy out of that kind of mess was always hard. But when it turned out to be Rusty it had just about wiped out Wes too. Thirty-some years of laughing together, sticking up for each other, understanding each other, all erased by one drunken misjudgment at the wheel. The image of Rusty in the wreckage had joined Wes's other demons—mental snapshots of the war, the dead buddies, the atrocities, the smell of death.

Usually, those demons slept. But an accident like this one stirred them up again.

At least he'd made sure Marty Hopkins was in the other corner of the county. She was Rusty's daughter, and like him hated to be protected, but Wes couldn't bring himself to send her on a job that could stir up her own sad memories. It was a comfort of sorts to him, being able to do right by Rusty's daughter.

Besides, that kid missing from New Concord was worrisome. No trace except for his prized new cassette, dropped near the highway. Wes wanted Marty on that job. If anyone could find the kid, she could. She was a real bulldog sometimes.

Shirley was watching him with a little frown. "Hey, Champ, let's get you into the shower, and then you can watch the end of the ball game."

The Reds were playing the Cubs tonight. "Not a bad idea," said Wes, and smiled at Shirley. She generally knew what he needed. "I probably won't solve all the problems of the world tonight anyway."

"That's right," said Shirley comfortably. "The world will just have to wait till tomorrow."

When Marty got home Aunt Vonnie was sitting in front of the TV with her foot up on the coffee table. "How's that ankle?" Marty asked. Aunt Vonnie had twisted it at the fireworks show, stepping wrong on the uneven ground.

"I don't know. I think the heat makes it swell up even more." She frowned at the puffy ankle. She was on her feet all day in her job at Reiner's Bakery, and Marty knew that couldn't help much either.

"Think you should see a doctor?" Marty emptied her gun, put it on its high shelf, and hung the Stetson and her gun belt on their pegs.

"Oh, it'll be okay if I can rest it."

"No big Saturday night on the town for you, huh? Where's Chrissie?"

"Upstairs. Packing for Memphis, she says."

"Yeah." They weren't leaving for another week. "Well, she's excited about seeing her dad."

Aunt Vonnie shook her head gloomily. She blamed Brad Hopkins for leaving Marty and Chrissie behind while he looked for work in broadcasting. Now that he had a job, she blamed him for trying to get them to join him in Tennessee. She probably would have blamed him for her turned ankle if he hadn't been two states away.

"I'll get some supper going. Tuna salad okay?" Marty asked.

"Yeah, and the green beans are coming along real nice," said Aunt Vonnie.

Marty went upstairs. Chrissie was flopped on her bed reading, one foot waving in the air, and Marty felt a great surge of love for her and sorrow for Johnny. "Hi, kid," said Marty, giving her a big hug.

Chrissie, tough as nails, wriggled away. "So, did you find Johnny?" the girl asked with elaborate casualness. She'd heard rumors, then. At ten, her daughter was alternately proud and ashamed of her mother's peculiar occupation, but always curious about it. Chrissie was sturdy and lively, with brown eyes like Brad's and dark curls. Marty thought she was beautiful. Today she wore jeans, an orange Elvis T-shirt, and bright orange dangling goldfish earrings that danced as she jumped up from the bed to follow Marty into her room.

Marty kicked off her shoes. "No, we didn't find him yet. We figure maybe he ran off for some reason, so we sent out a bulletin to other counties around here." She unbuttoned her shirt. "Do you know Johnny?"

"I met him and his sister Rosie once at that 4-H fair. The one when I made those blueberry muffins. So I don't really know them. But you know Valerie Woods? She knows Rosie. She used to go to the same school."

"Mm." Marty changed to shorts, T-shirt, and sandals. "Come on down to the kitchen with me. So what does Valerie say about Rosie?"

Chrissie trotted behind, goldfish bouncing. "Just that their families are friends so they see TV together sometimes. Is Rosie like a suspect?"

"No, no. I just have a feeling she knows more than she's telling. It's like she's scared to talk. But maybe she's always shy. Did Valerie say anything about her being easy to scare?" Marty put on some water to boil and started the tuna salad.

"No. I can ask her. She just said Rosie is good at playing the piano. And she said she has a really neat dog named Chuckles. He can walk on his hind legs all the way across the room."

"Really?" Marty remembered the little terrier. "I met Chuckles, but shoot, he just barked and jumped around. No tricks. C'mon, let's go out and pick some beans." They went out back to the garden, lush and mysterious in the steamy dusk. The vegetables, at least, were enjoying this weather. Marty asked, "Did Valerie say anything about Johnny?"

"No. He doesn't like the same TV shows so he sticks with his own friends."

"I heard he likes a band called Lily Pistols."

"Yeah. They're really cool. Sing about death and stuff."

"That's cool?"

"Yeah. Sort of." Chrissie stopped picking for a moment, suddenly very serious. This was the brother of someone her own age, someone she'd met, a closer link than she had with the adult problems Marty usually handled. "Do you think Johnny is in bad trouble?"

Everything will be fine, Marty wanted to say, it'll have a happy ending, I'll protect you from everything bad. But she had to be honest. Marty said, "He could be, honey. We don't know yet. So we're still hoping he's okay. We're still hunting for him."

Chrissie's eyes went very dark, looking at some mysterious interior fear, and she nodded slowly. "What if you don't find him?"

"We just keep looking. We ask some more questions. We hope somebody will remember something that will help. Hey." Marty hated seeing the kid worried like this. "Hey, do you want a Coke?"

"Okay."

She shouldn't give it to her right before dinner. But Marty found a can in the refrigerator when they went back in and handed it to Chrissie with a hug. "Hey, kid, we're working on it. We won't give up. I promise."

Walking the riverbank, the man carrying the lumpy feed sack took a deep breath, flaring his nostrils. The smells of mud and flowers, cattle and foliage, were strong when it was humid like this. The night rain had passed as the clouds lumbered on to the east, and the moonlight shone silvery on the rising river and gleamed on the water of the small creek that joined it here. Drops plopped from overhanging cottonwood and maple branches, laying a complex syncopated rhythm over the background gurgle of the stream.

He remembered another river from his childhood. A different river, but the sounds and odors were the same. He remembered sitting in a boat. His father, in a friendly, quiet mood, was teaching him to fish, telling him that Christ was a fisherman too. He remembered splashing naked in the moonlit shallows with his friend Stevie, the coolness of the water on a hot summer night, the hilarious fun of splashing

48

Stevie and being splashed, sputtering, laughing. His mother had found them and jerked him from the water, hissing, "Get dressed! Your father's going to tan your hide for being naked!" So he'd stumbled back into his clothes, pleading with her not to tell.

After that he'd stayed out of the river, though sometimes he was allowed to play with Stevie. They'd sail leaf boats, or scamper along the banks as cowboys, their small fingers becoming six-shooters that never missed, their eyes becoming keen and manly and able to spot every crook, their spindly legs becoming mighty steeds that thundered beside vast herds of cattle, beside besieged railroad trains, beside the Colorado or the Rio Grande.

That was long ago, before his great sin, before Morton's jeers. Now he inspected the moonlit riverbank cautiously, because so few people understood. But no one was near. In the riverside woods nothing moved except the warm breeze.

He knelt and opened the sack. It had been only recently, while he'd been working in Chicago, that things had come together for him and he'd understood himself at last. It had been a pleasant day and he'd taken a long walk south through Grant Park, enjoying the scudding clouds, the trees, the views of the lake. Then a sudden thundersquall had darkened the sky. As the rain splashed down he'd run up the steps of a giant building and found himself in the Field Museum, surrounded by elephants and dinosaur skeletons. He'd paid the admission and wandered through some of the halls filled with dioramas of prehistoric animals and people. Attracted by a full-size bison, he'd entered a hall devoted to Native American cultures, where a group of high school boys were inspecting an exhibit of a man in a bison headdress doing some kind of a dance. "Some of us laugh at the idea of clans and totems, or names like Sitting Bull," their teacher had told them. "But don't you find nature very spiritual? These people, like many other Native Americans, were affirming their spiritual connections with nature, with the universe. By identifying with certain animals, wearing their skins and skulls and doing dances sacred to that animal, they felt that they became part of the vast rhythms of life. They believed you had to have this deep connection to nature in order to be a true man."

"But didn't they kill the animals?" a freckled boy had asked.

"Sure, when necessary, but they did it as part of nature, not as someone outside nature trying to dominate it."

"The buffalo would still be dead. Eaten."

"Yes and no. Spiritually, the buffalo and the hunter would be one. They would both be immortal, connected in the realm of spirit. Eating the buffalo was part of that unity. You needed the spiritual connection to the wilderness, to your inner wildness, in order to be a true, whole man."

The freckled boy had shaken his head. "Shit, gives you something to think about next time you chomp into a Big Mac."

Anger at the freckled boy had welled up in him, anger at the stupidity of the laughing group. Luckily they'd moved on to the next room and he'd been left in peace. He'd crept into the Pawnee Earth Lodge to sit on the buffalo hides and understand himself for the first time. It was his true, wild, inner self that had nudged him to love the wilderness, to seek out parks and animals even in this great city. In the realm of spirit he was a true, whole man, connected to nature like the Pawnee, like the dancer in the bison skin and headdress. He'd understood that the skin was not a costume. The clothes men wore to work, or on the street—those were costumes. The animal skins were their true skins.

Now he drew his own skin from the feed sack, a magnificent shaggy bull with arching horns. Tor, he called his wild self. *El toro*, Taurus the bull. He looked about again, but no one was watching.

Tor stripped, donned the horned headpiece, picked up the sacred axe, and began to stamp rhythmically. He felt the ripple of his muscles beneath the shaggy, damp fur laid across his shoulders, felt the might of all nature in him as he stamped. He was courage and maleness, he was strength and rage. He was man, he was bull, he was ancient aurochs. Here, in this wooded riverside glade, he was powerful, whole, himself.

BLOODSTREAM

Tor stretched his arms wide, Christlike except for the newly risen axe in his right hand, and breathed deeply of the rain-scrubbed air. Those boys were wrong. Jeering Morton was wrong. He'd shown them how wrong.

But the sun was coming. It was almost time to hide again. Tor swung his great head landward. The silvery light glinted on the metal tips of his wide-arching horns. He changed back into his clothes, his everyday costume, and eased his shaggy skin into the sack. Then he climbed with easy strides from the muddy bank toward his secret home.

The Reverend Justin Jeffries lay wide-eyed in his tent. Beside him Bonnie breathed gently, and in the next cot little JayJay grunted, rolled over, and was silent again. The tent was large, luxurious by camping standards, and he could see through a clear plastic skylight that the moon had come out.

When he'd been small, some of his friends had told him that God was up there, in the sky, among the stars. That had puzzled Justin. He'd always felt that God was next to him, working in the world, inexplicable sometimes but always there. *Our helper He amid the flood of mortal ills prevailing.* When he was older he'd finally decided that people who thought God was in the sky were talking about how hard it was to grasp God's meaning. Why were there floods and hurricanes, why murders, why lost children, like this Johnny Donato? Justin had managed to dismiss the questions, content to live with the unknowable side of God's will as long as the divine presence was so obviously near.

And it was near, usually: in JayJay's laugh, in a sixteen-year-old camper's discovery of the joy of music, in a sunset, even in a good volleyball game or a woman's sweet grin.

Or was that divine? Especially if the grin belonged to the wrong woman? Were these warm, near things mere distractions from a more distant, austere divinity? Distractions, or worse—temptations, what preachers sometimes called the Devil's work? *For still our ancient foe doth seek to work us woe.*

Luther's God was not comfortable and near, nor was He remote among the stars. Luther's God was a mighty fortress.

The Reverend Justin Jeffries, who had always striven to tear down walls, wondered if perhaps he should be building them instead.

THE SECOND
SATURDAY IN JULY

8

OVER THE NEXT WEEK, THE WHITE RIVER DROPPED nine inches.

It was still swollen, still lapping at the lower trunks of some shoreline trees, still muscling its way through the trailing sievelike branches of bushes and trees it had torn up by the roots and then dumped downstream, half-beached. It still nudged at slower-moving things trapped in its bed— sunken logs, old bedsprings festooned with lost fishing line. But its mood was less boisterous. It retreated slowly from its high-water mark, and left behind a new edging made up of dead branches, gravel, broken bottles, and stones that it had been bowling along its bed like a rowdy child running with a kickball.

The sky cleared, but at night ghostly curls of mist condensed here and there over the waters. When they drifted aside, the river winked back at the stars.

It was not resting. It never rested. It had only slowed a little. And thunderstorms were on the way. Soon it could rage again.

* * *

Marty could tell by the way Foley's back stiffened that this call was major.

"Where?" he barked, lifting a shoulder to hold the receiver against his ear while he recorded the call. "Who? . . . Strand, okay, just west of New Concord. We'll be right over." He hung up and radioed Sheriff Cochran, who was driving home to lunch. Marty had already jumped from her chair and was on her way out the door, but she paused to get the full directions. Farm was on State 860, Foley was telling the sheriff, but what they'd found was down by the river. "They say it's a human bone."

Oh, shoot. Was it poor Johnny Donato at last? Marty yelled, "Tell him I'll meet him there," and bounded out to the parking lot. She hit the gas and the siren. She'd spent the week in frustration, worrying about Johnny whenever she wasn't working another case but unable to think of anything more to do, fielding Carl Donato's angry insults and Sue Donato's sobs. In two days she and Chrissie would leave for Memphis, and the trip was starting to feel like a betrayal of Johnny.

The sheriff was just pulling a roll of crime scene tape from the trunk of his cruiser when Marty's car screeched up, sending the gravel flying onto the Strands' blue Volvo. Sheriff Cochran straightened to his full six-four and adjusted the Stetson on his silvery head. "Glad you're here, Hopkins. Don't get out. Foley said someone would meet us—ah."

Marty was surprised to see Drew Brewster coming out of the Strands' dignified, old-fashioned farmhouse, past the bright annual flowers that splashed yellow, salmon, and magenta colors against a tall, trimmed hedge. In jeans and a light blue polo shirt, the big professor didn't look as comical as last time, except for his little mustache. The sheriff called to him, "Can we get the car any closer?"

"Uh—it's near the highway bridge, but it's hard to climb down from there. Too steep." Drew pointed a pudgy finger toward the woods that bordered the river at the foot of the long pasture. "We could drive across this field. Except the ground's still so muddy."

"Open the pasture gate. We'll give it a try," the sheriff told him. He climbed in next to Marty, grunting, "No sense both cars getting stuck in this mud. Pick him up when we get through the gate. Where are we?"

"The Strand farm."

"Doesn't belong to Walters, then."

"His place is the next one west, other side of the highway," she said. "This farm borders some of the New Concord backyards on the east, and the river down there to the north."

They watched the big professor close the gate, and Marty introduced him as he climbed into the cruiser. "What's going on, Mr. Brewster?" the sheriff asked.

Marty thought Drew looked tired. "I don't know. I wouldn't believe it but they showed me."

"Showed you what?"

"Bones. I'm pretty sure they're human. Justin thinks so too. I hope to God we're wrong. It's not a whole skeleton or anything."

"Where are they?"

"By the river, right at the edge of the water. He must have drowned and washed up."

They'd bumped across the pasture to the next fence. Marty braked and asked, "Is it much farther?"

"Just the other side of those trees. There's a clearing and a rock where people fish. It's a good place for a picnic."

The sheriff squinted at the trees and said, "Let's walk. If we're talking bones, there's not that much of a hurry. No sense cutting their fence."

They dodged between the barbed wires and crossed the Strands' second pasture. A tongue of the woods ran up from the river's edge along a small creek, barely big enough for a small boat, that was bridged near its junction with the river by a wooden plank bridge. Marty figured that the trail here must be a continuation of the footpath that followed the riverbank from the other side of town.

They emerged from the woods to find a tight knot of young people presided over by the muscular Reverend Jeffries. Long-faced Karen Brewster sat next to a pleasant woman with short curly brown hair who turned out to be Mrs. Jeffries. Bonnie, she insisted. She was holding the hand of a five-year-old boy. The remnants of a picnic lunch were still spread on a couple of blankets they'd placed on a broad, sunny rock that jutted twenty feet into the river. The water crashed against the upstream side but moved more slowly on the downstream side. Anxious young faces turned to them, and Marty's heart melted. When they were scared, these sixteen-year-olds didn't look much older than Chrissie.

The sheriff asked, "Is everybody here?"

"Except Nysa Strand," said Karen Brewster. "She stayed to watch over the—to make sure nobody disturbed anything."

"Was she the one who found them?"

"No. Russ found them." With a faint frown, Karen looked at the sixteen-year-old that Marty had interviewed a week ago, the same kid who'd been the last to talk to Johnny Donato. "He wasn't supposed to go that far away from us, but . . ."

Russ had a pointed chin and big eyes, and looked pale and genuinely unhappy. Marty suggested, "Why doesn't Russ come show us and tell us about it on the way?"

"Good idea," the sheriff said. "Mr. Brewster, you can wait here with the others."

Reverend Jeffries said in a low voice, "Russ, you up to this?"

"Sure." Russ squared his shoulders and marched off down the footpath.

A couple of others moved hesitantly to follow, but the sheriff said, "Wait here, please," and set off after Russ and Marty.

"River looks lower than last week," Marty said.

The sheriff nodded. After a moment he said, "Russ, there are a lot of footprints here on the path. Did all those folks come to look at the bones?"

"Not everyone." Russ's young voice was shaky. "Derek and Kenny were right behind me when I found them, and when we ran back and told the others, Justin and Drew went to see them. And Nysa."

"I see."

BLOODSTREAM

Too many people trampling on the evidence, Marty thought.

Russ said, "Justin and Drew say they look like human bones."

"Yeah, we'll see," the sheriff said gruffly.

"Is it—do you think—"

"We'll see," the sheriff repeated.

They'd walked a long way along the river. Just ahead, the riverside woods ended and big cement pylons loomed suddenly, carrying the Route 860 bridge. Russ didn't break pace as he continued under the bridge. The sheriff frowned at Marty, and she shook her head unhappily.

It was as they feared. On the far side of the bridge a barbed-wire fence ran down across the footpath and out into the river. Cautiously, Russ wriggled through and helped them hold the wires apart for each other before going on ahead. The sheriff murmured to Marty, "This the Walters place now?"

"Yeah," she confirmed.

"Shit."

"At least they had the sense to go back to the Strands' to call us. Walters is real touchy these days."

It wasn't much farther. Nysa Strand, her blond hair spangled with the sunshine that spilled through the cottonwood branches, was sitting on a log just where the river bent in to form a slight cove. "Hi, Miz Strand," said Marty. "This is Sheriff Cochran."

"Hello," Nysa said. She slid something into her crocheted bag and pointed. "They're right over there."

A broken femur. Most of a pelvis. They rested at the foot of a young maple tree, among sticks and pebbles recently dumped ashore. The river still licked at them, inches away. Marty swallowed and approached cautiously. They looked human, all right. She could see the prints of Russ's sneakers and some others, headed both ways on the muddy footpath. Near the bones there was a confusion of footprints. The prints told the same story Russ had: he'd gone ahead, found the bones, probably pointed them out to his friends, then all three had taken off to inform the others. Overlying the others, the most recent footprints were from small hiking boots like the ones Nysa was wearing. They were the only prints that circled around and past the bones, and returned, Marty saw.

She asked, "Did any of you pick up the bones?"

"I, um, started to," Russ confessed, his big eyes scared. "Then I saw they might be human."

"Must have given you a real turn," said the sheriff consolingly. But Marty could see that the big man was worried, his shrewd eyes under the steel-gray brows shifting from the bones at the water's edge, to the footprints on the path, to the woods and pastures that eventually led up to Dub Walters's fancy brick house. "Well," he said after a moment, "Miz Strand, why don't you and Russ go on back to your own property. I'll call the state crime scene fellas, and go break the bad news to Mr. Walters. Hopkins, you secure the scene."

"Yes sir."

Russ seemed eager enough to leave, but Nysa hesitated. Marty said, "We'll come talk to you as soon as we can," and the blond woman nodded and followed the boy away.

The sheriff gave them a moment. He probably wanted them well off the property when he spoke to Dub Walters. Then he said, "Hopkins, I may have to cancel your leave this week."

Marty's heart leapt. She'd get to work this case after all! Then she felt guilty because Chrissie would be so disappointed to miss the trip to see her father. "Yes sir," Marty said.

He handed her the crime scene tape. "Here, for all the good it'll do." He started up the bank.

She looked up at him. "Sir?"

He paused. "Yeah?"

"It's not Johnny Donato."

"Anything's possible in this business, Hopkins. But I'd say you're right. Hard to see how those bones could get so clean in only a week." He squinted in the direction of Walters's house. "One thing's sure, though."

"Sir?"

"It's going to be a grade-A headache."

9

DUB WALTERS WAS NOT A HAPPY CAMPER.

He stood in his kitchen door, tie loosened and belly jutting indignantly. Cool tendrils of air-conditioned air occasionally escaped around his bulk and soothed Wes's brow. Dub railed on. "Your little gal deputy brought all those kids last week to tramp over my fields. Now you want to bring in technicians, you say, maybe even goddamn divers."

"Yes sir. Trying to get all the evidence."

"Divers! Wes, you know half the town will be over here gawking. Fat lot of good it does to post my property. They just walk in anyway. And what the hell were those kids doing over here? The ones that trespassed and found these so-called bones?"

"I don't know, Dub. Probably just being kids. But now we've got to get the process rolling."

"It's that damn historic project. All those strangers."

"Come on, Dub, let's make that phone call. We'll find out what's going on a lot faster. Don't want to slow down the legal process."

Dub raised his beefy hands, palms out. "Help yourself! I'm not slowing anything down, Wes, I'm trying to tell you where to look for the culprits." He stepped back into the kitchen and waved Wes in. "You know I'm a real good friend to law enforcement. Question is whether law enforcement is a good friend to me."

"We do our best, Dub." Wes stalked past him to the kitchen phone and made his calls.

* * *

Marty headed back to the Strand farm. She'd cordoned off a broad area of the trail and riverside woods, stringing the crime scene tape farther around the cove to include not just the bones Russ had found but also something she'd glimpsed that might be a little knobbed sycamore branch— or might not. When Wes got back from calling the state evidence technicians he elected to stay at the scene and wait for them. He sent Marty back to begin getting statements from the picnickers. "You start with the ladies," he said, "and when you're done, go see the Donatos. Tell them it's not their boy. When the state cops get here, I'll leave them to it and come help you with the gents."

"Yes sir."

The day was warm, and steamy breath rose from the river and from the soaked landscape. Might as well be in that river, Marty thought as she ducked through the barbed wire that marked the boundary between Dub Walters's property and the Strands'. Just walking through this air was like swimming in a warm aquarium.

She listened to the dark mutter of the water and wondered where the bones had come from.

The river meandered back and forth from one side of its broad valley to the other. Here, at the foot of the Strand farm, it curved gently along the south edge of the valley, and the bank was abrupt, climbing sharply to the hills beside her. But across the water, the valley lay smooth as a bedspread, only a couple of low knolls breaking the flatness until it hit the steeper hills of the far side of the valley. If you followed this south bank past New Concord to the Brewster farm the situation reversed. There the river swung close to the northern hills, and the Brewster pastures on this side were mostly flat valley land.

She couldn't remember who owned farms on the other side of the river. Have to look that up. The nearest town on that side was tiny Beckerton, ten miles up the road.

There was a sound in the muggy air, very faint. Not the hum of insects, not the grumble of the water. A pulse to it. She listened carefully, and as she rounded a bend that brought her a first glimpse of the flat picnic rock, she heard more clearly. Voices. "Our helper He amid the flood of mortal ills prevailing." Young voices in glorious harmony. The musical arrangement was unusual, at once more archaic-sounding and more vivid than the version Marty knew. The singers were good, she decided as she came closer, better than the choir at Cedars of Lebanon Methodist that she heard every Sunday. In another moment she saw them, teenagers and adults in scruffy camp clothes standing in rows up the steep bank, all focused on the vibrant, upraised hands of a woman on the flat rock in the river. Nysa Strand, rapt, intense, pulled the shining music from them as though it was something physical, like beautiful thread from a spindle.

"Did we in our own strength confide, our striving would be losing." Marty slowed as she approached the clump of singers. In the last row Reverend Jeffries, wiry and muscular in a copper-colored polo shirt, sang an earnest bass with some of the taller boys, blond Kenny Ettinger and skinny Russ Pratt among them. The sopranos included Melissa Rueger and tall, clumsy Vicki Strand. Except she didn't look clumsy right now, Marty realized. Vicki's golden head was thrown back, and her strong, pure voice floated high among the others as her sister spun the harmonies of the old hymn into sparkling life. "Christ Jesus is His name," they sang, "from age to age the same."

For Marty the music suddenly crystallized why these people were here, why they dug for artifacts in the mud, why Bob Rueger and his church valued these long-ago buildings and long-ago stories. *From age to age the same.* Old Father Rueger's people had sung this hymn by this river, and Nysa's ardent reenactment braided together youth and history, past and future, humanity and divinity, into the shining present moment.

Marty forced herself to look around. Karen and Drew Brewster were not singing. She spotted them farther along the riverbank, packing one of the big coolers. She edged her way around behind the singers and joined them.

"Hi," she said quietly. "I don't want to disturb the singing, but we're expecting the state evidence technicians soon.

Mr. Brewster, could you go back up to the Strands' house and direct them, same as you did for us?"

Drew straightened, his jowly Oliver Hardy face sober. "Sure. Be glad to help. I've still got the key Nysa gave me." He set off along the path toward the little plank bridge that led to the Strand farm buildings.

Marty turned to Karen Brewster. "We'll want to interview everyone who saw the bones. And the crime scene people will need to look at shoes to match footprints. Maybe other things too."

"Crime scene? But the boy just fell in, didn't he? He couldn't have been killed!"

Marty said, "We have to keep an open mind until the technicians tell us what happened. It may not be Johnny."

"Oh, really? Oh, I hope not!" Karen said fervently. "I mean, the parents are so upset. They've been saying it's the historic project's fault!"

"I know."

"But that's so untrue and unfair! They shouldn't damage a positive project like this!"

"Damage?"

"With unfair rumors. We're trying to educate them, but if we fail Bob Rueger may take his money elsewhere."

"Well, we'll do our best to clear things up. Who all went to look at the bones?"

"First the three boys." Karen's comically expressive brows furrowed in concentration. "Russ Pratt, Kenny Ettinger, Derek Dunn. They slipped away after lunch. And when they came back with the news, Nysa Strand and Reverend Jeffries and Drew went to look. Bonnie Jeffries and I kept the other kids together here."

In the background Nysa had begun to drill the group on a musical phrase. "From age to age the same, and He will win the battle," they sang, over and over. Marty asked, "So everyone else was here with you?"

"Yes. Except Vicki Strand. She was over on our farm until half an hour ago, when she came for the music."

"I see. Now, think back to earlier in the day. Was anyone gone for a while?"

"No. Drew got here late, and Vicki, as I said. Everyone else has been here together since about ten o'clock this morning."

"Okay. Well, let us know if you think of anything that might help us clear things up."

"Okay."

The choir had finished and was breaking up. Marty hollered, "Just a minute, folks!" The babble of young voices stilled. "Just wanted to bring you up to date. The state crime scene technicians are on their way now. Sheriff Cochran and I will be taking statements from those of you who saw the bones, and from anyone else who can help us."

"Ma'am, please, was it Johnny?" asked Kenny Ettinger.

Marty said carefully, "The work of identification is just beginning. There's no particular reason yet to believe it's Johnny. Now, I'd just like to get the names of the people who saw it."

"Justin Jeffries!" sang out the muscular reverend. Marty nodded and wrote his name down.

"Nysa Strand," the choral director said quietly at Marty's ear.

"Okay, Miz Strand."

The three boys who'd found the bones filed up soberly to give Marty their names. Two others, eager for their place in the sun, blurted their names and launched right into an excited account of hearing sounds at night. "Kind of a roar," said Dave.

"There's always a kind of noise from the river," said Dave's friend. "But this was louder."

Marty asked, "Like a machine? A dog?"

"A machine," said Dave, while his buddy said, "Maybe like a cow."

Marty saw Drew Brewster puffing past, leading the state cops to the river trail. She waved them on before turning back to the boys. "Where did this noise come from?"

The boys looked at each other. "The river," said Dave at last. "Can't say any closer than that."

"Did anyone else hear it?"

65

"Don't know. We were awake, see. It wasn't loud enough to wake up anybody else in our tent."

"Okay, thanks, guys. Now, Miz Strand?"

But Nysa was nowhere to be seen. It was Vicki who looked around, startled. "Yes?"

"Oh. You know, that music was beautiful," Marty blurted. "You're such good singers."

"Thank you." Vicki seemed to glow. Marty felt that she'd done her Girl Scout deed for the day. It wasn't just Vicki's height that made her look clumsy, it was those extra-long arms and legs. Probably came in handy when she was handling a calf or a goat, but here in the world of humans it was good she had a voice to show off too. Something of beauty.

"Actually I wanted to talk to your sister about what she saw while she was waiting there for us," said Marty, getting back to business. "But since you're here, maybe you can tell me if you've seen anything that might help us."

"No." Vicki ducked her blond head apologetically. "I haven't been past the highway bridge since the river level dropped, so I didn't see the bones." She glanced up. "The river likes to leave things there. It's just where it turns north again, you see."

"You've found things there before?"

"Once I dropped a currycomb, from this flat rock right here, and found it two weeks later at that place. And there's a crab apple tree on the bank across from the Brewsters' farm. Every fall there are hundreds of crab apples that wash up there."

"I see. You know the river pretty well."

"If you're outdoors a lot, tending the animals, you notice things."

You would at that, Marty thought. Few people to distract you, seeing the same rocks and trees every day, you'd come to notice things like crab apples. Marty asked, "Any ideas where the bones might have come from?"

Vicki looked at her shoes. Then she said, "Nysa said it wasn't Johnny."

"We don't know yet for sure. Who did she think it was?"

"She didn't know. Do you think it's Johnny?"

"The crime scene technicians will try to make an identification and let us know." Marty studied Vicki a moment. She remembered the tall woman's hesitation the last time they'd talked. What had she noticed? "Do you have any reason to think it's Johnny Donato?" she asked gently.

"He drowned in the river, didn't he? But if this isn't him—"

"Why do you think that? Did you see him near the river?"

"Daisy was sick," Vicki said slowly. "It was raining, but I was looking for her near the path, to give her the medicine. Johnny said he was on his way home." She stopped.

Marty said, "Johnny was on the river path, you mean? Not the highway? Was this after he was seen running toward the barn?"

"Yes. But maybe he was on the highway later."

"Where on the river path?"

"Just this side of the hill behind the Brewsters' barn."

"Did you see him fall in?"

"No, no! I didn't see anything! But the river was still high. Still angry. And he disappeared."

"I sure wish you'd told us before. His cassette was found near the highway. Did Johnny say anything else?"

Vicki rubbed her face. "No. I'm sorry, I thought other people had told you."

"Did you see anyone else on the path?"

"A fisherman closer to town. I wasn't close enough to see who he was, and it was raining hard."

Marty wrote the information down. "Any impressions? Tall, short, fat?"

"Medium height, wearing a slicker, so I couldn't see more."

"What did you do after you saw Johnny?"

"I took care of Daisy."

"Okay, something else. A couple of the kids thought they heard a noise from the river last night. Kind of a roar, one said. Did you hear anything like that?"

"A roar?" A shadow of fright passed over the tall woman's face, then cleared. "A cow was bellowing last night. Like that?"

"Maybe that was it. These are city kids."

"But some of them know animals," Vicki said earnestly. "Melissa Rueger wants to be a vet."

"Yeah. One more question. I'm not accusing you of anything. It's just that Mr. Walters gets very annoyed by people on his property. I wondered why you were over there so often."

"The animals stray," Vicki explained. "He doesn't keep up his fence very well, and kids and fishermen break it down. I've repaired it four times this year."

"You repair it?"

"Yes. We used to call him but he got mad at us. So now we just fetch the animals back and repair the fence."

"Yeah, I think I'd do that too," Marty agreed. She looked around. "Do you know where your sister went?"

"She said she had to prune the vines, so she'd be at the labyrinth."

"The what?"

"It's on West Street in New Concord. Not a long walk."

"Okay, thanks, I'll take a look." Marty closed her notebook. The labyrinth. Might be a fitting place to talk about this mess, at that.

10

ON HER WAY TO WEST STREET MARTY TOOK A SHORT detour to the Donato house. She'd seen or talked to them every day for a week, but this stop was important. When she pulled up, Carl Donato was in the driveway, squatting in the shade near the garage. Even so he was sweating, his olive skin glistening, his red plaid shirt sticking damply to his muscular torso. He was working on a bicycle, Marty saw as she rolled down her window, a boy's bicycle. When he saw her he stood and walked down the drive to her cruiser. He wiped his brow with his forearm, and she could see fear in his eyes.

Marty leaned from her window into the heat. "Hello, Mr. Donato. There's no news about Johnny."

"Then why the hell did you stop by?"

"You see, sir, they found somebody else's bones down by the river. We didn't want you all hearing a rumor and thinking the wrong thing."

"Somebody else's? How do you know?"

"Well, it's not official yet. But the bones look like they've been there a whole lot longer than Johnny's been gone."

"Who is it?"

"We're still working on it, sir."

"Nobody knows a damn thing!" He kicked at a roadside stone. "Sue's after me—why didn't we this, why didn't we that. . . . But you can't wrap a boy in cotton!"

She ached for the Donatos. If Chrissie—but that thought was too terrifying to think. She said, "Yes sir, it's real frustrating."

"See, a boy's got to learn to stand up to the world. You can't coddle him!"

"Yes sir, you don't want to be too protective."

She'd meant it to be soothing, but Carl Donato exploded. "Then what the hell am I doing, working these hours? I'm trying to give them a safe place! Seventeen years I've worked for Helton, and it's no great joy. Long hours, wrecks your back. But you take it so your family can have a decent life. And then something like this happens, and your wife wants to know why you didn't do everything different!" He kicked angrily at the stone again.

"Sir, your wife is real upset too. It's natural to be upset. When she settles down she'll see that you did right by the family. Do you want me to tell her that what we found by the river isn't Johnny?"

"No, I'll tell her." He wiped the sweat from his forehead again, glowering at her. "Dammit, you find my boy!"

"We're trying, sir." She turned the ignition.

*   *   *

West Street dozed in the misty heat of the afternoon. Marty smelled hot foliage and muddy fields on the warm, damp breeze as she got out of the cruiser, and heard bees humming around the daisies and petunias. There were about a dozen simple New Concord clapboard houses on each side of the street, individualized over the years by a scattering of aluminum scroll porch columns, a few turquoise or mustard paint jobs, occasional tulip trees or giant sunflowers or miniature windmills in the front yards. No different from the Donatos' neighborhood a couple of blocks away.

Halfway along the row of houses was a wide stretch filled by a six-foot-tall chicken-wire fence planted with vigorous grapevines. As she walked beside it she glanced across the street, where one of the old civic buildings, a dormitory perhaps, had been outfitted with a pair of plate-glass storefront windows and a hand-lettered sign, now peeling, that proclaimed "Stern's Appliances." A second, more professional sign announced the presence of General Electric.

Marty came to a low gate in the vine-covered fence and entered. The area was large, four lots wide and just as deep, reaching back into the woods that bordered New Concord on this side. It was covered with grapevines. Far away, in the center of the field of vines, a tiny white building poked a pointed roof above the fluttering leaves. The grapevines were growing on chicken-wire supports, like the streetside fence but lower, perhaps three feet tall. Row after row of vines stood between Marty and the little building.

Above the buzz of insects she heard a faint clacking. She called, "Miz Strand?"

"Yes?" Nysa rose from the sea of foliage near the little building at the center of the field. She waved at Marty. "Over here, Deputy Hopkins!"

"How do I get there?"

"Go left. It's a long route, but you'll get here."

Marty went left. A sandy, crabgrass-studded path curved between two rows of exuberant vines. After twenty feet the path U-turned and she walked back almost to where she'd entered. Another U-turn and she was hiking the original direction, but farther this time. "Isn't there a shortcut?" she called.

"No, following the pattern is the point of the labyrinth." Nysa's voice was close behind her.

Marty turned, surprised to see the other woman only two rows away. "I thought the point was to get lost."

"That too," Nysa agreed. "But not to stay lost. Father Rueger's people believed this was a way to spiritual harmony. These days I think children understand that better than adults."

"Yeah, my daughter would love this."

"Oh, yes, bring her sometime! She'll like it. A labyrinth is an ancient symbol of life, because the path of life is mysterious and twisting. We don't know what direction we're going until we arrive."

"Well, that's true enough." Marty spoke across the three-foot-high curving rows of grapevine. The plants were robust, flinging out long, leafy branches that twined along their wire support. She could see infant bunches of grapes here and there among the broad, notched leaves. "I didn't know there was a maze here."

"We're in the process of reconstructing it. You probably noticed that the back half is still overgrown. But part of the central building was left, and we had Father Rueger's own plans in our family papers. This big lot borders our farm."

"I thought mazes like this were usually made out of hedges," Marty said.

"Yes, that's true. But vines grow faster, and Father Rueger was an impatient man. An enthusiastic man. Come along a little further and I'll meet you."

Meeting Nysa meant walking away from her for a while. Marty began to see what she meant about a spiritual experience. Trudging along this preordained path was hypnotic. Go halfway round, double back, double back again. The leaves danced, the insects droned, the warm, green-scented air bathed her, and time seemed suspended. But suddenly there was Nysa, striding gracefully along the narrow path toward her, the crocheted bag at her belt, a pair of long pruning shears in her hand.

71

"Good! Here we are." She smiled, brushing a vine leaf from her hair. "You see, there's only the one path."

"Father Rueger didn't believe in choice?"

"He believed in his angel voices," said Nysa, her voice tinged with bitterness. "And in doing everything possible to avoid sin. I suppose there's always the choice of crashing into the grapevines. Or of turning back, away from the center."

Nysa, even now, was turning toward the center. Marty, following a step behind, decided it was time to head for the main point herself. "I wanted to ask about what you saw at the river."

"You mean the bones? A pelvis, and part of a long bone from the leg, I think. And a little farther along that cove there's another bit of leg bone. Did you see that?"

"Yeah. I was hoping it was just a sycamore branch."

"I don't think so. What will happen now?" Nysa glanced over her shoulder, her blue eyes troubled.

"The state technicians will check over the scene, remove the bones, maybe look for the rest of them."

Nysa was silent a moment. Then she said, "The person didn't die recently. The bones were very clean. Very old."

Marty said neutrally, "Yes, it looked that way."

"Oh, it's not poor Johnny! I'm just sure! I live by the river. I've seen drowned animals. The water does sad things to bodies. It roughs them up, bloats them, but it doesn't strip them to the bone in a week. And also . . ."

When she didn't continue, Marty said, "And also what?"

"Here we are." Nysa turned left abruptly, and suddenly they were upon the little building at the center. It was round, about ten feet in diameter, and built of hand-chiseled blocks of native limestone. An entry arch had a flaming sun design carved above it, with some kind of figure carved within it. "The biblical 'woman clothed in the sun,'" Nysa explained. "A favorite Harmonist symbol. She awaited the end time in the wilderness. The labyrinth was an old European cathedral symbol too. They laid the maze designs into the tile of their floors. It was the same idea as Father Rueger's, the spiritual connection between a maze and our inability to see the design of our lives. But if we follow faithfully, we reach our appointed goal."

Marty touched the weathered stone doorjamb and said gently, "You were going to tell me something else about the bones."

Nysa studied her a moment, then said, "The important thing is that it's not Johnny Donato. Everything else is speculation."

"Speculation's fine," Marty said, hoping that Nysa was in the mood to talk. "You know Johnny, and the town, and the history project people. I'm interested in your speculations."

Nysa laughed and shook her golden head. "No, you don't know how I get carried away! I wish I could be logical and cautious, like you."

"You're logical enough," Marty said encouragingly.

"Not about the important things! I ran away when I was fifteen, with—no, you see I already got it jumbled. First you have to know that I've always loved music. I can't recall a time when I didn't."

Marty remembered Nysa's rapt intensity as she stood on the flat rock in the river, directing the hymn. "Well, you're good. That was the best hymn I've ever heard."

Nysa touched Marty's arm in delight. "Did you like it? It's such wonderful music. New Concord was known for its fine musicians, and Father Rueger appreciated them. I found the arrangement among his papers. He was a man of enthusiasms. It seems to be a family trait." She looked serious again. "Anyway, I've always loved music. Our family had problems, tensions, but they supported my love of music. They said I'd go to Indiana University, to the great music school there, when I was old enough. But when I was fifteen, I met Thom."

Marty decided not to interrupt just yet. Good information often came in the midst of rambling stories. Nysa leaned back against the stone wall of the building, her eyes far away. "He was attending Indiana State—we were living near Terre Haute at the time. It was spring, April I think, and there was a church picnic in a park. And some Indiana State students were having a picnic nearby. Thom had a little band, a rock band, and he was lead singer. My sister and I had gone for a walk and were attracted by the music, those great deep pagan rhythms we weren't allowed to hear at home. I told you my father was a preacher, right? And Thom sang, directly to me, I thought. Black jeans, no shirt, just a shiny silver vest that showed off his arms and the hair on his chest. My sister fell a little in love with him too. But I was sure he was my own special prince come to save me." Nysa's blue eyes flicked to Marty. "Some people say, well, everyone has crushes. Maybe so. I tracked him down, I sneaked away from school to go to the Indiana State campus, I lied and told him I was a freshman there. He—well, he liked me too. I wanted to learn the music, I wanted him, I wanted to change my life for him. Oh, it was all the clichés!" She touched Marty's arm. "Flaming passions, dreams come true. Thom was bright but moody, sometimes depressed. He called it the Beast, his depression. But for me it seemed wonderful, because he said I helped him conquer the Beast, I led him out of himself. I was fifteen, and it seemed glorious, helping him conquer the Beast! I was delirious with this new joy. There were drugs, yes, there was that magical alien music, but mostly there was his need, and mine. When he said I helped, he was so sexy, so very sexy! Do you know what I mean?"

Marty knew exactly what she meant. She shrugged. "Sure."

"I knew you'd understand! There's a Thom in your life too, isn't there? My parents—well, they found out, and that was that. My father went crazy for a while. It was terrible, not just for me, but for my sister, for my poor little lost brother. Especially for my brother. He finally ran away." Tears stood in Nysa's eyes, and she blinked. "Three, maybe four weeks I'd known Thom, and I'd wrecked everyone's life. So when Thom graduated I ran away and joined him."

Marty wondered why Nysa was telling her all this. But she nodded sympathetically. The other woman went on, "Thom was going to Chicago, and at first he was upset to see me. But I'd sacrificed everything for him, whether he wanted it or not. We drove off in his Honda. I remember I was wearing a tight black stretch top. I thought I looked so sophisticated in my stretch top! Mother always made us wear those floral blouses. We felt lucky at that—my father probably would have preferred gray woolen dresses like Father Rueger's folks. So off I went in my black stretch top, trying to pretend my father had never punished me, singing along with Thom in his Honda. And we talked, for the first time, really. Before that it had been just us against the Beast, and singing, and sex. And for such a short time! Now we talked. And I was trying to be upbeat, babbling about being musicians together, and Thom said, wait a minute, I'm going to law school, and you have to finish college! So I confessed I wasn't even in college, and he got it out of me that I was fifteen and my father wanted to save me from sin. Thom couldn't cope with that. He started swearing. Said I was too young. And I was, I was." Her grieving blue gaze found Marty's. "I think you might understand. I can feel it."

"Yeah, I understand." Marty had been nineteen, and even that was too young. She said gently, "Look, we're supposed to be talking about the case. The bones at the river. Johnny Donato."

Nysa swung through the stone doorway into the little building. "I'm afraid, Deputy Hopkins. Afraid for Johnny. Adolescence, the heat of sex—it muddies the vision. Is it just another turn in the labyrinth, or does it send us crashing into the vines? Is it a distraction, or is it at the center? Father Rueger tried to eliminate it. I tried to give myself to it. We both failed. Thom put me out of the car."

"He put you out of the car?"

"He left me behind. He stopped at a little town with a Greyhound bus station, and bought me a ticket back to Terre Haute, and drove away. I cried and cried. Do you know what I mean?"

"Yeah," said Marty shortly. Brad had married her, had put a cheerful face on it. He loved his daughter too, that was clear, and Chrissie loved him. But he'd left—oh, yes, he'd left, often. And maybe this time for always.

"It's sad," Nysa said softly. "So sad to know the rapture, and lose yourself to it, and then to be left behind. It is a terrible, terrible loss, at twelve, at fifteen, at thirty."

"Okay, look, let's be a little clearer." Marty pulled her thoughts around to the case. "You're saying that sex is at the center of Johnny's disappearance? A fourteen-year-old kid?"

"I'm afraid for him," Nysa said simply. "I don't know anything, it's just a feeling. A speculation. Logically, the center—well, the center isn't where you look for it, is it? It's where you find it."

And that was all Nysa was able, or willing, to say. Trudging back through the labyrinth to the cruiser, Marty told herself she'd better check with the youngsters again, see if she could find out anything about Johnny Donato's budding love life. And her heart ached—for Johnny, for young Nysa, for her own almost-fatherless Chrissie, and yes, for herself. Left behind.

11

WES COCHRAN DROVE PAST DUB WALTERS'S BIG house and down the lane. He parked the cruiser in the ragged row of state vehicles in Dub's lower pasture. Once Dub had realized that state investigation was inevitable, he'd decided to be sweet as pie to the state boys, letting them drive muddy ruts into his fields. But that didn't mean that Wes wouldn't be expected to view it as a big personal favor later.

The air was warm, heavy with river vapors, the smell of rotting vegetation, the sound of cicadas. He half walked, half slid down the muddy slope to the edge of the crime scene. "Hey there, Doc," he said. "What've we got?"

Dr. Altmann looked up from the bones he was arranging on a tarp. The coroner was a lean, fuzzy-haired man with glasses that looked like John Lennon's. Ten years ago, when

he was a general practitioner, he'd been asked to help iden-
tify the decomposed body of an elderly nursing home pa-
tient who'd wandered off. He'd liked the medical detective
work and the limelight of the courtroom appearance, and
had decided to run for coroner. Wes found him much more
competent than the alcoholic dentist who'd held the post
before. "Well, Sheriff," Doc drawled, gesturing at the tarp,
"I think I'm going to have to pronounce him dead."

"Yeah, you may have to at that." Wes nodded at the
bones, the broken pelvis and thighbone. "You said 'him.' "

"Pelvis is male, surprisingly juvenile in form," said Doc.
"But he's a real tall fellow—unofficial, of course. Can't give
you any numbers yet, but basketball scouts might call home
about him. Look at this femur." He fitted a couple of long
shards of bone together. "I'm hoping the guys will bring me
a skull, but they probably won't, the lazy oafs." He waved
dismissively at the divers who were dragging the nearby bottom of the river. The water was mustard-colored where they'd
roiled it.

"Mm. Any suggestions on time of death?" Wes asked.

"You wanna join our pool?" Doc's bright eyes beamed
through the spectacles at him. "Five bucks, you win it all if
you're the closest."

"Okay, okay, I'll wait for the lab report. Can you at least
rule out the last couple days?"

Doc Altmann nodded soberly. "Last couple days, yeah.
Last couple weeks."

"Well, I didn't think it was the kid we were looking for.
I'll see you around, Doc."

Doc Altmann turned happily back to his femur. "Last couple centuries, no. Can't rule that out yet."

Wes shook his head and climbed up the bank.

"The thing is, Brad, I can't come to Memphis until this
case is finished."

"Christ, Marty!" Even over the phone she could sense his
scowl. "All I ask is a few days! I've made arrangements for
time off and everything!"

"Yeah, I'm sorry. You know how this job is."

"I sure do. Why don't you get out of it? Do something more predictable? Don't you give a damn about your family?"

"Why do you think I took this job in the first place? Because it pays better than waiting tables! Because my mom was dying, and Chrissie had to eat, and you sure weren't bringing in much!"

There was a pause before his wounded tones came over the phone. "That hurts, kitten. That really hurts. You know I was working my butt off for you and the kid that whole time. Swear to God I was!"

"I know, Brad, I know." She shouldn't have yelled at him. He was doing his best too, she knew. Broadcasting was a hard business to break into.

"And now I've got something to show for it. It's great here, Marty, swear to God. And I want you and Chrissie to see."

"I want to see too. But I just can't, Brad."

"Don't you understand? I have to arrange for time off in advance! I can't just call up and say, Marty just blew in to town so I'm not coming in."

"I'm sorry, Brad."

"You really won't come?" He still didn't believe her.

"I can't."

"Christ! You are so—oh, hell!" His receiver slammed down. Marty hung up to the sound of a dial tone. Seemed like she spent all her time fixing other people's problems, and couldn't figure out how to fix her own.

She was in the pay booth at the Wilson 76 service station, at the intersection of the highway with Center Street in New Concord. As she walked back to the cruiser she spotted Rosie at the corner of her street, throwing a Frisbee. Rosie wasn't crying, the way she'd been last week. Marty approached slowly. The girl was playing with Chuckles, tossing the Frisbee while the little kinky-tailed terrier leaped for it. "Boy, he can really jump high!" Marty said admiringly.

"Yeah." Rosie, holding the Frisbee, glanced at her shyly. "He's a good dog."

"I like his crooked tail. It's cute."

"It was a mistake," Rosie said earnestly. "Johnny didn't mean to do it."

"Didn't mean to do what, honey?"

"Let the door close on his tail. But Daddy was mad at him anyway."

"Yeah. Well, Chuckles seems fine now. Can I pet him?" Marty leaned over the little terrier.

"Sure."

Marty rubbed the curly back. "I'm Deputy Hopkins. Maybe you remember?"

"You're looking for Johnny."

"Yeah. I wondered if you could tell me if Johnny has any special friends from Arizona."

"Maybe Russ."

"What about girl friends?"

"He thinks Ellie is pretty. I think Darlene is prettier but he says I don't know anything."

"Yeah, guys say that sometimes, but they're wrong. We really know a lot," Marty said. "Does Ellie know that Johnny thinks she's cute?"

Rosie shrugged. "I don't think so. He just acts silly when she's there. She's older. You know."

"What kind of acting silly?"

"Bragging, and walking on his hands, and saying he can ride cows and horses. You know, like in a rodeo. He can't really."

"Yeah." Pity squeezed Marty's heart to think of Johnny showing off for Ellie. Nysa was right about the awkwardness when hormones kicked in. At fourteen, even if you were tall for your age, you weren't cool. Walking on your hands and bragging—no, that wouldn't impress the older kids. "Did he ever have trouble with the people from Arizona?"

"Not really. They're pretty nice. Once Reverend Jeffries told us to leave when they were digging. And once that big woman sent him and George out of the barn because they were upsetting the cows."

"Why did Reverend Jeffries tell you to leave?"

"We were playing with the stuff they dug up. There was this thing, like a hammer only the other side was sharp?

79

But we weren't supposed to play with it." The girl patted Chuckles.

"Now, Johnny told you about cow witches, right?" Marty asked casually.

Rosie nodded, looking at her dog.

"Did he tell anyone else?" Marty asked.

The girl shrugged and hugged Chuckles till the little dog squirmed.

"Chuckles is cute, isn't he?" Marty said, struggling to restore Rosie to talkativeness. But Rosie did not respond.

Marty said, "Do you think Johnny told Russ Pratt?"

"No. Maybe George."

"Okay, honey. Thanks. Please tell me if you think of anything else Johnny was worried about. Or excited about. Okay?"

"Okay," Rosie said in a small voice.

"See, my job is to help people with their problems. But the people have to tell me what the problems are. Okay?"

"Okay."

"Thanks, honey. You're helping us a lot."

More than the parents, anyway, Marty thought as she climbed into the cruiser. She'd better check with Ellie. That would be the sparkly dark-haired girl who'd mentioned talking to Johnny shortly before his disappearance. And George was one of Johnny's best friends, the stocky New Concord boy who'd helped on the search parties. More kids to talk to.

Including her own. She'd promised to take Chrissie and her friend Janie to the mall when she got off work an hour from now. And after that she had to tell Chrissie that they weren't going to Memphis. A much harder job than telling Brad.

Marty sighed and nosed the cruiser back toward the Brewster farm.

12

WES COCHRAN RADIOED HOPKINS TO CALL IN. "BOB Rueger himself is in town," he told her when Foley handed him the phone a few minutes later. "Wants to talk to us. He's at his Rockland Mall office."

"Yes sir." Hopkins hesitated, and he could hear the whoosh of cars on the highway behind her. "I'll meet you there, sir."

"You worried about how late it is? You'll get overtime."

"See, sir, the thing is, I promised Chrissie I'd take her and Janie to the mall when I got off at four. Is it okay if I take a couple minutes to pick them up?"

"Hopkins, you saying your kid's little shopping trip is more important than a multimillionaire developer?"

"No, sir, but—well, yes sir, for two minutes, sir. See, I promised her. She's just at Janie's; it's not even much of a detour."

"Well, make it snappy."

Wes handed the receiver back to Foley, who said, "Sheesh. Women don't know how to put the job first."

"You're dispatcher, Foley, not departmental conscience," said Wes mildly, biting back the observation that Hopkins generally gave 110 percent to the job to make up for Foley's 90 percent. Plus being mom and dad both to that kid.

The Rockland Mall was not enclosed like the fancy new ones in Evansville and Bloomington, but it was the biggest shopping center in the county, L-shaped and boasting a JC Penney's and a Save-More Grocery. The Rockland Mall office was at the Penney's end of the building. By the time Wes found the right door Hopkins was already there. She

81

drove too fast, just like her dad. Don't think about that, Wes told himself. He nodded at her and opened the door.

A curly-haired blond woman in a green dress looked up from her desk. "Hi, Sheriff Cochran."

"How's it going, Janelle? D'you know my deputy? Marty Hopkins?"

"Sure. She did security for our Halloween parade."

"My uniform almost won the best-costume prize," Hopkins said.

Janelle smiled. "Let me tell Mr. Rueger you're here." She announced their names into the intercom.

Generally Wes's dealings with Rockland Mall concerned shoplifters, fender benders in the parking lot, security for Halloween or Christmas or Little Hoosier Miss festivities. He'd never been in this office. It was high-class, all right, with thick light gray carpeting. Everything else was vanilla ice cream color: walls, modern desk, file cabinets, sofa, even wastebasket. The only brightness came from a couple of wide-leaved plants by the small window, and a row of five architect's sketches over the sofa, labeled Lincoln Mall, Phoenix Plaza, Saguaro Mall, Riverside Mall, and of course Rockland Mall. The Rockland sketch was a glamorized ideal of this very place, showing a few outlined cars lined up neatly in the lot and a few outlined people filing by the carefully rendered storefronts. All the men were broad-shouldered, all the women slim, all the children placidly holding a parent's hand. Wes noted that there were no outlined sheriffs, and the architect had forgotten the little security cameras that scanned the storefronts. No crime or drunkenness there in Outline Mall.

"Sheriff Cochran! Deputy Hopkins!" A mid-height, square-built man in shirtsleeves and gray suit trousers burst from the inner office. He was fiftyish, tanned, with graying hair and an enthusiastic grin. Only his eyes seemed worried. "I'm Bob Rueger. Sure appreciate you coming by. Come on in."

Wes followed the other two in. Same carpet, but fancy wood furniture here, teak or something, and leather chairs.

A long way from his own chipped gray metal furniture. "So what can we do for you?" Wes asked.

"Well, it's about the situation in New Concord. Please, sit down!" Bob Rueger motioned for them to sit in the visitors' chairs, but propped himself against the front edge of his desk instead of sitting behind it. A good maneuver, Wes decided as he sank into the soft leather. Made Rueger seem informal and friendly, but gave him the advantage of height. Rueger continued, "My daughter Melissa called me last week, as usual. But her news wasn't usual. She said one of the local teenage boys was missing. She sounded worried. I reassured her and reminded her that I was going to visit the mall here this week anyway." He looked earnestly from Wes to Marty Hopkins. "Well, I drove out to see my daughter soon as I got here, of course. And she was very upset. Said they'd just found his bones in the river. Naturally, I want to know what's going on."

"Well, sir, at the present moment we don't think it's the Donato boy's bones," Wes said. "There's no positive identification yet, and it'll take time to get the lab report, but it appears that this guy died much more than a week ago."

"I see. I'm glad it wasn't the youngster my daughter knows. That's welcome news. I hope the boy's found soon. Donato, you said?"

"Yes sir," Hopkins said. Wes noticed the lively interest in her gray eyes and nodded for her to continue. "Is the fact that Melissa knew him the only reason you're concerned?"

"The main reason, of course. I called the Brewsters immediately, and they were sure the boy would turn up. I certainly hope he will." He leaned toward them with intensity. "But I'm also concerned with the New Concord historic project. The Donato boy's disappearance and this other death—could they be related?"

Hopkins said, "We're treating them as two different cases."

"Okay. And Melissa says the Donato boy left by the highway, although he was seen leaving her group, headed toward the barn."

"Yes sir, that's unclear. Another witness saw him beyond that point, on the river path."

Wes glanced at Hopkins. He hadn't heard that bit yet.

"So there's no connection. Good. The New Concord project is very close to my heart." Rueger relaxed and smiled his candid grin again. "You know, I'm descended from Emanuel Rueger, Father Rueger's son."

"Well, Mr. Rueger, you understand that the Donato boy was friendly with the kids in the church group, and they were among the last to see him. So naturally we've got to ask questions."

"Sure. Of course. I understand that," Bob Rueger said earnestly. "My concern is just that there's been opposition to the project. One thing I was trying to prove this summer was that the project would help the community. I don't know of a nicer bunch of kids than these. I'd think people would take more pride in their own history around here. Well, some do."

Opposition. Wes tented his fingers. He was aware of Hopkins's glance and knew her mind was running the same direction as his. He said, "Mr. Rueger, if you don't mind me asking, will you abandon this project if the protests continue?"

"Abandon it?" Rueger frowned. "No."

"Even if we turn up something serious?"

"Like murder, you mean? That's not likely, is it?"

"We're just supposing."

"I'd—well, the first thing would be to get the kids back to Arizona safely. I'd do everything in my power to help you solve it, of course. If it delayed the project, so be it. But I wouldn't quit." Rueger smoothed back his graying hair. "I didn't get where I am by being a quitter."

Hopkins said, "Excuse me, sir, but you didn't get where you are by doing historic projects, either."

Rueger laughed. "You're right, Deputy Hopkins. You want to know if I've lost my marbles, right?" His smile faded and regrets came into his eyes. "But you see, I haven't had much continuity in my life. As a kid we moved around—Ohio, Illinois, here. I started my career working on construction gangs all over the Midwest. Got a break in Kentucky working for a banker, remembered that this county needed a mall, and came back to build it. But it didn't need two, so I moved on, ended up in Arizona. Now, after years of moving around, I just have this hankering to find my roots. So somehow, when I heard about what that old German fellow, Father Rueger, had done, the story really grabbed me." He was leaning forward, intense. "Just think about it. My great-great-granddaddy! He led his people to a wild land, carved out a civilization in the midst of floods and malaria and Indians and wild animals. And look." He held out a fist and traced a blue vein with his index finger. "This is the same bloodstream as Father Rueger's! It amazes me, makes me proud." He stared at the fist, then grinned. "Oh, hell. Call it sentimental; maybe it is. Call it midlife crisis. But whatever the reason, I'm fascinated by this thing. I want to see it go smoothly."

Wes nodded. "I can understand that. In these parts, we don't always pay enough attention to our history."

"You should! It's a fascinating history. Maybe restoring New Concord will remind people. And it'll give the county an economic boost. You've got the Asphodel Springs Resort here, but no other big tourist attractions. A historic village will be very appealing. Sure, it's off the beaten track, but it could support a motel, some bed-and-breakfasts. And there are plenty of local ties. The Strand sisters—they're distant cousins of mine, it turns out! And the Brewsters have been very enthusiastic too."

And as he added people to his payroll he'd have even more supporters, Wes thought. "The opposition comes from Mr. Walters?" he asked.

Rueger nodded. "Yeah. I was surprised. When we built this mall, he was very cooperative. Of course, as Deputy Hopkins says, historic projects aren't malls. Though I really think it would benefit the county economically."

"It's not far from his house," Hopkins said.

"But it would be a good neighbor! And there's a highway

and a farm between him and New Concord!" Rueger said. "Anyway, that's why I started it so low-key, just to show the townsfolk that Walters was wrong and there wouldn't be any problems. And then one of their kids disappears, and a man turns up dead in the river . . ." He shook his head sadly.

"Well," Wes said mildly, "Dub Walters may be getting more crotchety in his old age, but I never heard of him murdering or kidnapping to get his way."

Rueger chuckled. "I wasn't accusing him. He's on the County Council, right? Respectable man. No, I was just explaining why I feel so regretful about this sad coincidence. And I want to let you know that if there's anything I can do to help you clear it up, I'll be happy to."

"Okay." Wes levered himself up from the chair and looked down at Rueger. "We appreciate your cooperation, sir. We'll let you know if something comes up. Hopkins?"

"The main thing we're after right now is information, Mr. Rueger," she said. "Melissa might tell you something that she wouldn't want to tell an outsider. You know, about the Donato boy, or about friends he'd made in her group, or about pranks he'd pulled."

"All right, I'll pass on anything like that. How about posting a reward?"

"Couldn't hurt," Wes said cautiously.

"I'll do it then," said Rueger. "Does five hundred dollars sound good?"

"Sounds great. I'll get Deputy Foley back to you to work out the details."

After the office door closed behind them, Hopkins walked a few steps with Wes. "Sir, sorry I didn't have a chance to tell you that Vicki Strand saw Johnny going toward the river path not long after he left the others. He didn't tell her anything so it's not much help, but maybe he didn't leave by the highway."

"What else did you get?"

"A couple of things from Nysa Strand. She didn't have

any evidence, but she talked about teenage sex as a possible problem. May just be her hang-up."

"Nobody else mentioned anything like that?" Wes asked sharply.

"Not yet. Like I said, it may just be her hang-up. But Johnny's little sister said he liked one of the Arizona girls, the one named Ellie. Checking that out will give me a reason to talk to the kids again. I'll keep my ears open for anything odd. Let's see . . . Johnny's father didn't have that much to add. Wants to know why we haven't found him, and what he's paying his taxes for."

"Well, he's worried about his kid. I'll tell him about the reward."

"Okay." They were standing at the arch that led into Penney's. "That's about it, sir."

"What'd you think of Rueger?"

"He was trying real hard to be a nice guy. And I guess the reward could help."

"It'll bring out the flakes. But sometimes even flakes have evidence." Wes hitched up his trousers. "Yeah, I thought he was trying hard to be nice too."

"Well, maybe he really is nice." She shrugged. "What do us working stiffs know about multimillionaires? And he's probably like Mr. Donato—really worried, wondering why we don't know more. His daughter's here, and the project involves his ancestors. Means a lot to him. He seemed really sad about growing up without roots. Funny thing, though— Nysa Strand seemed pretty cool toward him, even though he's supporting the historic project, paying her salary and her sister's. Plus he's a relative."

"Well, I don't love all my second cousins," Wes admitted. But he filed away this little discrepancy. Hopkins was pretty observant. "What do you think of the possibility that somebody's trying to cause trouble for the historic project?"

"I agree with you, sir: Murder and kidnapping seem too extreme for that motive. Still . . ."

"Yeah. Keep an open mind. You off to get Chrissie now?"

"Yeah, she and Janie are trying on swimsuits at Penney's."

"I don't see her at the pool often."

Hopkins grinned. "She likes the Reed Hollow quarry best, whenever the mean old sheriff's deputies aren't raiding it."

"Yeah. So did I, at her age. Have fun, Hopkins."

Walking back to the cruiser, Wes wished he'd spent more time at Reed Hollow with his Billy while he could. Too late now.

13

SATURDAY NIGHT, THUNDERSTORMS HIT NICHOLS county again. They were brief, and the last of them rolled on eastward by morning. The earth was left wet and steamy, the red mud thick and sticky, the foliage beaded with raindrops.

The White River gorged itself on the storms, swelling again, gaining speed and power. The rain continued to fall heavily upstream, and the river reclaimed the high-water mark it had so recently abandoned. Once again low branches were underwater, forming nets that caught the fast-food containers, aluminum chairs, broken toys, bottles, sticks, and other objects that the tipsy river scooped from the banks and rushed downstream.

One of the heavier objects had been dragging slowly along the stony bottom, well below the surface, until it had caught in a tangle of fishing line snagged under a rock. But the river was stronger now, and higher, and the object was puffing up so it was lighter. The river wrenched it from its makeshift anchor and sent it bobbing downstream for a quick quarter-mile. Then it jammed the object into the submerged branches of a small maple that had toppled into the water when its roots lost their grip on the dissolving bank.

The drunken river left it behind and reeled on.

At noon on Sunday the east was still dark with retreating storm clouds. But overhead the sky was a lighter gray, and after helping clean up after lunch, Marty kicked off her church shoes and said, "Hey, Chrissie, want to go for a walk?"

"Janie wants to come over," said Chrissie coolly, not looking up from the Sunday funnies. She hadn't forgiven Marty for canceling their trip to Memphis.

"Well, this walk is sort of connected to work, so I can go by myself. But I like to talk to you sometimes."

"It's connected to work?" Chrissie's eyes darkened with nervous anticipation. "Well—I can tell Janie to come later."

"Good. Tell her about four-thirty. And get on your mud shoes, because we'll be by the river."

Aunt Vonnie, sitting in her chair in her flowered Sunday dress with her sprained ankle propped up, clicked the remote to change channels and exclaimed, "Mud shoes? Can't you even spend your day off out of the mud?"

"You want to come along for the hike?" Marty teased, halfway up the stairs to change her clothes.

Aunt Vonnie snorted. "Get out of here."

As they drove toward the State 860 bridge, Marty said, "They say the river's up again." The Strand farm was on their right, its small, dignified farmhouse almost out of sight behind the tall hedges. On their left, Dub Walters's big brick house came into view. In a couple of minutes they were at the bridge. The rushing, muddy water was the color of old gold under the silver sky. Marty wanted to take a look at the other side of the river. No one had checked that out yet, except for a quick search of the nearest sinkholes. And she hadn't yet followed up on Nysa's comment about checking upstream. She drove across the bridge and pulled over onto the shoulder of the highway. "Okay, let's walk upstream on this side. See what's there."

"Where did they find those old bones?" Chrissie, wearing

her oldest sneakers, jeans, a glitter-design turquoise T-shirt, and matching turquoise-enameled stars in her ears, climbed up to balance on the bridge guardrail, looking out at the water.

"They were on the other side, about a quarter-mile downstream," Marty said, pointing. She was in jeans too, but her T-shirt advertised the Indiana Pacers and her earrings were the simple studs she liked for work.

"Can I see?"

"I was going to go the other direction."

"C'mon! It'll only take a couple of minutes!"

"Well . . ." Marty would have wanted to see too, at Chrissie's age. "Okay, if you don't mind staying on this side of the river. Mr. Walters doesn't like people walking on his land. And the state cops won't want us at the crime scene yet. They're bringing back the divers tomorrow."

Chrissie jumped from the rail to the sloping bank and started downstream. "Why not today? You work on Sundays sometimes."

"Sure. There has to be someone at the sheriff's office all the time, so we take turns. And if there's an emergency we have to help people, no matter when it happens, so we get called in. But the state cops are in charge of those bones now, and I guess they decided this wasn't an emergency. See, the guy's been dead for a while. And maybe they have to wait for the water to go down again."

The path on this side of the river soon petered out, but Chrissie forged ahead. The river, broad and brutish, slapped at the roots of the shoreline maples and hackberries. Occasionally a branch or plank bobbed past, and various objects—a bucket, a piece of an oar, a limbless doll—were trapped in branches of bushes that were half-submerged in the unruly water.

Chrissie paused and pointed across the river. "Is that it?"

Marty nodded. "That's the crime scene tape you see. The bones were washed up on the bank there. But the river's up now, so I think the water is covering the exact place we found them."

Chrissie squinted across the river a moment, nodded, then continued downstream. "I wish we were with Daddy."

"So do I, honey." Marty followed her daughter, grabbing a maple branch for support. The bank here was not as steep as on Walters's land across the river, but it was rough and slick underfoot. "But things didn't work out for this trip, and we'll have to go later. See, when you find human bones—"

"I know! You told me a hundred thousand times!" Chrissie gave a mighty leap to the next footing, setting the turquoise stars at her ears to bouncing. By some miracle she didn't slide into the river. She looked back and said, "But it's fun to be with him."

"We have fun without him too!" Marty protested, stung. The dark mood that hovered so near these days loomed closer. "What about the 4-H fair? And the Fourth of July fireworks? And that trip to New York last year?"

"I didn't say that wasn't fun! Sheesh, Mom, gimme a break!" Exasperated, Chrissie shoved her way through the next bush. "All I said was, it's fun to be with him!"

But that wasn't all she meant. Marty caught up and said, "It's complicated. But you're right, honey, it's fun too."

Chrissie paused and looked back. "They have sheriffs in Tennessee too, Mom."

So that was it. Marty took a deep breath. "I know. But getting a job is real hard." Impossible was more like it. It had been hard enough here on home territory, with a sheriff who'd known her forever, had been her dad's best friend, and had coached her childhood basketball team. And even so, Wes had kept her on dispatch at first. It had been eighteen months before she could talk him into sending her out on the road for even the quietest patrols. And for a job where knowing the turf was so important, she couldn't expect a Tennessee sheriff to take an out-of-stater's application all that seriously. Not to mention that she was an out-of-state female.

She would hate working as a clerk or waitress. She liked outdoor work. She liked helping people. She liked the pay and benefits. She liked this hot, muddy county.

Chrissie said, "Yeah, it's hard, but you'd have time to look around. Daddy has a good job. He says he's really set to climb the ladder now."

"I know that's what he says, honey. I hope it's true."

Chrissie hurled a muddy stone into the rushing water. "I think you hope he gets fired!"

"Of course not! Chrissie, that's a mean thing to say!"

Chrissie looked a little shamefaced and tried to change the subject, swinging her arm out to point across the river again. "What's that?"

Marty shook her head. "Chrissie, we've got to get this straight. Daddy and I are both doing the best we can, okay? I think Nichols County is best for my line of work, and he thinks Tennessee is best for his." At the moment, anyway; he'd tried Bloomington, Indianapolis, Chicago, New York, Alaska. "And I don't think we should give up our house and all our friends and Aunt Vonnie until we're really sure what we're doing."

"Yeah, okay, I know." Chrissie was still staring across the tawny river. "Mom, what *is* that?"

There was urgency in her voice. Marty turned and squinted across the water. They were downstream from the little cove where the crime scene tape still stretched. The bank was steep and rocky over there, and a small tree had fallen, dipping its crown deep into the snarling waters. Something was caught in its branches, something big and dark.

Marty turned and ran back toward the bridge, skidding on the wet rocks. She heard Chrissie close behind her. "Maybe somebody's old clothes," Marty said over her shoulder, hoping it was true.

"Maybe."

They ran across the bridge and clambered down the high, steep bank, dropping the last five feet to the footpath. Marty hoped that Dub Walters was somewhere talking to friends and not inspecting his land today. They trotted along the path, climbed around the crime scene tape, and continued downstream.

Marty heard the buzz of flies about the same time she saw the upturned roots of the maple. She said to Chrissie, "Wait here on the path."

Chrissie knew she meant it. Marty made her way through the woven vines and bushes to a spot near the fallen trunk.

She could see only the back of the body, because the face and arms and legs were still under the murky water, tangled in the maple branches. She fought back nausea and tried to be a cop. Observe, Hopkins. Get a grip.

It was a very fat person, blue jeans taut, black T-shirt stretched tight as sausage casing above the line of bare skin where the flies crawled. Not Johnny, Marty thought; he's slim.

But then the wind lifted a veiling branch for an instant, and she knew. *The river does sad things to bodies,* Nysa had said. *Roughs them up, bloats them.* It was a Lily Pistols T-shirt.

"Can I see?" Chrissie sounded scared.

"No, no." She did this job to protect her child, to banish these horrors from Chrissie's world. From Johnny's world too, for all the good it had done him. Marty's heart broke for little Rosie Donato.

"I want to know."

"No, honey, it's really awful." Marty remembered when her father died, her mother and Aunt Vonnie had sent her to stay a week on Dee Turley's nearby farm, trying to ease the blow by telling Marty her dad was sick. Of course she'd heard the truth from other kids, forced her friend Dawn to tell her when the funeral was, and bicycled to church, dusty and defiant, to witness her mother weeping, Wes Cochran blowing his nose during the eulogy, and the mysterious closed coffin that still formed part of the landscape of her dreams.

"But I want to know!" Chrissie insisted.

Who was she to deny Chrissie the truth? Shoot, the kid was right—truth was important too, even horrible truth. Another reason Marty did this job. She said uncertainly, "It's terrible, honey. But it's up to you."

Chrissie's eyes looked frightened, but she clenched her jaw and made her way through the underbrush to Marty's side. She looked quickly out at the river, turned away, and threw up.

Marty handed her a tissue and hugged her fiercely. Her daughter, so tough, so curious, so fragile. So like her. "C'mon, kid," Marty said, and cleared her throat. "We've got to call this in. There's work to do."

14

WES COCHRAN WAS STANDING BETWEEN DOC ALT-
mann and Marty Hopkins on the riverbank, trying not to
think about the hideous soggy lump the divers had just
hauled from the water and eased onto Doc's clean sheet to
be photographed again. Wes had asked Hopkins to do the
documentation and she was scribbling industriously in
her notebook about clothing, hair color, and condition of
the body. Doc Altmann's spectacles glinted as he watched
the photographer maneuver around the grim object. After
a moment Wes cleared his throat and asked, "Any
ideas, Doc?"

"Hey, Wes, I haven't even laid hands on him."

"But you've been looking at him like he was pretty as
a picture."

He wasn't. Johnny's body—if it was Johnny's—was pale
gray, almost white, discolored by raw, purpled blotches on
his puffed, lacerated face and hands. Hordes of flies crawled
lovingly across his skin where it was exposed. Wes and his
companions were all standing upwind. The photographer
held his breath when he could, and even Doc had a hankie
ready in case the breeze shifted.

"Pretty as a picture," Doc repeated, then called to the
photographer, "Hey, Kev, don't take too long. We want to
get him away from the flies."

"Flies are the least of his problems," grunted the photographer, shifting to a new angle.

"Not his. Ours. Those are land bugs contaminating the
scene now," Doc explained.

Hopkins glanced up from her notebook. "Contaminating the scene?"

"Yeah. Insects and worms can write a little history of where a corpse has been. On land, flies attack immediately, lay their eggs. The eggs hatch according to the species timetable. Usually there are several species. An entomologist can tell how developed they are and give a pretty good estimate of when death occurred, whether it was indoors or outdoors, whether the critters that laid the eggs were land or water critters, and so forth. I've made arrangements for an entomologist to assist on this. I'm hoping he can tell us how long this body was in the water—if he died there, or if someone put him in days later. So I don't want too many brand-new fly eggs lying around."

"Yeah, I remember in that course we took they said to collect samples of flies and maggots." Hopkins made a note and added, "His face looks like somebody really bashed him."

"Nah, that's probably postmortem," said Doc. Wes was amused at how talkative he'd become for Hopkins. "A body sinks facedown. The rear end floats highest, and the forehead and hands and knees and feet all get scraped over the rocks. See his sneakers?"

They were battered and torn, Wes saw, though the words "L.A. Gear" still showed muddily on the heels through a tangle of fishing line. The knees of the jeans were shredded.

Hopkins was squinting at the body. "What about the back of his head? And that wound on his side?"

Doc shrugged. "Can't tell till I look at him. But those could easy be postmortem too. If he was out in the channel, boat propellers could have done that. And the river's been carrying a lot of trash lately. Or maybe it slammed him sideways into a rock. On the other hand . . ."

"On the other hand what?" Wes asked.

Behind the John Lennon glasses, Doc's bright eyes zigzagged from Wes to Marty and back. "On the other hand, it's always safest to assume the worst, isn't it?"

Wes grunted. "Yeah, we'll do that. Not many kids go

swimming with their clothes on. Can you give me a ballpark time of death, Doc?"

"Maybe a week ago. We'll see what the entomologist says."

Kev the photographer walked upwind of the body and called, "I'm going down to get some shots of that fallen tree where they found him."

"Good." Doc turned to Wes. "If you want to do his pockets, we can all get on with our jobs."

Wes took a deep breath and approached the body. The jeans were wet and tight over the swollen flesh beneath, so it was hard to slide his fingers into the pockets. Twice he had to step away to take a breath. But finally he had the few items in his evidence box. "All yours, Doc," he said with relief. Doc signaled his men and they began easing protective bags over the mauled hands while Wes walked toward his cruiser. "Let's take a look, Hopkins," he said.

There were a few coins and a damp, pitiful billfold. It was plastic, once silvery. Inside were two slimy dollars, three photos blurred from their long dunking, and a video club card. They squinted at it carefully. "Yeah," said Hopkins at last. "It says Donato."

There was a bag of M&M's, torn open and containing the remains of a few chocolate buttons, their candy shells dissolved away into smears on the wrapper. The last item was in the best shape, a Swiss army knife that still functioned well. Wes refolded the knife, his throat tight, and looked at Hopkins. Her gray eyes glistened. He said, "Yeah. Let's talk to the Donatos."

"Yes sir."

It wasn't easy, talking to the Donatos. Sue Donato burst into screaming sobs when they showed her the billfold and collapsed onto her strawberry-colored sofa. Carl Donato was screaming too, but in fury. Wes motioned for Hopkins to soothe the wife while he faced the husband's rage. He'd been filled with rage too, when they told him about Billy. Wes stood stolidly while waves of abuse crashed over him. "Idiots! Fucking idiots!" Carl screamed. "You can't keep a kid safe! Johnny's smart! He'd never go into high water! He knows how to take care of himself! Hey, let me see this body, I bet it's not Johnny at all! Johnny's smart—your girl deputy's an idiot! You guys made a mistake, a fucking mistake! Let me see!"

"Yes sir." Wes knew that Carl was trying to stay tough when in fact he wanted to cry. "Let's step into the next room and—"

"No! Let's go see!" Carl started for the front door.

"Yes sir." Wes motioned for Hopkins to stay inside. Young Rosie was crying little hiccupy sobs while her mother hugged her and wailed. He followed Carl Donato onto the front walk. Carl yelled, "So where is it?"

Wes snapped, "Mr. Donato, don't you want to protect your wife? Sir."

"What do you mean?"

"Sir, I'm sorry to say the body's in pretty bad shape. It's been dead over a week, and—"

"See? What'd I tell you? You fucking idiots can't tell if it's Johnny or not!"

"That's right, sir. Nobody could tell. Nobody."

That made him pause. He glanced at the window next door and blustered more quietly, "So how can we know?"

"The billfold, sir. Johnny's cards in the billfold. The clothes. A Lily Pistols T-shirt. L.A. Gear shoes. Later our lab will check with your son's dentist to confirm."

The hammering of little details was breaking through the denial. Carl looked back at the front door and blinked rapidly. Wes had felt that way too. The guy needed to take some action. Wes said gently, "Sir, it'll save your wife the trouble of identifying his things if you do it. Somebody has to. Then we can get on with the search."

"Yeah, Sue." Carl coughed. "Sue's all broken up and hysterical. I'll do it."

"Yes sir."

Together they walked back into the house. Carl wrote out an identification while the female sobs from the sofa diminished slowly. "I can't make out the photos," he complained. "Don't know what they are."

"That's fine, sir. Just tell us what you're sure about."

It was another half hour before they could leave. Sue insisted on identifying the billfold too, but like her husband, she couldn't figure out the photographs. Hopkins, sitting on the sofa with her arm around the little girl, gave a tiny jerk of her head and Wes left the photos on the coffee table and herded the older Donatos toward the front door. He explained to them about the next steps in the investigation. Carl started yelling again about crazy faggots and departmental inefficiency, but Wes talked him down. At last Hopkins joined him, bringing the photos.

Getting into the cruiser, a low branch knocked his hat askew. Wes yelled, "Son of a bitch!" and wrenched the limb from the tree, crunching it several times over his knee before flinging it into the gutter. When he got in he saw Marty wiping tears from her cheeks. He radioed in to headquarters, then asked her, "What'd the kid say about the photos?"

She cleared her throat. "She thinks they're snapshots Johnny took. One of them is that Lily Pistols concert he went to in the spring, and the other two are of that girl in the church school camp he liked. Ellie."

"We'll talk to her next."

"I don't want to say anything bad about him. He wasn't bad, just a kid." Ellie's bubbliness was subdued over the news of Johnny's death.

It was getting dusky and some of the kids in the tents were lighting camp lanterns. Wes leaned against a tree trunk, staying in the background as much as he could, letting Hopkins say, "We know. But we need to know about his state of mind. You can probably help, Ellie. He was carrying your picture."

"Oh, God." Ellie looked away, embarrassed yet half-pleased at the power of her sixteen-year-old beauty. Wes had the feeling she'd giggle if it weren't for his own six-four hulk looming in the background. "I didn't encourage him or anything," she told Hopkins earnestly. "I tried to turn him off. He was just a kid."

Two years made so much difference at this age. Wes remembered his own stupidities at the gawky age of fourteen, as he shot up taller than all his friends, his feet too big and his heart too full of undying love for the aloof and well-stacked seventeen-year-old Annette across the street. The undying love had lasted most of a summer, until he returned to high school and basketball and noticed a nifty little cheerleader named Shirley. Forty-some years later, she was still nifty. Annette had married an appliance salesman and gotten fat.

Ellie's young figure was a lot like Annette's had been. Wes could sympathize with Johnny.

"He was kind of a show-off," Ellie said. "Dumb things like—see, I don't want to say anything bad about him."

"Hey, Ellie, we all do dumb things sometimes," Hopkins said. "It'll help if you just fill in the picture for us."

"Well, see, he bragged a lot. It's like he wanted to prove he was a man. He said he'd met Lily Pistols, and he said he was getting a Harley-Davidson motorcycle for his birthday." She giggled. "He said he could walk on his hands. He could, too."

"Yeah, acting like a kid," Hopkins sympathized. "Hard for you."

"Yeah! I tried to turn him off," Ellie said earnestly. "But he'd just come back with more bragging. Like I told him my real boyfriend was back in Arizona. And he wanted to know about him, and I said he was tall and a good singer and took me to a rodeo once. I was trying to let him know there was no hope, you know?" She eyed Hopkins anxiously. "I told Johnny he was a nice guy but I had a boyfriend already."

"How did he take it?"

"Okay. He seemed kind of sad but he went away. Then two days later he was back. Now his story was that he was going to ride in rodeos! I mean, he was such a kid!" Ellie shook her head in wonderment, the dark hair flopping across her face. She pushed it back. "I mean, I didn't even like the rodeo much!"

"So you didn't encourage him at all."

"No. I just said 'Suit yourself' and walked away. This

was all a couple of weeks ago. One of the other kids saw him trying to get on a cow, but Vicki Strand came out of the barn and stopped him. He still hung around and listened to the singing and asked questions about Father Rueger and stuff, but he didn't mention the rodeo again and I thought he was getting over it."

"Maybe he was. Can you think of anything else he did?"

"Not really."

"Well, let us know if you think of anything, okay?"

Lanky Vicki Strand was closing the pasture gate as Wes and Marty Hopkins walked from the campsite toward the Brewster home, where they'd parked the cruiser. They could see the rumps of cattle ambling off into the twilight. "Hi, Miz Strand," Wes said.

She turned to face them, wiping her big hands on her blue jeans. "Hello," she said.

He said, "You probably heard, we think we found Johnny's body in the river, a couple of miles downstream."

"That's so sad. Yes, Karen Brewster heard from Johnny's mother and told me."

Wes hitched up his trousers. "You were the last to see him, I hear. On the river path."

She looked stricken. "It's so sad!"

"After you saw him on the path, did you see anyone else?"

"Only that fisherman I told you about. I had to find Daisy. A sick cow. I had to go."

They hadn't found the fisherman yet. Wes asked, "Did Johnny say anything to you?"

Vicki covered her face with her hands. "No! I had to go! I'm sorry, I'm sorry!"

Damn women, always getting emotional. Wes nodded to Hopkins, who said soothingly, "Yeah, we're all sorry, Vicky. Maybe you can help with something else. A couple of weeks ago you had to stop him from riding one of the cows."

"Yeah. Johnny just didn't understand animals!" She still seemed wrought-up, but at least she wasn't hiding her face anymore. "With cows, you have to have patience, stay calm

100

and quiet. They have good ears and hate bangs and shouts. I mean, they weigh close to a thousand pounds, so you don't want to get them keyed up and nervous. It makes handling them so much harder."

"So Johnny was getting them keyed up?" Hopkins asked.

"Yeah. He was trying to crawl up on Daisy. She's old and peaceable, but even she was getting nervous. A couple of the younger ones were already jumping around, skitterish. So I told him to get off and get out, and not to come back until he'd learned to respect animals." She shook her blond head. "He just didn't understand animals! He broke his little dog's tail. Slammed a door on it. He said it was an accident, he didn't know the dog was following him in, but anyone knows a dog wants to be with its master. You have to watch!"

Wes asked thoughtfully, "You pasture the cows here, near the river?"

"Yeah, here or in the east pasture."

"Were they here the day Johnny disappeared?"

"Except while I was milking them."

"Miz Strand, if Johnny got a cow riled up, she could push him into the river, couldn't she?"

Even in the dusk, Wes could see that Vicki was upset by his question. "No, look, my cows wouldn't do that! They're gentle!"

"I'm sure they are, Miz Strand. But it's possible, all the same. We have to think of all the possibilities."

"Yes, I understand." But she still sounded shaky.

"Let us know if you think of anything else that might help us figure it out. Thanks, Miz Strand."

Wes dropped Hopkins at her house. He watched her run the rest of the way up the driveway, grab the basketball from her daughter's friend Janie, and sink a basket while the two ten-year-olds bounced around her screaming. He grinned as he headed back to Dunning. Marty had been worried that the girl would be stewing over the horrible experience of finding Johnny's body. She'd stew, sure, but the kid had a healthy streak of her mother's insistence on

truth and her mother's grit, and already knew that basketball could ease a lot of pain.

Back at the station he started his paperwork, but was soon
interrupted by a phone call.

"Sheriff Cochran? Bob Rueger here. I'm at the airport, on
my way out of town. Called my daughter to say good-bye
and she told me you'd found the Donato boy's body."

"It's a preliminary identification, Mr. Rueger."

"It was a drowning? I mean—Christ, I don't mean to
sound heartless, I'm a father too. But a drowning isn't as
menacing as other things that could have happened."

"It's still open, sir. We all hope it turns out to be nothing menacing."

There was a brief hesitation. "Sheriff, you're good at your
job. You must have an opinion."

"You're good at your job too, Mr. Rueger. You don't make
decisions until the evidence is in and analyzed."

A brief chuckle. "Okay. You're right. But I have a daughter there. They seem like good people, but a father wants
to be absolutely sure."

"Yes sir. We're giving it our best shot."

"Yes, of course. Well, I'll be in touch."

After he hung up, Wes gazed thoughtfully at the receiver.

Midnight, or after. It was hard to tell with clouds scudding across the moon and stars. Thong in hand, Tor lifted
his nostrils to the moist, warm breeze. It smelled of life and
death, growth and decomposition, earth and water. The cattle in the pasture behind him moved occasionally, munching
the thick grasses, lumbering down to the river's edge for
a drink.

He must have been very small when the rodeo came to
town, seven or eight years old, but it was still vivid in his
memory. He and his father had gone with some of the men
from church and their sons. He and Stevie were the smallest
boys, he remembered that. "You're always talking about
those TV cowboys. This is real," his father told them.

He remembered high wooden fences, red clay dirt, the
hot shadows of the crowd, all legs in jeans from his vantage

point. They blocked his view of the great mysterious animals that stamped and bellowed behind the fences. Then his father had lifted him to his shoulders, into the open air and hot sun above a sea of hats. "Watch that gate," his father said. "You'll see a real cowboy in a minute."

But it wasn't the cowboy that electrified him. It was the bull, a great rust-red longhorn that erupted from the gate like a tornado, all power, all motion. The cowboy clung to a band around the bull's chest, but to a small boy he seemed to be riding a great red tidal wave. The beast surged around the arena in enormous twisting leaps, and the ground shook each time he landed. The cowboy raked his sides with his bright spurs. When they passed close the bull's scent, his bellows, the flash of his pointed horns, and the flecks of his blood and sweat filled the air.

High atop his father's shoulders, he was screaming, screaming. The cowboy bounced on the broad back until the maddened beast slammed sideways into the arena fence. The rider shrieked and fell, sliding down the fence post, but before the clowns could lure the animal away those mighty hindquarters punched back once more, ramming the man's head against the post.

His father grabbed him down from his shoulders and stood him again in the shadows of the blue-jeaned legs. "Don't cry! Don't be a baby! Look how tough Stevie is!"

But he couldn't stop crying. The ground still shook with the victorious bull's every leap. Clinging to his father's leg, he trembled and wept.

"Don't cry," his father said again. "When I was your age I saw my brother bleed to death from a beating. I didn't cry!" But still he couldn't stop, until his father cuffed him hard against the jaw. The pain shocked him into silence at last as the salt taste of blood oozed into his mouth. His father said, "We don't always understand, but God has his reasons, so we mustn't cry. The ambulance is there. We'll say a prayer for that cowboy, okay?" And he drew the church friends around him and they all muttered a prayer, right there in the middle of the crowd, with the hot sun beating down and the ground still shaking from the triumphant beauty of the great bull's leaps.

He was no longer small. Now he was Tor, muscular, male, with shaggy shoulders and wide-arching horns. Slowly, he began to stamp and to whirl the bull-roarer on its thong. The earth shook as his deep song rolled across the night.

15

MONDAY MORNING, MARTY ARRIVED AT WORK ALready wrung out. She hadn't slept much. Chrissie was having nightmares, and so was she, nightmares haunted by Johnny and her other dead. In her waking moments she'd struggled to make sense of the mass of information they'd gathered about Johnny's life and his last hours, but too many questions remained. She vowed to root out the answers. But disappointment awaited her at roll call. Old Corky Dennis had called to report that burglars had hit his rental business on the outskirts of Dunning, taking several hundred dollars' worth of small machines. The sheriff sent Marty to take evidence there while he and the other deputies canvassed New Concord residents to find out if anyone had seen Johnny on that river path a week ago.

Shoot. But at least he hadn't taken her off the case. "When you're finished with the burglary, take a look at the north bank of the river. Someone could've used a boat," he'd told her.

The rental place was a sprawling one-story building that shared a broad asphalt parking lot with the 24-Hour Quick-Mart. It was painted in burgundy red and white, with cheerfully tipsy letters spelling out "Dennis Rent-All" along the roofline. Marty pulled in next to a blue Toyota and a black

Taurus. A short row of trailers, including a couple for live-stock, sat along the side of the building. On both sides of the door, big display windows were filled with a mixture of do-it-yourself and party items. The windows were rimmed with burglar-alarm tape.

Inside, Carolyn Russell was signing papers. The brown-bearded man behind the counter looked familiar, but Marty couldn't place him. "Hi, Carolyn," she said. "What's up?"

Carolyn was a slim brunette in a red polka-dot big shirt. Her daughter Malinda was one of Chrissie's friends. "Oh, hi, Marty. I need a pump. We've got water up to our ankles in the basement."

"It's been wet, all right," Marty said, grateful again that her house was on a hill.

The man behind the counter was watching Marty with a smile in his eyes. He was about six feet tall, sturdy rather than pudgy, and wore a burgundy-red Dennis Rent-All polo shirt. He said, "When I was in Benares, an old man swore to me that in 1907 it rained so hard the city actually slid four-point-six inches downhill."

"My goodness!" exclaimed Carolyn. "Could that happen to us?"

Marty was amused. "We could float down the river to the Wabash. Wake up in Illinois."

"And you'd be out of your jurisdiction," the man said, twinkling at Marty. "Here, Mrs. Russell, let me carry that pump to your car for you."

"See you later, Marty." Carolyn followed him out.

Marty glanced around the big warehouselike space, at the well-used and well-cleaned rototillers, punch bowls, lawn mowers. A set of long ladders and aluminum painter's scaf-folding in the corner attracted her eye. She lifted a section of scaffolding. The bearded man came back in, and she glanced at him. "If I decide to paint my house, could I put this scaffolding together myself?"

He grinned. "I bet you could, Marty LaForte, but most guys I know get a friend to help."

She stared at him, at the amused brown eyes, and memory stirred. "Dennis. Shoot! You're Romey Dennis!"

He nodded, still grinning.

"But I heard you were away! Overseas or something. Benares?"

"Oh, yeah. Romey the roamer. Been everywhere but the moon. I came back last week to help Uncle Corky."

"Well, shoot." Marty couldn't help grinning. Romey was a couple of years older than she was but they'd grown up on the same road, sharing kiddie pools and eventually becoming teammates on the kids' basketball team that Wes Cochran had coached. Romey was okay. She remembered riding with him in the backseat of the Johnsons' station wagon after one of the games. She'd been about Chrissie's age, ten or so, and they'd had a serious talk about what they wanted to do with their lives. At the time she was thinking about being a nurse because she liked to help people. "Be a surgeon," Romey had advised her, seeming infinitely wise at age twelve. "You're smart, and you'll make lots more money. Me, I want to travel. Maybe be an ambassador. We can go to Egypt or Nepal together and you'll run the hospital and I'll write treaties and stuff."

Marty had been thrilled at the thought that she could be a doctor. Nothing had come of it, of course. In high school and her brief stay at Indiana University she'd discovered she didn't even like lab work. She'd also discovered boys, and Brad.

"I thought you'd be an ambassador by now," she said.

Romey laughed. "Maybe someday. Life has its twists and turns. Look at you, working with Coach Cochran again. I figured you'd be a doctor."

"Yeah." Suddenly self-conscious, she pulled out her notebook. She hadn't expected him to remember too. "Well, tell me about this break-in."

He waved his arm at some empty shelves. "They took most of the small power tools. Saber saws, drills, even chain saws. They took blenders and toaster ovens. Here's a list for you, with serial numbers." He looked at her gravely. "Poor Uncle Corky. Just about killed him. He's over at the insurance agent's now. We've got a big deductible and he's worried about replacing the stuff. More than that, he's upset that someone would do this to him."

Marty inspected the back window. The glass was broken, still heaped under the window in a pile by the baseboard. "That window's high enough you wouldn't expect anyone to go through it."

"Yeah, but believe me, we're putting bars on now."

"Yeah. I'll get the fingerprint people over soon. Any ideas about when it happened?"

"I closed up Saturday about five. Everything was fine. And I came by yesterday to check one of the trailers that had a flat. Didn't go inside. But I drove around the back there, and I think I would've noticed if it had been broken then."

"So we're looking at last night, most likely. Okay. Do you have any ideas about who did it?"

"None at all. Lots of people come in here, or go to the Quick-Mart next door, so lots of people could've noticed that window."

"Well, I'll go talk to your neighbors. If you think of anything else, give us a call."

"Okay." He walked to the door with her. "Hey, you grew up nice, Marty LaForte."

Good old Romey. "Hopkins," she said. "Marty Hopkins."

He grinned. "Whatever. See you soon."

She checked the nearby businesses, but only the Quick-Mart had been open last night, and they hadn't noticed anything. She took the names of last night's customers and made some phone calls, but most of them were at work.

At last, about eleven o'clock, she was able to get back to the Donato case. She drove across the bridge, turned east, and a couple of miles later found a gravel road that led down to the water. Looking across, she could see the Brewsters' barn. She parked and walked downstream, back toward the highway bridge. The river curved along the northern edge of its valley here, and the banks were steep and sharp. Maples, sycamores, and thick tangles of vines slowed her. Across the river the valley was flat, the Brewsters' pastures sloping gently to the riverside trees. She glimpsed the red-and-white cattle through the branches. Some of their fence posts stood in water now. A cow dipped her muzzle through the wires into the river and then gazed across at Marty.

The walk flattened out as the river began to cross to the other side of its valley. A broad cornfield stretched to her right toward the steeper country. The bent, swordlike leaves were green and thriving in this rich soil. To her left, across the river, was New Concord itself, its neat houses lined up along the three main streets. She thought she saw a sheriff's cruiser parked on West Street.

She continued downstream. Across the water now were the steep banks of the Strand farm. The river, still high, had taken over the lower part of the creek that bisected the Strand farm.

On this side of the river, the crop fields ended abruptly. There was a rise in the ground, a low knoll that bulged into the river. No one had planted on it. There were lots of brick-sized river stones and lots of stickerbushes and maples. Marty picked her way through them, listening to the grumbling river a few feet below her as it gnawed at the base of the bank. It ran fast here, because the bulge in this shore faced a huge, flat rock that jutted out from the opposite bank. That rock must be the one where they had the picnic, Marty thought. The water whipped through its narrowed channel as though angry at the constriction.

Shoot. No answers on this bank. But they had to look.

The highway bridge was visible now, a quarter-mile away. She came down from the little rise, rounded a bend, and through the maples saw two men in T-shirts and vis-ored caps with the Goodyear insignia, packing up fishing gear.

"Hi," said Marty. "How's the fishing today?"

"Water's too high yet," said the shorter of the two.

"Yeah, it's been a wet couple of weeks. Who owns all this?" She gestured at the tangled woods.

"I thought this was a state road," said the taller one edgily. His skin was sun-reddened and black hair curled from under his Goodyear cap.

"Hey, I'm not saying there's any problem," Marty reassured them. "I just thought you might know."

Thawing a little, the taller one said, "I've never seen anyone there."

"Doesn't this place belong to some dude in Indy?" asked the shorter one.

"Nah, that guy said he was renting it from his friend."

"Well, seems to me his friend was in Indy too."

"Whoever owns it isn't farming it," Marty said, getting interested. "This is good flat farmland, right?"

The tall one shrugged. "Who can make a living farming?"

"Yeah, well, thanks."

This was worth checking. Marty returned to the cruiser and drove back to the Dunning town square. She stopped at Reiner's Bakery. "Hi, Aunt Vonnie, how you doing?"

Her aunt was sitting on a folding chair, her bad ankle up. "Hurts," she admitted. "This hot weather doesn't help."

"Here, I've got some Tylenol." Marty fished the container from her pocket.

Sad-eyed, motherly Melva Dodd, who'd been a Reiner before she'd married, came in from the kitchen with some of her family's famous hot blueberry pies. "Hi, Marty. Tell this stubborn woman to go home early today."

"No sirree. I'm earning my keep." Aunt Vonnie stood up and smiled at someone entering behind Marty. "Hi there, Phil, what can I get for you today?" She hobbled to the display case.

Marty left her aunt, hoping she wouldn't damage her leg further. She stopped at the drugstore for a chocolate bar, then crossed to the big limestone Nichols County Courthouse in the middle of the square. The courthouse basement was a remodeled maze of corridors and storerooms. Flo Duffy's office had a couple of high barred windows and a long oak counter blocking the public from the official record books in the rooms beyond. Flo presided over it all with Virginia Slims in her fingers and thinning hair that had been the same bright red ever since her divorce twenty-two years ago. This year she was wearing it frizzy.

"How's it going, Flo?" Marty put the chocolate bar down on the oak counter.

"No problems that ten million dollars couldn't fix." Flo's ashtray was shaped like a toilet seat and bore the message "Shit Happens." She tapped her cigarette into it, eyed the chocolate bar, and said, "So what brings you into my little den today?"

"I want to know who owns those farms next to the river, by the Route Eight-sixty bridge."

"Which side?"

"Both sides of the highway. North bank of the river."

Flo stuck her Virginia Slim into her bright red mouth, heaved a deep sigh, and stood up. She wandered into another room. After a couple of minutes she wandered back and put a piece of paper next to the chocolate bar. "Tax bills for both properties go to Alfred Shawn, Esquire. Indianapolis address."

"Yeah, the neighbors said it was a guy from Indy. Lawyer doesn't help much, though. I want to know who Shawn's client is."

Flo sat down again and slid the chocolate bar into her desk drawer. "Lawyers don't tell," she said. "You're law enforcement. You can find out."

"Nah, it's not worth a big deal. But if you just happen to hear something, let me know, okay?"

"Come back tomorrow," said Flo. "I like the ones with almonds."

"Done!" Marty grinned, and saluted the red frizz.

Across the street at the station, Wes was interested too. "Yep. I've known men who hide behind a lawyer so folks won't know how much they've got invested."

Marty said, "Flo may be able to tell us tomorrow."

"Yeah, you're right, Hopkins. We don't want to rattle any cages until we know what's in them."

"Did anything turn up in the canvass?"

"Nothing new."

"It's still too early for the forensics report, right?"
"Maybe tomorrow, Doc says."

As Marty drove home, she found herself brooding about Johnny. A lively fourteen-year-old, tall for his age, more interested in motorcycles than animals, still clumsy around girls and worried about being a real man. Interested in various kinds of music and in history. A handsome boy, to judge from his photo. What had pulled a boy like that into a hideous death?

There was an unfamiliar car parked in her driveway, a red Mazda with Arkansas plates. Who did they know in Arkansas?

A peal of laughter from Chrissie greeted her as she turned the doorknob. And suddenly strong arms were grabbing Marty, lifting her, hugging her. Dark eyes were grinning into her eyes, smiling lips were reaching for her lips and murmuring, "Hey, kitten!"

Marty glanced down in surprise at the revolver in her hand. She'd snatched it out in reflex when she was grabbed. She holstered it before she kissed him.

Brad was back.

16

AUNT VONNIE INSISTED ON GOING TO BED RIGHT after *Jeopardy!* "I'm all aches and pains now," she grumbled. "Just an old lady."

"Aunt Vonnie, that's not true!" Brad said. He and Marty were helping her up the stairs. "Your ankle will be better soon. And you know you're one gorgeous lady."

Aunt Vonnie's mouth twitched. "Hey, easy, fella, I've got no money to loan you!"

Marty saw the instant of hurt in his eyes before he answered, "No, really, Aunt Vonnie, it's God's truth. Sure there's women younger than you, but you've still got the prettiest hair and the prettiest mouth of anyone I know except for my two gals right here, and you know it."

Aunt Vonnie was vain about her mouth and blond beehive. She sat down on her mint-green satin quilted bedspread, pleased. "Quit your sweet talk, Brad Hopkins. I'll see you tomorrow." She waved them away.

Chrissie was not so easy to dislodge. She was wired and didn't want to go to bed. "Tell you what," Brad said, pulling a cassette from his duffel bag. "I was going to wait till tomorrow to give you this. But if you put on your jammies and promise to go up at ten-thirty, you can hear it right now."

"Is it another one of your shows?" Chrissie asked, eyes sparkling.

"An all-Elvis show."

Chrissie, vivid in the purple Graceland T-shirt he'd brought her, looked from Brad to Marty. "Yes!" she exclaimed, and sprinted off to change. She was no fool, Marty thought, amused; she'd get the tape and also an extra half hour past bedtime.

They sat on the couch, Brad in the middle, and listened to the show on Chrissie's little machine. Brad had focused on what he called "the many faces of love" in Elvis's songs, and the selections ranged from slow ballads to rousing rock. At "All Shook Up" Brad leaped to his feet, stepped across the recorder and the iced-tea glasses on the coffee table, did a quick shuffle, and said, "C'mere, Christine Hopkins, let's dance!"

Eagerly, Chrissie jumped up to join him. Marty tucked her feet under her, smoothed the aqua-blue skirt she'd put on for him, and watched them with delight. Her daughter bounced in her short yellow summer pajamas, her dark curls and tulip earrings swinging. She was athletic and quick, and he only had to suggest a step and she'd catch on.

But Marty mostly watched the man she'd married eleven

years ago. He hadn't changed much. Brad's brown eyes sparkled like Chrissie's, his dark hair tossed back and forth as he followed the lyrics, showing off shaky hands and weak knees as Chrissie giggled. He wore jeans and a dark blue shirt with the sleeves rolled up and the front unbuttoned. His little gold chain winked against his chest. Marty had forgotten how much she loved his hands, blunt masculine hands that somehow managed such expressive, graceful gestures. As the song finished he swung Chrissie up into the air, laughing at her laughter, and declared, "You're my buttercup!"

He eased her down onto the couch and his dark eyes turned to Marty. On the tape his voice said, "The King knew that love was the most beautiful and precious and serious thing in the world too. This next one is for the sweetest gal I know. Kitten, I'm lonesome for you."

"Mommy, that's you!" Chrissie squealed.

But Marty didn't answer. She was already caught by those magnetic eyes. He reached for her hand and drew her into his arms as the tiny machine played "Can't Help Falling in Love." They swayed together, and Marty forgot Chrissie, forgot the world, forgot all the thorny problems unsolved and unsolvable, forgot everything except the tickle of his mustache on her ear, the strength of his arms, the breathtaking nearness of his body. In the song rivers flowed surely to the sea, and Marty felt liquid too. Some things really were meant to be. It was easy to tell that he was as aroused as she was, and she pressed even closer. Under the music he breathed into her ear, "Stop that, kitten, or Chrissie might guess we like each other." That made her want to giggle but she managed to gulp it back, silent shudders running down her spine until he had to hold her up, smiling too.

Chrissie eyed them suspiciously when they came back to the couch. "I like the fast ones better."

"I like them all," Brad said, and hugged them both. For a few moments as they listened to the rest of the show, with Chrissie curled like a puppy in Brad's arm and the tingling promise of bedtime just ahead, Marty thought she was happy.

Chrissie kept her part of the bargain. She picked up the

tape recorder and said, "Well, I better go. You guys are starting to smooch already." Her tone dripped disgust.

"Maybe," Brad said, kissing her forehead and standing up as she did. "And maybe I'll have another iced tea. And maybe tomorrow you and I can drive to Spring Mill and go swimming. What do you say?"

"I say okay! Come tell me good night?"

"Sure thing, buttercup."

"I'll fix the iced tea," Marty said. "Or maybe a beer?"

"Tea's fine."

He joined her in the kitchen as she was pouring the tea and pressed close behind her, nibbling her ear. "Brad, stop!" she laughed. Tea had splashed onto the counter.

"You're right, kitten. I'll be good. We gotta talk."

"Yeah."

They sat at the breakfast table and she said, "So things are pretty good for you in Tennessee."

"Yeah, things are great." He sipped at his tea. "Sam— you know, my boss—says I'm getting more listeners, more advertisers. He's giving me a raise next month."

"That's great, Brad!" But something was knelling deep in her chest.

"That reminds me. I've been saving some these last three months." He pulled out his wallet and counted out four fifties. "I know you need some stuff around here."

"Yeah, that'll help paint the house. That's really great!" And it *was* great, after all the times they'd had to dip into the housepainting money to fix Brad's car or pay Brad's rent. She should feel like rejoicing. She moved the bills aside and put the sugar bowl on top as a paperweight.

"So, yeah, things are looking real good." He drank some iced tea. "See, I figured it out. I was trying to start too high. The guys that have the power in broadcasting, they don't want to give it up. In this business it's not talent that counts, it's who you know."

"Yeah. I see."

"So you gotta meet people. I heard Sam went to law school right up there at IU. I introduced myself, and we really hit it off, talking about Indiana and New York and so forth. And a few weeks later when a job was open he gave me a call."

"Yeah." She grinned at him. He was talented, dammit.

"So things are looking real good. But that's not what I want to talk about." He put down his iced tea and leaned forward, the dancing darkness of his eyes drawing her in. "Marty, I want you to picture rosebushes. A beautiful green garden, big back lawn, lots of trees, and the prettiest bushes. Just like we used to talk about. Looks like a magazine, you know? Looks like something in a dream. Nice house made out of fieldstone, with a two-story porch and columns." His hands were in the air, sketching the bushes, the columns. "It doesn't look big, but it's got these fireplaces, two or three, and it's got these beautiful French doors onto the upstairs balcony. Man, it's one gorgeous place!"

"Yeah, it sounds great, Brad, but what are you getting at?"

"It is great. See, now that I've got something steady with Sam it makes sense to be buying a place. And this is gorgeous. Plus there's a swimming hole only a quarter-mile away. Chrissie will love it. Swear to God, Marty, I saw those French doors and I could see you with one of those roses in your hair, standing there like a princess!" He reached across and touched her nose. "The cutest princess in fifty states. My princess."

She could almost see it too: roses, lawns, fieldstone, French doors. Ten years ago she'd dreamed with him of a place like that. These days, no. These days her dreams involved finding out how Johnny Donato died, catching the Dennis Rent-All burglars—things like that. She said gently, "Brad, this is my home. Right here."

"Shhh!" His finger moved down to her lips. "I know what you're going to say, kitten. You don't want to sell your mama's house, you like working with Wes Cochran, and so on. But I have something else to tell you first."

"Okay. But I'm staying here."

"Okay, okay, just hear me out for a minute, okay?"

She shrugged. "Sure."

He took a deep breath. "The thing is, kitten, I joined AA."

"AA?" She stared at him. "AA? What do you mean? You

always said you didn't have a drinking problem, Brad!" But part of her was remembering how hard it had been to believe him, how hard it was to keep herself convinced that she hadn't married a drunk, that he wasn't like those guys that she locked up every Saturday night. He was only a dreamer, she'd rescue him, he'd settle down someday, she'd told herself.

Watching her, he said, "Yeah, that's what I told myself for a long time. But it was getting bad, Marty. When I was in Alaska—well, you never saw the worst. But anyway, I woke up one day in an alley in Memphis and knew things were out of control."

"An alley?" Her heart went out to him. "God, Brad, you should have told me! Why didn't you call? I could have come to help!"

"I didn't want to drag you into it. But I finally admitted there was a problem and went to the meeting."

She said encouragingly, "But not a big problem, right? You never acted like a real drunk. Hangovers, sure, but you're not like Johnny Peters, always beating his wife and kids, or like Mrs. Seifert passing out with three kids—"

"So I was lucky. Look, Marty, are you saying you want me to start drinking again?"

"No, no! It's just that I never thought that was the problem."

"Well, it was. And I admit it. And I'm ready to change."

"Yeah." Marty rubbed her neck. Her dad, yes, he'd had a problem. But she'd never thought of Brad as a drunk. Well, maybe a couple of times— Face it, Marty Hopkins, you knew and couldn't admit it. You blinded yourself, but you knew!

"That's where I met Sam," Brad was saying. "At AA. All those years I was beating my head on closed doors. The minute I gave up and put things in God's hands, things started to happen."

"Yeah. That's good, Brad."

"See, I've been analyzing the past. And I know I hurt you and Chrissie, leaving you on your own so much, traveling all over the country like I did...."

He hesitated, and Marty suddenly knew with awful clarity that he was leaving out a phrase—that he'd cheated on her too. She pushed the thought back into the closet of her mind, where it had lived unacknowledged for years. He was right not to tell her—she didn't want to know. She shrugged. "We're doing okay. Chrissie is a real spunky kid. This is a good house, and I've got a good job. We miss you a whole lot, Brad, but—"

"Dammit, Marty!" His fist crashed onto the table. "Don't you even care about this family?"

"God, Brad, of course I care!"

"Well, I'm doing my damnedest to patch things up, and—" He took a deep breath. "Look, I know it was partly my fault. See, Marty, we were pretty young when we got married. We had to quit college, and with Chrissie coming so quick . . ."

Quick, as in five months after the wedding. Come to think of it, Chrissie's existence was due to a few too many beers in those far-off days when she and Brad were still discovering each other in the backseat of that ancient Buick. *There's a Thom in your life too,* Nysa had said.

"Anyway, I'm trying to do what I couldn't do then. Make a real home for you and our wonderful kid."

"Brad, *this* is a real home."

"There you go again, trying to run things! No wonder I—" He stopped himself and closed his eyes for a second before resuming in a quieter voice. "Look, kitten, I'm admitting I had problems, right? I was too young. And that's all water under the bridge now anyway. What I'm saying is, let's change things. Let's start over."

"Brad . . ." Marty rubbed her forehead. She wanted so much to help him, but it was hard to explain. "Okay, you say you're ready to change. That's good, okay?" she began. "But I've been changing for years. I had to change! I had to earn a living, and I did. I've kept up the house—well, except for the paint. And I've worked my way up in the job. I get commendations." *I've killed a man,* she almost said, but didn't. "See, I'm not that kid you used to dance with in Bloomington. I'm—"

"Sure you are." His hand was suddenly on hers, warm and urgent. "You still drive me wild when we dance."

She looked into his eyes and admitted, "Yeah. We still

turn each other on, don't we?" *Adolescence, the heat of sex, it muddies the vision.* Yep. Nysa's voice again. Marty tugged her hand away. "But I'm not that kid anymore, Brad. There's more to life than that."

"I know, kitten. That's why I'm here. I want to patch things up."

Patch things up. Could they, somehow? For the last five years he'd been gone so much, trying to get his break. Indianapolis, New York, Alaska, Chicago. And these last three months, Tennessee. With effort she'd taught herself to let go of their youthful dreams. To love Chrissie, to do her job, to rely on herself. And yet, and yet . . .

"Brad, look. It would be great. But I can't just—you know—"

"I swear to God, Marty, I'm changing! Don't you trust me?"

"Yeah, I trust you, but—" No. No, I don't trust you, something in her was screaming, not after all those years, all those crumbled dreams. "The thing is, I trust myself now."

He twisted up out of his chair, turning his back, punching the wall. For a moment he stood rubbing his knuckles and staring out the window at the darkness. Then he said quietly, "Yeah, you're right, kitten. One day at a time, that's always the hardest for me. We'll get there yet. Look, if you won't come, at least I want to take Chrissie to Tennessee with me tomorrow."

"What?"

"She can spend the week, like we planned. I'll bring her back on the weekend, or you can come get her."

"But how—you always said you couldn't take care of her!"

He looked back at her. "Chrissie's older than she used to be. So am I. I've got friends, and there's a nice pool and a library near the station. She'll be fine."

"I know, but . . ." But what? Marty couldn't put words on her objections. Brad was trying so hard. She should help him out. And Chrissie would love it. Adore it. A pang made her realize that part of her problem was jealousy. "Okay," she said, ashamed of herself. "I'll help her pack tomorrow morning."

"Great!" He came back to the table and picked up both her hands. "Kitten, I'm too impatient, I know. I didn't mean to rush you. It's just that I don't know what you want from me. I thought this was what we all wanted."

"Yeah." And he was right. Once, not so long ago, it had been what she wanted: to follow him to magical places, to merge with his sparkling life, to enable him to achieve wondrous things. That dream had died, or been outgrown. But what did she want from him now?

She said, "Shoot, Brad, I used to want it too. But now I want what I have here."

"God, Marty, you make it so hard!" He dropped her hands, kicked open the screen door, and went out into the night. She heard his car start as she rinsed the iced-tea glasses. But it wasn't until she was in her lonely bed that she cried, grieving for Brad and for the long-gone kid he used to dance with.

17

THE SCREAM OF AN AMBULANCE WOKE JUSTIN JEF-fries. It was after midnight. He tossed for a while, worrying. He'd helped the campers at the dig, led them in prayer, seen them into their tents. Ordinary activities, but Johnny's death had kept the youngsters subdued, often teary, all day, with an edge of hysteria and panic. He should be tired, not wakeful. But after half an hour Bonnie woke up and murmured, "Are you okay, Justin?"

"Yeah. Yeah, I'm okay, Bon. Just restless. I'll take a little walk and be back soon."

He kissed her, pulled on his blue T-shirt and shorts, slapped on a new layer of mosquito repellent, and went out into the soft, singing night. Cicadas strummed and frogs piped by the river, and from somewhere came a thin phrase of music. Justin cocked his head. There were a couple of lights still on in the tents. Was one of the campers playing a radio? No, the sound seemed to be coming from the other side of the Brewsters' hill, over where the long, flat meadows sloped gently to the water. He walked down to the river trail and turned toward the sound. The moonlight through the leaves dappled the path, occasionally dimming to black when a cloud crossed. The familiar path seemed changed, full of mystery, in the checkered light. Here by the river he heard the water's quiet splash and sizzle, and the frogs sang louder too.

The kids had been upset today as the sad truth of Johnny's death sank in. Last week they'd been excited and worried, but Johnny could have been anywhere so no one had given up hope. Yesterday, when Ellie told them that the body had been found, there had been tears and long faces, but it wasn't till today that the questions really started. Justin had prayed for the right words but didn't know if he'd found them. He loved working with teens, with young people on the edge of discoveries, but this discovery was damn scary. For him too. His charges were not much older than Johnny and most of them knew death as a threat only to their grandparents or to people who lived in far-off, dangerous places. Suddenly it had struck right in their midst. "He was just a kid!" they exclaimed, over and over.

Ellie, in tears, said, "I was praying for him, Justin! I was praying so hard! It didn't help!"

"Ellie, we can't tell God what to do," Justin said gently. "Our prayers share our thoughts with God. They communicate with God. But sometimes He answers our prayers in ways we don't understand."

"But how come he died?" Kenny insisted. "Why did God let him die? He was just a kid!"

"Compared to God, our minds are very small. It's pretty arrogant to think we can come up with quick answers, like it's just an algebra problem or something. Right? Let's say a prayer now, and reflect on the enormity of God and God's plan. Maybe we'll be granted a little strength and insight. Try to open yourselves to God's grace."

They prayed, and maybe some of them were visited by a sense of God's grace. But not Justin, not this time.

The footpath rounded a clump of trees. Here the far-off music was clearer, a woodwind of some kind, maybe a flute or a recorder. The piece was vaguely familiar, maybe Mozart, he thought. It ran sweetly through the night air, twining through the soft background chords of insects, frogs, and river. Justin paused to listen.

After a moment someone murmured, "It's lovely, isn't it?"

Justin jumped. "Nysa! I didn't see you!"

"Oh, I'm sorry if I startled you." In the dim, leafy patterns of light he saw that she was sitting on a boulder. She reached up to touch his arm lightly, apologetically, and sent a gush of desire roiling through his body. "I don't usually see you out here at night."

"No." He cleared his throat. "I was restless tonight. Decided to take a walk."

"And Vicki's music brought you this way."

"Is that Vicki?"

"Yes. A pack of dogs killed one of the calves this spring, so Vicki often camps out in the summer to be closer to the cattle at night."

"I see. What instrument is that?"

"An old wooden recorder I found in an antique store. Nice tone. I love to hear the music too, especially at night. It's a solace." He sensed more than saw her spreading her arms as though to embrace the river. "I feel in touch with divinity here. The water, the night, the river creatures, the music."

"Maybe that's why I'm here too," Justin said humbly. He felt for a place to sit and found a rock a foot away from hers.

"You feel the need for solace now too? A man of God?"

There was a bitter catch in her voice. The dappled moonlight glinted occasionally from her blond hair, but her face was shadowed. He said, "Of course I feel the need. Ordination doesn't make people less human."

"Fully human, fully divine?"

He chuckled. "Not me. That was someone else."

"But you're supposed to be the route to that someone."

"No. We have to stay very clear about that. People are saved by grace, direct from God. One-on-one. It's a gift. Nothing human brings it about. I was just trying to explain it to the kids tonight. Praying, the Church, all that, helps keep us open to God, but it doesn't control Him."

"Justin." She fumbled at her belt and pushed something into his hand. "Here, do me a favor, have a drink."

"What is it?"

"Red wine. Nothing fancy. Have some. Keep me from feeling like a slut, drinking by herself through the night."

"A slut?" Justin smiled at the thought. "Can't have that." He lifted the little flask to his lips. The wine wasn't bad. It was dry yet fruity, the breath of the grapes still in it.

"So the kids were asking for explanations tonight?" She took the wine back. Her soft fingertips brushed his hand and sent a fresh tingle into his every corner.

He made himself think of Bonnie and JayJay and poor dead Johnny, and cleared his throat again. "Yes. It's natural. For a lot of the kids, this is the first death of someone they knew. Especially someone their own age. They're very vulnerable now, just at the age when they're beginning to realize they're mortal too. And Bonnie and I are sort of their parents away from home."

"It's good they have you. Vicki and I have only each other now. Our sister committed suicide a few years ago, out in California. Hey, maybe we should adopt you for family too. A man of God." She gave a little laugh. "Listen, here comes the andante movement."

Justin listened. The sweet, slow phrases of the recorder lanced his heart and made him want to weep. The air was heavy with the scent of mud and growth and wine. And Nysa. He should leave, talk to her in the daylight, not now. But in a moment he heard himself murmur, "Luther said that only music and theology can give peace and happiness to troubled souls."

"Oh, but music can trouble the soul too!" There was that little catch in her voice again, like a sob. "This movement measures the length and breadth of agony. Don't you feel that?"

"Yes, but—but it keeps it in order, somehow." She needed help too. He couldn't abandon her now. "It makes sense of it."

"Sense? Well, yes, maybe in this piece." He heard her swallowing, then she went on. "But some of it tells us of chaos. Of meaninglessness. Of dread. Would Luther like Stravinsky, or Elvis, or Public Enemy?"

"I don't know. Maybe. He wasn't a narrow man. He knew about the demonic, about despair."

"And built a fortress against them in his God. Here, have another drink."

He sipped again and handed back the flask. "Did Vicki choose this piece for the sorrow in it?"

"I think so. Vicki is upset too. A young boy's life ended—" Nysa began to weep. In the dim, dappled light he saw her head sink onto her knees.

"Nysa, Nysa!" Awkwardly he reached to pat her trembling back, then withdrew his hand as though scorched.

"I'm sorry, Justin," she sobbed. "But it makes no sense! Music, theology—how can they explain the waste of a boy?"

"We can only pray and hope for strength and insight. We can't understand the ways of God," Justin said, hands clenched, aching to comfort her, to touch her.

"Nor the ways of the dead! The dead won't stay dead!"

"You mean eternal life?"

"No, not happily ever after. Not heaven, far away. I mean Mozart and Luther, Johnny and the bones, rule this life too."

"Nysa, I don't understand."

She rubbed her glistening cheek and took another swallow from the flask. "Gods die and rise again. You know that, Justin. Jesus dies and then comes Easter."

"That's right. Spiritual life is eternal."

"Do you suppose old Father Rueger was a god, Justin? Dying only to rise again, and walk in his town, and his labyrinth? Are we restoring New Concord for his spirit, d'you think?"

"I think you're a little bit drunk, Nysa."

"You're right." She held the flask up into a splash of moonlight. "Wine. The blood of Christ, right? Maybe I'll rise again too."

"Nysa—" What did she mean? Was she contemplating death, suicide? "Nysa, are you depressed?"

"Depressed?" Her head turned toward him. "Only drunk, Justin. Drunk with fear and terror and helplessness."

"Please, Nysa, don't do anything rash. I'll try to help."

"But you say you can't help, little man of God. You say it's between God and me, one-on-one, and God gets to make the rules."

"Sometimes God works through human love. I mean—"

"Sweet Justin." There was a smile in her voice now. "You mean *agape*, of course, not *eros*. But you know what?" The moon struck sparks from Nysa's hair as she tipped up the flask and drained it. "I bet God works through music, too, and theology and also . . ."

He felt her eyes on him, sliding along the splashes of silvery light that picked out his right shoulder, the front of his blue T-shirt, his sunburned left thigh. His voice was thick. "And also what?"

"And also wine. The blessed blood of the dying and rising Christ!" She stood up suddenly. "Good night, Justin. Sorry to run on like that. Don't worry about me. Thanks for listening. It helped."

With one last soft, apologetic, heart-jolting touch on his arm, she was gone.

Far away, Vicki's music shifted to a faster tempo. Justin hurried away from it, back to camp. All the lights were out in the campers' tents. Bonnie woke up, surprised by Justin's silent, urgent embrace, but amiable enough after a glance to make sure JayJay was fast asleep. A good wife, a good person, he told himself over and over afterward, lying there with his drained body and singed soul.

No music could be heard in this tent, only the cicadas and the breathing of Bonnie and JayJay, and very late, the faint bellowing of cattle somewhere out in the wine-scented night.

18

MELISSA RUEGER RAN FLAT OUT ALONG THE FOOT-
path, squinting against the early sun. It was warm already,
the river beside her steaming with mist, the air damp in her
nostrils. She was running hard because she was late. What
a ditz she was! Vicki and Karen had trusted her, and she'd
overslept! It had been a weird night for her, waiting for her
tentmates to go to sleep and then sneaking out to talk to
Kenny. Kenny was a really, really cool guy. He soothed her
worries about poor Johnny Donato and made her feel . . .
well, really awesome. But when she snuck back into her
tent, she'd heard that cow noise and started fretting again
about Johnny, wondering what had happened to him, and
she hadn't really gotten to sleep until nearly dawn.

Melissa was fifteen, almost sixteen now. She'd grown fast
the past few years, and was still catching up to a body that
had seemed too tall and awkward and basically weird until
very recently. She envied Darlene and Ellie, who'd become
shapely and at ease with boys so much sooner, but she'd
realized just this summer that she was catching up. Suddenly she could wear misses' sizes. She had hips now,
and a waist, and her breasts were finally the same size.
They weren't as big as Ellie's but they bounced a little
when she ran, and Kenny at least seemed to think she
looked adorable.

Kenny, Kenny! He made her feel so good. It was really
cool to be in love. He was a little on the short side, maybe,
and teased her sometimes about liking animals, but he was
the man for her. Probably.

However, even though Kenny was her love, animals remained her passion. At home in Arizona she had two spaniels, three cats, and a Morgan horse. At twelve, when one of the dogs had been hit by a car and rescued by the local veterinarian, she'd vowed to become a vet herself. "Plenty of time to decide what you want to be, honey," said her father. That meant he didn't really approve, but what did he know? She didn't talk about it much to him. But her heart remained true. She read the Herriot books and clung to her dream. That dream had seen her through rough days in junior high, when the popular kids called her a rich, stuck-up beanpole behind her back, just loud enough to be sure she overheard. It had seen her through the heartbreak when her first boyfriend in high school, the dork, had gradually quit phoning and then was spotted at the ice rink with Darlene. And it made this summer a joy, because for the first time she was learning about dairy cattle.

She was running up the hill now to the Brewster barn, streaks of sweat darkening her leaf-green T-shirt. The cows were nowhere to be seen. That meant that Vicki had already brought them all into the barn for milking, even Lucy and Florida, the two that Melissa was supposed to be caring for. She'd been so happy when Vicki had suggested it last week. "You'll get to understand them better if you're really in charge. I raised calves for 4-H when I was about your age, and it was wonderful."

"It'd be cool to raise a calf," Melissa had said wistfully. But since there wasn't enough time, caring for Florida and Lucy would be a good substitute. She'd gotten up early to milk them four days in a row, and was proud that she'd noticed Florida favoring one leg and discovered an overgrown hoof. With Vicki's help she'd filed off the overgrowth with a rasp, making the hoof neat and healthy again.

"When the ground's a little drier and harder, she'll keep her hooves neat just walking around," Vicki had explained. "But it's soft because of all the rain, so I'm glad you kept your eyes open. Florida doesn't walk around enough anyway, do you, old lady?" She'd rubbed Florida affectionately under the chin.

Melissa rounded the corner of the barn. No sign of the Brewsters today. Their pickup was gone too. Usually Karen helped with the milking. I must really be late, Melissa fretted.

The big door was ajar, and she slipped into the barn. The smell of cattle and hay and the stamping and rustling of the animals hit her first as she blinked to accustom her eyes to the dimness. She heard the rhythmic hiss-hiss of milk hitting a pail and located Vicki by the sound. Oh, rats, she was milking Florida. Melissa spoke softly so as not to startle the cows. "Hi, Vicki, I'm really sorry I'm late."

Several heads, spotted brick red and white, had swung around to peer at her. Cows were curious. Big, slow, and curious as kittens.

The hissing of the milk stopped. Vicki said, "I figured you weren't coming. Is something going on? Karen didn't come either."

"No, it's just that I overslept. I'm sorry. I didn't get much sleep last night. It's so awful about Johnny drowning."

Vicki stood slowly, her long frame unfolding like a step-ladder. "Yeah. Nobody's sleeping very well," she said. "Here, do you want to take over the milking?"

"Yeah, thank you. I'm really sorry I messed up."

Vicki looked at her in that shy way she had, put one big hand on Florida's back, and stepped away from the red-and-white cow. Melissa felt a kind of kinship with Vicki, because until very recently she too had felt large and gawky and shape-less, trapped in a body that didn't match her soul. And like Vicki, Melissa had turned to animals for comfort. Animals were awe-some. Here among the sweet-breathed cattle Vicki's height was an advantage, her shyness a virtue. Melissa understood.

The sad blue eyes were still on her. Vicki said, "You are sleepy, aren't you? Maybe you should have slept in."

"No, that wouldn't be fair to the animals. Or you. I'll be okay." Embarrassed by Vicki's scrutiny, Melissa sat on the stool and tucked her left shoulder in close to Florida's flank. Florida was a sweetie but every now and then she let loose with a kick, and sticking close was the best way to prevent the kick from building up enough speed to hurt. Melissa had been bumped a couple of times, but nothing serious. "Easy, Florida," she soothed. "Here we go, old girl." She began to milk two teats rhythmically, squeezing one, releasing it to refill while she squeezed the other, back and forth, squeeze, release, over and over.

Vicki said, "I'll take the others out to the pasture. I finished Lucy already."

Rats. She really had been late. Florida stamped a couple of times as the other cows ambled slowly out of the barn. Melissa crooned, "Easy, Florida, easy, old girl." Florida settled down again, munching on the grain, and Melissa got back into the rhythm. It made her feel dreamy, the smell of hay and fresh manure and the warm cow's flank, the sounds of a droning fly, the rustle as Florida's long tongue swiped the last bits of grain from her manger, the swish-swish of the milk squirting into the pail. It didn't seem so dark now that her eyes were used to it, but if she looked at the barn wall the light outdoors glared through the cracks and made her blink. She turned back to Florida. The cow got her name from a large brick-red spot on her side, right by Melissa's nose now, that was shaped a lot like a map of Florida.

Melissa shifted to the other pair of teats and resumed milking. Poor Johnny Donato. She felt guilty that she hadn't really liked him much. He was a pretty cute guy but he acted dorky, no matter what he looked like. He was always showing off, walking on his hands or teasing the goats. "He's just trying to get attention," Ellie told her when she'd complained.

Kenny thought that showing off was what got him into trouble. "Probably he was like trying to do some stunt, and he slipped on the muddy bank. I bet he hit his head as he fell in, because nobody heard him yelling for help. Plus he drowned pretty close to the shore, or they would've found him farther downstream. That's what happened—he was clowning around and slipped," Kenny told her firmly.

"Yeah, but I still don't know why God let him die."

"Maybe it was like a warning to the rest of us, to be careful. It's really slick along the river." Tenderly, Kenny had wiped a tear from her cheek. "Don't worry, Melissa, I won't let anything happen to you."

BLOODSTREAM

She'd been comforted for a while. But after he'd kissed her good night and she was back in her tent dropping off to sleep, she'd heard that cow bellowing somewhere out in the night. It was spooky, a deep-throated moan full of yearning and pain. It stopped after a few minutes but it left Melissa shaky, wide awake, and wondering if Johnny's ghost was crying out in the night.

Squeeze, release, squeeze, release. Her hands were getting tired of milking. "You'll have a great handshake by the end of the month," Karen Brewster had joked. Melissa slowed a little and glanced at the barn wall, and the back of her neck prickled.

Something was different. A shadow, blocking the sunlight she'd seen a few minutes ago through a couple of the cracks between the boards. A glassy glint, maybe an eye. Something was watching her.

It was outside, not inside.

Melissa didn't stare. She stayed cool, turning back to the milking as though she'd seen nothing, telling her heart to stop pounding. It was just someone passing outside, Vicki or maybe Kenny come to meet her, or a curious cow. Probably a cow. She'd spooked herself by thinking too much about Johnny's death and that bellowing cow last night.

There was a pitchfork leaning against the doorframe. She could grab that and stick the tines through the crack.

She wouldn't want to hurt a cow.

She stole another glance at the wall.

Gone! The sun sparkled innocently through the cracks.

Melissa stood slowly and looked around the barn. Everything was as it should be. Florida's spotted head swung around to look at her reproachfully.

"Sorry, old girl." Relieved, Melissa sat again. She finished the milking by massaging each quarter of the udder gently while milking its teat with the other hand, glancing at the wall occasionally. When she was done she poured the pailful of milk into the can and released Florida from her stall. The cow backed out slowly and dawdled to the door, pausing to snuffle the handle of the pitchfork leaning there. "Shoo, Florida! Shoo, old girl!"

Florida strolled out. She knew her way but she took her time, swiveling her ears at the chickens, sampling a weed by the fence. Vicki was standing by the pasture gate and opened it for them. Melissa followed the cow through, watching Florida's angular walk. "Her hoof is okay, don't you think, Vicki?"

"Yeah, we caught it early." Vicki latched the gate again.

"Was somebody around the barn just now? I thought I saw somebody watching me through a crack in the wall."

There was a hint of alarm in Vicki's face. She shook her head slowly. "From here, all I saw was cows."

"Yeah, could have been a cow." Melissa looked across the width of the barnyard. From here Vicki could easily have missed seeing someone on the other side of the barn. She said, "I thought I heard a cow mooing last night, real late. Did you hear it?"

Vicki nodded and gestured toward the west. "I was sleeping on the hill there."

"What was the problem?"

"No problem, Melissa." Vicki smiled her shy smile. "I check them. They're all okay, even Lucy and Florida."

"Yeah, but I was worried about them. That noise was so sad and spooky. And really loud. Awesome."

"Powerful." Vicki nodded. "But you mustn't worry, Melissa. I watch them. Nothing will hurt them."

"So how come the cow was so upset?" Melissa persisted.

"I don't know."

"Maybe a dog, or a snake?"

Vicki glanced at her, then down at her big shoes. "See, they aren't always upset. They bellow for lots of reasons. Like when they're in heat. Or when they want to remind each other of their strength."

"Oh."

"Don't worry, Melissa."

"Okay. See, I'm just asking because I want to be a vet."

"I know. It's good to worry about overgrown hooves or infected udders. You're going to be a good vet. You'll have to go to college but I can tell you'll be good."

"Thanks." Melissa was pleased and vowed never to oversleep again. "Um, I guess I better get back to camp for breakfast."

"So long," said Vicki.

Melissa ran toward the footpath. She glanced back as she turned onto it, and saw eight red-and-white cows and Vicki gazing after her. But then she slowed with a smile.

Kenny, looking adorably sleepy behind his aviator glasses, had come to walk her back to breakfast. Cool.

19

"OH, WAIT! I'VE GOTTA GET MY ORANGE T-SHIRT!" Chrissie rushed back into the house. Marty, in uniform already, glanced at her watch. In five minutes she had to leave for work.

Brad was standing by the open door of his Mazda. He reached for her hand and said, "Hey, kitten."

"Hey, Brad."

He'd come in late last night, very late. But he hadn't been drinking. She was sure. She'd mumbled a greeting as he crawled in beside her, and he'd thrown an arm over her and gone right to sleep. This morning Chrissie had been so full of excitement about going to Tennessee that they hadn't had a chance to talk.

"I was thinking last night," he said.

"Where'd you go?" She couldn't help asking. She'd always been too curious.

He waved a dismissive hand. "Just driving around. I had to think. See, the thing is, we've been apart a lot while I was checking things out. We've both changed, that's natural."

"Yeah, that's true."

"All those things we used to talk about—well, I've been

working my butt off trying to make those dreams come true."

"So have I, Brad. I haven't exactly been sitting around."

"Easy, kitten!" He raised his palm gently to quiet her. "I know it's been tough for you too. But you see, I'm not real clear on what you want anymore. You used to say you thought I had talent—"

"I still say that, Brad. It's true!"

"Well, the thing is, you gave me courage to keep trying. It's like you showed me the way. I'd be ready to chuck it all and I'd think of you and that kid and keep going. And I got there. And so it's really a shock when you turn around like this . . ." He shrugged eloquently.

Marty felt like an ungrateful worm. He was trying so hard! All the old desires were tumbling through her. She wanted to help him, to bring him strength and inspiration, to be at his side fending off threats to his shining talent, just as she'd done in the early days.

Just as she'd tried to do, she corrected herself. She'd tried, time and again. And time and again, he'd gone off in some new direction, on some new project, and pretty soon she was blaming herself because he needed rescuing again.

Last year she'd finally realized that she couldn't fix his life. *You're lucky if you can rescue yourself*, a wise friend had told her. Well, the job was teaching her how to do that much. And she sure as heck couldn't take care of Chrissie or Brad if she didn't take care of herself. She knew in her core that she couldn't give up what she'd built here.

But when she glanced at his hurt, dark eyes, she wanted to help. She wanted to so much. Could it be that, this time, he'd really changed?

Chrissie bounced out of the house and threw her orange shirt into the backseat. "Okay, let's go!"

"I'll try to get off next weekend so I can pick her up, Brad. Maybe we can talk a little."

"Think about it, Marty. Seriously."

"I will."

She hugged him, hard, and in a moment he responded,

pressing her close and kissing her curls. "We'll work it out, kitten," he whispered.

"We'll sure try." She stepped back and turned to her daughter. "Bye, Chrissie."

"Bye, Mommy." Chrissie gave her a perfunctory kiss and climbed into the car. Brad pulled out the seat belt for her before fastening his own. They rolled down the long drive-way and both waved as they turned onto the road.

Marty waved back, and was surprised to find tears sliding down her cheeks. Left behind. She swiped at them with the back of her hand, hurried into the house, buckled on her gun belt, and headed for work.

At the office, there weren't many new reports. Bobby Mason had interviewed almost all the people who'd been at the Quick-Mart Sunday night when the Dennis Rent-All break-in had occurred next door. No one remembered anything useful. Bobby hadn't talked to Andy Ragg, who'd stopped in for cigarettes about 1:00 A.M. Andy was a trucker and was now off in Fort Wayne, and wouldn't be back till this afternoon. Marty made a note to check with Andy then. There was a report from Child Protective Services, stating that Mrs. Seifert had agreed to attend an effective-parenting program, so her three boys would not go into foster care. Marty sighed. Mrs. Seifert loved her boys, true, but she loved bingeing even more. A couple of weeks and they'd be on their own again. A couple of years and they'd be locked up, if they weren't dead.

Dead like Johnny, whose parents had loved him, sheltered him, tried to protect him. What she tried to do for Chrissie. Damn.

She turned back to the stack. Karen Brewster had mailed her a photocopy of Nysa Strand's history booklet. The cover page, sea blue, said, "Father Rueger and New Concord: A History." Hardly tomorrow's news. Marty dropped it back into the stack and flipped through her notes of things to do. Too early to check back with Flo Duffy at the courthouse. Maybe she could catch Johnny Donato's buddy, what was his name? She found the note. George Muller. She knocked on Wes's office door.

"Yeah?"

She stuck her head in. "Hi. Anything new on the Donato kid?"

Wes frowned. "Naw. Doc Altmann's office said they hadn't finished the autopsy, because some shooter in a bar left a couple of bodies for the Dunning city cops and Doc's cutting them up now."

"They need the bullets?"

"Yeah, for a ballistics match. And the Donato kid may not be a homicide, plus he died over a week ago, so we get to twiddle our thumbs while they work the warm ones."

She said, "I thought I'd go talk to Johnny's best friend, sir, if you don't need me somewhere else."

"Might as well." He still looked grumpy. "See you later, Hopkins."

Like the Donatos, the Mullers lived in one of the old houses built by Father Rueger's followers. This one was painted white, with black aluminum-scroll porch supports and a picture window where the many-paned Rueger front window had once been.

Mrs. Muller answered the door, a short, pleasant-faced woman of about forty, with a high-piled blond hairdo that reminded Marty of Aunt Vonnie and her friends. She probably thought it made her look taller. She frowned at Marty. "Is it about that ambulance last night?"

"No, ma'am. I want to talk to your son about Johnny Donato."

"Oh, I wish you wouldn't! He's so miserable about poor Johnny. We all are."

"Yes, ma'am, I know. But he may be able to help us figure out what happened."

"Johnny just slipped, didn't he? The bank is so slick when the river is high."

"Yes, ma'am, that's what we're trying to confirm."

"I hate to bring it up again. It makes George feel so bad."

"Yes, ma'am. I have a kid a little younger than George,

and she'd feel awful too. But I think she'd feel a little better if she knew she could help us make some sense out of it."

"Well . . ." Mrs. Muller's eyes had softened. "Maybe so. He keeps talking about helping the search party. He's out back mowing the lawn. I've been trying to keep him busy. You'll go easy on him?"

"Yes, ma'am, of course."

Marty followed the racket of the lawn mower around the back corner of the house, and felt a pang of sympathy when she saw a stocky boy in a Lily Pistols T-shirt like Johnny's pushing the machine back and forth over the rain-lush grass. Marty waited for George to turn and start back, then waved her arms. He looked surprised, but put the machine on idle and came over to her.

"Hi, George."

"Hi." He eyed her warily, a short boy, tanned, his brown hair streaked lighter by the sun.

"George, I'm trying to find out what happened to Johnny. I have a few questions." They had to raise their voices a little because the machine was rumbling in the background.

"He fell in, right?" George's voice was about to change, deepening but still youthful. "Everybody says he slipped and hit his head and fell in."

"Who says that?"

"Mom and Pop and Uncle Pete. Same thing happened to a friend of Uncle Pete's when he was a kid. Uncle Pete saw it but they couldn't get him out in time."

"Did anyone see it happen to Johnny?"

"No, ma'am."

"We're trying to make sure that's what really happened."

"I thought there were like scientists who could tell."

"They can tell us some things. But they haven't finished their investigation yet. I just want to get it clear about what Johnny was doing that last day."

George's lower lip quivered. "I wasn't with him. I was with some guys riding our trail bikes."

"I see."

"I asked him to come along! But he liked this girl from Arizona—" Angrily, George brushed a hand across his wet

135

cheek. "I was tired of just hanging around those Arizona guys! They're older than us. They don't care."

"George, it's okay, friends don't have to do every single thing together."

"Yes, ma'am, but—" He stared down at his sneakers. L.A. Gear, like Johnny's.

"I know. When people die the rest of us keep thinking of what we should have done. It's tough. But try to remember the good stuff too. Anyway, you can help now."

"But I wasn't with him!"

"I know. But you know a lot about Johnny. You knew he liked Ellie from Arizona. His dad didn't know that."

"His dad? See, like if Johnny said he liked music his dad said it was for faggots. So Johnny didn't say much to him." His shrug was so dismissive that Marty found herself hoping that Chrissie never shrugged that way about her. Shoot, she missed Chrissie already. Left behind.

"That's the thing," she said, getting back to business. "He told you a lot more. And we've already talked to the people who saw him last. They've given us all the help they can."

"So what do you want to know?"

"Well, for example, some people said he was a show-off."

"No, not really!" George's indignation made his young voice crack. "He liked to try things, that's all! Like wheelies on his trail bike, and walking on his hands."

"Was he learning anything new?"

"He said he wanted to get into bodybuilding. And rodeos, but I thought that was weird. He always liked machines better. I think he thought Ellie would be impressed."

"Yeah. Guys do a lot of things to impress girls. And vice versa."

"Well, I don't!"

Not yet, Marty thought, but said, "Yeah, you seem like a practical guy."

"Yeah." George seemed pleased that she thought he was practical. "Johnny was always daring me to do things, but I wouldn't."

"Good. What kind of things did he dare you to do?"

136

"Like eating out of animal skulls. You know, Lily Pistols stuff."

"They do that? I *heard* they were weird!"

"Yeah. It's creepy. It's cool," George said casually, glad she'd been shocked, the young male proving how much tougher he was than a mere female.

"Did Johnny eat out of skulls, like Lily Pistols?"

"No. He said we should be looking for good bones, though. Like there's this one song, 'Pink Poison,' and their drummer uses bones to hit the drums. Real human bones. Johnny didn't have any human bones but he got the butcher at the Save-More to give him some beef bones. And he got this weed—he said it was a lily with a poison root, just like Lily Pistols sings about, but it looked like plain old Indian poke to me. He dared me to eat it like the Indians used to do, to prove they could be the chief. But I didn't. And later my dad said it really was poison. Indian poke is poison."

"Good you didn't eat it then. Did Johnny eat it?" She had a vision of Johnny, half-poisoned, collapsing on the riverside path, sliding into the water.

"No, ma'am, he didn't eat it. He only dared me to do it 'cause I didn't believe it was poison. He wasn't really trying to hurt me or anything, just proving he was right."

"George, you know we found those bones washed up near where Johnny died. Did you and Johnny have anything to do with them?"

George looked surprised. "No, ma'am! All we ever found was a rabbit skull. Johnny asked the butcher for a steer skull but he didn't have one."

Marty turned the page of her notebook. "Did Johnny ever talk about cow witches?"

"No." He glanced at her, startled, then at his sneakers again. His voice fell, and she could hardly hear him over the muttering of the lawn mower. "That was just a story he told. He was a good talker. Always said interesting things."

"You mean he lied?"

"No!" George was indignant now. "He wasn't a liar! He

just—you know, said crazy things sometimes, just to tease. That's not lying."

"I see. So what was this story?"

"Just a story." He fidgeted and looked longingly at the lawn mower. "See, I promised him I wouldn't tell."

She backed off for the moment. "Okay. Do you know if Johnny had enemies? Kids from here who didn't like him? Or maybe from Arizona?"

"Well, there's the Seifert brothers. They beat up on him once. They beat up on a lot of guys."

"Yeah." He was right—it wouldn't hurt to know where those pathetically angry boys had been that Friday afternoon. "Anybody else?"

"Not really. He got along. There's guys you hang out with, and guys you don't."

"What about the Arizona kids?"

"They mostly ignored us. I don't know why Johnny kept hanging out there," said practical George.

"You think maybe he annoyed one of them too much?"

The boy looked dubious. "Johnny's not dumb. I mean, those kids are bigger and everything. If they told us to scoot, we scooted."

"Yeah. George, back to the cow witches. His little sister seems really scared of them."

"She's just a little kid. He was only teasing." George squirmed in his black T-shirt, as though Marty was a teacher asking him to snitch on a buddy. Some things women weren't supposed to hear. "There's no such thing. He made it up, see?"

"Yeah, I see. What did he make up?"

"It was just like a comic book thing. A superhero bad guy. I promised him, okay? And I have to mow the lawn."

"George, it's probably nothing to worry about. But things have changed, and I bet Johnny wouldn't ask you to promise now."

"Ma'am, I can't." George stared stubbornly at his sneakers. His ears were red.

"Well, I'll let you think about your promise, George. Because things are real different now. Will you think about it?"

"Yes, ma'am." George scurried back to his machine and it roared into life once more.

Back in the cruiser, she radioed in. Foley's voice answered, "Hey, babe, about time! Boss says to get your butt over to the county hospital. Somebody about killed your professor friend."

"Professor?"

"Brewster."

"Ten-four." Marty hit the gas and the siren.

20

DEPUTY BOBBY MASON WAS WAITING FOR HER AT the hospital, his round young face bored. Marty asked, "What've we got?"

"Felony battery," Mason said. "Doctor says it's not a stabbing, just fists or possibly a small blunt instrument. Guy's out cold but they say they got him stabilized. Wife's hysterical, asking for you."

"So what happened?"

"She says she doesn't know. Near as I can tell, he went out for a drink. Clyde's in New Concord."

Marty nodded. It was a bar on the highway side of town.

"She got worried when he wasn't back by midnight. Called the bar, and they told her he'd left a couple of hours before. She drove around looking, found him down by the boat ramps. She called the ambulance but didn't think to call us till half an hour ago."

"You want me to talk to her?"

Mason shrugged. "She's asking for you. I'll go track down the bartender."

Marty spoke to the nurse and was directed to a room full

of monitors that beeped quietly. Karen Brewster, looking very small and not at all comical, sat by a hospital bed staring intently at a big still lump under the sheets. Amidst the tubes and wires, a bandaged arm was visible. Karen gripped the hand. Her anxiety was palpable. Marty murmured, "Hello, Mrs. Brewster."

"Do you think he just moved?" Karen whispered, still staring at the bed.

"I couldn't see." Marty came closer. Drew's face was puffy, ash-colored, and still. But there was a touch of pink in his cheeks. "Can you tell me what happened, Mrs. Brewster?"

"Someone beat him up! He's got a concussion, the doctor says!" Tears spilled down Karen's mobile face. "How could this happen to him? How?"

"I'm sorry, ma'am. You say he went to a bar?"

Karen leaned toward the bed. "Drew, can you hear me? Squeeze my hand."

The fingers she held twitched. "Oh, thank God!" Karen exclaimed.

"Professor Brewster?" Marty asked. "Can you hear me?"

There was no response. Karen said, "Deputy Hopkins, there's a killer loose around here! You've got to do something!"

"We're trying, ma'am. Now, he went to Clyde's, is that right?"

"Yeah." Karen took a deep breath. "See, we're trying to contact the neighbors informally. There's so much misinformation about the historic project." She choked down a sob. "I was going to go with him, but he said sometimes men were more open about their concerns if there were no women around."

"Yeah, I've noticed that too." Whoever had banged up Drew Brewster had been pretty open about his concerns. "Mrs. Brewster, are you saying the fight was about the historic project?"

"What else could it be? Drew is the sweetest man on earth!"

"Sweet" wasn't how Marty would describe Drew. In a

southern Indiana bar, she figured, he'd probably come across as a stuck-up airbag pointy-head. Marty asked, "Did Drew go to this bar often?"

"No. He only started this summer, to meet some of the neighbors."

"So he'd heard about local opposition to the project before he started going?"

"Yes." Karen fumbled for a tissue to wipe her eyes. "He just wanted to educate them about it. He was sure they'd approve if they understood."

"I see." Marty glanced at the professor's face, and saw that Drew's dark eyes were open, puffy but looking at her. "Professor Brewster, can you tell us who attacked you?"

"I don't—" Drew said thickly, and winced in pain.

Karen grabbed his hand again. "Oh, darling! Thank God, you're awake!"

"You don't what, Professor Brewster?"

"Don't—remember."

"You were in the bar," Marty prompted.

"Yes." There was a pause. "Clyde's."

"That's right, darling!" Karen exclaimed. "Then what?"

"God, my head hurts!"

"Of course it does, darling. It'll be better soon."

Marty said, "Did you have any arguments at Clyde's?"

"No. No, they listened."

"Were you alone when you left Clyde's?"

"Yes. God, it hurts!" His puffy eyes closed again.

"Yes sir. Did anyone follow you when you left?"

For a moment Marty feared that Drew had passed out again. Then he murmured, "I don't remember."

"Do you remember anything after leaving Clyde's?"

His eyes didn't open. "No. Nothing," he murmured.

"Well, if either of you remember anything, give us a call."

Marty radioed dispatch, eager to interview others who'd been at Clyde's, but Foley told her to cool down, Mason was covering it and she should break for lunch. Marty sighed. Well, it was getting late. The Three Bears wasn't far from the hospital, and she stopped there for a turkey sandwich and iced tea and a good think. Why would anyone attack Drew Brewster? Had he seen something, or said something, that endangered someone? Was it just ill will about the historic project, now that a local child had died while visiting it? It ought to fit somehow with Johnny Donato's death. But she couldn't see how.

When she paid she also bought a chocolate bar, with almonds, and picked up some M&M's for Chrissie. She was getting back into the cruiser when she remembered that her daughter was gone. A lump came to her throat.

Come off it, Hopkins, she's only been gone a few hours. You could fritter away your whole life missing people. Get back to work.

The Three Bears was at the intersection with County 405. It was only a few miles down the road to Andy Ragg's trucking business. If she couldn't work on the Donato case, might as well get that interview out of the way. Andy's consisted of a big parking lot, a long garage building, and a little aluminum add-on that served as office. A big air conditioner over the door dripped onto Marty's Stetson as she opened the glass door. Inside, the walls were covered with a pastel patchwork of invoices, clipped cartoons from newspapers, notices, schedules. Ruth Ragg rested both pudgy elbows on the wood-grain Formica counter as she talked on the phone. She raised an eyebrow at Marty and said, "Someone's here. I'll call back later, okay?"

Ruth was a broad-faced, blue-eyed, graying woman whose ample curves couldn't soften the toughness that thirty-some years of dealing with truckers had brought her. "Howdy, Marty," she said as she hung up.

"Hi, Ruth. Is Andy back yet?"

"Not for another couple of hours. He's on the road from Fort Wayne. What's going on? Deputy Mason phoned yesterday wanting to talk to him."

"Well, tell him to call us when he gets in, okay? We have a question about Sunday night."

"Sunday? Can I help? I was with him from, oh, four o'clock Sunday afternoon until he left for Fort Wayne Monday morning."

"We heard he stopped by the Quick-Mart for cigarettes."

"That he did." Ruth cocked a graying eyebrow at Marty. "And I waited for him in the pickup."

"You were there, in the Quick-Mart lot?"

"Yep."

"Hey, maybe you can help." Marty pulled out her notebook. "Was there any sign of anyone over at Dennis Rent-All?"

"Is that when the break-in happened? Sunday night? Now you ask, seems to me somebody was over there. Not people, a truck. Let me see." Ruth frowned and closed her eyes. "No lights on over there, just the Quick-Mart lamppost near me. But yeah, there was a pickup parked behind Dennis's."

"What'd it look like?"

"Chevy, maybe eight years old. Couldn't tell the color, it was way too dim. Some light color. Big dent in the left rear fender."

"Great!" Marty wrote it down. "You didn't see the license, then?"

"Only part of the truck with any light on it was that fender. You're lucky I can tell you the make, young lady."

"I know, I know! You've been great, Ruth. I'll check this out. And listen, when Andy gets back, you can ask him if he noticed anything more."

"I'll ask, but it won't be any use. I'm the noticer in the family."

"I believe you. See you soon, Ruth."

The afternoon was warm and steamy, the sun glowing in the hazy sky. Marty looked anxiously at the chocolate-almond bar she'd left in the cruiser. It looked pretty soft. She flipped the air-conditioning to max, placing the chocolate over the vent. By the time she got back to the Dunning courthouse square it seemed acceptably rigid again.

She stuck her head in Reiner's Bakery. "Hi, Aunt Vonnie. Gotta hurry. But I wanted to know how you're doing."

"Still hurts," her aunt admitted. "Melva said that driving probably made it worse. She said I should stay with her a couple nights, cause we come in to work at the same time."

"I could drive you," Marty said.

Her aunt snorted. "No sirree! The hours you keep, I'd never know how long I'd have to wait for you."

"Suit yourself. I'll see you later."

She hurried across the street into the courthouse and downstairs to Flo Duffy's lair.

"Hey, Flo. Sharp outfit."

Flo placed her Virginia Slim in her vulgar ashtray and stood up to twirl like a model. She wore a saffron-yellow pants outfit. The top, styled like an oversized man's shirt, tied at the waist and was unbuttoned over a green-and-rust jungle print T-shirt. The little green alligators at her ears peeked through the frizz of red hair. "I'm going to retire to Borneo," she announced as she sashayed toward the counter. "Just getting in practice."

"You'll knock 'em dead, Flo. Any word on those properties?"

Flo became serious. "I've got a little ethical question, Marty. A little question of loyalties." She leaned across the counter, almost into Marty's face. "I can't promise that I won't mention that you've been asking. You understand?"

Someone important, then. Marty said, "You may have to tell I'm asking even if you don't give me the answer. Is that right?"

"Right."

"Well, might as well tell me then." Marty slid the chocolate bar across the counter. "You can always claim police brutality."

Flo beamed and picked up the candy. "In questions of loyalties, I'm loyal to chocolate. Okay, we're talking about two farms, one on each side of the state highway, across the river from farms owned by Dub Walters and by Nysa Strand. Is that right?"

"That's right."

"They're both owned by Dub Walters."

"Shit," said Marty.

Flo was already halfway back to her desk, peeling down the candy wrapper. She shrugged her saffron-yellow shoulders. "Hey, what can I say? Shit happens."

144

21

"CRAZY DAY," DOC ALTMANN TOLD WES ON THE phone late Tuesday. "Couple of shootings, and two folks dead at the nursing home. Looks like food poisoning. I just now finished the Donato kid's autopsy."

"Yeah." Wes found himself gripping the receiver tighter. "What did you find?"

"You've got some work to do, Wes. Kid was dead before he hit the water. There's a lot of postmortem scuffing from the river, and a few of the chop wounds could have come from a boat propeller, but we've got at least three stab wounds that could have caused death. Homicide, definitely."

"Stab wounds. A knife?"

"Nope. Something pointed, maybe like a stake you drive into the ground. We've got chop wounds too from a two-and-a-half-inch-wide blade, not real sharp. Maybe a small hatchet. Plus we've got contusions from a one-and-a-half-inch-diameter blunt object, like a hammer."

"Holy shit." Wes rubbed a hand through his hair.

"Yeah. Somebody tried to turn this kid into ground round. Best we can tell from the condition of the body, all the blows came at about the time of death, and he was dropped in the river right away."

"Holy shit. All those weapons—a gang, do you think?"

"Your problem now, Wes," said Doc cheerfully. "You'll have the written report first thing tomorrow, full of juicy details. Now, your other case, those old bones? My expert is voting for a hundred years old."

Wes was still turning over Johnny's wounds. Hammer, hatchet, tent stakes. Ground round. The local toughs didn't go in for that kind of thing. They'd divided themselves into three or four gangs, did drugs and beat each other up occasionally when somebody's manhood was challenged, but it was usually for a reason, however misguided. Todd Seifert and Clayton Wall had got into armed robberies, but Wes had got them convicted and sent away last year. Clayton was still locked up but Todd, supposedly reformed now, was out on probation. Time to look him up, maybe. "A hundred years!" said Wes belatedly.

"Give or take a few decades," Doc said. "Male with some oddities. Very long legs, but a juvenile pelvis. Maybe some hormone problem."

"Well, Doc, we're not likely to find any hundred-year-old killers even if you rule it homicide. We'll get moving on the Donato kid."

"Okay. You'll get both reports tomorrow morning."

"Thanks, Doc." Wes replaced the receiver. Hammers. Hatchets. Stakes. He wiped a hand across his face. How could a fourteen-year-old kid get into that kind of trouble?

He looked at the photograph on his desk, Shirley and their son Billy at sixteen, grinning at him.

"Foley!" he yelled.

"Yessir?"

Wes surged from his desk and leaned out from his office doorframe to look at the dispatcher. "Where's Hopkins?"

"Last time she called in she was headed back to Dunning from the hospital. She talked to that professor who was in the bar brawl. Mason's following up on that."

"Good. Get her here." Doc Altmann's call about the Donato boy had given a new, dark edge to the assault on the professor. Wes asked, "Where's Sims?"

"He was down south, checking a vandalism call."

"Well, get him here too. We got a definite homicide on the Donato kid."

By the time Marty Hopkins arrived fifteen minutes later, Wes had almost finished rereading the Donato file. He said, "Doc says homicide on the Donato kid. You think the Brewster assault is connected?"

"Hard to tell, sir. He's just waking up, doesn't remember much."

"Shit." Too often, assault victims blanked on the moments preceding the attack. "What kind of injuries does he have?"

"Concussion, ribs, bad bruising. The doctor thinks he was hit with fists, maybe a stick too. Guy looks terrible."

"Mason's checking it out, right? Anything else?"

"Flo Duffy says Dub Walters owns those two farms across the river from where we found Johnny. Only he's not letting on about those two properties—he's handling them through some Indianapolis lawyer. Even the neighbors don't know he owns them."

"Shit. I wonder what old Dub's up to." He squinted at the map on the wall, then shook his head. "Can't see how it connects with Johnny Donato, though. Doc Altmann says the kid was beat up before he was thrown in the river."

"Oh no." There was pain in Marty's gray eyes, but she was thinking, making connections. "Professor Brewster was beat up too."

Wes still had to remind himself sometimes that he wasn't supposed to protect Marty. She was his buddy's daughter, okay, but she'd dealt with ugly deaths before, she'd discovered this body, she was not the little girl he'd coached in peewee basketball twenty years ago.

He said, "It was ugly, Marty. Kid was beat up with a hammer and a hatchet and a tent stake, or something along those lines."

She winced at his words. "God, that's brutal! Poor kid!" She took a deep breath and said shakily, "Brewster was worked over, but nobody mentioned hatchets."

"We'd better ask," Wes said.

"Yeah." Her expression became thoughtful. "Well, God knows we've got tent stakes nearby this summer. And hammers and hatchets are easy enough to find around most people's houses. Or barns. Although there's something . . ." She frowned, worrying over it. "Sorry, can't place it."

"Maybe it'll come to you. Meanwhile we've got a lot of

new questions to ask. Hopkins, does this sound like a gang to you?''

"Could be, sir. This whole thing—well, it's muddled. But there are so many kids involved. Teens, just on the edge of growing up. Nysa Strand thought—'' She frowned. "Sir, was Johnny molested? Sexually?''

"Doc didn't say. He would have if there was evidence. Why?''

"Well, Nysa didn't give any specifics, but she seemed to think the trouble sprang from sex and youth. There are so many teenagers around. And then there's the Lily Pistols thing.''

"The rock group?''

"Yeah. Johnny's best friend was a New Concord kid named George Muller. I talked to him this morning, and he was pretty forthcoming about a lot of things. Said Johnny was interested in witches, death, poisons—all the stuff Lily Pistols fool around with. Johnny was a big fan.''

Wes frowned skeptically at his metal wastebasket and pushed it into the corner with his foot. "You're thinking it could be connected to a music group?''

"I don't know. It's a weird group. And George mentioned the Seifert boys.''

Wes snorted. "There's always the Seifert boys.''

"Yeah, but—see, sir, their situation is so bad. I can see why they're mad at the world. That family is like a textbook on how to raise bad guys.''

"Yeah. Gotta admit, I thought of Todd Seifert too.''

"George said something else, sir, probably nothing. But he was holding back about one thing. It sounds crazy, I know, but it might be important. George said Johnny made up a story about a cow witch, whatever that is. Then George got tongue-tied and wouldn't say any more. Wouldn't tell me what the story was.''

Didn't sound like much. Why was she worried about it? Wes studied Hopkins a moment. Her instincts were usually good. He said, "And you think this is important.''

"Yes sir. I think—it's not logical, I know.'' She ran her fingers back through her curly hair. "But George had strong feelings

148

about it, and Johnny's little sister Rosie had strong feelings about it. I didn't want to press her, she seemed so frightened. George wasn't frightened, but he really seemed—embarrassed, I think. Just didn't want to talk about it. Anyway, it's those strong emotions that make me think it's important."

Wes nodded thoughtfully. Why would George be embarrassed? Well, for one thing, he was thirteen. For another, Marty was a woman, in the same category as mothers, teachers, and girlfriends. No matter how much she tried to be a regular guy, there were things you just didn't mention to mothers, teachers, or girlfriends. Especially if you were thirteen. He said, "I'll have a word with the kid tomorrow. Man to man. And if he's still too bashful to talk, you can have a word with Rosie."

"Man to man," said Hopkins.

22

TOR WAS A NIGHT CREATURE. IN THE SUNNY HOURS he stayed in his workday costume, laboring like other people at a job that was all right but didn't allow him to be fully himself. He knew that he had to pretend to be ordinary or he'd be in danger. There were secrets that you couldn't tell even to your family, because although they knew part of the story, they couldn't understand it all.

Sometimes he thought with longing of the Pawnee he'd studied in the Field Museum in Chicago. They were not like most men today, swaggering and bragging about their accomplishments. They had linked themselves with nature. They had made themselves whole. Sometimes he wished he could come out of hiding and explain the truth to people, explain the Pawnee way. But he was afraid to risk it. He'd risked telling the truth to Morton, and Morton had jeered.

So Tor was cautious. But he was restless these days. The moments at the dark river's edge that fed his soul seemed less nourishing now, and he had to come out more often and stay longer.

For years, he hadn't emerged at all. When he was small his father had tried to teach him not to cry, but he'd never been able to learn, no matter how many times he was slapped or called a girl. He had learned instead to run away, to cry in secret. He could trust Stevie, but not parents, not adults, not other children. His parents made that clear. Most of the kids at school were not to be trusted, his father explained. Their parents weren't raising them right. His mother made sure he never visited anyone except kids who went to Sunday school or children's choir. Stevie qualified, so he'd been allowed to visit, to watch TV or to read about the West, about outlaw kings, about cattle drives, about rodeos. They'd learned to sing cowboy ballads and play the harmonica.

And then, when he was eleven, came the confused times. There was a problem already, a family crisis he hadn't understood, except to know that his father was bleak and angry. He'd been glad to get away to watch TV at Stevie's because his family was so upset. Then, riding their bikes around the neighborhood, they'd stopped for a rest and Stevie had noticed the picture in someone's trash. "Hey, look," he'd said in a funny voice. They'd both looked at it, and then they'd pedaled off with it to a private place under a bridge and looked again, and laughed raucously. But they both knew their young lives had changed forever. Stevie told him to hide the picture, but he hadn't hidden it well enough. He remembered his father's rage, the searing pain, the move to a new town, and he remembered crying in secret every night in that new house because he missed Stevie and because there was nothing friendly left in the world.

His parents had tried to help him adjust, getting him books and new clothes and a guitar, but he remained fearful and his father pretty much avoided him except to preach about overcoming sin. Every now and then he'd slip away to the banks of that new river, remembering the days of cowboys and Stevie. He didn't fit anywhere now. The other kids at his new school seemed alien beings. The girls were distant, ignoring him, and he didn't really know how to talk to them. The boys were rowdy and disdainful.

Finally he'd made friends with Morton, because they both wanted to learn to play the guitar. Morton lived on a working farm, and they'd practice chords outside his barn. It was okay for a while, until that summer they both started growing so fast. Morton's voice changed and his shoulders broadened and he started swaggering and bragging. Then, one terrible evening, he'd bicycled to Morton's farm to practice some songs—"Red River Valley," he remembered, that was one. As he'd put his guitar in its case afterward, his friend had slipped a muscular arm around his shoulders and kissed him clumsily on the cheek. "No! Please!" He'd jerked away, horrified, and told Morton it was impossible, it was sinful. He'd tried to explain why. But Morton was revolted, embarrassed, and finally angry. "You're saying I'm a faggot?" he'd jeered. "You're the faggot! You're a monster!"

Looking back, Tor realized that it was the jeering that had first awakened the blinding rage of the bull within him, made him grab the pitchfork, made him lunge at Morton like the great red bull lunging and kicking at that cowboy. At the time he'd been frightened as soon as it was over, frightened and shaky, and he'd dropped the pitchfork and begun to run. Bicycle to the river near the freight station, rinse the clothes and ditch the bike in the night river, ride north, hide. After that had come the wasted years, trying to build what looked like a normal life while knowing that he would have to hide forever, filled with rage and helplessness. At last he had seen those exhibits in the Field Museum, and he had found this place and realized that here on the dark riverside he could at last emerge, he could be himself.

But he longed for a true companion, a helpmeet.

The sun would rise soon, spilling golden spangles across the black water. It was time to hide again. It was too late to view the church school tents. The young people would sleep soundly for another hour, but the older ones who began the breakfast would soon be rising. And soon Vicki the cowherd would have to collect the cattle, calling them to the barn for the morning milking. He knew her hours, her chores, her daily routines, her music, her pride in the lovely voice and hair, her shame about the tall, awkward body. Vicki would never be anyone's helpmeet. He tossed his head, and his great horns glinted silver in the early light. His helpmeet would be soft and yielding, regal and gentle, young and motherly and understanding.

A gleam of light topped the eastern hills. Tor plunged into the deep woods, back to his dark home.

But later, well-hidden again, he emerged just far enough to peek at the blond girl who was stroking Florida's head.

She was beautiful, and gentle, and rarest of all, she stirred his loins.

She started to look in his direction and he retreated hastily into the dark. But he had decided. He had found his helpmeet.

23

MARTY'S FIRST JOB WEDNESDAY WAS TO STOP BY THE hospital to see Drew Brewster. She found the big professor almost sitting up in bed, lumpy as a rockslide on the crisp sheets. He was finishing breakfast. "How're you doing, Professor Brewster?"

"Broken ribs, broken head," he grumbled, his Oliver Hardy mustache twitching.

"You sound better than yesterday."

"Well, today I can tell how much it aches."

"Do you remember any more about what happened?" She pulled out her notebook.

Drew Brewster's plump fingers closed on his coffee cup. "No," he said quickly. "I remember the bar. I remember who was there, at least their first names. I remember walking out of the air-conditioning into the warm night. Then it's all a blank."

Something didn't ring true. She prodded, but Drew couldn't or wouldn't tell her anything more. "Posttraumatic amnesia," he declared, and gave her a brief lecture on it. She checked with his doctor, who admitted that Drew's wounds might have come from a hammer instead of a stick, but definitely not a hatchet. Then she left to join the other deputies in a search for weapons.

By 10:00 A.M. it was clear that they'd drawn a blank there too. They'd looked at hatchets, axes, and pickaxes in every house and outbuilding within a couple of miles of where Johnny had died, and all the blades were wider than the two and a half inches that Doc specified in his report. On the other hand, there were plenty of hammers and tent stakes that filled the bill. But Marty was increasingly convinced of what she'd feared from the beginning: The murder weapons had been hidden, most likely pitched into the river, never to be seen again.

She stood by the pit of the archeological dig, near a fence with a yellow climbing rose sprawled along it, talking to the Arizona teenagers working there. Reverend Jeffries was supervising their activities but it was clear that everyone was just going through the motions, distracted by Johnny's fate and by her questions. None of them remembered any hatchets. She decided to ask Kenny Ettinger about cow witches too.

"Can't help you with that either," he said apologetically. "Never heard of cow witches." His aviator glasses slid down his nose and he pushed them up. He'd been digging and his finger left a smudge of dirt on his nose.

"Okay. Are any of the kids here fans of Lily Pistols?"

Kenny shrugged and glanced at Melissa Rueger, who was sifting dirt in the pit. "Not fanatic fans. Lily Pistols are kind of weird. Bones and things. I mean, some of their stuff is interesting, but most of us like other groups better."

"Do you know who owns Lily Pistols tapes?"

"Most of us have a couple. Probably Russ has the most. He's got a huge collection of tapes and CDs back in Arizona and he likes their stuff."

"Okay, Kenny, thanks. Let us know if you think of anything."

The sun smoldered in the hazy sky and the air was fragrant with roses and mud. Marty's uniform shirt clung damply to her back as she walked over to Justin Jeffries. The man looked deeply weary today, red-eyed. He'd had a bad night, clearly. "Hi, Reverend Jeffries. How're you doing today?"

"Okay." Jeffries straightened up, leaned on his shovel, and smiled at her warmly enough.

"We've got a couple of new leads, so I have a few more questions."

"Yeah, what is this with the tent stakes?"

"Just something we have to follow up, sir. Now I wanted to ask if you've seen a small blade, around two and a half inches wide, thicker than a putty knife. Maybe a small hatchet."

She saw his face draw tight as he jumped to the right conclusion. "Good grief," he said, and stared at her.

She prodded gently, "Have you seen a little blade like that?"

"No. Good grief, what—" Suddenly he paused and his eyes widened. "Wait. Wait a minute." He was talking to himself. "That was two full weeks ago, and it went missing the next day. . . ."

Memory stirred. He'd shown her the artifacts they'd found, and something was missing from the collection. "Reverend Jeffries, are you talking about that hand axe?"

"Yes." He looked at her, his face still taut with shock. "See, we didn't find out till a week later that it was missing."

"It was missing when I spoke to you."

"But see, I figured Ben Stewart had taken it—he's the

professor from Ball State who's supervising this dig. He takes the more valuable finds for safekeeping. I forgot to ask him about it and then the next week he asked me. He hadn't taken it after all. He was pretty upset about losing it."

"Can you describe it?"

"I can give you the exact measurements. Darlene?"

The curly-haired blond girl holding a notebook looked up. "Yes?"

"Let me see the book." Reverend Jeffries strode to her side, took the book, and began leafing through it as he returned to Marty. "It's here somewhere. The kids were excited when we found it. It was a tool that Father Rueger's people used for final fitting of logs and pegs. Trimming and hammering both."

"Hammering?" The word bonged in Marty's head.

"Yes. A Rueger hand axe is like a little hatchet, a handle with a small blade, but instead of having a blunt back like most hatchets today, the back end of this blade was shaped like a hammer. They could trim a wooden peg, turn the tool in their hand, and hammer the peg in. No wasted motion."

"And it disappeared two weeks ago." Marty's nerves hummed. This was it, this was it! Hammer and little hatchet in one. Not very sharp, Doc had said. After a hundred years in the dirt it wouldn't be. She and the other cops would have to go through the motions of looking for other possibilities, but even if it was now at the bottom of the river, this was it.

"Yes. We found it in the morning, and everybody admired it—including a bunch of kids from town who came by—"

"Was Johnny one of them?"

"Johnny." Jeffries closed his eyes a moment. "Yes! He was there. I remember him clowning around on his bike. Johnny and George and three or four other boys were there. Anyway, Professor Stewart told us what it was that afternoon, and I figured he'd taken it to the university when I missed it the next day. Look, here it is in our book."

He'd found the notes. Item number 74, hand axe: a note on where they'd found it in the earth, and careful measurements. The blade was 2⅜ inches wide and rusty. Marty copied all the information carefully.

Jeffries watched her. "Is this—I mean, does this have anything to do with how Johnny died?"

"Reverend Jeffries, we don't know yet. Best not to start any rumors, okay?"

"I understand."

"Now you told me last week that you put the things you find in that room and lock up."

"Yes, but not during the day. We're right here, so there's no need . . ." He trailed off, realizing what he was saying and shaking his head. Marty felt sorry for him.

She asked, "Who has keys to the room?"

"I do, Professor Stewart does, Drew and Karen Brewster. Melissa Rueger may have a spare key—her father owns the property. I think that's all."

"Have you missed your key at any time?"

"No." He shook his head. "It's on the ring with my other keys, and I haven't lost them."

"I'll check with the others. This is very helpful." She hesitated. How to ask the next question? "Reverend Jeffries, you have a pretty large group of teenagers. Are there cliques?"

"A group this size, there are always subgroups."

"Are any of the subgroups especially difficult or rowdy?"

"Not really. Unless you count volleyball games. We're all rowdy then."

So what did you expect in a church school camp, Hopkins: Crips and Bloods? "Sir, can you tell me anything about cow witches?"

"Cow witches? I have no idea. What are they?"

He was no help with Lily Pistols either. She closed her notebook and thanked him, and left him looking worried, slowly bending back to his work.

After calling the sheriff to tell him about the hand axe, she drove the short distance to the Brewster farm. Karen Brewster was picking flowers in the field next to the driveway. She wore jeans, work boots, and a gray vest over her white T-shirt.

"How are you doing, Mrs. Brewster?"

"Oh, God." Karen straightened and blinked foolishly at Marty. "Have you caught that drunk yet who beat up Drew?"

"We're working on it. I have a few more questions."

"Sure. I'm going to the hospital in a few minutes. They're releasing him today, I hope. He'll have to stay in bed a while. I thought he'd like some flowers in his room."

"Yes, ma'am. Now Deputy Sims already looked in your tool shed, right?"

"Yes. What's all this about tools?"

"We need to know if you've missed any tools in the last month. Especially hammers or hatchets."

"But Drew got hit with a baseball bat! Or—you don't mean Johnny?" Karen went rigid and stared at Marty. "But he slipped, didn't he? He just slipped and fell in!"

"No, ma'am. Now, I'd appreciate it if you could tell me if any of those tools have gone missing in the last month."

Karen had paled. "No. Just that screwdriver." She licked her lips. "My God, you mean it wasn't just a crazy drunk? God, I have to go to Drew!" Karen started for her red pickup truck.

"Please, just answer a couple more questions! We're trying to catch the guy!" Marty followed.

Karen slowed but didn't stop. "Okay. I'll try."

"Okay. First, we saw all the tools you have?"

"Yeah, except for a lost screwdriver I told Deputy Sims about."

"Okay. Can you tell me anything about cow witches?"

"Cow witches? No, what are they?"

"A couple of the local kids mentioned them. What about a rock group called Lily Pistols?"

"Lily Pistols. Some of the kids have talked about them. They had a concert up at IU last spring so there were posters and T-shirts around. I've never heard them myself." Karen had reached her pickup and unlocked the door.

"Their songs involve death sometimes. They use bones and skulls in their shows. Have there been any signs that someone around here was trying to copy them?"

"Signs?" Karen threw her wildflowers onto the passenger seat.

"Have you seen any bones? Or lost any livestock?"

Karen shook her head so hard her braids lashed the air. "No. No, look, this is crazy! The only bones were on the Walters farm! What terrible things are you saying?"

"Take it easy, Mrs. Brewster," Marty said.

"Look, you don't understand. Things are getting better! Drew was about ready to quit the farm last year. Our first school folded, and we weren't making progress in setting up a new cooperative community. He said it was getting to be too much, the farm plus the teaching load." Karen waved an arm at the gentle meadows sloping to the river, the hills sudsy with Queen Anne's lace, the gray house and big barn. "But I love it here. It's home. I can't believe there's a monster loose here, just when things are getting better! It's just a drunk!"

Marty had to sympathize. Nobody wanted to believe there was evil in their own community. "Yes, ma'am, I understand. The sooner we straighten out this boy's death, the sooner things will be back to normal. Now, have you had any problems with livestock?"

"No. Nothing unusual. Florida's calf was killed by a pack of dogs this spring, but that was the only problem. We sold most of the other calves for pretty good prices, considering most folks these days think they're runty stock. It's all been fine, until this problem came up! This is a happy place!"

"Yes, ma'am."

Karen climbed into her pickup and slammed the door, then leaned out the window. "You know, you should talk to Dub Walters. He's tried to cause trouble for the New Concord project from the beginning. He doesn't understand the value of history, and of being in tune with the environment. I mean, God, he's a car dealer!"

She made it sound as though car dealers were one step away from cannibals. Marty said, "Yes, ma'am, we've talked to Mr. Walters, and checked his toolshed too. We'll keep that in mind."

"And he doesn't like kids!" Karen added. "He could be behind this trouble!"

"We'll check it out, Mrs. Brewster. Now, I haven't seen Vicki or Nysa Strand around today. Do you know where they are?"

"No. Vicki could be anywhere, checking the animals. If they're not home, you could come back around four o'clock when we have music practice. They're both here for that."

"Okay. I'll try at their house. Thanks."

Marty followed Karen's pickup down the long graveled Brewster driveway to the highway, where the hopeful little sign still hung: "Rivendell, A New Community." The trouble with new communities was that they were made up of the same old type of people. Father Rueger's new community had failed; so had Karen's Rivendell. But shoot, so had the community Marty worked for; Johnny Donato was proof of that. Nichols County people went to church, read the Bible, talked about loving their neighbors—and some of them did, she had to admit. Some of them cared for the sick, gave to the poor, taught the children. Some poor fools even worked their butts off in the sheriff's department trying to help folks over the rough patches, trying to keep them from hurting each other. But after all that effort they were helpless against the senseless rage that had killed Johnny Donato. What kind of community treated its kids like that?

Maybe Chrissie was better off in Tennessee.

Shoot, if Marty couldn't do any better than this for Johnny, maybe she'd be better off in Tennessee too.

She floorboarded it and hit seventy on the short stretch between the Brewsters' and the Strands'.

24

NO ONE WAS HOME AT THE STRAND HOUSE. THE leaves of the plants in the old-fashioned dooryard rippled in the breeze, but the Volvo was gone and no one answered Marty's knock. She looked at her watch. Lunchtime, almost. Maybe she could pick up Chrissie and Janie and treat them to a Big Mac and a—oops. No, Hopkins, you idiot, Chrissie's in Tennessee. Shoot. When a case got her down, like this one, seeing her daughter reminded her of why she did this job.

This morning she'd had hopes. Maybe Professor Brewster would remember something, and maybe it would be relevant to finding Johnny's killer. And later, when Reverend Jeffries had remembered the hand axe, she'd had hopes that someone would know who'd taken it. No such luck. She couldn't think what to do next.

Time to take a break from this sad case. She was supposed to follow up on the Dennis Rent-All break-in when she could. She picked up the mike.

"Nichols County three twenty-one," she said, identifying her car.

"Hi, baby doll."

That meant Sheriff Cochran wasn't on the radio to overhear. He'd bawled Foley out, but the dispatcher still needled her whenever he knew the boss wasn't listening. Marty didn't make an issue of it because she knew it would give Foley too much satisfaction.

"I'm at the Strand place off State Eight-sixty near New Concord. Has anything come up for me?"

"Sure has, baby, right between my legs."

Shit, didn't the idiot care that there were citizens with police scanners? He probably thought it was funny. She said coolly, "I'm going to Dennis Rent-All to follow up on that break-in, then I'll take a lunch break. I'll be back in New Concord before four."

"Ten-four, sweetie. When are you taking your lunch break with me?"

No need to answer. On the way to Dennis Rent-All, she didn't spend much time being disgusted at Foley. She spent it feeling bad about Johnny Donato. If only she could do something!

Come off it, Hopkins, quit banging your head against the wall. Get professional. You know you can't win 'em all.

But damn, she wanted to win this one for Johnny. It had something to do with Chrissie, something to do with making the world fit for her daughter to live in.

The black Taurus was again near the Dennis Rent-All door, next to a five-year-old Ford pickup. The tinkle of the little bell made the two men crouching by an orange riding mower look up. Old Corky Dennis, the leather-faced, twinkly-eyed man who'd run the business for years, stood up warily. His nephew's brown-bearded face broke into a delighted grin and he bounced to his feet the way he used to when he was twelve. "Marty! Hey, good to see you! You here to rent that painting equipment? Or is there something to report?" He raised his palm in salutation.

"Hey, Romey!" Smiling, she gave her old teammate a high five. "Not much news, I'm afraid. Hi, Mr. Dennis."

"Hi, honey," said Corky Dennis. "Wes hasn't caught the bastards yet?"

"No sir, but we're working on it."

Like Romey, Corky wore the burgundy-red polo shirt embroidered with "Dennis Rent-All—you CAN do it yourself." Thin wisps of hair trailed across his sunburned head. He shook his head, his lips tight. Marty felt for the old man. Shoot, she'd feel betrayed too if someone broke into her place. She said, "We've got one bit of information. There was a light-colored Chevy pickup here Sunday night about one A.M. Dent in the left rear fender. Do either of you recognize it?''

Something flickered in Romey's eyes, but he shook his head. The old man was shaking his head too. "What color did you say?''

"Light-colored is all we've got.''

"You got the license plate?''

"No, it was too dark, and the witness was pretty far away.''

"All this crime. I can remember when old Sheriff Wyatt and his wife and a couple of deputies used to run this county and the jail and all, and we didn't have the crime we have now.''

"Didn't have so many people either, Uncle Corky," said Romey. "You know, when I was in Marrakesh an old man told me that one of his friends had a herd of camels. Some people from another tribe came sneaking over one night and stole three of them. Well, the man was so upset that he began to comb the hills, searching for his stolen camels. Never did find them. But weeks later, when he got back to his herd, he found that four had died of malnutrition and six more were sick. And all because he didn't appreciate what he still had.''

Corky frowned at his tall nephew. "You were never in Marrakesh, Jerome Dennis!''

"Sure I was, Uncle Corky." Romey waved a sturdy arm at the door. "When we get home I'll show you the stamp on my passport.''

"Well, lemme look at this machine." Corky squatted by the lawn mower. "You'd think Tim Post would know better than to run it across that stony field.''

So the old fellow had decided to take care of his remaining camels. Marty grinned at Romey. "Let me know if you think of anything. I'm off now to get a hamburger.''

"It's your lunch break? Hey, let's go to the Pebble Creek! I could use a burger too." Romey practically lunged for the door and held it open for her. "Uncle Corky, I'll be back soon.''

Corky's only response was to unscrew something on the

162

mower, muttering, "I can't believe Tim Post could be this stupid."

Marty followed Romey's Taurus half a mile to the Pebble Creek Diner. "Hamburgers are above average," he informed her as they got out, "and you have to go all the way to Reiner's Bakery on the square to get peanut butter pie this good."

Marty smiled. She led the way into the diner, a rustic place with a stuffed bass over the lunch counter, fishing lures on the wallpaper, Johnny Cash music, and half a dozen men in ball caps with feed-company logos talking at the lunch counter. Marty waved a hand at them, slid into the corner booth across from Romey, and dropped her Stetson on the seat beside her. "Medium hamburger, iced tea, separate checks," she told the beefy blond waitress who brought ice water.

"Rare burger and a beer." Romey looked up at the waitress and Marty studied his profile, thinking that Nysa Strand was right about the vast changes adolescence brought. In manhood Romey was broad-chested, with a strong brow and jaw. A faded scar ran along his cheekbone into the short brown beard. But the skinny, rambunctious boy Marty remembered still glowed in the lively eyes, the grin, the way he tilted his head to look up at the waitress, just the way he used to sight at the hoop. "So how's it going, Mary Lou?" he was asking. "Your little Mikey over his cold yet?"

The waitress nodded. "Better. His cough's gone."

"I told you that special Indian tea would work!"

Mary Lou laughed. "C'mon, he would've got better anyway!"

Romey looked smug. "Mebbe yes, mebbe no."

She laughed again and went to get their order. Romey turned to Marty. His eyes were a warm, clear brown, the color of brandy or maybe maple syrup. "Hey, teammate, it's a treat to see you."

"Yeah." He was right—it was a treat. Seeing Romey took her back to those lively childhood days playing for the Stonies, the teamwork, her sharp inside jump shots, her dad and Coach Cochran cheering themselves hoarse, an intoxicating sense of infinite possibility. She propped her chin on her hand and grinned at him. "Hey, remember when the station wagon got a flat tire on our way to play the Little Pistons? Everybody telling goofy jokes?"

He grinned too. "Why did the Little Pistons practice free throws in a music store?"

"They wanted to break a record!" She giggled. "Why did the Little Pistons play their new cassette to the cattle?"

"They heard it was in steereo!"

By the time Mary Lou brought the drinks, they were both hooting with laughter and Romey was pounding the table at the remembered silliness of their young selves. The other customers glanced at them occasionally, amused. Still chuckling, Marty squeezed lemon into her iced tea. "Good old days."

"Yeah." Romey nodded. "The Stonies were a great team. Saw Coach Cochran the other day. He looks good with that silver hair and the spiffy uniform you guys wear."

"Yeah. You know he had a heart attack last year."

Romey frowned in concern. "No, Uncle Corky didn't tell me."

"Well, he's doing fine now. Getting more exercise and eating right. But he complains about no desserts."

"I bet he does! He sure had his share in his day. Remember that church supper, he had five desserts and no vegetables?"

Marty laughed. "Yeah, my mom was mad. Said he was a bad example. So then my dad went and got five desserts too."

"They were good buddies, your dad and Coach."

Mary Lou returned with the hamburgers, and Romey cupped a hand to his mouth and stage-whispered, "Let's do it, Marty, quick, before old man time gets us too. I'm talking peanut butter pie." He twinkled at her. "How about it? You want five pieces?"

She laughed. "Whoa, I'm on duty, you goofus! But I'll take one."

Mary Lou penciled the order onto her pad and left, humming along with Johnny Cash. Marty dribbled ketchup on her hamburger and said, "Okay, Romey Dennis, tell me about the truck."

"Huh?" Then he grinned. "How do you do that, Deputy Hopkins? Am I that transparent?"

"Only to your old teammates. C'mon, Romey, out with it. That's why you came to lunch with me, so tell me."

"That's one reason why I came to lunch with you. But see, there's a problem. I only know one light-colored pickup with a dent in the fender, and it belongs to one of Uncle Corky's best friends. There's probably some good explanation, like it wasn't his at all. I thought I'd have a quiet word with him before bothering you with it."

Marty eyed him coldly. "You want me to take over your rental business while you do the sheriffing?"

Some guys would have been miffed. Romey laughed. "You haven't changed, Marty! Never would let anybody do your job, not even carry your gym bag!" He lowered his voice again. "But hell, you're right. If we two can't be teammates, who can? It's Herb Frick. Lives about five miles out of Stineburg. But—"

"Yeah." Marty swallowed the bite she was chewing. "I'll be careful, Romey. And I won't tell him you suggested I talk to him. So it'll never get back to your Uncle Corky."

"Good. The old guy is really devastated," Romey said. "And I can't believe Herb had anything to do with it. Jeez, he and Uncle Corky go fishing together maybe forty times a year!"

"Okay, I'll bear that in mind. Now, you said there was another reason you came to lunch?"

"Nothing about the break-in." His brandy-colored eyes were intent on hers. "I just want to catch up on your life."

She took another bite. "Well, I've been with the sheriff's department six years—"

"Start earlier. I was thirteen, maybe fourteen when your dad died and you left for Bloomington."

Johnny Cash switched to "King of the Road." Marty ate her last fry. "Well, I was in Bloomington about ten years. I finished high school and started at IU. Joined a sorority for a year. Our team won the tricycle race."

He grinned. "Wish I'd seen that! Did you play any basketball?"

"A little in high school and freshman year at IU. Girls' team—just wasn't the same."

"What happened next?"

She shrugged. "Got married, quit college, had a kid."

"A girl, Uncle Corky said."

"Yeah, Chrissie. She's great. Anyway, when Chrissie was three my mom got sick and moved back here, and after a year I moved back too. Mom died a few months later. Coach had been elected sheriff again and he gave me a job as deputy when I passed the tests."

Mary Lou brought the peanut butter pie and the checks, and Romey started right in on the pie. "I bet you aced the tests."

Marty grinned. "Yeah. I'd worked security for a while at IU so I knew a little more than the farmers hereabouts."

"This job agrees with you. You look good, Marty. Are you divorced?"

"Not—no." She stabbed at her pie. "Your turn, Romey. From age fourteen."

"Well . . . I finished high school here and went east to college. Maryland. Did languages, graduated, went abroad. Almost got married once, but it didn't work out. Mostly I worked for a travel agency, doing tours for American dancers and rock groups, people like that. Couple of years for Oxfam, trying to set up marketing cooperatives in Central America." His face went bleak.

"Bad stuff, huh?"

"Horrors. There was a war on. After that I taught English in Egypt, toured India with a backpack, and so forth."

He was right about the pie—it rivaled Aunt Vonnie's. "So you really have been all those places you say."

"Most of them, yes."

"Farthest away I've been is New York," she said wistfully. "I'd sure like to visit other places. I'm curious."

He grinned. "Yes, I remember. Ever been to the ocean?"

"Not exactly. Dad had some money once and took us to the Indiana Dunes. I was about eight. The beach was great."

166

"On a real ocean you can surf. I bet you'd like surfing." He nodded slowly, a smile twitching the corner of his mouth. "Yeah, I can definitely see you surfing."

Suddenly she could see herself too, and him, riding the great rolling waves, tuned in to sun and foam and eternal waters. She looked away and picked up her iced tea. "Sounds like fun. Romey, how come you came back?"

He gestured at his half-eaten dessert. "I needed a hit of peanut butter pie."

"No, really. Are you running from the horrors?"

Romey shook his head in a quick, firm negation. "Can't do that. Real horrors stay with you." He looked at her closely. "You must know that, Marty. The job you've got—"

"Yeah." She glanced at her watch, but an image of Johnny's hacked and bloated body swam across her vision. Time to go, time to go.

"What is it, Marty? You look so sad all of a sudden."

"Another case I'm working. That kid who died in the White River. I guess there are horrors everywhere."

"Yeah." His eyes held hers a moment. "And delights everywhere. Don't forget delights. The Taj Mahal and the Sphinx, sure, but also family, friends, swimming in the quarries, Little Pistons jokes."

"And peanut butter pie." She smiled at him, put on her Stetson, and stood up. "Hey, gotta go. Tell your uncle we're working on it, and we'll let him know if we learn anything. Good seeing you, Romey." She picked up her check and put a dollar tip down on the table.

His big hand closed over hers, gently, just for a second. "Good seeing you too, Marty LaForte."

"Hopkins, you goofus," she said.

Head tilted, he grinned up at her. "Whatever. See you soon."

25

WES COCHRAN HITCHED UP HIS TROUSERS AND studied the boy who stood across from him on the Muller porch. George Muller was thirteen, sturdy, wary, and sad. Wes wished he could toss the kid a basketball and practice dribbling or something, instead of tossing him a bunch of questions that raked up his sorrows.

Wes's too. Seeing kids made him miss his Billy all the more.

Well, he and George would have to face up to it. He said, "I hear you did a real good job on our search team, George."

"I tried, sir."

"You've been a good friend to Johnny. We've got just a few more questions now."

"Yes sir. But you see, I wasn't with him. I don't know what happened." There was raw sorrow in the boy's face. "He slipped, didn't he? Just fell in?"

This job was a real bummer sometimes. Wes steeled himself and said gently, "I'm sorry, no. Someone beat him up and pushed him in."

"Beat him up? Who? How come?"

"That's what we're trying to find out. See, when something like this happens, we get a whole team together. We have scientists and law enforcement officers and witnesses and friends, all on Johnny's team. I want you on his team too."

"Yes sir." The news was sinking in and George's lower lip was trembling. "But I don't know how to help."

"Your job on the team is to give us background, so we have a good picture of Johnny's life. Hell, George, you've

already helped a lot. Ellie from Arizona, and Lily Pistols—
that was important stuff you told Deputy Hopkins."

George nodded miserably.

"Now, you told Deputy Hopkins that Johnny liked to say
interesting things. Like daring you to eat Indian poke."

"He was just teasing me." George's voice was small and
choked.

"Hell, I know that, George. Guys do that kind of thing.
And you said there was some crazy story about cow
witches."

"Yes sir." George glanced at the house door.

Wes lowered his voice. "We don't have to tell your parents. Let's walk over to that tree in the corner of the yard,
okay?"

The boy started down the steps with him, but protested,
"See, I promised Johnny—"

"I know. But being a guy's friend is a kind of promise
too. It's a promise to do the right thing for him. To be on
his team."

He let George think about it as they crossed the lawn to
the big sycamore. A few knobby twigs and white curls of
bark lay in the grass under the tree. When they reached the
shade Wes pushed his Stetson higher on his forehead and
lowered his rump to the fence rail so he didn't loom so far
over the kid. He said, "It'd help the team if you explained
about it."

Without looking at him, the boy kicked the tree. The trunk
was blotchy whites and grays, a complicated camouflage
pattern. "It was just a story. See, we went—"

He paused. Wes waited. Bees hummed and a jay in the
next yard squawked.

"See, we had to, um, sneak out at night. You won't tell?"

"I'll have to tell a couple of deputies who are helping me
catch the killer. But except for that, I won't tell, and neither
will they," Wes promised. "When did you sneak out?"

"Back in June. See, Johnny heard you could catch more
fish at night. And he said if I was a real man I'd go with
him, so I went along." He glanced furtively at Wes, who
nodded approval. George seemed to take heart and went on

less hesitantly, "I crawled out my bedroom window and everything. We went to that big fishing rock on the Strand farm. And the fishing wasn't that good, maybe the river was too high. Anyway, after a while we heard this noise upstream. Well, Johnny was getting bored, so he wanted to see what it was. We started toward it. The noise kind of drifted on the wind—you know, louder, then softer. At first we thought it was in town, but it wasn't. We followed the river path all the way past town and started along the Brewsters' path."

"Must have been pretty dark."

"The moon was still up so we could see okay, except where the trees got real thick. And the noise was getting louder. It was just some cow mooing, I could tell by then. So I said I was going home. And the noise stopped before I even got back to my window."

"But Johnny didn't go back home with you?"

"No sir." George kicked the mottled trunk again.

"But he told you about it later?"

"Yeah. It was just a story."

"I bet he said it wasn't a cow."

"He said it was a cow witch. You know, just trying to make me feel bad because I didn't go."

"So what's the difference between a cow and a cow witch?"

"He said it was half man and half cow."

"I don't get it."

"He was teasing, okay? He said he sneaked up behind some bushes and peeked. And this thing was on the riverbank, like a man except he had big cow horns and hair on his shoulders, and like boots with hooves on them. And Johnny said he had something in his hand that made these loud mooing noises. I don't know what."

"You keep saying 'he.' But you call him a cow witch?"

"Yeah, Johnny said 'he' because some witches are men."

"Why did he think this one was?"

"Because this man wasn't wearing—um—" George stared down at his sneakers.

No wonder the poor kid wouldn't tell Hopkins. Wes too

was glad to be out of earshot of George's mother. He scratched his armpit and said, man to man, "Yeah, I get it. The guy was naked except for the boots and headpiece. And Johnny could see his dick."

"Yeah." George seemed relieved at Wes's casual manner. "He said it was—you know, really big."

"Yeah, that's pretty weird, all right." Shit, what kind of a pervert got his jollies from jerking off while he mooed on the riverbank?

George said, "Yeah, it was just a crazy story. He was just teasing me 'cause I didn't go with him."

That was the most likely possibility, Wes had to agree. Johnny had made up the story, or maybe got hold of some porn magazine and transferred a story to the local riverbank to tease his friend. "You're probably right," Wes said.

"Yeah, there was no man. It was just a cow mooing and he made up the rest."

"Yeah. Did he say anything else about this cow witch?"

"No. He said as soon as he got a good look he slid on out of there. He said he wasn't scared."

Wes shifted his seat on the fence rail. "Did anyone else ever see anything like this?"

"Course not. Johnny made it up."

"Did Johnny ever mention it again?"

"No. Maybe because—see, I teased him too. If we heard a cow I'd say, 'Oooh, it's a witch, but I'm not scared.' He got mad at me so I quit doing it."

"Okay. George, you're a real good teammate. Now, is there anything else that might help us find the guys that did this?"

George straightened, an earnest, sturdy boy. "Sir, if he got beat up I bet it's the Seiferts."

"Yeah. We'll definitely check them out. They're the ones that already beat Johnny up once, right?"

"Yes sir." The boy looked at him squarely. "Johnny talked back to them. I always stay out of their way. But if you need someone to help catch them, I'll come."

Wes was touched. "Thanks, George. We have armed deputies for arresting people. That's their job. Just like yours is telling us about stuff Johnny was interested in."

"I just wish—" George's lip began to tremble again.

"Yeah. I wish the same thing. But things happen and a man's got to go on."

"Yes sir." George nodded manfully.

Wes clapped him on the shoulder, ignoring the boy's tears. He wasn't all that far from tears himself. "Thanks, George. I'll talk to you soon." He headed back for his car.

Dub Walters was waiting in his Buick next to the station parking lot. When Wes got out of the cruiser Dub got out too, slamming his door with a loud clunk that didn't bode well. Wes sighed and turned to face the music. "Hey there, Dub."

"What do you think you're doing, Wes? Just what do you think you're doing?" Dub's low tones made Wes remember being twelve, smoking cigarettes under the railroad trestle with his buddies, hearing his father's quiet, angry voice behind him.

He shook off the memory. Best way to handle anger was with reason. "The Donato kid was murdered and we're trying to find his killer," he said calmly. "That's my job."

"It's not your job to harass property owners! We're not criminals!"

"Nobody's harassing you!" Wes raised his palms in a gesture of peace. "But we—"

"What do you mean, nobody's harassing me?" Dub was shorter than Wes but outweighed him and sure as hell felt a lot more ornery right now. Wes could see a vein throbbing in his temple. "This is what I've been saying all month! You've got murderers loose, you say. You've got burglars breaking into businesses. You've got vandals and teenage thugs out at my shopping center. And what do you do about all that? Zip! You send your cunt deputy in to ask about deeds!"

"No need to insult the ladies, Dub. Take it easy."

"Take it easy? Listen, Sheriff Cochran, I've been a good friend to you and your department for years. You think the money for jail improvements will go through if I say no? And after all these years of helping you out, I make a suggestion about cutting crime at the shopping center. And bang, you find bones on my property. Bang, you find a goddamn body on my property. Bang, you're poking your nose into my property records. That's not harassment?"

Thank God Professor Brewster had gotten himself beat up at the city boat ramps instead of on Dub's property. "Dub, I'm as sorry as you are that your place is so close to the action on this case. But—"

"Just coincidence. Is that what you're saying? Miles of riverbank and your deputies just happen to find bodies on *my* farm? Twice? And I'm supposed to believe it's coincidence?"

Wes held on to his temper. "Hey, Dub, we have to investigate. We've got no choice."

"You don't have to go nosing into property records. You think the voters are going to want the sheriff snooping into their private business every time they make a suggestion to him?"

"The voters." Wes paused, letting Dub remind himself that voters also weren't real keen on County Council members who used inside information to speculate, that Dub's political viability was on the line too. No need to spell it out; that was probably why he was so upset. Wes went on mildly, "Voters like to see the county lock up criminals. See, we didn't know who owned those properties. It was a discrepancy, so we had to check. I mean, hell, for all we knew it was owned by some satanic cult that killed children."

"What the hell are you talking about? Are you crazy?"

"We've got a murdered child, Dub. We check everything, okay? Now we know it's you, we can eliminate that line and look somewhere else."

"I want you to do more than eliminate that line. I want you to shut up about stuff that isn't your business. I want you to get that nosy—so-called lady deputy off my back."

"Done," said Wes.

"Done. You mean it?"

Wes shrugged. "Look, we had to know. We could have sent off official requests for information, left a big paper trail for the reporters to follow, and so on. We didn't. We went the quietest way, just us and Flo. Nobody else has to know about it. Your business is your business."

"And let's keep it that way."

"Sure." Wes gave him a big toothy smile. "You've always been a good friend to us, Dub. I won't forget."

Dub hesitated, probably clicking off his options, realizing that he'd gotten all he could from Wes on this round. Then he nodded shortly. "Remember, I won't forget either."

Wes watched the big Buick pull out of the lot. So learning that Dub owned those two properties had given them a weapon to use against Dub. Good to know it gave him some power. But he didn't know why.

He did know that the campaign contribution he'd hoped for looked pretty unlikely now.

He had the feeling that, of the two guys he'd just talked to, young George Muller was more of a man.

Back inside the office, Wes studied the big county map on the wall. Why did old Dub stick to that farm anyway? Why had he secretly bought more land? It was a remote part of Nichols County. State 860 didn't do much for it. It had a good bridge, and was used by people in that part of the county as a shortcut to State 37, which led to Bloomington and Indianapolis. In the other direction, though, it wound its way along the unpopulated side of the huge Naval Ammunition Center; he'd never been able to figure out why the Navy kept ammunition in the middle of the nation with no body of water around except for the river. On south of the Navy property, 860 soon fizzled out ... where? He pulled a state map from his drawer and looked it over.

Ah.

State 860 quit in the middle of nowhere, he was right. But up here were Indianapolis and Bloomington on State 37. Down here was Evansville in the southwest part of the state. People had been talking for years about a superhighway linking the two areas. They'd talked about several possible routes, mostly on the other side of the naval property. But you could also extend 860 a few miles toward Evansville, turn the whole thing into superhighway, and you'd cut an hour off the time it took to get from Indianapolis to Evansville.

And you'd have a bunch of valuable new business sites in Nichols County.

Dub was gambling on that. And didn't want it known yet. Probably had his eye on more properties to acquire.

Such as the Strands'.

Wes looked back at the blowup on the wall, with the two pins marking the sad sites where they'd found Johnny's body and the old bones on the riverbank.

Dub was a greedy bastard, okay. Most folks were when they got the chance. But most folks weren't killers. And West could see no connection yet between Dub's greed and the death of a teenaged boy.

He decided to file the information for now, and get on with the investigation.

26

"I'M SURE TIRED OF THIS RAIN," MELISSA SAID TO Kenny. "It's a drag, having to come back after lunch." They were sitting apart from the others at the dig, finishing up a corner of the old pit while the others started a new pit nearby. Melissa stretched and wriggled her tired shoulders. Kenny watched her grape-colored T-shirt when she did. It made her feel powerful, having a guy think she looked so good. It made her feel pretty and powerful.

But Reverend Jeffries was nearby, so Kenny stayed cool. He just said, "Yeah, it'll be good to get back to Arizona weather."

"Yeah. Except I'll miss the cows. I really love the cows."

"Won't your dad get you a cow if you want?"

"Daddy's pretty weird about animals. I mean, he likes dogs all right, but big animals freak him."

"What do you mean? He got you a horse. That's big."

"Yeah, but he makes me board Flash at the riding stable, and it took like three years of begging to get Daddy to do that much."

"He doesn't like big animals?" Kenny's eyebrows rose behind his aviators. "So naturally Missy-Lissy gets the bright idea of being a vet."

"Hey, you're not exactly following in your dad's foot-steps!" Kenny wanted to be a computer engineer instead of a lawyer like his father.

"Being an engineer is respectable. A vet is kind of weird."

"It is not!" she said hotly, then saw that he was grinning his adorable grin. She melted. "Hey, don't tease!"

"Okay. Hey, what would you do if you found out I hated animals?"

"But you don't! We got to talking that first time because we were both petting the goats!"

"Yeah, but that's 'cause I thought he was Russ's dad."

Melissa laughed. Russ's dad had a little beard. "No, really, Kenny. You liked the goat, you said."

"Really, I thought you were cool-looking and I figured you'd hang around the goat awhile, so I went over."

Melissa was glad he thought she was cool-looking, but she wasn't sure she liked the rest of this story. "You mean you were just pretending? You didn't like the goat?"

"No, no. The goat's okay, silly. I'm just asking a simple question. If I hated animals, wouldn't you give them up?"

"What if I hated computers?"

"How can somebody hate computers? They aren't even alive."

"But what if? It's the same thing as what you're asking me."

"No it's not. You don't get it. What's a guy supposed to think if you'd rather be with some old cow instead of him?"

Melissa didn't want to fight. She said, "C'mon, Kenny,

that's not true." He still looked sulky, so she added, "Please?"

"Well . . ." Kenny lowered his voice even further. "Meet me tonight again, okay? Prove you like me a little bit."

"Okay!" They smiled at each other, and her insides felt all fluttery. It was really cool, being in love. "But—"

"But what?"

Melissa stuck her trowel into the earth again. "You know, I went by our tree this morning on the way to milk Florida. It was like real early. And I got this real spooky feeling, like someone was watching me."

"Probably some raccoon. Or some cow!"

"Yeah. It was like, you know, sometimes you see an animal and you look again and it's not there. Like rabbits can camouflage themselves? They're really there, but they look like something else?"

"Yeah."

"It was like that. It happened yesterday too, when I was milking Florida. Something looked at me through the cracks in the barn wall. All I could see was the shadow." She shivered, remembering. "It was spooky."

"Hey, don't be scared, Missy-Lissy. Nothing's going to happen to you."

"Things do happen! What about Johnny?"

Kenny shook his head firmly. "I still think he fell in. He always clowned around."

"Then how come the sheriff is asking all those questions about hammers and things?"

"Okay, look." Kenny was cuter than most guys who liked computers, but he was very logical, and Melissa could tell that a fit of logic was on its way. He held up a dirty finger. "Number one, the river's full of rocks and sharp branches. Didn't have to be a hammer, you see. The body must have been bashed around a lot in the high water."

"Oh, God, Kenny!" Melissa clapped a hand to her mouth.

"Hey, I'm sorry, Missy-Lissy." He did sound sorry. "I just don't want you to be scared, okay? I know it's awful to think about, but we have to look at the truth. He probably fell in. Number two"—he held up a second finger—"Johnny was kind of a weird kid and he probably had enemies around here. Some of these locals are bad news. So even if somebody did beat him up, his problems have nothing to do with us.''

''What about Professor Brewster?''

''That was just a bar fight. Plus Professor Brewster is a local too. We're not. I mean, why would that drunk care about us?''

''What if he's somebody really weird? Some psycho?''

''Your dad checked this place out for us, right? Would he send you anyplace there was danger?''

''No.'' She couldn't argue with his logic.

''Don't be paranoid. If there was a psycho around here your dad would have heard about it. And by now we would have heard about it. And we haven't. Johnny's the only one, and he probably slipped.''

''I guess so.'' Everything he said made sense. She was comforted, mostly.

Kenny said, ''Tonight, if you want, we can go find Florida. See what she does at night. Would you like that?''

''Cool!'' Melissa beamed at him. He did love animals! She had nothing to worry about.

27

''OKAY, TAKE IT EASY, MRS. DONATO,'' WES SAID into the receiver, but the sobbing at the other end didn't slow. ''You'll be home about four-thirty, you said? We'll send someone out to talk to you.''

Poor woman. He hung up, ran a hand over his face and looked into the main office. Hopkins was filling out reports, her least favorite activity. Grady Sims was just coming in from outside. Wes said, ''Sims, Hopkins, in here a minute!''

He held his office door open for the two deputies, then propped his rump on the edge of the desk. "Several things. First, Carl Donato didn't come home last night." Hopkins looked stricken, and he added, "He's gone to work. His wife just called from his boss's office and he made all his deliveries yesterday and today. But she's upset 'cause she hasn't seen him since Monday night."

Grady Sims was tall, all angles, and Wes thought he could have been a college basketball star if he'd had more speed. As it was he hadn't done too badly for the Dunning High team, but he hadn't received any scholarships and ended up doing a tour in Vietnam. Although he had a few gray hairs now, he'd kept himself fit. Not that he'd ever get fat, but he didn't even have the little potbelly that skinny guys develop when they go flabby. Or the big potbelly Wes had grown before that heart attack made him get serious about his diet. Damn ticker.

Sims asked, "What's he driving?"

"His van. I'd like you to get out a bulletin on it."

"Yes sir. Does his wife have the plate number?"

"She says it's one of the company vans. You better check with Helton Gas."

"Yes sir."

"Hopkins, you run on out to New Concord and talk to her. Now." He cleared his throat, looked at his two deputies, and temporarily chickened out. "So what did the Seifert boys have to say for themselves, Sims?"

Sims cleared his throat too, as though in imitation of Wes. "The Seiferts say just what they always say: They're innocent and why are we bugging them? That Mrs. Seifert, she just about bit my head off. The two younger ones say they were at the video game arcade. I checked it out and it seems to be true. See, their car's been laid up two weeks waiting for a part, so they hitched a ride with the lady next door, and she backs their story."

"How about big brother Todd Seifert?"

Grady shrugged an angular shrug. "He coulda done it. I'm not convinced. Couple reasons. One is, it's not his style. When he beat up people in school, or poor old Jess Parker when he caught Todd shoplifting, well, he pretty much hit them around the head with his fists. And it was just fists, no weapons, or he'd still be locked up for Parker."

Hopkins said thoughtfully, "I was thinking that too—not his style. He might change if he was in a gang, you know, guys egging him on. But after the Wall kid got sent away the Seiferts have pretty much stuck to family."

Sims said, "Yeah, that's right. Todd says he was watching TV and his mom backs him up."

Wes snorted. "That's what they said when Parker got beat up too. That's the one thing he *wasn't* doing, I bet. Now, you said there were a couple reasons."

"Yes sir, just a feeling." Sims looked uncomfortable. It was always embarrassing to admit something was just a feeling, even though in the end a lot of police work was based on hunches. Sims cleared his throat again. "I asked to see their toolroom. The mother says fine and leads me toward this boxed-in back porch where they keep stuff, and she starts in again about how we're always bugging them. But the kids gave each other this look, you know? Right then I was thinking maybe they did it. But when I started looking over the hammers and things I swear they kind of relaxed. So yeah, they've been up to something, but whatever they did, they didn't do it with a hammer or an axe."

"Maybe they did it with that hand axe and couldn't remember if they'd thought to toss it in the river," suggested Wes.

"Yes sir, could be." Grady didn't sound convinced.

"Okay. Now." Wes couldn't put it off any longer. "I spoke to that kid, George Muller. He was Johnny's best friend. Hopkins thought he was holding back about one story that Johnny told him. Well, I can see why the kid didn't want to say anything in mixed company."

Hopkins was leaning against the doorframe, her curls bouncy, her tan skin warm-toned against the deep brown of the uniform shirt. She'd pulled out her notepad. "So there was something?" she asked eagerly. "Cow witches?"

"Not exactly. All we've got is a dirty story Johnny came up

with. That's what George thinks, so there's no need to spread this around. But I figure you guys should know, just in case." He cleared his throat. Sounded like a bunch of frogs in here, people clearing their throats. "These two kids snuck out to the fishing rock late one night about a month ago. Heard a cow mooing on the Brewster riverbank. They started to investigate but George got cold feet and went home. Next time he saw Johnny, Johnny said he'd gone on, peeked through the bushes, and saw a naked man wearing cow horns on his head, hooves on his feet, big erection, making a mooing noise."

Both deputies were staring at him. Wes said testily, "Look, *I* didn't make it up, Johnny did! Or maybe George. Or maybe neither one of them made it up and there's really some pervert out there doing that stuff." He shrugged. "Did you see any cow horns laying around at the Seiferts'?"

Sims almost choked. "No sir, I surely didn't."

Hopkins was looking thoughtful. Wes said, "You got something to add, Hopkins?"

"Not really, sir, it's just that I was remembering those Arizona kids who said they'd heard a cow bellowing at night."

"Yeah. Check with the Arizona kids too after you talk to Mrs. Donato."

"Okay. I still haven't asked the Strands about that hand axe. I'll ask them about this guy too."

"Okay, but keep it general. Just as if they've seen anyone strange along the riverbank."

"Yes sir."

"If they *have* seen something, use your judgment. Sims, you check the town kids. Not the little sister, that's Hopkins's job. See you soon."

Hopkins closed her notebook and they started out. As she opened the door, Wes said, "Hopkins!"

"Yes sir?" She turned back, letting Grady go on.

"One more thing." He lowered his voice and she closed the door. "You haven't mentioned to anyone that Dub Walters owns those properties across the river, right?"

"No sir."

"Good. Don't."

"Walters is upset about it?" Her gray eyes sparkled with eagerness. "I could ask the neighbors if—"

"Hopkins, no! I want this real clear: No questions about those properties to anyone, okay? And if you run across something else that points toward old Dub, just tell me and I'll take care of it."

"I'm not supposed to check out leads if they involve Walters?"

"Correct." She looked so unhappy that he added, "Look, I'm glad you thought to check with Flo Duffy. It got Dub mad, okay, but that's because it gave us a weapon to use in dealing with him. Now that we've got it, it's my job to make sure we play it right."

"Yes sir."

He glanced at his watch. "If you're going to talk to Mrs. Donato and the Strands, I better give you overtime."

"Thank you, sir." She gestured with her notepad. "I could sure use the money now. Housepainting fund."

Wes smiled. Marty'd been trying to save enough to paint her house for four years now. Things kept coming up, she said. "You think you'll make it this time?"

"Yeah. I was working on the Dennis Rent-All burglary and they had housepainting stuff for rent like electric paint strippers and long ladders. Even scaffolding. Got me wondering if I could do it myself."

"Yeah, I bet you could. Good to see old Romey back, isn't it? I still remember you two in those games. He'd distract everybody while you snuck inside and then he'd slip you the ball. Real smooth for eleven-year-olds."

"Yeah. I could always depend on Romey. Some of the other guys always wanted to take the shot themselves, even when I was in the clear."

"You weren't real shy about taking shots either." Wes smiled at the memory of those lively kids storming around the court. "Shit, I wouldn't trade those years for anything."

"Me either, sir. Boy, in those days I thought I could do

anything." She was smiling too. Then a touch of caution entered her eyes and he realized she'd remembered her other teammate, his lost Billy. She looked down at the notebook in her hand and said, "Well, I better be going to New Concord now."

"Go," said Wes.

28

IT WAS ONLY FOUR O'CLOCK, AND MRS. DONATO wouldn't be home from talking to her husband's boss till four-thirty. As Marty passed the Frick farm it occurred to her that she might as well check out that pickup with the dented fender. She turned into the graveled driveway that ran past the house all the way to a tractor shed out back, and pulled up by the front door.

It was a ranch-style house, painted yellow, with purple and white petunias spilling out of the porch planters. A television blared inside, and it took five minutes of pounding on the door and hollering before Herb Frick came beaming to the door. "Why, hi there, missy," he said, adjusting his hearing aid. "Now what brings you here?"

"I'd like to take a look at your pickup truck, sir. Just routine."

"Sure thing. Come along here, it's parked out back." He was a big, bluff man with reddened skin and bib overalls. "What's all this about?"

Marty followed him around the corner of the house. "We got a bulletin on a light-colored pickup and we're checking where they all were Sunday night."

"Well, this baby was parked right here," Herb said,

thumping the side of his pickup. It was a Chevy, beige, with an obvious dent in the back fender.

"You didn't take it out Sunday night, sir?"

"No, missy, I sure didn't. I was watching TV."

"Does anyone else ever drive it?"

"The missus, sometimes. She's the one put the dent into it. Course she won't admit it. Ain't that a woman for you?" He shook his head in amazement.

This truck sure looked like Ruth Ragg's description. There was a crunch of gravel behind her and she turned to see Mrs. Frick approaching, a rangy woman in a candy-colored blouse. And a hearing aid. She confirmed everything her husband had said—they both watched TV Sunday night, went to bed at ten-thirty. "And don't let him tell you I made that dent! He did it himself and didn't notice. He's hard-of-hearing, you know."

"And ain't you worse, Alice? You could be hit by a sixteen-wheeler and you wouldn't hear it!"

Marty left them and the TV shouting at each other. Romey was right—Herb and Alice Frick weren't real hot suspects for the Rent-All break-in, no matter what their truck looked like.

State 860 eased its way around gentle limestone hills toward the White River. Overhead layers of heavy clouds blanketed the sky. The lowest of them were ragged, dark, rat-tailed clouds scurrying east, threatening rain but moving fast enough that Nichols County had a chance of escaping this time. Marty hoped so. She'd had enough wetness this summer to last the whole year.

There were no cars in the Donato driveway, and no one answered the bell except a frantically yapping terrier. Poor Sue Donato. Poor Rosie. How could a guy run out on his family just when they needed him most? Marty left Sue a note saying that she'd be at the Brewster farm and would be back soon.

But no one was there either. Choir practice, that must be it. Marty headed for the river path and the pasture beyond the hill, where the tents had been raised. In fact, the group was just finishing, singing the last verses of "When Christ to Jordan's Shore First Came." As before, Nysa Strand stood before them, radiant and intense even on this dark day, her white blouse trimmed with old-fashioned crocheted lace that shimmered like foam on water as she moved her arms. As before, Reverend Jeffries stood among the basses and tall Vicki Strand among the sopranos, and the other singers were the same kids she'd talked to so often, some graceful, some awkward, all merged now in an old, old hymn of vivid beauty. And as before, Marty felt pulled into another sort of time, where Father Rueger's followers blended with the youthful voices, yesterday and tomorrow touching in this shining moment. The singers seemed to feel it too. Even Reverend Jeffries, who'd seemed so harried and worn when she'd spoken to him this morning, appeared joyful as he chugged out the bass line of the beautiful hymn. Marty noticed curly-haired Bonnie Jeffries sitting in front of one of the tents, hugging her wiggly son and gazing pensively at her husband.

When Nysa dismissed her singers at last, Marty moved fast. She headed off Vicki Strand. "Miz Strand, excuse me. I have to ask you and your sister some more questions."

"Questions? Okay." Vicki pushed back a lock of blond hair.

"Let's go catch her."

The two walked over to where Nysa was collecting her music into a portfolio. Marty said, "That music is so beautiful!"

"I'm so glad you like it!" Nysa was flushed with happiness, her fair skin rosy and her eyes alight.

"It's wonderful. I have a few more questions, for both of you. Could I talk to one of you now, and meet the other in about five minutes? I'm supposed to do this one at a time," Marty explained.

The sisters exchanged a glance. The blue eyes were very similar, large and sad. Nysa touched Vicki on the arm. "You have to bring in the cows soon. Do you want to go first?"

"Okay," said Vicki.

"I'll meet you down by the river," Nysa said to Marty.

She closed her music portfolio and swung off down the hill, a slender woman in blue jeans and a lace-trimmed blouse. She waved to the Jeffries family by their tent and continued on toward the river.

Marty had pulled out her notepad. "We looked at your tools yesterday morning, that's not the problem. But I wondered if you'd seen the hand axe they dug up a couple weeks ago."

"A hand axe?"

"A small hatchet with a hammer attached. They found an old rusty one here. Do you remember seeing it?"

"A couple weeks ago. Yeah." Vicki frowned at the ground and rubbed the back of her neck. "But didn't they lose it? Justin said it was missing. Asked us all to look around for it."

"That's right. And you haven't seen it since?"

"No." The sad blue eyes flicked toward Marty. "Why are you asking about it? Do you think it had something to do—"

"We don't know for sure."

"Everyone's been saying he fell!" Vicki's face tightened with dread.

"We're just checking," Marty tried to soothe her. "Now, we're also asking about a strange guy who's been seen on the riverbank at night."

"What kind of guy?"

"You've seen someone on the riverbank at night?"

Vicki shrugged. "Sometimes."

She was a hair too casual. Marty's eyes snapped up from her notebook, and she decided to add some detail. "He moos. And wears some kind of a costume with cow horns."

"Cow horns?" said Vicki. "I think they're bull's horns."

"Bull's horns? You've *seen* this guy? What does he look like?"

"Big, muscular, powerful." Vicki gazed toward the river, a little smile on her face. "Horns on his head, very long and spreading. Bull's horns, I'm sure. Big deep voice when he bellows."

"Vicki, you've got to tell us about this kind of thing! It's your duty as a citizen, understand?"

Vicki looked around at Marty, stricken. Marty took a deep breath before adding more gently, "Now, when was he here?"

"Don't remember." Vicki was reluctant now. "Maybe this spring."

"He's been here more than once?"

The tall woman looked like she wanted to run away. "Yes."

"At night?"

"Late at night, always."

"You said this spring. Can you be more exact?"

Vicki rubbed the back of her neck, but finally said, "Maybe May."

So Johnny had been telling the simple truth. He'd seen the guy in June, George had said. "How often has he been here?"

"Once or twice a month." Vicki's brow puckered. "Maybe more often recently. Maybe once a week."

"Where does he show up? This farm, your farm?"

"Different places. The first time was on the fishing rock on our farm. But he goes up and down the river."

"Okay, this could be important. Do you have any sense of where he comes from, where he goes? New Concord, maybe?"

"Maybe." Vicki looked down at the ground. "I don't know."

"What are the farthest points where you've seen him?"

"What do you mean?"

"Does he go on the other side of the highway bridge?"

Vicki said, "Look, I only have business on these two farms! I don't know what people do other places!"

"Look!" Marty began sharply, then pulled back. Though reluctant, Vicki was being real helpful, and she didn't want to upset her. "See, I'm just trying to find out what I can, because this is a real unusual guy and unusual things have been happening. You've seen him on the riverside on both sides of New Concord. Do you have any sense of whether he goes farther? Along the path, maybe in a boat?"

"Maybe. He's very strong and fit."

"What does he do, exactly?"

She shrugged.

Marty said, "You said he bellows?"

"Yes. A big, low voice, like a bull. He pets the cows, he looks at the river. He dances." She shrugged again.

"Did you ever speak to this guy?"

"No! No, he shouldn't—he shouldn't be disturbed."

"Good. Don't disturb him. Did you see his face?"

"It's like a bull face."

"The mask, you mean. It covers his face?"

"Yes."

Marty adjusted her Stetson. "Miz Strand, why didn't you tell us before this?"

"I don't know." Vicki looked away, clearly upset, her big hands rubbing nervously up and down the sides of her jeans. "There was no problem. Up till now, there was no problem."

"Did you tell anyone?"

"No. There was no problem."

"Well, weren't you afraid he'd hurt you? Or the cows?"

"No. Oh, no." Vicki looked back at Marty, her eyes lustrous. "The cows like him."

"They like him?"

"They're pastured outside at night in the warm months. They know when someone isn't good for them. They like him. They let him pet them. I know he won't hurt them."

"Weren't you afraid he'd do something else weird? He's naked, right, except for the bull face?"

"Yeah."

"Well, God, he might hurt you!"

"No, I—" Vicki rubbed her forehead. "He seems—kind to me. He seems so—lonely."

Marty looked at Vicki in dismay. What kind of feelings had this gawky, unattractive woman developed toward this weirdo? Had her own loneliness blinded her to danger? Or was she right, was it just a secretive guy performing some odd but innocent ritual, just harmless dress-up? Either way, Vicki seemed much too trusting. Marty said as forcefully as she could, "Look, Miz Strand, we're talking about a loony here. Maybe he had nothing to do with Johnny's death, okay? But maybe he did. So if you see him, or hear him bellowing, or anything, don't approach him. Okay? And call us right away. We have to talk to him. Okay?"

Vicki looked down at the ground again. After a moment she said, "Okay." But Marty didn't like that hesitation.

"You call us, now. I'll talk to you again soon, okay?"

Vicki nodded and struck out across the pasture to collect a couple of the red-and-white cows. Marty watched her a moment, then headed for the river.

29

MARTY FOUND NYSA A FEW YARDS ALONG THE footpath, looking up the hill toward her sister. She glanced quickly at Marty, then uphill again. "You said something that upset Vicki," she observed.

"Yes, ma'am, I'm a little upset too. She's seen a weird guy along the riverbank here several times. Naked except for a headpiece with horns. Bellows like a cow. And she didn't tell us."

Nysa was holding her music portfolio in one hand, a flask in the other. "Damn," she said. "Do you want a drink?"

"No thanks. Have you seen this guy too?"

"No. I think I've heard him." She drank and tucked the portfolio under her arm to cap the flask and return it to the crocheted bag at her belt. "Vicki asked me once if I'd heard the bellowing the night before. I said yes, and wondered if one of the cows was in heat. No, but everything was okay, Vicki said. I decided to believe it."

"Well, I'm not sure you should believe it. She says she hasn't spoken to this guy, but I'm worried. He sounds like a serious nutcase, and your sister isn't taking him seriously.

She claims he's kind and won't hurt anybody. Anything's possible, I guess, but how can she know?"

"How can any of us know?" Nysa studied Marty a moment, as though trying to decide how to phrase her comments. "You know, they say that back in pagan times, the first maze was modeled after the river Meander. But I think it was modeled after our minds. Twisty, walled pathways—we don't even know ourselves. How can we know anyone else?"

"Well, yeah, that's exactly my point. It's better not to be too trusting."

"Would you mind if we walked along the river?" Nysa started along the pathway, and Marty fell into step. "I love this riverbank, don't you? 'A savage place! As holy and enchanted/ As e'er beneath a waning moon was haunted/ By woman wailing for her demon-lover!' The river's rising again."

A savage place. A demon-lover. Marty suppressed a shiver and looked down at the churning brown waters beside her. It was true—the river had gained inches since she last saw it, though the weather had been dry. "Must be raining upstream."

"Yes. All those clouds." Nysa waved her hand at the dark, ratty clouds. "Tell me: those bones—the bones Russ found after the picnic? Have they done tests on them yet?"

"Oh. Yeah, some. They're saying they're about a hundred years old."

"I thought so!" Nysa beamed. "They're from the old New Concord cemetery, I'm sure! The lost cemetery!"

"Yeah." Marty made a note. It'd be good to get one thing cleared up. "I remember you mentioning that cemetery. It was supposed to be on your property, but you couldn't find it."

"Yes. The records say it's on this side of the river between the town and the ferry—that's where the bridge is now, at the old ferry landing. That's all our property." She looked across the licking waters. "Maybe the cemetery is underwater now. You can see how the river undercuts its banks. Over a hundred years a river can change a lot. I looked everywhere along our bank, and couldn't find the cemetery."

"So you think the river covered it over? Well, the bones sure came from somewhere." Marty made another note. It was spooky to think of a drowned cemetery under the mud. She hoped the river didn't bring up many more bones. She had plenty to do without having to check the contents of old cemeteries.

"The river has its secrets. 'Caverns measureless to man,' " said Nysa. "Do you know the poem?"

"What poem?"

" 'Kubla Khan' . . . 'Five miles meandering with a mazy motion/ Through wood and dale the sacred river ran/ Then reached the caverns measureless to man/ And sank in tumult to a lifeless ocean:/ And 'mid this tumult Kubla heard from far/ Ancestral voices prophesying war!' That always makes me think of Father Rueger listening to his voices and building his town by the sacred river, just like Kubla Khan. And now Father Rueger's an ancestral voice too, isn't he, prophesying to us?"

"I don't know about Father Rueger," Marty said, getting back to business, "but I prophesy trouble if you and your sister don't steer clear of this strange guy on the riverbank."

"I've steered clear. You're worried about Vicki? Vicki's surprisingly strong."

"It's—look, I hate to read things into it, but it's like she thinks this guy with the horns is kind of romantic."

"Maybe he is!" Nysa slowed, her earnest blue eyes fixed on Marty. "You think he's strange. A nutcase. A monster. But why? He's naked, you say, late at night. But what if no one is meant to see? He wears horns, you say, and he makes noise. But what if no one is meant to hear? It's odd, yes. But I think it's terrible to have no room for oddness! It's terrible to force people into the same pigeonholes!"

"Maybe so. All the same, I have to investigate."

"Deputy Hopkins, you're odd yourself. Don't people tell you sometimes that yours is a man's job?"

"Yeah, sure. But so what? I can do it."

"Of course you can. But some people think there are only

two ways to be. Real men, real women, nothing else. And a man who thinks law enforcement is a man's job will be very upset when he sees you do well. He thinks he knows what a real man is, and you attack his most basic ideas. And if those basic ideas are wrong, he doesn't know who he is anymore."

Poor old Foley, Marty thought. Maybe he didn't know who he was.

Nysa went on softly, "In school my little brother wasn't allowed to do what other boys did. My father was very strict. And the other boys called my brother a sissy, and beat him up. Those children were so eager to prove they were men. They turned into monsters instead."

"Yeah, I remember catching it in high school because I was athletic. Girls weren't supposed to be good at sports. But you're right—boys who didn't fit the pigeonholes had a worse time than I did. I feel for your little brother. Did he come out of it okay?"

"Oh, yes! He's a wonderful person. But he still has some problems to work on."

"Kids can be monsters, all right."

"Yes, we all be monsters when we're afraid. Like my father. Or Thom. Handsome, admired by so many. He loved me and left me behind. You too, loved and left behind. Who are the true monsters? A lonely man on a riverbank, or those who leave love behind?"

Her words echoed through the back tunnels of Marty's heart. Left behind. Monstrous, yes; Nysa was right. Yet it was an everyday tragedy, fed by everyday blunders. She said, "There's plenty of pain in the world, you're right. But—"

"Yes! So much pain. And yet—there is joy too. Thom gave me moments of pure joy. We must seize the joy."

"Not if it risks your life!" Marty exclaimed, seeing where Nysa was headed. "Look, for the sake of your sister, you've got to call us if this guy shows up again! Let us check him out. If it's just coincidence that he turned up about the time Johnny was killed, there's no problem. We aren't monsters who beat people up because they're different. If this guy isn't doing anything illegal, well, shoot, you all are welcome to any joy you can get out of him. I don't care. But we have to check him out."

"All right." Nysa touched Marty's arm imploringly. "Something's happened, hasn't it? You seem so sure there's a problem now—you've learned something?"

"We have some new questions. Did you see the hand axe they found at Bob Rueger's dig a couple of weeks ago?"

"Hand axe. That little tool with a blade and a hammer on the same handle? No, I haven't seen it since the day they—" Nysa stopped so suddenly her frothy blouse swirled about her. "This morning you were asking about hammers—oh, no, you can't mean that poor boy—"

"We don't know yet."

"Oh, God." Nysa leaned against a maple trunk. "That poor boy! And you think—" She tucked her portfolio under her arm, fumbled at her belt, and pulled out her flask. "Do you want a drink?"

"No, thanks."

Nysa tipped it into her mouth. "And you think that the man with the horns is involved?"

"Too early to know. But I sure want to ask him some questions."

"Yes, of course. That poor boy! Like a sacrifice—Father Rueger said we must sacrifice all for the kingdom of heaven's sake." She raised the flask again.

Marty caught her wrist gently. "Hey, let's lay off for a minute, okay? What are you telling me about Father Rueger? Is there a connection with Johnny's death somehow?" Past Nysa, she noticed a blond woman and a man in a coverall running along the path toward them from New Concord.

Nysa said, "I don't know. I don't know!"

"But you suspect something?" Marty asked urgently. "You talk about a connection. But Father Rueger's been dead a long time. Do you mean Bob Rueger?"

"Bob Rueger? He's looking for ancestral voices. But he won't find them here. Vicki and I, yes: Father Rueger is our ancestor. But—"

"Deputy Hopkins!" called the blond woman. It was Sue Donato.

"Oh, dear." Nysa focused on the approaching pair.

Sue Donato was gasping for breath. "Deputy Hopkins, you've got to—find Carl! Please, please!"

"Take it easy, Mrs. Donato. He's okay. He's going to work, so it'll be easy to find him."

"That's just it! When I was leaving his boss's office, I met Harry—" Sue turned a tearstained face to the man in the sage-green Helton Gas coverall next to her.

Harry was wiry and weather-worn and decidedly uncomfortable. He kept his dishwater-blue eyes on the river as he said, "I thought Carl was just staying home with his family, and forgot to call in. And the guy had enough trouble already. I figured he didn't need our boss coming down on him. So"—he looked at the ground—"I got together with a couple of the guys and we did his deliveries for him."

Damn, damn, damn. Marty asked, "So nobody's seen him at work either?"

His pale eyes met hers at last. "The last person to see him was Sue here, two nights ago."

Her portable radio didn't work well in the valleys. Marty raced up the pasture to her cruiser. She saw Karen Brewster helping her bandaged husband from their pickup truck, but she didn't pause to greet them before radioing dispatch.

30

LATE WEDNESDAY, DOC ALTMANN CALLED. WES was looking at the first responses to their bulletin about Carl Donato and his van—a couple of them from the Kokomo area looked promising. He hunched his shoulder to hold the receiver to his ear while he dug out the Donato file. "We like the measurements on that hand axe," Doc said. "They fit most of the blunt force trauma and most of the chop wounds. If you need extra evidence, we've got one weird-shaped blunt wound to the back that was made with the side of the thing. The marks that don't fit are most likely postmortem, the river scuffing him around."

"I see."

"Course it would help if you folks would get me the actual object. Theory's all very well for you'n me, but juries don't like measurements. They like weapons. Preferably bloody."

"We'll try, Doc, but my bet is the weapon's in the river now. Even if we find it, it'll be clean. How about those puncture wounds?"

"That's more of a problem. The tent stakes you sent don't look very likely. Diameter's too big, and they don't penetrate to the depth of the wound if they're only inserted to the level where the diameter's right. The taper's too abrupt."

Wes tried not to think of what Doc had to do to the body to reach these conclusions. "We'll keep looking, then. Maybe some kind of pointed iron? A piece of a railing?"

"Could be. It's a little tricky to predict from the condition of the wounds. On some of them our local fishies had a banquet."

Wes flinched. He'd been thinking of catching something on his day off for Shirley to fry up. Maybe he'd give that project a skip for a while.

Doc continued happily, "But we got a few wounds that were pretty clean so even a jury will see that they match the weapons, if you'll just get me the weapons."

"We're working on it. If we could get a better idea of exactly where it happened we could call in the divers again."

"He was last seen—what, three miles from where he washed up?"

Wes squinted at the large-scale map of that corner of the county that he'd posted on his wall. "Yeah, roughly, but that's as the crow flies. By the time you add in the curves, it's twice that far by river."

"Yeah, the state divers won't want to do that much work. Lazy bastards."

"Oh. One other thing," Wes said. "Hopkins called in a few minutes ago and reminded me that there's talk of an old cemetery at New Concord. Hundred, hundred and fifty years old. Nobody knows where it is exactly."

"You're talking about those old bones now. Yeah, could be. People usually don't put cemeteries in bottomlands. But stranger things have happened."

"That's for sure. Thanks, Doc."

Wes hung up and studied the map again. It was true—most cemeteries were on hills. Most people didn't like to drop their dear deceased Aunt Maude into a hole that filled with water as you dug it. Well, he'd worry about that later. The cemetery had waited a hundred years, it could wait a little longer. There were more urgent things to do. He phoned Kokomo and a couple of other departments that might have spotted Carl Donato and asked them to follow up, then turned to the other news Hopkins had called in: Vicki Strand had corroborated Johnny's unlikely tale about a guy wearing cow horns! Wes was astounded. Who the hell could it be? He'd send the night shift down to the riverside to take a look tonight, and reinterview people in the New Concord area tomorrow.

But first he had an important call to make.

The boy's mother called him to the phone. Wes said, "Hi, George, this is Sheriff Cochran."

"Yessir," he squeaked. Then in a more grown-up voice, "Yessir."

"Got some news for you. Somebody else saw the same crazy thing on the riverbank that Johnny told you about."

"Huh? But he made that up!"

"Yeah, I thought so too. But this other person said the same things Johnny did, so we have to check it out. And I just wanted to let you know that we're going to be asking people about it because of the new information. Didn't want you to think I was breaking my word."

"Oh, no sir, I won't think that."

"So that turned out to be real good information you gave us. Let us know if you think of anything else. And thanks."

He hung up and looked at the map of the river. Hopkins said the guy had been spotted on the Brewster property, and on the other side of New Concord on the Strand property. Of course, the guy may have gone beyond that. Wes looked carefully at the area around the highway bridge. Three Walters properties there, three of the four corners where the highway crossed the river. The Strand place took up the fourth, southeast corner. A little south of the Strand farm, the highway bent east toward New Concord, and was lined on both sides with a series of smaller lots as it approached the town. The town itself stretched mostly north from the highway toward the river, though a few small houses and businesses, like Clyde's Bar, had been built south of the highway.

Looking at the smaller lots along the highway, memory stirred. He'd known someone who lived in one of those lots. Who was it? A name, a face, seemed to glimmer, unrecognizable yet somehow familiar, in the mist of his mind. You're getting old, Coach. Well, maybe it would come to him later.

Past six. Time to call it a day for now. Wes signed a couple more papers and closed up shop. At the dispatch desk, Roy Adams had long since replaced Foley. "I'll be back before midnight to talk to the night shift," Wes said. "Beep me if anything comes up on the Donato case or the Brewster case."

Adams said, "Yes sir. You'll be at the church supper?"

"Ah, shit, I forgot it was Wednesday! Yeah, I'll go straight over there. Thanks, Adams." He couldn't miss the church supper. It might sound like a leisure-time activity, but he got more done there than in hours at the office.

The Cedars of Lebanon Methodist Church parking lot was nearly full. There were a couple of departmental vehicles. Mason, it looked like, and Hopkins. Wes slid in the back door, nabbed a plate from the nearest table, and joined the end of the line.

"Hey, Wes." "Howdy, Sheriff." "How's it going, Wes?"

He smiled and nodded and traded jokes with the folks and waved at Mason across the room, but his eyes roamed busily over the crowd until he saw Shirley. She was ahead of him in line, just now dishing something onto her plate, saying something to Melva Dodd, turning to look around the hall before going to her table. There was a little worry line between her eyes until she spotted him. Then the frown disappeared and she smiled, the same mind-boggling smile that had won his heart forty years ago when he was the star of the high school basketball team and she was its bounciest cheerleader. Shit, you'd think after forty years a guy would get immune. He grinned and gave her a small wave, still listening to Hank Russell's observations about the Cubs game the day before.

Something niggled at his mind, and he realized that while the happy babble in the room had kept on, a silence had fallen to his right. He glanced over at a small group of people standing there. Aha, Chuck Pierce. His noble opponent in the sheriff's race, a sandy-haired, pale-eyed fellow in a blue shirt and tie. Chuck was standing between his wife Abby and Pastor Kemble. They were all staring at Wes as though he had a gravy stain on his shirt. Wes said to Hank Russell, "Hey, Hank, hold my place a minute, okay? Gotta check in with the pastor."

Pastor Kemble was a soft, chunky man with a good preaching voice, dark eyes, and stick-out ears. Wes strode over and shook his hand heartily. "Hi, Pastor. Howdy, Chuck, Abby." He loomed over them all.

"Hi, Wes," said Pastor Kemble. "Terrible thing, that poor boy from New Concord."

"Yeah, we're working overtime on that."

Chuck Pierce said, "Your lady deputy working overtime too?"

Now what did he mean by that? Marty didn't fool around. But there was a hint of a smirk on Chuck's lips. Wes said, "When a kid gets killed, we all work on it full steam."

Chuck sobered up, but Abby Pierce looked up at him like a banty hen and said, "Where's her little girl?"

Wes glanced out at the crowd and saw Marty at the far

end of the room, just settling her Aunt Vonnie into a chair at one of the long tables. She'd had time to change out of her uniform and was wearing a short red skirt and a white T-shirt thing with ties at the sleeves. She'd pulled back her curly hair with a red band. Vonnie, in a pale flowery dress, was laughing at something Romey Dennis was saying.

Marty was laughing too. Wes thought she looked very carefree and pretty. Maybe that's why Abby was making comments. He looked down at his rival's short wife and said, "The kid's in Tennessee visiting her dad. He's got a temporary job down there." All of Brad's jobs turned out to be temporary.

Pastor Kemble nodded. "Ah, I see. Nice that she can visit."

"Yeah. Well, I better get back in line before I starve," Wes said. "Good seeing you all."

He went back to his place in line. Old Mrs. Shaw toddled toward him. "Hi there, Wesley."

"Hi, Miz Shaw, how you doing?" She'd been his fourth-grade teacher.

"Pretty well, thanks. But you know, we're having such a problem on our street with stray dogs. They killed a calf near New Concord this spring, I hear! I think there are five or six . . ."

Wes nodded politely as she went on. The line moved up to where he could see the food: macaroni and cheese, baked fish with paprika, Clara Johnson's beef stew, plates of chicken, mostly fried, scalloped potatoes, pickled beets, green beans with bacon, Edna Brown's German potato salad, Laurie Evans's three-bean salad, and four Jell-O salads of various colors. One of them was a red-hot salad made with the fiery little candies. Most of the dishes were at least half-gone. He gazed longingly at the beef stew, but took Shirley's low-fat baked chicken and green beans like a good boy. He couldn't help peeking at the dessert table, laid out like a preview of Paradise for hungry Christians. There was a strawberry pie, three chocolate cakes, brownies and chocolate chip cookies, a big angel food cake with strawberries, a pretty fruit bowl filled with chunks of honeydew and lush red watermelon. Shirley would want him to choose fruit when the time came, but he decided to negotiate for the angel food. If he skipped the whipped cream it would be low-cholesterol.

He gave Shirley a hug as he sat down.

"Well, hi, Champ! Glad you made it," she said.

"Yeah. I'm glad too. Hi there, Johnsons."

"Hi, Wes." The couple across the table were Nichols County natives, solid German-Scandinavian stock, gray-haired but with the fair, sun-reddened complexions that told of their youth as blonds. Gus Johnson added, "Hot enough for you?"

"And then some."

"Champ, you should have taken Melva's baked fish," Shirley said. "She says it's fresh-caught."

"I was more in the mood for chicken," Wes said without explaining why he didn't want fresh-caught fish.

Romey Dennis, on his way back to his seat at the far end of Wes's table, stopped by. "Hi, Coach. Hi, Mrs. Cochran."

Shirley beamed at him. "Mr. Dennis, you're old enough to call me Shirley now."

He grinned. "Okay."

"How's it going, Romey?" Wes asked.

"Pretty good." Romey was in jeans and a green-and-purple striped shirt. He'd grown up more muscular than Wes would have expected from the skinny kid he used to coach, and the short brown beard squared off his face. But his quick grin and alert eyes were the same. He was serious now. "Of course, Uncle Corky's upset about that break-in."

"I'd worry about him if he wasn't upset," Wes said. "We're working on it, tell him."

"Yeah, Marty told me you had a lead. Didn't say what."

Wes didn't know of any leads. She was probably just being polite. He said, "Yeah, we'll let you know soon as something works out."

"Okay. Aside from that, business is pretty good. When I was in Chichicastenango I talked to an old woman named Luz who wove sashes and belts for tourists. She lived out of town in a little hut but buyers trekked out there to get her stuff. I asked her the secret of her success and she said her things were better and cheaper, and most important, she *told* people they were better and cheaper. So Uncle Corky and I have started running ads in the Bloomington papers. 'Drive a little, save a lot' kind of thing."

"Good idea."

"Just like the Stonies, right, Coach? Gotta hustle. You and Luz teach the same lesson. Well, see you soon."

Shirley smiled after him as he made his way down the table. "He was a nice little kid, too."

"Yeah. He and Marty were the same size that year, remember? And both of them scrappy as hell. They sure look different now."

Shirley laughed. "Ain't hormones grand?"

"Still scrappy, though, both of 'em." He ate some chicken. "Say, Shirl, didn't we know somebody who used to live up on Highway Eight-sixty? Edge of New Concord?"

"The people who moved to Florida?"

"Yeah, I believe you're right."

"Oh, what was their name? Quick? No, Joanne Quick is the librarian. Quinn. Was it Quinn?"

"Ed Quinn. That's right."

"Ed and Vilma Quinn. They went to Tampa," she said.

He leaned sideways to give her a smooch on her smooth pink cheek. "Who needs computer ID searches when you're around, Shirl?"

She smiled, curiosity in her eyes, but she knew better than to ask why he wanted to know. He changed the subject.

He managed to be one of the first at the dessert table. Shirley had allowed the angel food if he left off the cream and took some watermelon salad too. He stopped off to see Vonnie on his way back. "How's the ankle?"

"Well, you know, driving seems to make it worse. So I'm going to stay with Melva a couple of days and she'll drive me."

"Good idea. That should get you back in your dancin' shoes."

Marty Hopkins arrived, carrying two pieces of chocolate

cake, he noticed enviously, one for Vonnie. "Sir, I had a thought on my way home. Can I talk to you a minute?" She jerked her head toward the back wall by an empty table.

"Sure." He followed her to the quieter spot.

She spoke in a low voice. "It's about the Seifert boys. They live on Milo Road, right? Parallels State Eight-sixty."

"Yup."

"Well, see, their place backs up to Herb Frick's place on State Eight-sixty. So I stop by Herb's again, he tells me to look wherever I want to. I drive as far as I can on his little access lane. I get out, cross a little field, go over a fence into the woods. I can look over a fence into the Seifert property now, and there's this little plywood shack in the woods. I peek through a crack in the wall and there's a bunch of stuff in there. Chain saws, electric drills, and so forth. All painted that kind of burgundy red they use at Dennis Rent-All."

"Son of a gun!" said Wes. "Let's get a search warrant. What made you look there?"

"The geography just hit me," she explained. "Plus Grady said the Seifert boys' car broke down two weeks ago. But a pickup just like the Fricks' was at the scene. I got to thinking, the Fricks are just about stone deaf. You have to bang on their door for ages before they come. Late at night there's no way they'd notice if a Seifert boy came by and hot-wired their pickup truck."

"Son of a gun," said Wes again. "I'll get Judge Relling to sign a warrant tonight and send Mason out. And we'll need to get the state fingerprint boys to check the machines in the shack. Oughta print the Frick truck too."

"Tell the guys they'll have to bang on the door real loud at the Frick place."

"Okay. Good thinking, Hopkins."

She looked more mournful than proud. "Sure wish there was something we could do for those Seifert kids."

"That's the downside of our job. We don't get called until it's too late to help the bad guys. Our job is to help the good guys, like Corky Dennis. Focus on that."

"I just hate to give up on a kid. But you're right." She managed to smile. Made her real pretty, that smile.

Wes watched her go back to her seat, a tough, smart, sweet woman in a skirt the color of his watermelon chunks. Rusty would be real proud of his girl.

He called Adams and told him to track down Judge Relling and beep him when he had. Only then did he sit down to his hard-earned angel food.

31

JUSTIN CLOSED THE BOOK. "SO THAT'S HOW TOMMY Tugboat got to the big ocean."

JayJay wriggled onto his stomach and hugged Bobo Bear. "Was Tommy Tugboat's river like this river? Out there?"

"Yeah, pretty much."

"It's blue in the book. This one is brown."

"Rivers are different colors. It depends on the weather."

"Does this river go to the ocean?" JayJay yawned.

"Yeah. It joins other rivers and makes a bigger river, just like Tommy Tugboat's river." Justin put the book on the stack. "Okay, JayJay, time for a prayer."

They knelt together and JayJay asked God to bless mommy and daddy and grandpa and all the campers and Gruff the goat and his friend Skip in Arizona and Tommy Tugboat and Bobo Bear. Then he lay down on the cot and let Justin fuss with the sheets. "Read another story," he murmured halfheartedly.

"Tomorrow, JayJay." Justin kissed his son, turned down the lantern, and went out through the tent flap.

Bonnie was mending socks outside, her hair a soft cloud in the lamplight. She looked up and smiled. "Get him settled?"

"Yeah. He gets tired trying to keep up with the big kids."

"They're very good with him." She handed him the mosquito repellent as he sat down on the camp chair next to hers. After a moment she said, "Honey?"

"Yeah?"

"I, uh, I think I'm pregnant again."

"What? Really?" He stared at her. "That's great! I mean, I'm stunned! But that's great!"

"Yeah. Don't tell anybody; it's way too early." They'd lost one early about a year after JayJay's birth, and Bonnie had found the well-meaning condolences of acquaintances unbearable—"You're young, you'll have others," or "Thank goodness you never got to know the baby." She'd spent hours weeping in her room.

"Honey, that's great!" Justin finally moved, knelt by her camp chair, and hugged her. "That's great!"

"I just pray—" she said with a little catch in her voice.

"Yeah. God will see us through." He squeezed her tighter and caressed her soft hair. He loved Bonnie, he loved JayJay, he would love the new one. The cruel temptation he faced this summer would soon be behind him. God would see him through.

Bonnie murmured, "I just worry—you know, with a child killed this summer—I worry."

"Honey, it's not an omen or anything. We have to trust in God's plan for us."

"I know." She took a deep breath, and he realized how close she was to tears. "But sometimes it would be nice to see the future a little, so we could prepare."

"I know."

"And you have so much on you now—you've been so distracted and sad, trying to help the kids through it. All that extra counseling. It's a strain."

"Yes." And that wasn't the only strain. Justin felt a guilty pang. "You're a real help, Bonnie. I couldn't manage without you." A lot of the girls had gone to talk to Bonnie instead of him. Ministers' wives had an unfair, unpaid burden.

"We're partners. I like to help," she said.

"Yes." He gave her another squeeze. "That's what God wants, for us to help each other."

They sat companionably while the campers slowly settled in. He saw Kenny and Melissa kiss briefly before separating to go into their tents. Then Bonnie stretched, yawned, and went in to get ready for bed. Justin sat for a while in a confusion of love, joy, and guilt, trying to fathom God's plan. Helping each other—it was easy to say, but in fact only God could help. And yet, human love had such a major role in His plan. Sexual love, with its little miracles like JayJay and this new child, and of course the act itself was one of God's delights. Or sometimes the devil's delight, he reminded himself. *For still our ancient foe doth seek to work us woe.* Sexual love brought with it heavy obligations. And to meet those obligations, God had created nurturing love, like his love for JayJay or his love for the youth group. Love that connected people to each other in God, love that made them vessels of God's grace.

Was he meant to be a vessel of grace for Nysa? A nurturer? His reactions to her were so passionate, so lustful, fight them though he tried. But she was not a tramp or prostitute trying to arouse his lust. That would be an easy situation to avoid. Nysa was different, a bright and sensitive and talented woman who was in great pain, weeping at the riverside about the loss of a boy, tormented by other, unknown sorrows. "The dead won't stay dead," she had sobbed to him. "Gods die and rise again. Maybe I'll rise again too."

Had she meant suicide?

That had been Monday night. This was Wednesday. For two days he had been worrying about her. Did God mean for him to counsel her? To talk her out of suicide? Was the electricity between them a sign that he was meant to save her? He couldn't bear the thought of a world without her sweet, ardent brightness. What was God's will?

But he mustn't confuse God's will with lust. Was Bonnie's new pregnancy a sign that he should stay away from Nysa?

He must keep himself open to God, be ready to respond to God's voice.

God was very still tonight.

Justin heard frogs and cicadas, soft water sounds, an occasional breeze in the trees. He heard murmurs and rustling from a few of the campers' tents. He heard occasional snatches of recorder music from across the hill, Vicki serenading the night. He longed to go to the river, to make sure Nysa was safe. He closed his eyes, waiting for God to tell him he should go. Or stay.

A fitful rain started at midnight. He doused the lantern. Were those voices he heard down by the river? Half dozing, he thought he saw a blond camper coming back to her tent from the latrine, and later, a light bobbing by.

Much later, he heard a cow bellowing.

But God was very still tonight.

32

MELISSA PATTED LUCY'S RUMP AND WATCHED THE red-and-white cow amble into the pasture. "She didn't give much milk this morning either," she said to Vicki.

"What? Oh, it's been months since she had her calf." Vicki glanced at her across the fence. She was on the barn side of the gate, sliding in the latch. "We'll have to breed her again soon, I think."

Melissa yawned. She'd been out real late with Kenny. It was so cool, being in love. Even the night rain seemed warm and friendly when you were in love. It had been embarrassing when those two deputies went by with their flashlights, but Kenny had answered their questions politely and then when they'd left he'd imitated the deputy and broken her up. She said to Vicki, "Sorry, didn't get much sleep."

"I didn't either." It was true; Vicki looked hollow-eyed

and edgy. But she spoke kindly to Melissa. "It's a difficult time for all of us."

"Yeah. Will you send Lucy away to a bull somewhere?"

"No. Artificial insemination. You better learn about that if you're going to be a vet."

"Yuck."

"A lot of veterinary work is yucky." Vicki looked out at the cattle, slowly making their way toward the trees at the edge of the pasture. The rain had passed and it was another warm, gloomy morning. "I'd like to have a real bull some-time. One of this type of cattle, the strong runty ones." She hesitated and added, "We were going to keep Florida's calf last spring and let him grow up. But the poor thing was killed." Vicki turned away to blow her nose, and Melissa realized how much she'd cared about that calf.

"Yeah, Karen told me. That's sad," she said gently. "That's why I want to be a vet, to save animals like that."

"You're a good person, Melissa." Vicki sounded choked up.

"Well." Melissa didn't know how to respond. "I guess I better get back to camp for breakfast." She waved her hand and started across the wet pasture.

"Okay." Vicki waved back, then rested her hands on the top of the gate. When Melissa got to the bottom of the pasture she looked back and Vicki was still standing there, gripping the gate before her with both hands as though she wanted to vault over, her blond head bowed between her arms. She seemed very sad to Melissa.

Kenny was late today. He usually met Melissa here at the corner of the pasture to walk her back. She felt a stab of disappointment. Last night had been very intense, even in the rain. Maybe this morning he'd overslept. Because of her. As she walked the path beside the swollen river Melissa smiled to herself, thinking of the power she had over him.

He wasn't at the breakfast table either, the long folding table they set up near the kitchen tent so Bonnie Jeffries and the breakfast-duty crew could serve everyone quickly. She slid onto the bench next to Kenny's tentmate Derek. "Is Kenny still asleep?" she asked him.

"Asleep?" Derek was gawky and pimply but had nice brown eyes and was always willing to help out with stuff. "No, he was up early today. I thought he went with you."

"Really? He didn't. He didn't meet me afterward either."

"That's weird."

"Yeah. Did he say anything yesterday about going anywhere?"

"No." Derek looked at her sideways, then away. He lowered his voice. "I think he went out of the tent again last night. But he always comes back."

Melissa's cheeks grew hot. She and Kenny had been so careful not to wake their tentmates! Those two deputies were bad enough, but this was really embarrassing! She said stiffly, "Well, he didn't tell me where he was going today."

"Yeah, I believe you." Derek frowned at the tent that he and Kenny and four other guys shared. "But I don't know— Look, did you guys have a fight or something?"

"No! Why do you think—" Melissa stared at Derek and suddenly felt clammy. If he didn't know where Kenny was, and she didn't know, something was very, very wrong. She said, "No! No!"

"Melissa? Is something wrong?" Reverend Jeffries was at the kitchen end of the table, helping to hand down plates of pancakes.

"It's Kenny! Oh my God! Where is he?" Melissa scrambled off the bench, poised to run back to the footpath.

"Melissa, wait!" Reverend Jeffries's voice was commanding. Derek had jumped up from the bench too and now grabbed her arm. She shook it, but couldn't get free.

"Wait, Melissa, we'll help," Derek said.

"But we've got to find him! What if . . ."

"Who's seen Kenny this morning?" Reverend Jeffries asked.

The campers seated at the table glanced back and forth at each other. Ellie said, "He usually goes down the footpath in the morning to meet Melissa."

"Did anyone see him today?"

Heads shook. Forks were still.

Melissa knew they were all thinking the same horrible thoughts.

Reverend Jeffries said, "Let's go look. Derek and Melissa and everyone else on that side of the table, go toward the Brewster place. The rest of us will go along the footpath toward town."

In an instant, the campers were up and hurrying toward the river. Derek was still holding Melissa's arm and she ran beside him as fast as she could, although something was screaming in her head, "Danger! Danger! Danger!" She wondered if it was screaming in Derek's head too. Sometimes in her dreams she'd heard Johnny Donato scream like that. "He just fell in, he knocked himself out somehow and fell in," Kenny had reassured her after those dreams. "It's natural to be upset, Melissa. You're sensitive. Of course you're upset." And he'd hugged her tighter and stroked her hair. But Johnny's voice was back now, screaming "Danger!"

They reached the footpath and Melissa's brain, wandering among the screams, realized that she'd just come this way and he wasn't there. She shook Derek's hand from her arm and turned toward town instead.

"Melissa! Justin said—"

She didn't wait for Derek to finish. Last night she'd left Kenny on the path that led to town, not this one that led to the Brewsters'. She raced along the footpath toward the other group. She had almost reached the stragglers when a shout went up somewhere ahead of her.

She heard Reverend Jeffries exclaim, "Oh, dear God, no! Here, give me a hand, Russ."

She heard Ellie scream, and some of the others.

She heard Reverend Jeffries say, "I'll do mouth-to-mouth. Russ, go call 911. Run to the Brewsters', it's closest."

Seconds later Russ sprinted past her. His face was horrified. Melissa heard sobs and wondered if it was Russ crying. She hurried along the path toward the shouting voices.

The sobbing continued.

She heard Ellie's strained voice. "It's Melissa! Stop her!" Suddenly arms appeared, lots of arms, and as she struggled to get away from them, to move on, she heard Ellie say, "Dear God, please give us strength. Please!"

"Please, God, please!" Voices and those sobs were all around her.

Melissa took a deep breath and lunged from the encircling arms.

Reverend Jeffries, she saw, was bending over a still, stiff form, blowing in its mouth, striking its chest. It was blond like Kenny, and it wore Kenny's clothes, but it couldn't be Kenny, could it? Kenny had nice tanned skin. This thing had ugly cuts on its face and arms. Kenny wore glasses, and this thing didn't have any.

The sobbing continued.

Melissa realized it was herself.

She sagged back into the nest of arms.

33

"THOUGHT I TOLD YOU TO FIND THOSE WEAPONS, Wes." Doc Altmann peeled off his latex gloves as he climbed the riverbank to where Wes stood.

Kenny Ettinger's body was being bagged by Doc's assistants. It was an awkward job because the body was still steel-hard with rigor mortis. Doc had given it a careful look-over before he set his crew to work.

"Same weapons?" Wes asked.

"Same size wounds, anyway. They'll be easier to measure than the Donato kid's. This happened just a few hours ago." Doc's steel-rimmed glasses were sliding down his nose, and he poked at them to put them back in place. "He's in full rigor except for the jaw, and I think the preacher broke the rigor there trying to get his airway open for mouth-to-mouth. Unofficially, let's say the kid died at three A.M., give or take a couple of hours."

"Thanks." Wes knew that Doc must be pretty sure of himself to do him the favor of estimating time of death before the autopsy. Wes glanced at Doc's crew, a Dunning funeral director and his assistants, as they struggled with the body bag.

Doc wasn't his usual bouncy self today. "I feel for the preacher," he said. "Trying to give CPR to a stiff is not a real uplifting experience."

"None of this is." Wes turned his head as Marty Hopkins walked up. She looked angry, her eyes the color of the storm clouds rolling by overhead. "Hopkins. What's the report?"

She might be angry, but she'd learned to keep calm and to-the-point on the surface. "He was last seen for sure around eleven last night by his roommates," she said. "But one roommate thinks he might have gone out again much later. Apparently Kenny and Melissa Rueger have a thing going. They've been sneaking out very late when they think everybody's asleep."

"What does the girl say?"

"That's the thing. Karen Brewster called Bob Rueger right away, and he sent his local lawyer over. Buzz Sheldrake, the guy who handles the Rockland Mall business? Buzz took charge of Melissa and got some doctor to prescribe tranquilizers. He won't let me talk to her."

"Shit. What does Rueger himself say?"

"Don't know, sir. Apparently he's flying here right now with Kenny's parents. I can't get in touch."

"Any chance the girl herself did it?" Wes mused.

Hopkins shrugged. "Probably not, sir."

Doc Altmann objected, "The blows were solid and angry. You can feel the rage. But they weren't superhuman. An angry woman could have done it, yes."

"But not Melissa!" Hopkins protested. "Of course we have to talk to her. But she managed to convince all the other kids that she was devastated, practically in shock. They know her pretty well."

"Mm." Wes frowned. "Old Buzz Sheldrake oughta know better. Oughta give us a shot at the kid."

"We don't have as much money as Bob Rueger, sir," Hopkins observed.

"That's God's truth," said Doc.

"Sir, did Bobby Mason see anything last night?"

"It was quiet, he says." Wes shook his head glumly. Mason and Doerfer, the rookie on night duty with him, had had a busy night. Judge Relling had issued the search warrant around ten-thirty, and they'd served it, recovering the stolen items from the Seiferts' hut in the woods. Todd hadn't been home, but a few hours later they'd returned and taken him into custody. Meanwhile they'd done a couple of patrols along the river footpath. Wes had given them Vicki's description of the horned man, but they hadn't seen anyone dressed like that. Wes said, "They walked the riverbank twice and didn't see anything suspicious. Of course, a kid wouldn't look suspicious, or a fisherman."

"Maybe they'll remember something after they think about it."

"Maybe. And let's hope Rueger lets us talk to his daughter soon. He seems a reasonable man. Probably just wants to be here when we talk with her."

Hopkins asked, "Anything else I should know before I go back to the interviews? The thing is, a lot of the kids are going home today."

"Shit. Well, of course they would. You've talked to the boy's friends, and the girl's friends?"

"Yes sir. I haven't spoken to Reverend Jeffries yet, but his wife says they're staying till tomorrow or Saturday. A couple of the kids can't leave right away because their parents aren't home. The Jeffries are going to stay with them in the Brewster house tonight, and tomorrow night if necessary. So anyway, he'll be here a couple more days and I figured it was okay to leave him and the Strand sisters for last."

"So what's the timetable so far?" Doc Altmann asked.

"Yeah, give us a rundown of his last day," Wes agreed.

Hopkins adjusted her Stetson. She looked grim today, Wes thought, angry and frustrated, just as he was. In the humid air her face was shiny with sweat. She flipped back in her notebook. "Okay. Yesterday Kenny did the usual activities with the rest of the group. He worked at the dig in the morning and I interviewed him about hammers and so forth along with everyone else. He had lunch with the others, then returned to the dig for a while in the early afternoon. At free time midafternoon he and Melissa played a game or something on his computer. They wandered off down the footpath, but most of the time they were in sight of a couple of the other kids. They both were in the choral group at four. After that he was on dinner duty, Bonnie says, and helped chop salad and make tea and lemonade. Had dinner, played volleyball with the group, went to his tent at bedtime, and read for a while. So did Melissa. Normal day. Nobody so far had heard him say anything about early-morning plans."

Doc Altmann shook his head. "How could a kid like that get into this kind of trouble?" He waved toward the awkward bag that his assistants were loading into their van.

"One of his roommates thought he heard him go out again."

"What time?" Wes asked.

"He doesn't know. This is the kid named, let's see, Derek. Derek says a couple of times recently he's heard Kenny moving around real quietly at night. He figured he was sneaking out to see Melissa. Last night he was only half-awake so he didn't check the time. But he did think it was strange for Kenny to go out, because it sounded like it was raining."

"It started raining after midnight, right?"

"Yes sir. Bobby Mason would know more exactly."

"Yeah." Wes rubbed his face. "And maybe he'll remember something that'll help."

"Good." Marty didn't sound very hopeful. She was probably right, too. Mason and Doerfer had probably walked along the footpath with flashlights and loud talk, the heavy-footed law, easy to avoid. "Do you think they're going to let us talk to Melissa Rueger soon?"

"Hope so."

Doc Altmann's men had finished loading the van. The funeral director yelled, "Hey, Doc!"

"Coming!" Doc waved at him.

"Dr. Altmann, sir?"

"What is it, Hopkins?" He turned back.

"You said the wounds on Kenny might have been made by that hand axe, right?"

"Probably were."

"Did Kenny have those other wounds too? The tent stake kind?"

"Yeah. Except none of the tent stakes fit, so far."

"Sir, could they have been made by cow horns?"

"Cow horns?" Doc thought a minute. "Possible, yeah. But bring me the cow, okay? Because I've never met a cow who could use a hand axe."

Wes nodded at Hopkins. Should have thought of it himself. The weirdo on the riverbank wore horns! So maybe he was there last night. And Mason had missed him. Hell.

Hopkins's mind seemed to be running along the same lines. She said, "It's not surprising our guys didn't notice him if he's a local. Could be they drink with him. Even if they don't know him, he'd know where to hide, if he was local."

"Or if he'd been living here all summer."

The van beeped. Doc Altmann said, "Keep me posted," and trotted over to his vehicle. A moment later it left, lurching slowly over the rutted pastureland toward the highway.

Hopkins said, "Sir, I better try to talk to the Strands. They weren't around this morning. But Vicki especially seems . . . well, almost sympathetic to this guy. And she's the only one I've found who's seen him, except for Johnny. She may know something. That worries me."

That worried Wes too. "They weren't around this morning?"

"I didn't see her, but Vicki was around, according to Karen Brewster. She said she'd been in to milk the cows but didn't have much to say. And Karen says Nysa doesn't usually get up early. No one's seen her yet today."

"Mm. Hope she's okay."

"I'll try to find her." Hopkins pocketed her notebook. "Any other instructions?"

He studied her tense, bleak face. "You going to be all right on this?"

"I feel like a goddamn failure, sir. I've got a kid too."

"Stow it, Hopkins. How you feel is beside the point. I'm asking if you can think straight."

"Yes sir. I can think straight and work hard."

"Good. Use the emotion for fuel."

"That's what you used to tell the Stonies." She grinned shakily. "You've been trying to teach me that all my life, Coach."

"So go do it, Hopkins." He punched her shoulder lightly and went to join the state crime scene technicians who were methodically inspecting the riverbank below.

He knew what she meant. Two boys, on the verge of bright young manhood, brutally hacked and gored—he felt like a failure himself. He'd given it his best shot, throwing most of his troops into investigating the first death, hunting for the weapon, patrolling the riverside at night—and even so, another kid had died.

Back at the office an hour later, he looked at the map. Here was the point on Dub Walters's property where Johnny's body had washed up, here was where Kenny's had been found, pushed into the river but snagged underwater by a bush that had been covered by the high waters. If he'd been pushed a little farther out—yeah, he might have fetched up on the shore just about the same place as Johnny. About the only good thing was that Kenny's body had been found on Brewster land instead of Walters land.

Could old Dub be behind any of this? That was a big chunk of land he'd assembled. Naturally he hated the idea of a federally protected historic project. It would diminish the likelihood of a superhighway and the big profits Dub envisioned. Still, it was a long way from hating the feds to butchering two boys.

But who else would benefit?

Well, try a different angle. Doc had said there was lots of anger in these killings. Todd Seifert was an angry kid. He'd attacked Johnny Donato before, George had said, and if a rich kid like Kenny looked at him the wrong way he might get mad. Mason and Doerfer hadn't arrested him till three o'clock last night. Where had he been before that?

Other questions lingered too. Where was Carl Donato? None of yesterday's rumors had turned into strong leads. Who had assaulted Professor Brewster?

Nothing seemed to fit. Better collect some more facts. Wes picked up the phone to find out if Mason and Doerfer had remembered anything more about their patrol last night.

34

"ROSIE, HONEY?" MARTY GOT OUT OF THE CRUISER and waved at the little girl jumping rope all alone in her yard.

Rosie turned big sad eyes on her and walked over slowly.

Marty leaned down to her level and pushed back her Stetson. "Rosie, you know we're still trying to find your father."

"Yeah."

"Did he tell you where he went?"

"No. He said he'd get ice cream on the way back."

"And he hasn't called or anything?"

"No. Maybe he found the man who hurt Johnny."

"Was he looking for the man who hurt Johnny?"

"Maybe." The little girl looked at the jump rope in her hand. "Daddy says it's some faggot."

Marty blinked. "Well, whoever it is, we're trying to catch him too. And I hoped you could tell us more about that cow witch. We found somebody else besides Johnny who saw it."

"Is the cow witch a faggot?" Rosie whispered.

"I don't know. Did Johnny say anything else about it?"

"See, he told me not to tell or the cow witch would get me."

"The cow witch won't get you. Anyway, somebody else already told, and that makes it okay for you to talk about it too."

Rosie thought about it and finally accepted Marty's logic. "I think Johnny was scared. He said he was going to catch it. Lasso it like in a rodeo, and then beat it up." She looked down at the rope in her hand. "But I think he was scared."

"Yeah, I think so too. Why do you think so?"

"After he saw it—he said he needed a gun. But Daddy keeps the real gun with him, and Johnny said nobody was afraid of a BB gun. So he got a little hammer thing to carry around in his pocket."

Marty tensed. "A hammer thing?"

Rosie held out her fingers to show the size. "I told him he shouldn't take it."

"Can you tell me what it looked like?"

Rosie shrugged. "Just a hammer thing."

"Tell you what. I'll bring you a picture and you can tell me if it's a picture of Johnny's hammer. See you soon, honey."

Marty returned to the cruiser and headed for the Brewster farm. Sounded like Johnny had taken the hand axe, and the weapon had been turned against him, and then against Kenny. Which didn't get her any further, she thought gloomily as she turned in at the Brewsters' Rivendell sign.

There was a knot of people around the Brewster kitchen door—Karen Brewster, Reverend Jeffries and his wife Bonnie, and many of the campers. Their faces, sad and drawn, turned toward the cruiser. But she wanted to find Vicki Strand, and drove past the house and on into the barnyard. The big barn door was ajar and she stepped into the warm, straw-scented dimness. The silvery light that slashed through the cracks in the wall was all she could see for a moment, but she could hear the clunk-clunk of someone at work. She called, "Hello?"

The sound stopped and a hesitant voice from somewhere above answered, "Hello."

"Vicki, good. I want to talk to you a minute."

"Okay. I'm just forking down some straw."

"You heard what happened?"

"About Kenny, yeah. But the cows . . ."

"Cows always need attention, don't they? No matter what happens." Marty could see her now, a hazy form high in the loft of the barn.

"Do you know—is Melissa okay?" Vicki asked anxiously.

"She's upset, of course. One of her father's men has taken charge of her. A lawyer."

"Taken charge?"

"Taken her to a doctor. I haven't seen her, I just heard she's being taken care of."

"A doctor? Oh, no! Is she hurt?"

"No, only Kenny was hurt. But of course Melissa's upset. I guess her doctor figures she needs tranquilizers."

"Oh. I see." Vicki sat down next to the ladder, letting her legs dangle from the edge of the loft. She gripped a pitchfork in one hand. A bar of light fell across her face and the shoulder of her pink plaid shirt. "Yes, maybe tranquilizers are a good idea."

Marty's eyes had adjusted, and even from below she could see that Vicki looked strained, haunted. Probably could use a Valium herself. Marty said gently, "Vicki, Melissa will be okay. Sad, but okay. But—maybe this is bad news for you, but we have to find that man you see sometimes on the riverbank, the man with the cow—with the bull's horns. We think he might have killed the two boys."

The pitchfork twitched and Vicki pressed her other hand to her eyes. "No. No."

"It's tough to face, I know. You say he's been kind to you."

She whispered, "Yes."

"See, if he killed the boys, he's probably—well, partly crazy. We have to find him to help him stop the killing. You understand, don't you?"

Vicki was silent, then drew a deep, shaky breath. "Yes. You're right. We have to stop the killing. What will happen to him?"

"We'll have to lock him up for a while. Maybe doctors can help him. The court will decide."

Vicki shook her head slowly.

Marty said, "Vicki, we have to find him. If you can help us, please do. He might be a killer."

"No! Maybe . . . maybe an avenger."

"An avenger? What do you mean?" Marty asked gently, wondering what those young kids could do that needed avenging.

"I don't—" Vicki was shaking her head again, and massaging her brow.

"Did he tell you he was avenging something?"

"No, he doesn't talk to me."

"Well, what makes you think he's an avenger?"

"He's not a killer." She looked very confused, still rubbing her forehead. "I don't— Maybe the kids hurt him."

Marty could see bragging Johnny, armed with the hand axe, approaching the muscular horned man—but why? "Why would they hurt him?"

"I don't know. Because he's different."

Kids were like that, yeah. A lot of grown-ups too.

Marty's neck was getting tired. She said, "I'm coming up, okay?" and climbed up to sit on the other side of the ladder. She tried to look Vicki in the eye but she was still staring down at the barn floor, still rubbing her face distractedly. Marty asked, "Who is he, Vicki? I mean when he isn't wearing that bull mask? You've guessed, haven't you?"

"He—he hides in the daytime. He likes the night."

"Yeah, I know that. Where is he in the daytime, Vicki?"

Vicki shook her head. There was a dull gleam of tears on her face. Marty was sure she knew more.

"Vicki, we've got to stop the killing, right? Please, tell me the rest!"

"That's all!" Vicki was sobbing openly now. She shifted the pitchfork to her other hand.

Marty leaned toward her across the top of the ladder. "Okay, I'm sorry, I know this is a shock. We're all shocked about Kenny. Please, Vicki, get ahold of yourself. Tell us where he is."

Vicki shook her head helplessly. Big, noisy sobs rolled through her long body.

"Vicki, think! If he's basically nice like you say, he doesn't want to be a killer, he wants to be a good man. Right?"

She was still sobbing. Shoot, this was useless. Ought to take her in until she cooperated.

But Vicki's grief made her pause. Better give her a minute to get used to the idea that her romantic fantasy was dead. Then, even if she didn't give them the information, they could watch her, and she might lead them to him.

"We can help him, Vicki. Think about it," Marty urged. "Pull yourself together. I'll be right back, and you can tell me about it."

She swung down the ladder and out into the gray daylight. It was common enough in police work to find women devoted to the wrong men, and Marty had spent plenty of sad hours trying to get information from some loyal wife about her husband the burglar or drunk driver, and plenty more urging some bruised and bleeding woman to press charges against her brutal boyfriend or husband. But this guy was twisted beyond everyday drunkenness or brutality. And Vicki's reactions made Marty uneasy. Other women might suffer because of their men—shoot, Marty herself had suffered some—but most of those women had other possibilities, more in their lives. . . .

Come off it, Hopkins, who are you to judge? You with a broken marriage and nightmares and a bad case of the glooms. Vicki had good things in her life too—music, a loyal sister, work with the animals she loved. She wouldn't gamble it all on a guy who didn't even talk to her.

Or would she? There was something so poignant about the gawky, shy woman latching her affections onto that strange beast of a man. What attracted people to each other? Shoot, after ten years Marty still wondered at times how she'd ended up with Brad. He was sexy, sure, but plenty of guys were sexy. Brad had made her feel attractive and sexy too, at a time when her sorority sisters—like her high school friends before them—were telling her to dress differently, to act more feminine, to give up her favorite sports and play down her athletic ability, though they'd been quick to put her on their tricycle race team for the big weekend. That sense of infinite possibility she'd known as a kid playing for the Stonies had been slowly jabbed to death by their comments. Going out with handsome Brad had shut them up.

And Brad had big dreams to make up for her dying ones. That had appealed to her in those college days, when she was first getting a glimpse of the great world beyond southern Indiana. New York, stardom—silly adolescent fantasies, but Brad's descriptions were so easy to believe. And when she got pregnant she'd believed his dream about marriage too, about how he'd go to New York to get his career launched and then she and Chrissie would join him in a delicious, exciting life. Once, in a low mood, she'd asked him if she wasn't just a drag, if he wouldn't do better without her and Chrissie. "I need you, kitten," he'd said earnestly. "You keep me going. You show me the way." She'd lived in the glow of those words for months.

I need you. Magic words. She needed to be needed. That's why she loved this job. That's why she'd stuck with Brad so long, because it felt so good each time he needed her help—even though when she tried to follow up, to tell him how to avoid problems in the future, he'd get irritated and call her a selfish nag. Then she felt used and discarded, about as worthwhile as a chicken bone or a watermelon rind in the dump.

But the moments when she could help him were wonderful.

Nysa had said something like that. Thom had told young Nysa that he needed her to conquer his depression and moodiness, that she led him out of himself. It was glorious, she'd said, and sexy. Sexy to be needed. Yes.

And was poor, gawky Vicki caught up that way, sensing the deep need of the sick man on the riverbank, hoping for the glory and sexiness of rescuing him? Marty shivered for her.

She went into the Brewster kitchen, where Karen and a couple of the campers were leaning against the kitchen counter watching Ellie talk on the phone. "Okay. I'll try back in another half hour," Ellie said, and hung up. She didn't look sparkly today. Her eyes were red-rimmed and frightened.

Marty said, "Hi, Mrs. Brewster. How's your husband doing?"

Karen turned with an angry frown. "Rotten! He's resting here, but he's not himself. Moans in his sleep, says great books are irrelevant! Why doesn't your stupid department do something?"

Her husband is injured, Marty reminded herself, her hopes for the history project disintegrating, her peaceful farm life shattered by horrible deaths. Go easy on her, Hopkins, she's real close to the edge. Marty folded away her annoyance and said, "Yes, ma'am, we're still working on it. May I use the phone?"

"Help yourself." Karen shrugged and tossed a braid back over her shoulder.

"In private, ma'am," Marty said.

"Oh, sure. Let's go, kids. Official secrets." Karen pushed off from the counter where she'd been leaning, yanked the door open, and held it for the three campers before following them outside.

Marty picked up the phone and dialed dispatch. She glanced out the window at the barn, but saw no sign of Vicki.

"Three twenty-one," she said when Foley answered.

"Howdy, three twenty-one."

"I'm at the Brewster farm. Need to talk to the sheriff, not on the radio."

"Radio's all he's got right now."

And he might be listening, because Foley was minding his tongue. Marty said, "Ask him to phone here. Important, but not life-or-death." She gave the number and then, still holding the receiver, pushed down the cradle and waited, glancing out at the barn from time to time. The remains of breakfast were still on the oak table and the countertops. A confusion of rain gear, including Drew's long black umbrella with the steel tip, hung ready on the pegs next to the door.

After five minutes Karen stuck her head in the door. "Finished?"

"Almost. Thanks." Marty had been inspecting the baskets of vegetables, mostly zucchini, on the counter by the sink. She held up the receiver. "Another five minutes."

Karen rolled her eyes but went away, slamming the door.

The call came three minutes later. The sheriff said, "Hey, Hopkins, what can I do for you?"

Marty kept her voice low. "Sir, I think Vicki Strand knows where to find our suspect. She's real upset about it. Seems to like the guy for some reason. I'll talk to her again but if she won't talk it might be good to get someone to tail her. She may try to go to him."

"Tell you what. Grady Sims isn't far away, checking out a problem at Collier. That old timber bridge is going. I'll get him in plainclothes, maybe fishing gear. He's a good tracker. Where is she now?"

"In the Brewster barn."

"Okay. Keep an eye on her, but don't follow."

"You want me to stay on the interviews, then?"

"Correct."

"Ten-four, sir."

She went out to the group by the porch. "Okay, Mrs. Brewster, thank you. The kids can get on with their phone calls. Reverend Jeffries, could I ask you a couple of questions?"

"Sure. Back in a minute, Russ." He joined Marty on the porch. She could see the barn over his shoulder.

"I want to know if you heard anything unusual last night."

"It's terrible! I think God wanted me to do something last night—but I didn't, I didn't!"

"Take it easy, Reverend Jeffries." Marty looked up from her notebook. "God wanted you to do something? What?"

"He wanted me to prevent this terrible thing! Last night I couldn't sleep. I wanted so much to walk by the river— but I fought it." Reverend Jeffries wiped his hand across his mouth. He looked ravaged, as though he'd been in a war, or sick for a week.

"You fought it," she repeated, still not understanding.

"I thought it was my duty to stay here with the campers. I never dreamed God wanted me—there—"

"Yes sir, God's hard to figure out sometimes. Now, were you awake when it started to rain?"

Jeffries squinted, as though getting back to physical details was an effort. "Yes. Around midnight, maybe a little after. I doused the lantern but I still felt restless, so I didn't go in the tent. I waited under the flap till the rain stopped."

"Did you see or hear anything down by the river?"

"I thought I heard a voice once. And a little later a flashlight went by. This was after the rain stopped. And even then I didn't go!"

"Sir, do you remember what time the flashlight went by?"

But the Reverend Jeffries had buried his face in his hands and was repeating, "I didn't go!"

"Sir . . ." Marty felt for the guy, but this was getting them nowhere. "Sir, I don't know as much about God as you do. But I can tell you a couple of down-to-earth things. First, we had deputies walking the river path last night. And they missed it. So I don't know how you think you could have helped. If you'd been there and met the deputies, it would have confused things."

"There were deputies there?" He looked up, puzzled, and wiped his mouth again.

"Twice. Not all night. You can't be everywhere along the riverside all night. And the other thing I wanted to say was, what if you'd left all the kids here and gone away, and then something happened at the camp? Who knows? Maybe you were meant to stay at the camp."

Jeffries sighed. "Maybe so. But I can't help thinking I was meant to be on that footpath."

"Yes sir, we all wish we could have prevented it. Now, what time did the flashlight go by?"

"After the rain stopped. Maybe half an hour later."

He was still upset, but at least he was with her again. Marty pressed on. "That would be about two-fifteen?"

"Two-thirty, maybe."

"Okay." That would be Mason and Doerfer going by the second time. "Now, did you see or hear anything else?"

"A little after that I heard . . . well, footsteps nearby. I looked, but all I saw was a camper going into a tent. Melissa Rueger, I thought. It was her tent. I thought she'd just been out to the latrine or something."

"Did you see Kenny at this time?"

"No!" A spasm crossed his face. "No. And in fact I did glance around for him. They're so obviously fond of each other and I wanted to be sure nothing had happened—oh dear God." Realizing what he'd said, he rubbed his mouth again.

"Yes sir, you were doing your best, sir." She turned the page. "Now, after that, did you hear or see anything else?"

"No. Just the night sounds."

"Did you hear a bull bellowing?"

"Oh. Oh, yes, I did, very, very late. I was nearly asleep, but I heard it. I've heard it other times, too."

"Can you tell me what time that was?"

"Not really. Later than the other things I remember. Maybe three-thirty A.M. I think I'd dozed off in the camp chair."

"Anything else?"

"No. I went in then and got a little bit of sleep."

"When did you get up?"

"Six A.M." He managed a small grin. "That's why I'm not much use today. I usually get more sleep."

Marty wrote down the time. "What did you do next?"

"It was . . . well, normal for a while. I was dressed in fifteen minutes or so. Bonnie went to start breakfast and I got our son dressed, then went to help her. The campers started drifting over and helped set up the tables. About a quarter to seven I said a blessing and we started."

"You didn't miss Kenny?"

"I knew he wasn't at the table. But you see, he usually waited for Melissa to finish with the cows. They were usually a few minutes late. It wasn't till she got back around seven that we realized nobody had seen Kenny for hours."

"I see." This fit with what the others had said. She wished she could talk to Melissa. "And then?"

He took a deep breath. "When I realized he wasn't here I—I divided the campers into two search parties. Mine went toward town. Russ spotted him in the river caught on that bush and helped me pull him up."

"Did you remove anything—clothes, anything in his pockets?"

"No."

"Did you notice anything else while you were pulling him out? Objects in the water, maybe?"

"No. I was focused on—on—see, he was just rigid! I sent Russ to call you and I—I gave CPR, tried to, but it was so hard to—" His hand went to his face again, and Marty realized why he kept wiping his mouth.

She said gently, "Reverend Jeffries, you did a real good job, I think."

"I just wish—"

"Yes sir, I know. Maybe—well, maybe if you pray—"

He met her eyes and connected for a moment. "Thank you," he said with a shaky smile. "I've forgotten my lines, haven't I?"

"Anybody'd be upset, sir."

"Yeah."

"Well, let me know if you think of anything else. Even if it seems unimportant. You'll be here another couple days?"

"Until tomorrow afternoon, anyway. We hope all the kids are taken care of by then."

"All right." She closed her notebook. "Have you seen Nysa Strand this morning?"

"No." The man flinched as though she'd struck him. Strange, Marty thought. "No. She's usually not around in the mornings. Is she—okay?"

"I suppose so. I just want to talk to her too."

"Her sister's down by the river, I think."

"By the river? I thought she was in the barn."

"She came out just after you did, while you were making that call."

"Damn!" Marty jumped from the porch. "Sorry, sir. Which way did she go?"

"Toward town."

"Okay, thanks, I gotta go."

Marty raced to the barn. No Vicki. She galloped down the pasture to the riverbank trail. Shoot, she'd been so sure Vicki could lead them to the man with the horns! But the tall woman was nowhere in sight.

She did find Grady Sims, in jeans and his Pacers cap, baiting a fishhook. He'd made good time. She said, "Hi. The fish you're after went past about fifteen or twenty minutes ago. Sorry."

Grady started packing up. "Downstream?"

"Yeah. Good luck."

On the way back to the cruiser she checked through the barn more thoroughly just to be sure, but Reverend Jeffries was right: Vicki wasn't there.

35

MELISSA RUEGER WOKE UP IN A PRETTY BEDROOM with ruffled white curtains and fuchsia-and-white wallpaper. Where was she? She sat up slowly, pushing back the sheets. What a ditz she was, not even knowing where she was. She was dressed, she saw, in her cutoffs and peach-colored T-shirt. No shoes. She remembered putting on the T-shirt, long ago, in the dawn light, before she went to milk Florida and Lucy.

What time was it? Was it time to milk them again? Her brain wasn't working right. She felt a wild panic, a sense that something was terribly wrong. But when she looked at her watch, she saw that it was only two o'clock. She had time.

But where was she? She got out of bed and went to the window. A wrinkly-looking silver sky stretched over a suburban landscape, a subdivision similar to places back in Arizona where most of her friends lived, except that here the land rolled in little wooded hills and the lawns and bushes were thick and green. She could see a wing of this house, brick with white trim, similar to the ranch-style house beyond the hedge. Both houses faced onto a wide blacktop street that curved away past other ranch houses and over a little cement bridge before disappearing behind a hill. She didn't recognize any of it. Where was she? Why was she so logy?

She needed a bathroom, and turned back into the room. There were three doors. One was a closet; the next was a small, pink-tiled bathroom. When she'd finished she looked at herself in the mirror. Her face looked shocked and miserable. She ran her fingers through her blond hair and tried to smile, but something inside seemed to keep her face locked in that sour position. Something she didn't want to know.

The third door opened and Melissa turned to see a plump, gray-haired woman in white bringing in a tray. "Hi, honey, I heard you were up. How are we doing?"

Melissa stared at the tray. A hamburger, french fries, salad, ice cream. She said, "I'm starving!"

The woman chuckled happily. "You missed breakfast, poor thing. I thought you'd be ready for this. Here, now." She set the tray on a small table and pushed it next to the bed so Melissa could sit down. Melissa picked up the hamburger. Pickles. She hated pickles. She fished them out and took a big bite. After chewing for a moment she mumbled, "Where am I?"

"Poor thing, it's confusing, isn't it? You're at Buzz Sheldrake's."

"Who?"

"One of your father's friends. Your father's on his way, flying here. Mr. and Mrs. Sheldrake are taking care of you until he gets here."

Melissa chewed for a moment. Sheldrake. Skinny, bald, horn-rimmed glasses. She could almost remember, but something in her didn't want to remember. She ate some fries and asked, "Where's Reverend Jeffries?"

"He's still at the camp, helping the other kids get organized to go home."

Melissa didn't remember anything about going home. She went on stuffing her face with fries and salad and mumbled, "I'm sorry, I don't remember who you are."

The woman burst out laughing. "Of course you don't, honey—you were sound asleep when I came on duty! My name is Peggy, and I'm here until the Sheldrakes get back from the luncheon."

"Thank you." Melissa picked up her milk and saw a tiny plastic cup with two pills in it. "What's that?"

"Your pills, honey. Dr. Pierson thinks you'll be a lot calmer if you take some more."

Calmer? Unbidden, the closed door in Melissa's mind inched open. Calmer. There was a danger she would not be calm. She was upset; she looked upset in the mirror. A terrible thing had happened. Truly terrible. She realized that tears were running down her cheeks. She was crying for Kenny. Kenny was dead. She would never see him or touch him again.

She threw herself onto the pillow to sob. Peggy said, "Now, now, honey, be brave! We don't want you crying. Here, take the pills. The others have worn off!"

Not cry? How could she not cry? What was this fat old woman saying, that Kenny wasn't worth crying about? Melissa realized she'd slept most of the morning, and felt guilty. Lovers wept for their lost loves. They didn't sleep!

But she didn't think she could explain to someone as old as Peggy. She looked at the pills and sobbed, "In a minute," and began eating the ice cream.

"You'll feel better when you've had the pills," Peggy said.

Melissa drank some milk and made herself stop sobbing.

"Here, honey, take the pills," Peggy urged.

"I'm not crying," Melissa said politely. "I'll take them later."

"No, no! Dr. Pierson says I have to make sure you take them. Here you are, honey."

Melissa shrugged, placed the pills in her mouth, and drank the rest of her milk.

"There, that's a good girl! You'll soon feel much better. Now I'll just get this tray out of your way." She bustled out.

Melissa got up, closed the door after Peggy, and spat out the pills she'd hidden in her cheek. She didn't want to sleep. She wanted to cry, to weep, to wail out her sorrow and despair in a giant voice. But not here. She wanted to be comforted and warmed, but not by that stranger. She wanted . . .

She wanted her animals, gentle, loving creatures that made her feel connected to nature, to soothing nature.

Kenny loved animals too.

Florida's calf had been killed. She wanted to hug Florida, to tell her she knew now how she felt, to feel the warmth and strength of the great friendly creature. Maybe later she'd talk to Ellie or to Bonnie Jeffries, but right now she didn't want other people. Especially not stupid Peggy or the dorky Sheldrakes.

She didn't know where she was. But she knew where she wanted to be.

Melissa threw the sticky pills under the bed. Her sneakers were there, pushed under the edge. She put them on, bunched up the sheets so if Peggy peeked in she'd think she was sleeping there, and then unlatched the window. As quietly as she could, she slid up the sash and screen, and with a quick glance around to be sure no one was watching, she slipped out.

The prickly foundation bushes scratched her bare legs and arms. It was warm and muggy. She managed to close the window but couldn't reach the screen. She pushed her way out through the plantings and raced across the little side yard to the tall hedge at the fence line, so as to have it between her and Peggy's eyes. But as she followed the hedge toward the thicket of trees behind these properties, she panicked for a moment. How could she get to the Brewster farm if she didn't know where she was?

Then a plan came to her.

The street crossed a little bridge near here, and a bridge meant a creek. Melissa edged along the bushy fence line toward the creek. It was a wide creek, brown and full today.

Its banks were lush with bushes and, a little farther along, trees. There was even a path, muddy and in places overrun by lapping water.

Melissa wasn't crying. She felt guilty for a moment, but realized that Kenny wouldn't want her to have an accident, fall in or something, just because she was blubbering over him. She'd grieve for him when she got there.

The path was muddy, and she was leaving footprints. She ran back and forth a few times, then took off her shoes and walked in the water for a long quarter-mile before emerging onto a grassy bank and putting the shoes back on.

She hurried along the path, heading downstream toward the bigger river and the friendly beasts.

Tucked into a big four-poster in his own bedroom, Drew Brewster looked worse than he had the day before. Marty decided it was because the bruises visible below the bandage on his chubby face had turned theatrically dark. Photographed in grainy black and white, he could be Oliver Hardy the morning after a big fight scene.

He was as grumpy as Oliver Hardy too. "Another kid killed! Why don't you do something?"

"We're trying, sir. Have you remembered any more about the attack on you?"

His puffy eyelids blinked. "No. But it's not logical to connect my attack to the murders. This was just some hard-working man who had a few too many. You should be looking for the murderer."

So he thought he'd been attacked by someone who wasn't the murderer. Interesting. Marty said, "Yes sir, but we want to keep an open mind. Let me ask a couple of things. Did you ever see a man wearing cow horns? Not necessarily when you were attacked, but ever?"

"Cow horns? Some kind of a Viking costume, you mean? God, no. Not around here. Of course at the university kids wear weird costumes sometimes. But around here people have lives to lead."

"What about a combination axe and hammer?"

231

"That hand axe? I never saw it. I'm sure the person who attacked me didn't have one."

"Why are you sure, sir?"

"Because—because I was bruised, not cut. Blunt instrument, the doctor says."

"And also because you remember what the attacker was holding?"

"No," he said too quickly, then added glibly, "I see what you're driving at. If he only used the hammer side it would look like a blunt instrument. Well . . . that's possible, I suppose."

He was hiding something, Marty was sure of it. But why? Generally people wanted their attackers caught and punished—unless their attackers could in turn hurt them again. Marty asked, "Professor Brewster, the man who attacked you—did he threaten you somehow if you went to the police? Maybe threaten to hurt your wife?"

"No. That is—I don't remember. I'm blank on the whole episode. Did I explain about posttraumatic amnesia?"

"Yes sir. Did he threaten to tell your wife something you don't want her to know?"

"Listen, I don't remember!" The professor sat up straighter and pointed a plump finger at her. "People here have hard enough lives without false accusations!"

Marty closed her notebook. "I hope you do remember soon, sir. You may be right that your attack had nothing to do with the murder of the boys, but the sooner we clear it up, the sooner we can devote more time to finding the murderer. Do you understand?"

"Yes." He leaned back on his pillow, his fleshy chin sinking into his jowls, and Marty felt that his weariness, at least, was genuine. "Yes, I understand."

Back in the cruiser she sat for a moment, thinking about how the hefty professor might look in a Viking costume, before heading back to Dunning. It was time to do a real good background check on Drew Brewster.

36

"YEAH, WE SOLD THOSE TWO PROPERTIES TO AN ARIzona feller, named Rueger," said Ed Quinn's faraway voice.

"I see." Wes switched the phone to his other ear and leaned back in his desk chair to look at the map of Highway 860 on his wall, the little lots along the New Concord stretch of the highway. "Did he tell you why he wanted them?"

"No. Didn't have much in the way of direct dealings with the guy. I thought he wanted some sort of fishing retreat, but my old neighbors say he rented the places out. You'd know better than I would."

"Yeah, I think that's right. Funny place to look for rental property, though. Why not stick to Arizona?"

"Hey, who cares? His money was good. Not that he gave me a whole lot of it," said Ed.

"Was there pressure on you to sell?"

"Well, you remember Vilma had this rheumatism, always worse in the winter—"

"Yeah, but she had that for years. I mean, pressure from Rueger."

"No. Dub said the guy wanted someplace near the river and I'd better grab the offer before something else came on the market."

Wes tensed. "Dub? Dub Walters?"

"Yeah, he was the broker."

"He arranged the sale for Bob Rueger?"

"What's the problem? He's in real estate, right? See, I was complaining one day at the Three Bears about how I wished I could move to Florida like my brother. And Dub was having a cup of coffee there. He called me the next day and said he had a buyer who might be interested."

"So he set up the deal."

"Yeah. Dub took his seven percent, but I figure he earned it. I wish he'd got another couple thousand out of the guy but heck, it was in the ballpark."

"And you like Florida?"

"You wanna hear about our weather?"

Wes looked out his tiny window at the muggy, gray day outside. "No, thanks!"

"I miss you guys sometimes." A wistful note had crept into Ed's voice. "But Vilma says she's a lot more comfortable these days. And my brother's teaching me deep-sea fishing."

"Sounds good. Listen, Ed, send us a card sometime, okay?"

Wes was still frowning at the map when Hopkins knocked. "C'mon in," he said.

"Sir, any word from Grady Sims?"

"He called a few minutes ago. No sign of the Strand woman yet."

"Too bad." Despite her mild words, there was tenseness in her face.

"You're worried, Hopkins."

"Yes sir. I really think she knows something about this guy. And she was upset enough to do something stupid."

"She knows he could be our bad guy?"

"I tried to tell her. Shoot, I wish I'd—see, she'd quit cooperating, she was just crying, and I thought I'd get more out of her if I let her pull herself together. And if she didn't tell us anything I figured we could watch where she went, maybe find the guy that way. But she slid out while I was on the phone with you."

"Grady may catch her. He said the Volvo's gone from their place. We've sent out a bulletin on the car."

"Good." She brushed back a curl. "Sir, I just talked to Professor Brewster. He still claims that he doesn't remember what happened."

Wes squinted at her. "And you still don't believe him."

"Okay, look. We've got a guy, goes to a bar, leaves his wife behind. How come? Well, Mason didn't hear anything about arguments or hitting on women or anything. But Brewster leaves the bar around eleven, and his wife doesn't find him till nearly one o'clock. Maybe he sees a woman on the street afterward and makes his move, and the boyfriend takes exception. He wouldn't want his wife to know."

"That's been known to happen."

"Or it could even be a guy he propositions. He'd want to hide that from his wife too."

"And he'd want to hide it from the university, and from the cops. Or his taste might run more to kids—"

"He was already beat up when Kenny died. But he was home from the hospital."

"Yeah. There are lots of things he might want to keep quiet. Drugs, gambling. I'll call Bloomington and see if they've got anything on him around the university."

"Good. Anything else, sir?"

"Bob Rueger's expected in town before five, they say. And we can't talk to his daughter before that. Mason and Doerfer did see a couple of kids necking last night. They were in a hurry to get back to the Seiferts' to see if Todd had come back, so they just told them it wasn't real safe there and they'd better get back to camp. Both blonds, boy had glasses."

"Yeah. That was them. So we've got Kenny alive when?"

"Two thirty-five."

"That fits. Doesn't narrow it down much, though. We've got to talk to Melissa."

"Yeah. Close the door, Hopkins."

She did, with a questioning look. Wes said, "One last thing. I just found out that Dub Walters was the broker for Bob Rueger when he bought some of that New Concord property."

"Huh! They don't act much like buddies now."

"No, they don't. Maybe they had a falling-out. Look here, Hopkins." He pulled out the state map. "Here's Indianapolis, four big interstates. Here's Evansville down here, another interstate and connections to Memphis, Little Rock, New Orleans. And here's our little State Eight-sixty."

She nodded slowly, looking it over. "Yeah. But I thought if they ever built that highway it was supposed to go on the other side of the naval center."

"I thought so too."

"But if it's on this side—yeah, Dub could make a lot of money. Except Rueger's historical project messes him up, doesn't it? The Brewsters have applied for federal historic protection."

"But it hasn't been granted yet," Wes pointed out. "Dub's fighting it. Says it's communism."

"Yeah. So that would explain a falling-out. You don't suppose Dub would—no, he wouldn't!" She stared at Wes, horrified.

"I don't think he would either. He might get someone to rough up Professor Brewster, but not the kids. Still, this thing sure got rid of the historic project for now."

"It sure did." She frowned at the map. "Course—maybe Rueger and Walters just pretended to fight."

"How do you mean?"

"Suppose they want to buy the Strand farm. Dub can't get them to sell. But Rueger's related—shoot, maybe that's why Dub invited him on board, knowing that Nysa's so proud of the family history, hoping the Strands would sell to him."

"So the historic thing lets them play good cop-bad cop. And the kid getting killed cancels the historic project, which Rueger maybe planned to cancel all along? Pretty roundabout." Wes scowled. "Plus Dub is still on County Council. Still votes on our budget. Keep your ears open, Hopkins, but previous instructions stand. You hear anything, don't follow up. Tell me."

"Yes sir."

He looked at her hard. "And I want you to get some sleep tonight, Hopkins. You look ragged."

"Yes sir. Um—same to you, Coach."

Wes nodded and she went out. When the door closed he rubbed his forehead. She was right—he was ragged too. Doc Hendricks wouldn't approve of this stress. But what the hell could a guy do? It was one thing to keep Marty off Dub's case. But somebody had to ask some questions, and that meant him.

And shit, he just couldn't think of a polite way to ask Dub if he'd been mooing on the riverbank last night.

Marty flopped down in her desk chair and glared at the stack of papers. She wanted to be doing something, arresting someone or rescuing someone or interviewing someone. Not sitting here like a lump waiting for Grady Sims to find Vicki Strand, waiting for Nysa to return, waiting for Rueger to give the go-ahead to talk to his daughter, waiting for forensics to call back with more information about the crime scene.

She picked up a paper and stared at it blindly. The trouble with waiting was that all her fury and frustration had no place to go. She was overflowing with anger at whoever had killed Johnny Donato and Kenny Ettinger and turned her friendly home community into a place of terror.

Unwelcome visions shoved their way into her mind, though she struggled against them. Pale, lifeless Kenny, deep, river-washed cuts on his head and body, rigid on the green riverbank. And behind him Johnny, swollen and stinking in the brown water. And behind him that man she'd had to shoot last year, his eyes staring and his hand reaching toward her through endless time. And the other dead she'd known, accident victims and homicide victims and old-age victims, and her mother at peace at last in her bed with Aunt Vonnie closing her eyes, and before that a closed coffin that everybody said held her dad although twelve-year-old Marty could not believe it for years.

Get a grip, Hopkins. Crawling among yesterday's dead won't stop this killer today. And getting the paperwork done might help. She focused on the piece of paper in her hand, a half-finished report on her interview with Drew Brewster. Okay, finish up the reports. Had to be done sometime. She turned to the computer and set to work, ignoring the visions.

Half an hour later she looked at the clock. Better give Nysa a little longer to get back. She sifted through the remaining papers. She'd finished everything to do with this case and there were only old unfinished reports on barroom brawls, dogs running loose, speeders, and the usual teen rowdiness—graffiti on somebody's barn, a couple of minor drug busts, vandalism, shouts and gunned motors late at night. The only thing left in the stack that was connected to Johnny's and Kenny's murders was that copy of Nysa's history of New Concord. Shoot, might as well get that out of the way.

She skimmed over the first part—Father Rueger's youth in Germany, joining Father Rapp's New Harmony settlement on the Wabash, becoming impatient with Rapp's group, persuading some of them to join him miles up the White River. "A place of God's benevolence and beauty," he'd written, and named it New Concord. His industrious and celibate followers had built a church, homes, barns, granaries, and mills, and had planted fields and vineyards, all within three years. The fourth year they built the labyrinth, the fifth year two big dormitories and a school for the handful of children. Apparently a few couples had been having some trouble being "eunuchs for the kingdom of heaven's sake." The children were treasured, but the wayward parents were punished. How? It didn't say.

The next section was about their food, hearty German farm fare. The New Concord folks drank wine but frowned on hard liquor, though they distilled it to sell to their neighbors, along with their cheeses and merino wool. Then came a section on clothing, the gray wool dresses and dark suits Nysa had already described to her. The next heading was "Discipline." Father Rueger was very strict. Horribly strict, Marty decided as she read on. People who shirked their work, even for reasons of illness, were denied the communal dinner that night. A woman who had eaten some cheese meant for market was sentenced to having four teeth pulled. A runaway teenager was brought back, whipped, and had three of his toes cut off. In the seventh year, a second child was born to one couple; the man was castrated "like a bull calf," Father Rueger's letters reported, and the woman was "treated with lye." "Matthew 19:12—Eunuchs for the kingdom of heaven's sake," Father Rueger explained.

Marty shuddered. What had happened to "the place of

238

God's benevolence"? The law Marty tried to enforce was clumsy sometimes and frustratingly slow, but those problems seemed trivial compared to Father Rueger's bloody justice. "If thy right eye offend thee, pluck it out!" his letters exclaimed. Nysa wrote that he believed he was doing the culprits a favor, destroying the source of their sin and thus saving their souls.

But through it all, they sang. The last section in Nysa's pamphlet was the longest, about her specialty, their music. They sang at their church services, they sang at work, they sang the blessing at meals. They sang Luther's hymns and their own arrangements of music by many composers, even Bach and Beethoven. Father Rueger's son was a gifted musician, apparently, known for his beautiful voice and his skill at choral arrangements. Their music and the faith that God would soon smile upon them compensated for the cruelties of religious discipline and of frontier life. Or so Nysa Strand believed.

Marty wasn't so sure. She dropped the pamphlet back into the file and went over to the little refrigerator to get herself a Coke, pondering Father Rueger's story. There were cults today, too many of them, similar to Father Rueger's in their attempts to discipline people into perfection. Most, she hoped, were not as cruel as Rueger's. But she could sympathize sometimes with people who wanted to force others to be good. She wondered what Father Rueger would do to Johnny and Kenny's murderer. At the moment the idea really appealed to her.

"Any word yet from Grady Sims?" she asked Foley on her way back to her desk.

"Not for a while, baby," said the dispatcher. "Hey, are you the one who got Grady that soft job, fishing on duty? When you gonna do that for me?"

"Next time there's an opening, Don. Anything to get you out of this office."

"I like every opening you've got, babe," he leered.

Enough. Marty dropped her Coke can in the trash, put on her Stetson, and headed for the door. "Don," she said, "you ever thought about becoming a eunuch for the kingdom of heaven's sake?"

"A what?"

"Matthew 19:12. Think about it. Might improve your personality." She slammed the door and jumped into her cruiser.

Just in time, too. A TV van pulled up and people started unpacking cameras. Poor Sheriff Cochran. Marty gunned the motor out of the parking lot.

But Nysa Strand wasn't back yet. Marty asked about her in town and at the Brewster farm. No luck. By the time she finished asking, her shift had been over for half an hour.

When she called in, Foley had been replaced by Adams on dispatch, who told her that the sheriff wanted her to knock off and get some rest, but stay in touch.

On the way home she stopped by Melva Dodd's brick ranch house, where Aunt Vonnie was staying. A yellow blaze of marigolds stood tall along the low chain-link fence. Sweat ran down Marty's forehead as she waited for Melva to answer the doorbell.

"How you doing, Aunt Vonnie?" she asked when she'd been admitted and taken to the fruitwood-paneled family room off the kitchen.

"Melva's taking real good care of me." Aunt Vonnie was sitting before the TV in a recliner, her ankle propped high. She frowned at Marty. "But you're looking weary."

"Yeah. Real bad news. It'll be on TV. Another kid got killed last night."

"Dear Lord! What's happening to this place?" Aunt Vonnie said. "Honey, please, be careful. Wes shouldn't let you work on these killings."

Marty didn't feel like fighting that old fight. She shrugged.

"Things didn't used to be so terrible," Melva said darkly. "It's everywhere. My niece worked over at the Asphodel Springs Resort. Says all those rich people take drugs. Awful."

"Maybe not all, Melva," Aunt Vonnie said uneasily.

"But last year that Klan thing, now these poor children!"

"We must trust in the Lord," Aunt Vonnie said.

Marty felt even more depressed. "I better get on home," she said. "Lots of laundry. Can I bring you anything, Aunt Vonnie?"

"Well, I was just thinking, it's so warm I could use my halter top. The turquoise blue? Melva's garden is nice to sit in in the morning, but it gets hot so fast."

"I'll drop it by. See you soon, Aunt Vonnie."

She didn't feel like heating up the kitchen, so she picked up some Kentucky Fried Chicken on the way and called Tennessee as soon as she got home.

"Hopkins," said her daughter's voice.

"Hi, Chrissie, honey." Marty was ridiculously happy to hear that voice. "How's it going?"

"Okay. I'm going to go swimming tonight."

"Tonight?"

"Yeah, Daddy has to go to a meeting, so his friend Tiffany is going to teach me how to dive."

"That's nice," said Marty cautiously, while questions buzzed in her head: Who's Tiffany? How close a friend? But it wouldn't be fair to ask Chrissie. She added, "You be careful, now."

"Okay. See, Tiffany is a lifeguard on weekends."

"Great! Bet she's a really good diver, then."

"Yeah. She's neat."

"Is Daddy there?"

In a moment Brad said, "Hi, kitten."

"Hi. How's everybody doing?"

"Real well. How about it, kitten? You going to come on down here?"

"No. Bad news today, Brad. Another kid was killed."

"And naturally you think it's up to you to solve it all." She could hear the bitterness in his voice.

"I've got to help! My God, we're talking about murdered kids!"

"Yeah, well, listen, Marty, nobody's indispensable. You won't really be missed."

She closed her eyes. Was he right? No, she did as well as

any of the guys. Better than most. And she knew more about this case than any of the others did.

Not that she'd done Kenny Ettinger any good.

She said, "I've got to work this case, Brad."

"Don't you even care about our family?"

"Brad, you know I do!"

"I'm off the sauce, I've got the job we've been waiting for for years—"

"I know, Brad, that's great. Really."

"So why won't you come here?"

"I've got work to do, Brad, just like you. Listen, I'll talk to you tomorrow, okay?"

"Kitten, I just don't understand you anymore. It's like I don't even know you. What do you want from me?"

"Good night, Brad."

"Kitten—oh, hell. Good night."

She put down the receiver and stared at it blindly. What did she want from him?

Do you want me to start drinking again? he'd asked when he was here.

No, of course not, she thought, why should I want that?

Because then he'd need me.

Oh boy. Better think about that one later. Better do the laundry now.

She changed into jeans and a Big Red T-shirt and put in a load of sheets, then sat down in front of the TV to finish the chicken. Kenny's death was on the news, and there was good old Coach Cochran, looking serious and asking for public co-operation. After the program she put in some more laundry and tried a game show. But the house seemed so empty without Chrissie and Aunt Vonnie, and Kenny's pale, rigid body kept intruding in her thoughts, and even though she was exhausted she knew it would be worse if she tried to sleep.

She called her friend Dawn and lucked out. Joe was home watching a ball game so Dawn could leave the kids with him and meet her at the mall. They'd talk and have a soda, and maybe she'd find jeans on sale for Chrissie. Marty headed out to the cruiser again.

37

"SHE'S BEEN KIDNAPPED! WHAT KIND OF LAW EN-forcement lets a girl get kidnapped?"

Wes pushed back his Stetson and gave Buzz Sheldrake a once-over. The slim, bald attorney's dignity was completely shattered. Wes had never seen him with his tie askew and grass stains on his shirt. Wes said patiently, "You say Melissa is gone?"

"Yes, of course!"

"You say she was kidnapped. Do you have a ransom note? Any kind of communication?"

"No." Buzz Sheldrake licked his lips.

"Okay, sir, just tell me what happened."

"I don't know what happened! He got in the window somehow, and—"

"Sir, could you show me the window?"

"In the bedroom, of course!" Buzz's skinny arm waved at the back of the house. "What kind of—"

"Pipe down, Buzz," said Bob Rueger wearily. He'd been sitting in an armchair, leaning forward with his elbows on his knees. Now he stood and beckoned Wes to the hallway, taking charge automatically, though his voice was flat and dull. "Sheldrake put her back here, side of the house. She was sleeping, he says. Doctor gave her tranquilizers because she was taking it pretty hard. The nurse said she woke up for lunch—"

"Nurse?"

"Peggy Jackson, used to work at the county hospital. Buzz got her to come in while he and Nan went to lunch with a client."

243

"Is this nurse here?"

"No, he sent her away when he got back. Melissa was sleeping then, he says." Rueger indicated a bedroom with expensive wallpaper in a white and reddish-pink pattern. The bedclothes were a mess, sheets and spread dragging the floor, and the windows were closed. "When I landed I called right away, and he said he'd wake her and tell her I was coming. She was gone when he went in."

"That's right!" Sheldrake had followed them. "What kind of law enforcement—"

"Buzz, I said pipe down!" Rueger flared with the first emotion he'd let himself show. "Let the sheriff ask the questions."

Wes looked down at the lawyer and saw panic in the man's eyes. Well, Buzzy-boy was right to be panicked: He'd screwed up royally. Wes said politely, "Mr. Sheldrake, I just wanted to know if this was what the room looked like when you discovered that she was missing."

"Well, yes, I suppose so. Who would do such a thing?"

"Sir, were both the windows closed?"

"Yes. Well, the kidnapper left the screen on that one open."

Wes inspected the indicated screen. It was closed now. No obvious marks of entry. He'd have to check outside too. "Did you close the screen, sir?"

"Yes, of course! Somebody got in! I had to lock it!"

Idiot. Wes turned back into the room. "What about the bed? Were the sheets off?"

"Well, no. They were kind of clumped up on the middle of the bed. I thought she was sleeping there at first."

Wes stared at him a moment. "Mr. Sheldrake, can you just briefly tell me exactly what you did after you got home?"

"Well, Bob called and said he'd be here, so Nan and I went in to wake her up, and—"

"That was the first time you looked in?"

"No. Peggy and I peeked in when Nan and I first got back, and we saw that she was sleeping."

"What time was that?"

"About three-thirty."

"And Mr. Rueger called at what time?"

"Four-forty," said Bob Rueger.

"So you went in to wake her up at about four-forty?"

"Yes." Sheldrake licked his thin lips. "For a minute I didn't realize she was gone, because of the way the sheets were clumped up. Nan pulled down the covers to make sure she wasn't in there somehow, and I shook the spread. See, we'd already looked around."

"Where did you look?"

"In the bathroom, the closet, under the bed. We looked through the rest of the house too. Then I noticed the storm screen was open and went to look outside too."

Bob Rueger said, "It took forty-five minutes to get here from the airport, because I had to drop Kenny's parents at the funeral director's. When I got here he and Nan were going door-to-door asking the neighbors if they'd seen her. Nan's still out there, doing the next block. Buzz and I came back to call you."

"She might have crawled out the window herself," Wes said.

Bob Rueger nodded. "I hope so. But the problem is, even if she did, she was heavily tranquilized, the doctor said. I talked to the nurse on the phone, and she saw Melissa take the two pills. So I agree with Buzz on this. If she did get out by herself she wouldn't have gone far. And if someone was after her she sure wouldn't have put up a fight."

"Yeah." That cleared up another question Wes had been wondering about: If someone wanted to kidnap Melissa to get at Rueger's money, why do it now instead of taking her from camp? The answer was that at camp she'd been undrugged, alert, and usually surrounded by people.

"One more question," Wes said to Buzz Sheldrake. "You said when you went in to wake her, the bedclothes were bunched up so you thought she was still there at first. Now, did it look any different at three-thirty, when you and the nurse looked in?"

"She was—" Buzz Sheldrake licked his lips. "She—my God, you're right, it looked the same."

Rueger's fist crashed down on the vanity table. "Dammit, you idiot, that means nobody's seen her since lunchtime!"

Wes got on the radio and deployed the troops, setting them to work canvassing the neighborhood, asking about a sleepy blond girl, possibly drugged, and about vehicles in the area. He had Adams call everyone in, Sims and Hopkins and even Foley to take over dispatch so that Adams could join the search. Then he went out to take a look at the window area.

There were prints in the soil around the foundation plantings, all right. Three sets, four? Wes got Mason to secure the scene—not that it did much good after Buzz had already steamrolled across the evidence. He called for the state evidence technicians. They bitched because she hadn't been missing long, but after he explained that she was a witness in the White River murders they agreed to come right over.

Hopkins arrived last. She'd been at the mall when the call went out and it had taken time to get home to change back into her uniform. He briefed her and put her in charge of the Sheldrake house. She looked disappointed but said, "Yes sir."

"Mason talked to a guy at a service station who saw a blue pickup with a blond kid in it. I'm going to check that out."

"Yes sir."

"State evidence technicians will be here before long. We're not real sure it was a crime, but if it was it's been pretty well trampled on by Sheldrake, so try to keep him out of the relevant areas and make sure they don't forget to take elimination prints."

38

IT WAS AFTER FIVE. BONNIE AND KAREN BREWSTER were fixing dinner, assisted by the handful of campers who hadn't yet been able to get flights to Arizona. Justin was exhausted, filled with his own guilt and grief, unable to confide in anyone. The youngsters needed his help. He could admit his horror and sorrow to them, but he couldn't admit the most dreadful truth—his conviction that he could have prevented the tragedy somehow if he had trusted the stirrings of his heart, God working within him, and gone to search for Nysa on the riverbank. He hadn't known it was God. He'd thought God was silent, and instead He'd been calling to Justin.

Or had He?

That was the second dreadful truth: that Justin could no longer sense God's will, hear His voice, as he could in the old days.

He couldn't confide such things to the young people who came to him in tears, looking for strength and insight. Ordinarily he could share his thoughts with Bonnie, but she too was wrung out from the demands of the youngsters, who asked her for counsel just as they asked Justin. In any event, he couldn't have revealed to her more than the vaguest outlines of the problem. It was unthinkable to burden her with his complicated, shameful feelings for Nysa.

He walked along the river trail, making himself pass the familiar, suddenly ghastly place where Kenny's body had lain. The police tape kept him at a little distance, thank goodness. There was the spot in the river where Russ had seen the body, there were the footprints in the muddy margin—some his own—where they'd struggled to drag the body from the water, there was the grassy meadow's edge where he'd tried to blow life back into the rigid form. He shuddered, wiped his mouth, and walked on.

The path continued through woods for another quarter-mile, then passed the first backyards of New Concord. Here was East Street, where he'd helped dig up the axe the murderer had used. Here was the public boat access, here was Central Street leading to the old church. Next there were more houses, then West Street. Halfway along West Street he could see the big old dormitory building, now used for businesses, facing the green hedge that bordered the labyrinth. Finally he passed the last backyards and entered the strip of woods that bordered the river. Nysa's land. Justin hesitated. It was still a good hour till dinnertime. He took his small Bible from his pocket and walked on.

These woods were no different from the others, maples and hackberries, sometimes willows and sycamores, vines wrapping the trees and fence lines in a rowdy, leafy net. And yet Justin found himself sniffing the humid air for a hint of wine, of Nysa. He crossed the little bridge over the creek that ran through her property, and soon came to the flat fishing rock where she'd stood on the day of the picnic, the day they'd found those old bones. Strange, those bones, like a drumroll announcing the tragedies to come. Boastful, dark-eyed Johnny, and Kenny with his aviator glasses and computers and youthful love for Melissa.

Justin blinked back tears and opened his Bible. "As a hart longs for flowing streams, so longs my soul for thee, O God." Yes. He felt parched, graceless. He walked out onto the fishing rock to look at the flowing streams. Most days the waters rushed by in the narrowed channel a couple of feet below the flat top, and the wider section below the rock formed a quieter pool. But today the river poured over the lower end of the rock and even the pool boiled angrily, collecting a swirl of logs, broken benches, fence posts, plastic bottles, and other debris at the downstream end. The brown waters hurled logs and branches against the rock, as though trying to chip it away.

BLOODSTREAM

Justin felt chipped away too. The man he had once been was disintegrating under the onslaught of meaningless death, meaningless love. "My adversaries taunt me, while they say to me continually, 'Where is your God?' " Who was Justin Jeffries, and why had he ever believed he could minister to God's people? He had no answers. He could leap into that swirling water right now and be drowned or pounded to death by logs, and would it make any difference at all? "All thy waves and thy billows are gone over me."

A picnic bench bobbed past on the swollen river.

He closed the book. This wasn't working. He'd hoped that this walk would clear his head, help him face up to what had happened, give him a direction. No such thing. He was still lost in morbid confusion. He tucked his Bible into the pocket of his khakis and trudged back the way he'd come.

But he didn't want to go back. When he reached the bridge over the little tributary creek he didn't cross it, but turned away from the river. Too many memories along the river kept his mind confused. He didn't know where this little stream led. It might be more soothing. It was a creek that twisted back and forth across the Strand farm but came roughly from the southeast. Must be the one that ran under the highway as it passed New Concord. He could walk back to the Brewster farm along the highway and still be in plenty of time for dinner.

Dense woods bordered this creek, although he could see pastures through the trees to his right. On his left the creek hurried, higher than usual, splashing over rocks and swirling several inches up the tree trunks. The trees on the other side were thick at first, but as the creek curved closer to town, he began to glimpse fences and flower gardens, then a long, even stretch of green that puzzled him for a moment until he realized he was looking at the back of the labyrinth.

"Hello, Justin."

Yes. That's why he'd come, hunting her. Kenny killed, his sweet wife pregnant, his very God forsaking him, and what did he do? Roamed the countryside looking for this woman. She was across the stream where a little spring gushed from the rocky bank and poured into the creek. She was sitting on a fallen log, wiping tears from her face. His body tingled for her. Helplessly, Justin leaned back against a tree.

"You're very quiet, Justin. Are you all right?"

"I'm—no, I feel terrible."

Her sorrowful blue eyes fixed on him like a comforting angel's. "We all do. Where are you going?"

"Just walking."

"That helps sometimes." She stood up. "Do you want a drink before you go on?"

"Uh—no, thank you. That doesn't help, really."

She shrugged. "True. But when nothing helps you might as well get pleasure where you can."

"I'm trying to think. Trying to discover what *will* help."

She smiled sadly. "God will help."

He slid down the creek bank, looking for a way to cross. "Yes, but—"

"No, no, I'll come over. I know the way." She stepped quickly across the creek, her practiced feet finding the half-submerged stepping-stones. "You told me God gives us grace. We can't control it."

She was too near. He clambered back up the bank. "We can try to stay open to grace."

"Let's walk," she said, motioning back the way he'd come. In the humid gray light her beauty had a sheen that almost choked him. She went on, "God gives us grace. God gives us wine too, and music, and human love. And God gives us two murdered boys."

"Nysa, we can't always understand. But God is working through history, somehow. Perfecting His creation."

She frowned. "And do you really want to be part of that history, Justin? Blood and ugliness and horror?"

"We don't have much choice, do we?"

"We can leap into the killing river."

He took a deep breath. God wanted people to use their talents to help their neighbors. He must try to help her, to counsel her, despite his own despair. "We can try to pray. Hope for strength and insight, and hope that evil will be overcome."

"Doesn't that make God too small? Overcoming evil, as though he's responsible only for the good? I think God is bigger and wilder than that. My God is the god of joy and also of horror. My God is the god of pain and also of bliss."

"So is mine," said Justin stoutly.

"My God is mad. Insane."

He laughed uneasily. "Guess I can't go that far."

"Maybe you can. Have some wine."

He hesitated, then accepted the flask and sipped. "Thanks. Not insane, Nysa. Beyond our comprehension, yes."

She took back the little bottle. "Wine. The blood of Christ, right, Justin? Maybe you're right—your God is a god of horror too. Crucifixions, crowns of thorns, agonizing death, abandonment, despair."

"To redeem our souls!" Justin cried. "That's what's important. There's a purpose, a meaning!"

"And Kenny? And Johnny? And—other children who suffer or die?" There was a sob in her voice. "What's the meaning there?"

He shook his head. "Nysa, I can't tell you. Luther spoke of the masks of God, God working through imperfect people like you and me, or even through things terrible and incomprehensible on the surface but used by God to work out His purposes in history."

"Masks of God." She nodded. "I like that, Justin. God behind things, wearing horrible masks sometimes. Except . . ."

"Except what?"

"You see, Justin, my God *is* the mask. Horror, joy, despair, delight—there's nothing behind it. That's it."

"No, Nysa." No wonder she was so despairing, so tempted by the killing river. "We must trust that there is meaning. We must hope."

Her smile was full of pity. "Sweet Justin! You know so little of pain. I want to take your soul and shake it hard before I give it back to you."

She didn't understand. "I know pain, Nysa! Losing Kenny—losing Johnny—a few years ago, losing my father—"

"My father is dead now too. Another man of God, Justin.

He used to preach from Romans, 'God did not spare his own Son but gave him up for us all.' I can never forgive him for that. His own son!"

"It was to redeem us all from our sin and guilt."

For a moment they walked in silence. The river's roar was nearer now. She said, "Children live in promise, and they die. Lovers meet and cannot join in love." She touched his arm, a scorching touch. "Men of God cradle our sore souls and send us to bleed in their causes. My God rules it all, Justin. My God is mad."

"God cares, Nysa! He cares for Kenny and Johnny, for you, for all of us! God is fully in every grain of sand, yet the whole universe can't comprehend Him. He's in everything finite, yet transcends everything. He's fully human, yet fully divine."

She stopped, turning toward him. "Well, then, he's just like my God, isn't he? He's mad too."

His hands were fists in the pockets of his khakis. "There's good in the world, too, Nysa. That's God. Flowers, children, love—"

"Love. That's right, Justin, love. And lust, is that good?" She stepped close to him, her mournful blue eyes looking into his, her soft lips so close. "Suppose you give me pleasure, Justin. Is that God? Or evil? Or a mask?"

"I don't know." He bent toward her lips, a man ensnared. But her finger stopped his mouth. "No, Justin, you can't."

"But Nysa—don't you want it too?"

"Oh, God, yes, of course I do! But it's impossible—you can't give me pleasure, not sexual pleasure. And yet"—she stepped back a few inches—"and yet the mad God maddens us with lust."

Suddenly, vividly, Justin glimpsed his own stained and shaken soul and made his choice. He turned in horror and ran like a madman.

It was evening, way after milking time. Melissa's feet were sore and wet in soggy sneakers, her arms and legs scratched by thorns and bitten by mosquitoes, and she was still trudging beside the broad, brown, endless river under a gloomy sky. It was the right river. She'd glimpsed a highway sign as she made her way under one of the bridges: "East Fork, White River." But she didn't recognize the town names on the other signs, and she wasn't even sure she should be walking downstream instead of upstream.

She'd seen cows occasionally, but they'd always been huge black-and-white holsteins, not the small, tough, red-and-white cattle of the historic project.

The river on her right kept swinging from one side of the valley to the other. It was turning again now, flowing north to the next bend. The skimpy riverside trail left the steep hillside and widened a little as the river meandered out across the flat bottomland. Branches and stickers still lashed at her, but the trail was muddy now, not so rocky. Up ahead the river had reached the north edge of the valley and was slowly turning west again. On Melissa's left the woods were thinning out, and she could glimpse pastureland through the trees.

And what was that noise? A cow? She turned toward it, climbing carefully through the barbed wire only to be jabbed by a wild rose on the other side. But her heart bounced up when she saw the reddish-brindle color of the cow. "Daisy, old girl, how are you?" she crooned. "Where's Florida?"

Daisy's big eyes regarded Melissa and she chewed rhythmically, as though considering the question. Still murmuring, Melissa came closer and rubbed her forehead. She and Daisy were in the woods on the eastern edge of the Brewster place, she saw, and the cows were scattered across the pasture. She didn't see Florida, but with dusk approaching it was hard to see far in the riverside woods. She said goodbye to Daisy and worked her way cautiously through the underbrush.

Her peripheral vision caught a shape, a tiny movement, and she turned to look, but there was nothing there but nodding leaves and branches.

She moved on, skin prickling, like that day in the barn.

Kenny had said she was paranoid.

A few yards farther on she found Florida under a big maple, chewing her cud methodically, swishing her tail at a fly, and looking at Melissa with soft, wise eyes. "Florida!" Melissa made herself slow down and speak quietly so as not to spook the animal. "I've got so much to tell you, old girl!" She reached the cow and hugged her around the neck, and suddenly tears gushed. Kenny! Kenny! She buried her face in the warm, hairy neck and sobbed.

A figure was quietly climbing the riverbank toward them. Florida swiveled her ears but went on chewing.

39

MARTY SLUMPED ON BUZZ SHELDRAKE'S LEATHER sofa, watching the dark clouds roll by outside. The sun would set in another hour. Her mood was darkening too. At Adams's call she'd hurried back on duty, fueled by the adrenaline rush that Melissa's disappearance brought on, only to be posted here to wait in boredom while others did the work. The state evidence technicians had looked around outside first, and now were bustling about in the back bedroom, muttering things to each other, occasionally guffawing. There was a woman on their team, but even so the guys treated Marty with about the same respect they'd show a school crossing guard. "We'll be out of here in a jiffy, miss. Just go have a seat, now," the fat guy had said when she hovered eagerly in the hall, hoping to hear about what they uncovered.

Nan Sheldrake, after telling the sheriff that none of her neighbors had seen Melissa but several had spotted a beat-up brown van with Kentucky plates, had brought Marty the mug of coffee that she clutched now. Then Nan had fixed dinner for Buzz and Bob Rueger, and was now cleaning up the kitchen while the two men made phone calls from

Buzz's home office. Rueger was trying to reach the governor. Fat lot of good the governor could do, Marty thought.

Fat lot of good she could do either, stuck here sipping her coffee and brooding. There were so many problems, maybe connected to the murders, maybe not. Where was Carl Donato? Their Kokomo lead had fizzled out. Where was Vicki Strand? Where was Nysa? Who had beat up Professor Brewster, and why wouldn't he tell them what he knew? And the one that hit closest to home: Where was Melissa? Melissa's disappearance stirred up Marty's worries about Chrissie. Shoot, she missed her daughter. At dead-end times like this, when the job she usually loved was frustrating, she kept herself going by reminding herself that she was at least taking care of the family. But the family was disintegrating—Brad suddenly sober and responsible, but making new friends, such as Tiffany. Settling down, claiming he was making a home for Chrissie and her, but too far away. Calling her his princess, courting her, courting his daughter—and Chrissie so very vulnerable to her charming dad ...

Marty's throat was tight. She hadn't admitted it to herself before, but she was scared. Because of Tiffany? Yes, but even more because Brad could so easily take Chrissie away from her. Oh, she could hire a lawyer, fight it in court, but the legalities weren't really the problem. Chrissie was the problem. Marty remembered herself at ten, charmed and delighted by her own lovable, boisterous dad. Her mother seemed a grim and weary background figure, always nipping their adventurous plans in the bud. If she'd had to choose, at age ten, she would have gone for the adventure and romance that her father represented. Why wouldn't Chrissie do the same?

She'd vowed it would be different for her daughter. But maybe it always came out the same.

Quit feeling sorry for yourself, Hopkins. You're on the job.

Yeah, some job. Collecting overtime for cooling your heels. Cheating the taxpayers. Marty stared out at the dusk and tried to imagine herself as Brad's princess in Tennessee.

Nan Sheldrake came in with the coffeepot. "You ready for some more?"

"Thanks. Just warm this up."

Nan poured her some and went to join her husband and Bob Rueger in the den.

After a few minutes the technicians came out and Marty jumped to her feet. The fat, grizzled man smiled at her. "Chapman," said his nameplate. "Well, you can tell your boss we're all done."

"Sir, did you get the elimination prints from the Sheldrakes?"

Chapman's smile disappeared, but he snapped his fingers and one of the men hurried into the den. Chapman led the rest out to the cars. Marty followed and asked, "Anything we should be on the lookout for, sir?"

"Your boss can call me. Chapman," he said, as though she couldn't read.

Marty felt her mouth tighten, and thought she caught a glimmer of sympathy from the dark-eyed woman technician. C. Hardy. The fingerprint man came out, and as they loaded their gear Marty touched Hardy's sleeve. "Please. A girl is missing," she said quietly.

Hardy glanced at Chapman's broad back and murmured, "No blood. Couple of sticky Dalmanes under the bed. Prints and hair have to be tested."

"I owe you," said Marty, stepping back as Chapman turned to frown at them. Hardy jumped into the van and they rumbled away.

Marty radioed the sheriff. "They're gone, sir."

"What'd they find?"

She couldn't tell him on the radio—might be overheard and get Hardy into trouble. "Um. Well, sir, they said you should call."

There was a brief pause. "Ten-four," said Coach.

Five minutes later his cruiser pulled up. Marty met him at the door. "Chapman, right?" he said.

"Yes sir."

"I'll phone. What'd you hear?"

"No blood, other stuff has to be tested. Two sticky tranquilizers under the bed."

The sheriff looked at her a moment. "Shit. So she may not be doped up. We better widen the circle."

"Yes sir. And it's a long shot, but I've been thinking where she might go if she wasn't sleepy. I figure either the airport to meet her dad, or else back to the camp."

"I sent Mason to the Brewsters', thinking she might have called someone to pick her up. Nobody's seen her or heard from her. And no one saw her walking that direction, or trying to hitch a ride."

"You've checked the creek down the street here?"

"Yeah, a mess of footprints there, could be the right size. Mason brought back another pair of her sneakers from the Brewsters', so we know that much. But the prints lead back up the bank too. Still . . ." The sheriff thought a moment. "You're right—that camp is in the center of this mess. Go give it a look, Hopkins. I'll send Sims to the airport." He sighed. "Me, I gotta talk to Chapman and maybe even the goddamn governor."

Tor was filled with excitement. It was almost time to come out of hiding. Almost, but not quite. He maneuvered the boat through the angry river. Melissa said, "I don't like this!" and peered over the side.

He said, "Be careful, Melissa. Don't fall in. Only a real strong swimmer could get out of this current."

She held still then, frowning. He kept the boat far out until he'd passed the town, then drove in hard to the south shore. Even so the current was so strong that he almost overshot the mouth of the creek.

When he reached his destination he helped her from the boat. She said, "Really, I've got to get back."

"It's only a few more steps."

He led her through the hidden door into the cool interior and lit a lantern. She looked around at the ancient shelves, the stone slab floor, the little spring burbling at the end of the room, and walked over to inspect the photograph he'd cut from a magazine and pinned to the edge of a shelf, a great red longhorn bull. "Nice picture," she said.

He'd known she would like it. She'd like him too, when he came out of hiding.

If she didn't . . .

But she would.

40

AT THE BREWSTER FARM, KAREN ANSWERED THE door, accompanied by a fidgety JayJay. "Hi," she whispered. "They're praying."

"Hi, guy," said Marty, ruffling JayJay's hair and glancing into the living room. Reverend Jeffries, looking miserable, was murmuring something to four young people and his wife.

"I'm watching the kid while they pray," Karen explained on the way to the kitchen. She was calmer than last time, but her lean, mobile face was sad. "Wish I could pray. Those boys killed, Drew hurt and depressed, and it may be all up with our farm. Bob Rueger won't hang around if his daughter's kidnapped."

"You know for sure she's been kidnapped?"

"That's what Buzz Sheldrake told Drew."

Marty frowned. "I'd like to talk to Drew."

"You mean she wasn't kidnapped?" Dread and hope chased each other across Karen's face. "But that might be worse. What—"

"We don't know for sure. You haven't seen Melissa, then?"

"No. But I haven't been out of the house much. Justin took a walk before dinner. You could ask him."

"Have you seen the Strand sisters?"

"No. But when I went out to milk the cows they'd been milked already. So Vicki's around."

Marty was relieved. Sheriff Cochran had called Grady Sims off his search for Vicki so he could help hunt for Melissa, and Marty had been worried about the tall woman. "Let me talk to Drew."

The professor was in his big four-poster bed, a stack of papers on a bed tray before him. "I had my secretary ask my students for reports on this week's poems." Drew looked unexpectedly despondent. "They don't understand. Some come right out and say it's not relevant to their future. I always believed that poetry was worthwhile for anyone, but maybe I should rethink my position. What can Coleridge or Eliot say to people working eighty-hour weeks as accountants or salesmen?"

Or as cops, Marty thought. She said, "Yes sir. Your wife said you thought Melissa Rueger had been kidnapped."

"That's what Buzz Sheldrake said on the phone."

Marty asked, "So you don't have any other information that she was kidnapped?"

"You mean she wasn't?"

"No sir, I'm just trying to collect evidence. You've got a pretty good view from your window here." She gazed out across the darkening pasture. The river gleamed like dull silver at the end of the vista. "Have you seen anyone pass by?"

"Not many. Two kids walking toward town, later a fisherman. Couple of people in a boat too, over toward the other side."

"That's a bad idea, with the river so high."

"Yeah, I agree. Couldn't see who they were. Guy and his girlfriend, maybe."

"Did you see the Strand sisters?"

"No, but Karen says Vicki milked the cows tonight, so she's around."

"Okay, thanks. Let us know right away if you see anything of Melissa or the Strands."

The low drone of Reverend Jeffries's voice had stopped.

She poked her head into the living room. "Has anyone seen or heard from Melissa?" They all shook their heads. "Reverend Jeffries, could I talk to you alone?"

"Sure." He joined Marty in the kitchen.

"Karen said you took a walk before dinner."

"Yes," he said, so guardedly that Marty went on alert.

"Did you see Melissa Rueger?"

"No. Deputy Mason asked that too. We were praying for her."

"Did you see any sign of her at all?"

"No." He looked worried, but there was a tinge of relief too.

Marty changed directions. "Did you see anyone else?"

"A few people when I went past town. I was on the river path." He looked away and rubbed the back of his neck. Marty waited, knowing there was more. "And I, uh, saw Nysa Strand for a couple of minutes."

This was it. He was worried about Nysa, for some reason. "What did Nysa have to say?"

He balled his fists and stuck them in his pockets. "She was—very upset, I think. We talked about God and evil."

"Did she know where Melissa was?"

"Melissa?" His thoughts had clearly been elsewhere. "No. That is, I didn't ask her. I didn't even hear Melissa was missing till I came back for dinner."

"Did Nysa tell you anything more about Kenny's death, or Johnny's?"

"No clues, if that's what you mean. It was more a theological discussion, about why terrible things happen."

Marty wouldn't mind knowing why terrible things happened, but right now her job was to find Melissa, and Jeffries didn't seem to know anything about that. She asked, "Where did you see Nysa Strand?"

"On the bank of that creek that runs through her property."

"Near the river?"

"Farther upstream, about where the maze is."

"Sir, why were you walking up that creek?"

260

He rubbed his neck again. "The river had—bad memories. I was going to come back by the highway."

"What time did you see her?"

He shrugged. "Five-thirty or six. Before dinner."

"Did she say what she was doing there?"

"No. I got the impression that she was . . . thinking. Reflecting."

"Very upset, you said. Why did you think that?"

"She was crying. And saying strange things."

"What kind of strange things?"

He hesitated. "Saying God is mad."

Marty heard stranger things than that from drunks every Saturday night, but maybe preachers weren't used to it. "Is that all that worries you, Reverend Jeffries?"

He looked at her in anguish. "I don't know why she's so unhappy!"

"I see," said Marty, and suddenly she did see, the little tragedy of a good man, husband, father, clergyman, besotted with a woman not his wife. She wondered what Nysa's feelings were as she headed out into the dusk to look for Melissa.

Down by the river she saw no footprints. The heavy cloud layer and the sinking sun made the evening gloomy. In the east it was nearly black already. She walked that direction for a few minutes, squinting at the footpath. In low places the river washed over it. The water had a deep-throated roar as it rushed logs and other objects downstream, slamming them into standing trees or newly submerged rocks. No wonder the old bridge at Collier had given out. Some of those wooden beams sliding by probably came from it.

The cows were grazing placidly in a loose collection near the eastern woods. Melissa loved animals, and had responsibility for a couple of them. She would have been here, like Vicki, if she could, Marty thought. The cows watched Marty with gentle, interested eyes and chewed thoughtfully, but offered no clues.

She was using her flashlight now. On the dark shore under some foliage she found a couple of footprints and some skid marks. A boat? With the river so high? But Drew had seen a boat in the last half hour. She squatted to shine her light on the mud. The prints seemed to belong to two people, one much larger than the other. Marty ran upstream, keeping to the grass and woods, and soon spotted a few more of the smaller prints. Melissa's? Had she come in a boat, or gone in a boat? Marty called "Melissa!" a few times. A couple of curious cows strolled closer, but no one answered.

She thought a moment. Maybe Melissa wanted to see where Kenny had died. She cut across the farm to the other side of the loop in the river and again followed the river path, this time south toward New Concord. The police tape was still up where Kenny had been found. No footprints here.

She went back to the Brewster farmhouse. It was full night now. She phoned the Strand house, but no one answered.

What do you do when you come up zero, Hopkins? You keep on trying. She drove to New Concord, crossing the intersections with East and Central Streets. West Street crossed the highway just before the tiny bridge over the creek that ran through the Strand place. Not a chance in the world that Nysa would still be there, but hey, what else was there to do? She turned down West Street and parked by the labyrinth, then radioed Foley.

"Hi, babe."

"I'm in New Concord. West Street by the maze, across from the appliance store. I saw some footprints on the riverbank that could be Melissa's."

"Could be. You're not sure?"

"I'm looking into it. I'm going over to the Strand farm on foot and down the creek to the river. Get me some backup, okay?"

"Everybody's busy, babe, hunting for that rich guy's kid."

"So'm I. Well, send someone as soon as you can."

"They'll come when I tell them you want somebody to watch your backside."

Marty keyed off without answering. She checked her flashlight, followed the weedy path beside the labyrinth that led from West Street to the Strand property, and started down the little tree-lined creek.

"Yes, Governor. We're covering all the bases," Wes said.

"You need more manpower?" said the telephone.

"Well, sir, we're already getting good cooperation. The state crime scene technicians have already been here, and the state police are working on the vehicles that were seen in the neighborhood at the time of the disappearance. My deputies are focusing on the local scene."

"Look, Cochran, this is a major situation. And Bobby Rueger's a good man. I went to high school with him, you know."

"Yes sir," Wes said mildly. The son of a Helton Gas driver gets killed, the father goes missing, and nobody pays attention. But the daughter of the governor's high school buddy disappears and suddenly they're willing to call in the National Guard. "One thing would be a big help, sir," Wes added. "Could I suggest that we hold off the media announcements for now? This is still very open-ended. We don't want a lot of reporters jeopardizing the investigation. Tipping off the criminals and so forth."

"All right," the governor said. "I'll call the state police and see if they need any help tracking down the escape car. Check back in a couple of hours, okay?"

"Yes sir."

Wes hung up and turned to Bob Rueger. "The governor's doing all he can," he reported. "He'll keep the media out of it and make sure we get assistance tracking down the vehicles."

They were sitting in Buzz Sheldrake's wood-paneled den. Buzz muttered, "I don't know how you've left this guy loose so long! What kind of law enforcement do we have in this county?"

Bob Rueger, brooding in one of the black leather library chairs, suddenly stood up. "Sheriff, I need to stretch my legs. Will you walk with me?"

"Sure thing." Wes knew what the guy must be feeling. And it'd be easier to talk outdoors.

Buzz Sheldrake stood up too, but Rueger said, "Buzz, would you stay here to catch the phone calls? If somebody wants ransom I want to be sure the message gets through."

Buzz sat down again. "Yes, of course."

Out in the steamy night, Bob Rueger loosened his tie and took off his lightweight summer jacket. He slung it over his shoulder and asked, "Seriously, Sheriff, what do you think?"

"Seriously, it looks open-ended to me, just like I told the governor. Maybe we'll get a ransom call. Maybe we'll find out she just got confused and ran away. Maybe we'll find her in that brown van or that blue pickup people saw. Maybe she hitched a ride out to the airport or back to camp. We're checking it all."

They were walking slowly down the sloping street. Rueger said, "My secretary tells me you lost a son, Cochran."

"Yes sir."

"He was seventeen."

"Yes sir."

"All right." He took a few more steps. "Look, I know I didn't have to call the governor. It was just—I couldn't think of what to do."

"Yes sir."

"I wanted to do something. Anything."

They'd walked as far as the little cement bridge, and leaned side by side on the guardrail to look down at the creek. The gurgling water glinted in the streetlight. Overhead the clouds had thinned a little, and a hazy, circular glow showed that a moon lurked somewhere above. Wes cleared his throat. "One thing you can do, sir."

"Yeah?"

"I don't mean to be nosy, and I know it probably has nothing to do with this. But it would help if I had the whole picture of what you're doing here."

"I explained that, didn't I? A small development in connection with a historic farm and village. Like a small New Harmony. Kind of a tip of the hat to my roots."

"Yes sir. So you bought property and arranged for the Brewsters to host the campers from your daughter's church school group. And you hired the Strand sisters to assist."

"I wanted the neighbors involved. I also set up accounts with local grocery stores and drugstores. Public relations."

"Yes sir. But despite your efforts to be neighborly, there's been opposition."

Rueger shrugged. "I've thought of that, of course. But every project a developer suggests will generate some opposition, at least until people see how it benefits the community."

"Yes sir. That's our reading too. We've heard grumbling from a few folks, but nothing extreme. Now, I know this probably isn't related, but you do own quite a bit of property in New Concord. Historic village, I know. And the main grumbler is Mr. Walters, and he also owns a lot of property—three of the four farms by the Eight-sixty bridge."

Rueger had become very still.

Wes went on, "Now, we know that Mr. Walters arranged some of your purchases for you. I mean, why not, he's in real estate."

"Why not."

"And if you look at Route Eight-sixty on the map, and think about Indianapolis and Evansville and all those interstates, and then you think about who the governor went to high school with, and you realize you've never seen any plans for the proposed historic village—"

"Well, that'll depend on the archeological results."

"Yes sir. But I have seen a plan in your office for a huge development called Riverside Mall."

Rueger sighed. "How many people have you told about this?"

"None outside the department, sir."

"You heard it from Walters?"

"No sir. Worked it out—a scrap here, a scrap there. Walters wasn't real happy when I asked him about it."

"I bet he wasn't. So how many people know?"

"I don't think he's spreading it around. I know I'm not. But you can see why I'm kind of puzzled about what you really want, and what Mr. Walters really wants."

Rueger gazed at the water. "I don't see how this could have anything to do with Melissa's disappearance."

"Like I say, it's probably not related. But it's confusing, what with you pushing for the historic project, and Walters pushing against it, and a giant mall being planned behind the scenes."

"Yeah." Rueger kicked at the bridge guardrail. "Okay. I was looking to invest in southern Indiana because I knew the governor liked the idea. And the name Rueger naturally caught my eye in a Nichols County brochure. It was a good area. But when I checked with Dub he said there were some artsy newcomers who'd fight a development. They were the kind who'd prefer a historic village, he said. So I said, why not? I'll cozy up to them, you lead the opposition. You win, of course, but by then I'll have the land."

"Well, sir, excuse me, but if someone found out you were just using them, wouldn't they get upset?"

"No, no, we'd have a historic component," Rueger protested. "Not a federal preservation district, but I want to leave a few old houses, and spread out restaurants and such along the riverfront. Keep it classy, so it's not like every other mall on the road."

Wes thought that still sounded like a lot of pavement. He said, "From the highway to the Brewster place is a lot of acres. Rockland Mall won't look like much next to this one."

"Oh, somebody will want those little places even if we move the main tenants to Riverside." He glanced sideways at Wes. "But how does this help with my daughter?"

"You haven't had any kind of falling-out with Walters?"

"Didn't think I'd had." He stared grimly at the water.

"What is it, sir?"

"Nothing. He's got nothing to gain from crossing me." Rueger stepped back from the guardrail and faced Wes. "I don't think we've gained any ground."

"Well, sir, I know it's a stretch, but let's suppose somebody else knows you want to develop a regional mall, and they want to stop it. They may think these problems will drive you away. Or let's suppose somebody wants the mall but thinks you favor the historic project. Again, they could be trying to drive you away. Or let's suppose somebody who likes the historic farm project found out that you were really opposed to it. They could be real upset."

"Or they could want my money. Ransom still seems the most likely."

"Yes sir. That's the most rational possibility."

"Rational." Rueger looked down at his shoes, then kicked the guardrail, jaw clenched. In a moment he said, without looking at Wes, "She would've called by now if she was all right."

"Kids don't always think about how much we worry."

"Yeah. Look, get back to work, Sheriff."

"Thank you, sir." He started back to his cruiser without adding, I've been working.

41

MARTY HADN'T GONE VERY FAR ALONG THE CREEK behind the labyrinth when her flashlight picked out a bump in the mud. She squatted to look at it, but it was only a cow hoofprint. Several hoofprints. Strange that a cow would be taking a drink in these woods, squeezed between the little creek and the town. Across the creek here were more woods, and beyond them . . . Marty wasn't sure how far from the highway she was, but she might well be beyond the Strand house and yard by now. So maybe this cow had wandered across the creek somehow from a pasture on the Strand farm. Or had come up from farther downstream, where the creek bent away from the town in its progress toward the river.

A small streamlet gushed into the creek just ahead, one of the many natural springs that formed part of the drainage in limestone country. Above it was an indentation in the bank, probably worn away by the same streamlet.

A flashlight beam hit Marty full in the face, blinding her.

Marty dropped into a crouch and flipped her own light to her left hand. She aimed it just above the other beam while she fumbled out her gun with her right. Bad show, Hopkins, she scolded herself. You could be dead meat.

But she recognized the other face even as she heard the gentle voice. "Deputy Hopkins! I'm sorry, I didn't know it was you!" Nysa switched off her flashlight.

Marty took a deep breath and holstered her gun. "Hi. I'm glad to see you. Why are you out here tonight?"

"I was walking down to the river and saw your light over here, so I checked."

Still shaken, Marty demanded, "Why are you going to the river at this hour?"

"Sometimes when I'm sad it makes me feel better. 'Five miles meandering with a mazy motion, through wood and dale the sacred river ran. . . .' It's so eternal. Do you know what I mean?"

"Yeah. I remember sitting by the river when I was a kid and my dad—" She'd been as scared back then as she'd been a minute ago, whenever her dad came home boisterously drunk. Usually her mother got him calmed down, but every now and then he'd start throwing the furniture around. If it was daytime Marty would slip out on her bicycle to a friend's house or to a quiet place where she could think. A couple of times she'd gone as far as the White River, riding down the public access ramp near Dunning to sit on a stone and watch the river slide by. It was a solace.

"Did your father beat you too?" Nysa asked softly.

"Not often. But he totaled a few chairs." They'd started walking slowly along the creek bank toward the river. Marty turned the conversation back to the investigation. "What I was wondering about, Reverend Jeffries said you were feeling very sad and upset."

"Dear Justin! He doesn't know much about sorrows. About the dark side of the divine."

"Miz Strand, have you, um, been having an affair with Reverend Jeffries?"

"An affair? Oh, no. Unless you count affairs of the soul."

"He seems real unhappy about it. Because it's not physical?"

"No. It'll never be physical. He's unhappy because he wants it and thinks he shouldn't. He's struggling against himself. Working through the labyrinth of his own soul."

"Ma'am, I'm sorry, but hormones are pretty strong. I don't run into many affairs of the soul that don't turn physical pretty soon."

"This one won't. It's more complicated than you know."

Marty took a different tack. "He said you thought God was evil."

"Not exactly. It's just the old, old questions. If God is all-powerful, and allows evil to happen, how can he be all-good? If God is all-good, and evil happens even so, how can he be all-powerful? If God is all-good and all-powerful, then how can evil be evil?"

That didn't sound like a very romantic conversation to Marty. "Well, my question is really what made you talk about that stuff. Had you learned something new about the man who wears horns?"

"No. Nothing new."

"Why do you defend him?"

"Don't you think that all God's creatures deserve love?"

"Sure. But if they break the law I'd rather have them deserve love in jail. I mean, think of those murdered boys! Shoot, that even makes me sympathize with old Father Rueger's bloody justice a little bit, when I think . . ." Marty trailed off, because Nysa had breathed in sharply and her steps had slowed. "What is it?"

Nysa asked, "You know the history of New Concord?"

"I read your booklet." Marty stopped too and shone her light at some foliage so that Nysa's face was illuminated in the bounce light. What was so important about that little pamphlet? Marty said slowly, "Rueger believed in eye-for-an-eye justice, didn't he?"

"Partly. Mostly he believed in avoiding sin." Nysa wiped at her cheek.

"And you told me . . . " Marty groped through her memory. *Did your father beat you too?* she'd just asked. "You said your father admired him very much."

"Yes."

"And he beat you. Right?"

"Yes." Nysa was sobbing now.

Little pieces were sliding together in Marty's mind. "Your father found out about Thom, you said, and punished you. He must have been furious."

Tears glistened on Nysa's face as she nodded.

"He didn't—oh, God, Nysa, what you did was a sin in his eyes! Father Rueger used lye—"

" 'If thy right eye offend thee, pluck it out!' " said Nysa bitterly. "Or at least turn it into a mass of scar tissue."

"You were his daughter! You were only fifteen!"

"He was a monster, all right. But he believed he was doing God's work."

Marty threw her arms around Nysa. "My God, I can't— how cruel! My God, Nysa!"

The other woman sobbed on her shoulder for a moment. Marty stroked her back, horrified at Nysa's loss. No sex, no marriage, no children ... But her cop side was still awake, trying to reconcile this ghastly new history with the beautiful sad musician sobbing in her arms. She asked gently, "What did you do next?"

"I told you: I ran away to Thom, who didn't want me. He left me with a ticket home, but I couldn't go back to my father."

"Good! Good!"

"I traded it for a ticket to Indianapolis. I didn't know anything except church music, so I went to a church. I met a wonderful woman there. She helped me; I made up a background story, and she eventually helped me apply to music school. And after a few years I heard that my father was dead. I used the inheritance to buy this farm and took care of my mother until she died."

"You wanted a connection to this horrible past?"

Nysa nodded slowly. "I needed—an explanation. A meaning. When the man who should nurture and care for you turns against your body like that, you can run away, you can hate, you can rage. But you want there to be a meaning. And once he was dead I could begin to understand. My father was abused, and his father, and probably Father Rueger, and on into the past. Each one reaching through children's pain to hurt the future. Dying but rising again. Like God. When I learned about Father Rueger I saw that my father did love me in a monstrous way."

Monstrous, yes. "So Reverend Jeffries . . . does he know?"

"Not the details. I told him it was impossible, that's all." Nysa stepped back, but her hand still rested on Marty's arm. "Maybe you fault me for talking to him at all. And at first, yes, maybe I wanted him to suffer because he's a minister too. But it was good to talk with him about the depths of God. And also—well, as you say, hormones are pretty strong, and I've got plenty of them. Justin is an attractive man, after all, and reminds me of what I knew with Thom."

"Yeah. Yeah, I understand." No children, no sexual pleasure, only inconsolable desire. And anger. What a hellish life that minister had left his daughter!

"But you need more than bitterness and rage." Nysa started slowly downstream again. "For me, music is a total delight. The joyful side of divinity. I feel blessed. It gives me such a feeling of wholeness—no, it's beyond wholeness. It's like being in touch with divinity. It's like a marriage, a marriage to a god."

Wholeness. Yes, Nysa had not been defeated. "I'm glad," Marty said. "I was wondering about—what's that?"

Her flashlight had caught a bent board ahead, painted a glossy brown. A small boat, she saw, with an outboard motor. It had been pulled into the creekside bushes.

Nysa exhaled in a little moan.

Marty ran the flashlight beam around the boat and nearby ground. It was stony here, and except for some broken twigs there was little she could see. "Is this your boat?" she asked.

"Yes."

"Yours and Vicki's?"

"Yes."

"Is Vicki here? Nearby?"

"Maybe. Probably."

"And that man with the horns?"

Nysa was sobbing. "Please, I can't betray him again!"

"You can't—" Marty turned the light on Nysa's tear-streaked face. "Because your sister's in love with him? Or because—wait, you said—didn't you say you had a brother too? A lost brother?"

"He finally ran away too."

"Your father drove him out?"

"No. My father loved him, but he got in bad trouble with a boy at school and ran away. But please, you have family. Please try to understand."

"Police trouble?"

Nysa looked down at the rocky ground. "Yes."

"Rape? Robbery?" Marty demanded, a terrible suspicion growing in her mind. When Nysa didn't answer, she said, "Did your brother kill somebody?"

Nysa rubbed her cheek.

"Did he go to jail? To an institution?"

"No. He escaped the police. He went into hiding."

"And now he's hiding on this riverbank, isn't he? And you and your sister protect him. Nysa, for God's sake, he probably killed those boys!"

"No! He's gentle, he's good!" There was fear in Nysa's voice. "Please, please understand! Back then it wasn't his fault, it was the other boy! And I can help him! When we get enough money I'll take him to a doctor— He hates doctors, but I've been trying to get together enough money for a really good one."

"Nysa." Marty picked up the other woman's hand. "Please, listen. I think you're right about the doctor. I know you want to help your brother. I want to help your brother too. But first we have to find him. Stop him. Then help him. Do you understand?"

Nysa drew a deep breath. "The trouble was my fault at the beginning. And it was so hard to find him! I spent all my money on detectives. They found him, finally, in Chicago two years ago. Working part-time at the Lincoln Park Zoo, sleeping in the park. I brought him here. He's happy here. And he's so gentle! He couldn't have done those things!" She spoke intensely—too intensely, Marty thought, as though she were trying to convince herself too.

Marty looked around at the dark foliage. "Do you know where he is now?"

"No." It sounded like a sob.

"But you can guess."

"I don't bother him. He can talk to me whenever he wants."

"We have to find him!"

"Please. My brother couldn't have done those things!"

"Maybe not. Maybe you're right, your brother didn't do it. But he may have evidence. We've got to stop the killer, Nysa."

"Yes, but—I can't betray him. Please."

"Tell me where he is, Nysa."

"I can't."

Marty thought about taking her in, but that would take too long. She was close now, she could feel it, too close to leave the hunt. Vicki and her brother had been in that boat, the couple Drew Brewster had seen, and she knew in her bones they weren't far away now. She needed backup, but if Foley did his job she'd have some soon. She said, "Okay, look, I'm not finished with this talk. I want you to think real hard about how you can help. And I want you here, near the footbridge, when I come back. Do you understand, Miz Strand? If you're not here, or if you interfere in any way, I'll have to take you in. I mean, I know you've had terrible things happen. But we can help your brother better together. That's part of my job too. Do you understand?"

Nysa bowed her blond head. "Yes."

"The killings have to stop."

"Yes. Of course."

"Go on, now." She waved the weeping Nysa toward the footbridge ahead. Marty kept the flashlight on her until the creek turned and bushes hid her from sight. She'd never seen anyone look so downhearted. Marty felt like crying for her too.

42

NO, NO, NO! MELISSA HURLED HERSELF THROUGH the woods. She hadn't seen what she'd just seen, no! She had to get back to—

She slammed into a tree trunk. The physical pain snapped her mind back into action. She could hear his footsteps behind her, so he could hear her too. But she couldn't be silent in the dark. She kept crashing into bushes and trees. Wait! There was faint moonlight to her right up there. He'd fear the light.

He said he just wanted to talk. But she couldn't, she couldn't!

She swarmed up the bank. A hedge. Push through it— no, there was chicken wire running behind the leaves. Over it, then. She jumped and scrambled and fell to the other side.

Another hedge! Melissa ran along the narrow path between them. It turned, led back, turned again.

She could hear his steps. Get out of here! She threw herself over the second hedge, only to find herself on another path between hedges. Panicking, she scrambled over the third.

Her foot caught on a vine and she crashed down. Fiery pain shot up her leg.

Melissa sucked in her breath to keep from crying out. When she tested the leg she almost blacked out from pain.

The footsteps still came. She lay down and rolled under the hedge, tight against the chicken wire, and tried not to breathe.

JayJay had heard about Tommy Tugboat and turned out the bedside lamp all by himself and said his prayers. Now

274

he reached up sleepily to his father. Justin hugged the thin, vibrant child's body close to him. His son, his joy.

God had not spared his own Son.

What unthinkably enormous love for humanity that implied.

Holding the boy, Justin felt a sort of peace. He was still full of grief for Kenny, for Johnny, for his impossible love, and yet strength was seeping in somehow. God loved him. God cared.

They'd set up JayJay's camp cot next to the double bed in one of the Brewsters' spare rooms. Gently, Justin let his sleepy son lie down again and kissed his forehead.

Kissed it.

If he'd kissed Nysa, he couldn't kiss JayJay now, he realized.

The ghastly kiss of life he'd attempted on Kenny haunted him. But it hadn't hurt him, and in fact had almost ennobled him. Kissing Nysa, though, would have been a betrayal not only of Bonnie, but of all his deepest commitments, of his soul. That must be why she'd told him of the mad God, he realized. She'd said, *I want to take your soul and shake it hard before I give it back to you.*

He was filled with gratitude. She'd made him acknowledge the fact of his—of their—desire, and made him acknowledge its impossibility. She'd taken him to the depths of temptation and despair and then nudged him to choose God.

It was over. He'd learned what God had wanted him to learn, and God's strength was returning now. And yet he felt uneasy. Why?

Because she didn't know why he'd run from her. He'd been so horrified at what he'd almost done, he'd left her behind without explanation.

Justin realized that there was one more step to take before this chapter of his life was done. He must apologize, and thank her. It was the least he could do.

He closed the bedroom door gently and found Bonnie in the kitchen talking to Karen Brewster. "I'll be back in a few minutes," he told them, picking up a flashlight by the kitchen door and heading out into the night.

Marty walked upstream toward the labyrinth along the bank of the little creek, back toward her cruiser. She'd better take a minute to radio in the new information that Nysa had just given her about her brother. Her heart ached for Nysa and Vicki, trying to rescue their brother even though he'd been involved in that long-ago homicide and, she feared, the murder of Johnny and Kenny. He had to be stopped. But Marty's heart wept for them all. What horrors their childhood had held! She thought about the violent man she'd had to kill last year, what he'd had to bear as a child. She thought about what the Seifert boys were going through right now. Nysa was right: The brutality and violence went back through generations, reaching through children's pain to hurt the future. What a ghastly sort of immortality that was, each horror explained by the one before.

Explained, but not excused. Because most hurt children overcame it. Nysa was not brutal. She seemed to believe that her father, like Father Rueger, had in his twisted way wanted the best for his children. She'd gone on to find a reason for life and joy in her music. It was like a marriage to divinity, she'd said, bringing a feeling of wholeness, and beyond wholeness. Marty understood what she meant. Hugging her daughter, or now and then in Brad's arms, she'd felt it too—though so often she felt fragmented and guilty when he was around, never able to do enough to fix his problems. But most often she felt that special wholeness when she was using her body and mind to the fullest—like those happy days in peewee basketball, when everything seemed possible. Or on the job, maybe helping a battered woman, or figuring out that it was the miserable Seifert boys who'd stolen the Dennis Rent-All tools, or a few minutes ago, when it hit her that the man she was hunting was Nysa's brother. A moment of insight like that brought her a fierce joy, even when what she grasped was horrible or tragic.

Something was tickling at her mind now as she climbed

the bank toward the labyrinth and her cruiser parked on the far side. Something about the creek bank. Below her, just above creek level, the streamlet tumbled from the indentation it had worn into the bank. The indentation ran back to a vertical, foliage-covered wall where the spring emerged. But there was something else about this place. Marty paused, frowning. What was it? Something about Nysa. She'd met Nysa here tonight.

And so had Justin, hours earlier.

Why would Nysa be here, twice, at exactly this point on the creek bank?

She'd seen that hoofprint the last time she was here. Not much else, because Nysa had flashed that light in her eyes and distracted her. But she'd had a chance to look around, hastily, and had seen nothing amiss.

Nysa's light had been off until she used it to dazzle Marty. Marty switched off hers.

The night was warm and humid, still overcast, but the clouds had thinned enough that the moon silvered a misty circle in the sky. Here near the top of the bank she could see a few lights in New Concord houses, far across the broad blackness of the labyrinth beyond these trees.

She couldn't hear much, because the creek gurgled noisily over the limestone below her, and cicadas sang in the background. She could barely hear the car whose lights moved along West Street on the far side of the labyrinth. But she heard—or thought she heard—a woman's voice, distant and muffled. In one of the houses on West Street? She couldn't make out the words, but there were pauses in the faint cadences she could hear. Maybe a phone conversation.

She looked down toward the creek, letting her eyes adjust to the darkness. There was something, maybe, a faint gleam of some kind in the bushes halfway down the bank. She squinted at it, pushed the nearest branches out of the way, and stepped closer. Yes—a faint glow. She held on to saplings and slid cautiously down the bank to where it leveled off in a small terrace. The creek ran below her, the vines of the labyrinth rustled above, and here at the middle level the spring emerged from a low, horizontal slit.

And so did a faint, wavering light.

As she stepped closer, a branch snapped and she froze, but the muffled voice continued. She hesitated, then switched on her light again, keeping it well away from the slit where the flickering light glowed, and directing it at the foliage beside it. Yes, behind the leaves was rough-cut stone, shaped by humans into a wall. The stone was covered with vines and weeds grew from the joints. About seven feet up, her light found a horizontal lintel stone, smoother than the others and featuring a flaming sun with a woman's figure inside. The New Concord woman clothed in the sun.

Below the carved lintel—yes, there was wood behind the draped vines. A door.

The light was seeping from under a door.

She could no longer hear the muffled voice.

Why a door in the bank? Then she remembered Nysa talking about the old springhouse near the labyrinth, where Father Rueger kept his milk cans. It hadn't been restored, she'd said. But there was a light.

That didn't mean Marty should go in now. She tried her portable radio, but down here in the creekbed so far from the station it didn't work. She'd have to go back to the cruiser if she wanted to call in. But Foley shouldn't have to be reminded. She'd wait. She climbed up the bank again to the point where she could see her cruiser far away on West Street. As soon as her backup arrived she'd signal them and go down. She thought about running over to West Street to tell them to hurry up, but that would risk losing track of whoever was down there behind the door.

She heard the voice again, though with difficulty. The rushing waters of spring and creek combined with the singing of the frogs and cicadas to blank out other noises. If she strained she could catch a faint murmur. It still sounded like a phone conversation, one-sided. But there couldn't be a phone in there, could there? Maybe the woman was speaking to herself.

Or maybe speaking to someone who wouldn't answer.

Maybe speaking to a man who'd been in hiding for too many years, a man who never spoke.

Maybe the woman was pleading for her life.

Where the hell was that backup?

Marty strained to hear what was going on.

Rats. It was impossible. She hesitated, then pulled out her handkerchief, tucked the corner into the band of her Stetson, and hung the hat on a tree. The guys should be able to see that from West Street when they pulled in next to her cruiser. Then she scrambled down the bank again to watch the door.

43

"DUB, IT'S TIME WE HAD A TALK. MAN TO MAN."

Dub Walters stood broad as a backhoe in his front door, a glass of Scotch in one beefy hand and the other on the doorknob. He was in a short-sleeved yellow business shirt with no tie, collar unbuttoned. The light from his living room hit his ear and jowl, shadowy with the beginnings of the stubble he'd shave off tomorrow morning.

"Is it about the Rueger girl?" Dub asked.

"Yeah."

"Come on in. I don't know a damn thing, but come on in." There was worry in his voice. He stepped back so Wes could enter, then closed the door and led the way past the living room and back into the kitchen. The room was done in honey-colored oak cabinets with green polka-dot curtains. The countertop was marbly white. Dub put down his Scotch and said, "You're on duty, I guess."

"Wouldn't mind a glass of water."

Dub got some ice and filled the glass from the tap. In the fluorescent light Wes could see the strain lines in his face.

"Here you are," Dub said. "Now, what's this about?"

"Thanks. Now, I know you would have told us anything about Melissa Rueger's disappearance that you knew."

"Damn right."

"But what I need now is some straight talk on how things are set up in this corner of the county. Hard for us to see what's gone wrong if we don't know what's normal."

"You know as much as anybody," Dub protested.

"Yeah, I know more than most," Wes admitted. "But there's things I'm not real clear about."

"Such as?"

"Okay. The Donato kid is from here."

"I don't know anything about him."

"His father agreed with you about the historic project being no good for the area."

"Jesus, that doesn't mean we're buddies! A drink in the same bar every now and then, that's all!"

"So you don't know anything about his disappearance either?"

"Nothing!"

"What about Professor Brewster getting beat up?"

There was a glint of satisfaction in Dub's eye, but he repeated, "Nothing."

"Okay." Wes sipped some water. He hadn't really expected Dub to admit to anything, but he decided to wait before telling him what he'd heard from Rueger. "Tell me about this historic New Concord thing."

"I knew those teenagers would be trouble!" Dub said.

"Yeah, you were right. But to help the Rueger girl we need facts. So tell me about this history project."

Dub shrugged. "Okay, I'll try, but you know as much as I do. Bunch of kids on a Bible work camp project. There's a minister and his family along to supervise. And some professor, I hear he's from Ball State, in charge of the historic stuff they dig up."

"Is Rueger paying him?"

"No. Expenses, maybe. And the prof gets free labor from the kids, and gets to write up the stuff for publication."

"Is Rueger paying the Brewsters?"

"Not much. Drew got some kind of a fee for organizing

the historic farm side of it, and they got something for leasing that pasture for the camp."

Wes nodded. "Who brought in the Strand sisters? They're getting paid."

Dub finished his Scotch. "Brewsters must have told Rueger about them. See, the church group needed a music teacher, and Nysa Strand knows all that local history. Rueger wanted both taught, so she looked like a bargain."

"But Rueger got a Ball State professor to work for free."

"Yeah, but Nysa's local, right? Rueger didn't want the project to look like a bunch of outsiders."

"Yeah, I can see that. And Rueger hired her sister too. Why not some other local?"

Dub put his empty glass carefully on the counter. "Nobody knows much about farming anymore. When Vicki came to live with Nysa, they went out and got a couple of those mutt cows they're so proud of, from the Lincoln Boyhood Home, I recollect. So when Rueger mentioned adding a Conner Prairie component to the historic village, Drew Brewster remembered those cattle and suggested hiring her."

"And Rueger was willing to bankroll all this."

"Yeah. He's kind of nutty about his ancestors."

The same bloodstream, Rueger had said proudly. Well, you could say that old Father Rueger was a developer in his day. New Concord probably looked just as glitzy to the log-cabin pioneers as Castleton Corner looked to folks today.

Wes said, "Okay, the way I read it, the guy's bought a lot of the houses in New Concord, and he's paid a little to get the church school camp here—probably writes it off as a charitable donation. And he's paying quite a bit to get the Strand sisters in line. Is their place mortgaged, Dub?"

Dub's eyes had narrowed. "What are you getting at?"

"Suppose Rueger buys up the rest of New Concord. He's already got half of it, and I bet he can control the vote on the publicly owned stuff as well. Now, it seems to me he might get a hankering to own the Strand place too. His ancestors as well as theirs, right?"

Dub, still cautious, said, "Could be."

"Or you might get a hankering to own that place too. For symmetry."

"Look, Wes, we've agreed not to talk about this. It's got nothing to do with it."

"I know, Dub. I'm just trying to get the big picture. Rueger told me the two of you are going for a regional mall when the new highway goes in." He was pleased to see Dub blink. "Now, I know all this isn't happening anytime soon. But if any of this has leaked out it could look real threatening to some people. They might want to get some sort of pull on Rueger."

"They oughta know kidnapping is not the way."

"Lotta things people oughta know." He put his glass of water down on the white countertop. "Dub, who holds the Strand mortgage?"

"Indianapolis bank."

"And you and Rueger are trying to buy it."

He hesitated, then nodded curtly.

"Okay. On to the Brewsters. Rueger says he wants both sides of the town, the Strand farm and the Brewster farm."

"Yeah, we got the Brewster mortgage already."

"Risky, isn't it? What if they keep up payments?"

Dub shrugged. "Our project is pretty far down the road. Meanwhile, if they pay, we don't lose. If they don't pay, we win."

Wes leaned back against the counter and folded his arms. "Okay, now. I've got a picture in my head, Dub. Big super-highway from Indianapolis to Evansville. Big bridge over the White River. Big classy regional mall stretched along the riverbank. Special easy-access lanes from the mall to the development here on your property. But I don't see how your places across the river fit in. Rueger didn't explain that part of the plan."

"You told Rueger about those places?" Dub squawked.

Uh-oh. "He's your partner, isn't he?" Wes asked innocently.

"Godammit, Wes Cochran, that's it!" Dub's fist crashed onto the countertop so hard the glasses jumped. "That's the end! You blundering idiot! You've been trying to get me from the beginning!"

So that's why Rueger had seemed off-balance. Before Wes told him, he hadn't known that his partner was doing a little secret investing on his own. Come to think of it, the other side of the river would work just as well for a mall, right? But Dub, as the local in charge of real estate, could tell Rueger those places were unavailable, that they should concentrate on shaking loose the Strands and the Brewsters.

Dub's ranting was sputtering to a close. Wes said, "Sorry. But you see the problems I get into when I don't have all the facts."

"You'll have problems, all right, Cochran! Weak heart, right? And weak head besides! Hiring that cunt deputy to sleep around with your men—"

"You'll push me too far, Dub!" Wes glared at the other man. "Whoever told you that was lying."

"Heard it with my own ears! You think nobody else has police band radio?"

"Heard what, Dub?"

"Heard her talking to her sweetie! Anybody could tell what was going on."

"Dub, I don't have the foggiest idea what you're talking about."

Dub took a swig of Scotch and said, "Well, maybe I misinterpreted it."

He'd backed off too fast. Wouldn't have done that if he'd made it all up. But what the hell could he be talking about?

He remembered Chuck Pierce's question at the church supper, right in front of the pastor. Whatever it was, it was going to be a headache.

He said, "Dub, seems to me we're at a standoff. Now, I didn't say anything to Rueger until I knew he was working with you—"

"The hell you didn't!"

"Okay, I'm saying it was an honest mistake. If I can help the two of you work out the problem I'll be glad to."

"Stay the fuck out of it!"

"Okay. Done. Now, I'm not talking about the mall project

to anybody else. Not unless I'm forced to." He locked eyes with Dub. "So I want you to think—"

The white phone on the wall rang. Dub picked up. "Walters . . . Yeah, Don, he's here." He handed it to Wes. "For you."

It was Foley. "Sir, just wanted you to know, the state cops stopped a brown van with Kentucky plates down near Jasper, and they think they've got our bad guy."

44

BACK DOWN AT THE SPRINGHOUSE DOOR, MARTY couldn't hear the woman's voice above the chortling creek. She tried the door gently and it swung open. A glow spilled across the stone threshold, but no sound came from within. Marty waited a moment, gun ready, then leaped into the room, shouting, "Police! Freeze!"

No one was there. The spring burbled at the far end, and old shelving rotted along the sides. It was cool enough to store milk, all right. A pair of oars lay against one wall, and a gunnysack. She glanced into the sack. Jeans—somebody's clothes. There was a slotted stone with a thong attached, and a camp lantern turned low. There was a ball of twine and some wood shavings. Tacked to the edge of a shelf was a picture of a huge red longhorn bull.

On the stone slab floor, there were muddy marks. Footprints. But whoever had been here was gone now. She gave one more look around the little room, but there were no doors, nothing more.

She'd focused on the light, on a possible confrontation, when she'd come. Now she turned her flashlight on and inspected the muddy ground outside the door. There were footprints, all right. Her own. She swept the flashlight around beyond her own messy trail and finally was rewarded with another print. Middle-sized, nobody huge. And near it, another one—no, just a cow. She followed the trail, more a matter of broken branches than actual footprints. It led up the bank, slanting toward town.

There was that voice again, just a murmur over the cicada and creek sounds. Marty hesitated.

She was nearing the edge of the trees here. The moon behind the ragged clouds lit the vine leaves of the labyrinth with a dull shimmer. Marty switched off her flashlight. She couldn't see anyone. Where was the voice coming from? She took a few more steps in the direction the trail had been leading.

Yes. It was getting stronger.

Who was it? Where?

Here was the labyrinth, the outermost row of vines on their chicken-wire supports. Marty followed it toward the corner.

She could almost make out words now. It sounded like pleading. It sounded like Vicki. Pleading with her brother?

It was coming from inside the labyrinth. "We can work together." Something something. "I know you're here. Please."

The moon showed dimly for an instant and Marty glimpsed someone in the maze, a few rows in. Instinctively she ducked below the level of the vines. How could she reach them? She tested the fencing. There was little space below the chicken-wire support, but every eight feet or so there was a support post. Marty grabbed the top of the nearest and pulled herself over.

Vicki was saying something about animals. She, at least, hadn't noticed Marty's approach yet. Marty was on the sandy path now between two of the vine hedges. She fumbled her way to the next support post and again pulled herself over.

A branch snapped.

Vicki stopped talking.

Marty, in combat crouch with her back to the hedge she'd

just come over, looked wildly in both directions, but saw nothing. Then the moon gleamed through for a moment and lit the next turning. Marty gasped, "Police! Freeze!"

The creature was tall, the nostrils and glistening eyes of his bull's mask about six feet up, his spreading horns arching up another ten inches, the points glinting in the moonlight. Shaggy hair covered his shoulders, but his body was naked and hairless. His arms and legs were long and smooth, his skin very pale. Vicki had said he was powerful, muscular—but that didn't seem quite right, Marty thought. Impressive, yes; tall and strange, yes. But under the shaggy wrap his shoulders were not very broad, his flat, hairless chest and waistless torso were puny, his long arms and legs were not well-muscled. He wore short boots outfitted with hooves underneath. His penis was small and droopy, but he'd tied some kind of a G-string underneath it that supported—oh dear God. Marty felt nauseated as she recognized a bull's scrotum, nearly a foot long, dangling between the creature's legs.

In his right hand he held a long wooden handle that had been lashed to an iron head of some sort. Marty flashed a glance at it and recognized the hand axe. A shiver crawled up her spine.

He didn't speak, but from the viny darkness behind him came the woman's muffled voice. "Why are you here? You shouldn't be here!"

"Vicki! Is that you? Where are you? Are you all right?"

The man with the horns stamped his foot and Vicki cried, "Talk to Tor! Don't talk to Vicki!"

"Okay, okay." Marty's mouth was dry, and she licked her lips. "Okay, Tor. Is that your name? Tor?"

The creature's great head inclined gently.

"Tor. Okay." She held her gun steadily but licked her lips again. "We've got a situation here, Tor. Maybe we can work something out."

"Drop the gun," Vicki said from behind him.

"Hey, I'm not allowed to drop the gun." Marty squinted into the gloom. The moonlight darkened. She couldn't see

Vicki. "Vicki—um, Tor, is Vicki all right back there? I can't see her, it's too dark."

Tor didn't look around.

Vicki said soothingly, "Don't worry, we'll get rid of Deputy Hopkins."

Vicki was on Tor's side, then. No big surprise, but it complicated things. And there was Nysa, Marty remembered suddenly. Nysa, who could come up behind her at any moment, who had refused to betray her brother because she still felt such guilt of having brought their father's brutality down on him.

Their father, who admired Father Rueger.

Father Rueger had used lye on the sinful woman. The man, he'd castrated like a bull calf.

Reality shifted for Marty, slipping like a kaleidoscope into a new pattern as the moon glowed again. A eunuch for the kingdom of heaven's sake. The man before her had never gone through adolescent changes, had grown tall without growing masculine. Romey Dennis flashed into her mind, how much he'd changed: broad shoulders, beard and body hair, firm jaw, low voice.

Low voice.

The last pieces slipped into place. Nysa's brother was her sister! Tor was Vicki. Not a man, not a woman, not a child, but suspended in a terrible place somewhere between.

Couldn't they treat him? Hormones or something? Nysa had talked about doctors. About getting money for doctors. He was afraid of doctors, Nysa had said, but—

Watch it, Hopkins. No time now to fix his life. Remember that men and women and even children can all become murderously angry. And who had more reason for anger than Tor? Horror washed through her, horror at what had been done to Tor, horror at how he'd struck back at young Johnny, young Kenny.

She steadied her gun. "Tor," she said. "I'm glad to see you. I've been wanting to talk to you."

"You shouldn't be here," said the huge creature in his woman's voice. "You shouldn't know my secret."

Marty licked her lips. Who had Vicki—no, Tor—been talking to before? She had to get him talking, to try to ease her way into the twists of his thoughts, to communicate somehow. She said, "And Nysa's secret too, right? Is Nysa here?"

"No! Nysa knows Vicki, not Tor! She's never seen me!"

But she'd guessed something, Marty thought, and had tried to protect her brother. She said, "Okay, good, it's just us. Let's talk about it, okay? Secret talk, just you and me. And let's put away our weapons."

"No! It's a sacred weapon."

"Yes, I can see that. See, the trouble is, it's harder to talk when we've got the weapons out."

"What do you want? Why are you here?"

"I want to talk to you. I want to find out about your secret place, and the nights on the riverbank."

"That has nothing to do with you!"

"Okay, you don't have to say anything if you don't want to. But I bet I could learn a lot about life from you."

"Yeah." He hesitated. "First drop your gun."

"Yeah, I want to put it away too. But I can't as long as your weapon is out. Let's talk about putting it down, okay?"

"It's a sacred weapon."

"Okay, let's talk about something else, then." Marty steadied the gun. "Let's talk about—about bulls. Are bulls sacred too?"

"It's not for you to know!" cried Vicki's muffled voice from inside that mask. "It's for Melissa and me!"

Melissa. Dear God, it was Melissa he'd been talking to. Where was she? Why so quiet? Then she remembered the words she'd heard. "I know you're here somewhere." Melissa was hiding. Tor didn't know where she was either. Marty said in a loud voice, "Well, Melissa's going to stay quiet, I bet, so we can talk."

"No!" The bull's head jerked around to scan the labyrinth for the girl, his great horns silhouetted against the dimming sky. He must think she was deeper in the labyrinth. But Marty had no time to reflect, because Tor turned back to her. "You're like the others. You want to kill me." He raised the axe.

She couldn't shoot. She didn't know where Melissa was.

BLOODSTREAM

Marty lunged back and to the left, but the springy vine fence prevented escape. She grunted in pain as the axe slashed down against her right arm, slicing skin and bruising bone. Her gun fell from her numbed fingers. There was no time to recover it, because the axe was swinging up again.

Marty attacked, diving straight for the smooth-skinned, flat chest, butting Tor against the springy wall. The axe head sliced into the sandy path behind her. But he outweighed her and caught his balance quickly, and raised it again. She faded to his left, away from the axe, and he shoved her in the face, trying to push her back where he could swing at her. Marty used his push to help carry her back along the path and down onto her gun. She grabbed it, and new pain sizzled up her cut right arm. Then the axe swung up again and Marty focused on it, the one point of significance in the universe. She was crouched, off-balance, at the base of the hedge. The axe started its downward swing and she rolled away, shifting her gun to her left hand.

Where was Melissa? And even if she knew, she was a lousy shot left-handed. She flashed on that other man, the man she'd had to kill last year, who still visited her nightmares—

Don't think of him, Hopkins. Think of Johnny, of Kenny, of that axe. Pull yourself together.

Time for a new plan. Get behind some of these springy vines. She scrambled over a hedge and Tor hesitated, glancing back across the labyrinth. Maybe he realized that taking Melissa hostage was his best ticket out of here. Distract him, Hopkins. Marty got her feet under her and stood, shouting, "I don't want to shoot you, dammit, but I will! Drop that weapon!"

"Melissa?" he called softly.

"Melissa's nearby, don't worry," Marty said soothingly. "She doesn't like it when you make me shoot."

"Don't shoot."

Marty backed up a step, farther from that long-handled axe. Her good left hand was wrapped around her useless right, holding up gun and hand alike. She wanted to make a break for it, take her chances that she could outrun Tor in his costume. Those wide horns and strange boots couldn't be easy to move in. But she couldn't leave Melissa alone, and she couldn't let Tor escape now. She had to hold him somehow until her backup arrived.

But how? She had to get him talking. She had to feel her way into that troubled mind and connect somehow.

She said conversationally, "I won't shoot unless I have to. Tor, when I talked to you before—remember when I talked to you and you were Vicki?"

"Vicki is a place to hide."

"Yeah, I see. You aren't really Vicki, you hide in Vicki. Is that the way it is?"

"Yeah."

"Well, see, I like you when you're hiding in Vicki, so I thought I'd like you when you weren't hiding."

"I have to hide. Father said I had to hide, I had to pretend to be a girl."

"But here, in this secret place, you're not hiding. You're not hiding from Melissa or me."

"Where is Melissa?"

"Nearby. You know, it's not exactly the same, but I kind of know what you mean about hiding in a body. I kind of do that too."

"What do you mean?"

"Well, I like to play basketball, boys' rules. And I like to drive fast, and practice shooting on the range. They say women aren't supposed to do those things, but I like to. And—"

Tor said, "But you have breasts, and a uterus."

"Well, yeah. But what I'm saying is, that's only important if I want to have a baby. All the other stuff I do is just general human stuff. Men can do it and women can do it. So it doesn't make any difference if I have a man's body or a woman's body."

"But it does make a difference! The biggest difference of all! You don't understand. I was supposed to be a man!"

His anguish twisted Marty's heart. But she had to go on, had to distract him with these forbidden thoughts. Her arm was aching with exhaustion, but she didn't dare lower the gun, didn't dare let him see that her right hand was useless.

He'd forgotten the weapons for the moment, but still gripped the deadly long-handled axe in his right hand. "I guess I don't understand," she admitted. "How does it make a difference?"

He struggled to explain, his soft woman's voice earnest and hesitant. "People don't like it. People like men. They like women. They don't like someone different."

"People like someone special," she said.

"Nysa says special. Other people hate you. They beat you up on the way home from school, over and over. They call you weirdo. They call you freak. They call you fairy. But a fairy's a man! They call you lezzie, but a lezzie's a woman!" His narrow shoulders heaved and a choked sob escaped. Marty felt like crying too. She'd said weirdo herself. Weirdo. Nutcase. What would she have done, faced with such cruel brutality against her body, such cruel intolerance against her spirit?

Remember Johnny. Remember Kenny. She wouldn't have done that. She cleared her throat. "Most people don't understand, that's for sure."

Tor pounded the axe handle against the sandy path. "But Melissa will understand! She loves animals. She's good, like Nysa. She'll be my—where is she?"

"She's waiting for us to put down the weapons."

"Where is she? Is she out there?" Suddenly Tor lunged forward, vaulting the hedge with an ease that chilled Marty's blood.

"Stop!" Marty cried, dodging right, away from the axe.

But he wasn't swinging it at her. He jumped the last hedge and ran into the trees, automatically allowing space for the spreading horns, and Marty realized that he'd practiced moving in the awkward costume until he'd become skillful. "Melissa!" he called in Vicki's voice.

"Stop, dammit!" Marty pulled herself over the vines.

He ignored her, galloping into the night. Marty scrambled after. The moon's faint glow didn't reach far into these woods. Her right hand still wasn't doing much, so she stuck her gun in her belt on the left side and grabbed her flashlight. He paused, then started down the creek bank. She tackled him, slamming her shoulder against him, then rolled away before he could regain his balance and swing the axe.

"Stop, Tor!" she yelled, hoping her voice would reach West Street, hoping someone was there to hear. "Melissa liked you when you were hiding in Vicki. Maybe you'd better hide again, take it slower! You want her to think you're a freak too? A weirdo? You know she'll think that if you try to force her!"

"No. No!" he screamed, as though she'd wounded him, and lunged down the bank toward the creek, heading downstream.

Marty followed grimly. Where was Melissa? Safe in the labyrinth, she hoped, and now on her way to town, to safety. And where was her backup? Had they heard her yells? And how was she supposed to collar this guy with one hand? But she wasn't going to let him get away now.

He ran down the trail, following the creek toward the river, amazingly surefooted amid the trees. Marty had no headgear to worry about—she'd left her Stetson hanging on a branch back there as a signal to her backup when it came. Even so, she had trouble with the rough trail, and despite her best efforts the gap between them widened as he approached the river. But she was near enough to see him run across the bridge, and on down the riverside footpath. She lost him a moment at a bend in the path, but then saw him again, slowly stepping onto the half-submerged fishing rock.

Someone else was on the rock too. Nysa Strand stood in the faint moonlight, the river foaming about her feet. She stretched out her hands toward the tall horned man. "Welcome, Victor," she said.

45

"YOU AREN'T SUPPOSED TO SEE ME." TOR'S VOICE was gentle, hurt. The moonglow through the thinning clouds was not strong enough to show more than dim shapes, trees and river and half-submerged rock, and a slim shadow that was Nysa and a taller horned one that was Tor. Marty stepped onto the broad rock and stopped, pulling her gun from her belt. She tested her right hand. She could move her thumb and index finger, but it sent pain rocketing through her arm. Stick to the left, Hopkins, and hope you don't have to shoot at all.

Nysa said, "You're my brother. It's okay if we see each other."

"No. You thought I was Vicki. Happy, well-adjusted— well, resigned at least—" He struck the axe against the rock. Marty steadied her gun.

"I know you are Victor, not Vicki," Nysa said. "I remember you from before! A little boy who loved his dog and wanted to be a cowboy when he grew up. A little boy who didn't like schoolbooks but loved Wild West stories, and liked to sing and pound on drums, and liked baseball when his father allowed it, and teased his sisters with ice cubes down their backs."

"That was before!" His voice was choked.

"Yes, but you're my brother now too! And you're wonderful. Your voice, your hair, your spirit—wonderful. Victor, I know you didn't do those terrible things. You're my brother."

Nysa was deluding herself. "Tor isn't Vicki," Marty called over the throbbing ache in her arm.

Tor turned and took an angry step toward Marty. Nysa said, "He's Victor. He's my brother."

"Nysa." Marty licked her dry lips. She didn't dare take her eyes from Tor, but she wished she could tell what Nysa was thinking. "Nysa, look at his weapon. Just look."

"I see," said Nysa. Then, almost pleading, "But you didn't do those things, Victor, did you? You found that axe somewhere. You didn't take it from the historic project."

"No. I didn't."

"Where did you get it?" Marty demanded.

Tor took another step toward her, but Nysa repeated softly, "Where did you get it?"

He swung his head to look at his sister. "He wanted to kill me. And he'd seen me. He wasn't supposed to see me!"

"Who, Victor?" Nysa's hands were still stretched toward him, but her voice was sad.

"The boy who hurt the cows. Johnny. See, that morning I was late getting back, and Melissa was coming to milk the cows, and I didn't have time to go back and put away the horned crown, so I hid it in a sack in the barn. Then it started raining again and I thought no one would be on the footpath, so I started to take it back. And he came running along the path and bumped me, and the sack fell open."

"And then what?"

"And he said, 'You're that cow witch! You're that freak! That faggot!' And other bad things. And he said he was going to tell his father. And his father would beat me up."

"I see," Nysa sighed.

Marty saw too. Johnny was right: Carl Donato would have beat him up. Carl Donato holding a few beers might have killed him.

"It was just like Morton. I had to stop him! I came out and grabbed him. He had that hand axe—just the metal head, I put on the handle later—and he pulled it out of his pocket and started hitting me. So I hit him with the horned crown and—stopped him. I had to stop him."

Marty felt sick. Stopping him—that's what cops said when they meant shooting, maybe killing. That's what they told her she'd done to that man last year. *You had to stop him,*

Coach had reassured her, *he was trying to kill you.* That was true. But Johnny couldn't have killed Victor, could he?

Damon Seifert and his broken bottle could have killed you, Hopkins. Johnny was two years older, tall and muscular, and backed by a father who wanted to eliminate faggots and freaks, who wanted to wipe out whatever didn't fit his pigeonholes.

Tor said, "I took the axe away from him, and—"

"Hush," said Nysa, glancing at Marty. "I don't have to hear any more. I understand. You're my brother."

But Marty didn't want to let this moment of talkativeness slip away. She couldn't coax him to say things, as Nysa could, but maybe she could challenge him. "I don't believe you!" Marty burst out. "If you'd ... stopped him, you would've been covered in blood! Nobody saw you covered in blood! You're lying!"

Nysa raised a cautioning palm, but he'd jerked around to face Marty. "It was raining! And when I hit him with the horned crown it pushed him into the river, and afterward I pushed him farther out so he'd float away. The river washed me, and the rain."

"Well, that was smart," Marty said. Her left arm was so tired it hurt almost as much as her right. "But I can't believe you stopped Kenny too! It wasn't raining then!"

"Yes it was!"

Nysa's hands fell to her sides. "Victor, Victor," she mourned.

He turned to Nysa again. "I had to stop them!" he explained earnestly. "They said bad things—and Johnny wanted to kill me. And he hurt the animals. And he stole the axe and cut me with it. And he saw me. If people see me they want to kill me. And Kenny saw me too. I was watching Melissa that night, making sure she got back to camp all right. And he came up behind me and told me to stay away from her. Just because he has—"

He struck the rock again with his axe. Marty knew what Kenny had and figured she'd better change the subject. She asked, "What bad things did they say?"

"They—they—" The horned head drooped and he started

to whimper. She began to have hopes of taking him in without further struggle. If Nysa played things right . . .

Marty asked gently, "Did they say weirdo or something?"

"Yeah. Weirdo, freak, monster—like Morton, he said I was a monster—"

"Victor." Nysa stepped toward him, arms out. "You're not a monster!"

"Of course I am."

"If you're a monster, so am I! It happened to me too!"

"No, Nysa." Tor's womanly voice was calm and dignified. "You were already a beautiful woman when you were . . . wounded. I was a boy. I grew up so now I'm not a boy. I'm not a woman. I'm not a man. I'm something different, something monstrous. They're right."

"They're wrong! You're not monstrous!"

"But Father said so! He said, 'Now you're a monster, but you can hide it by dressing like a girl.' "

"Father was wrong!" Nysa said. "Wrong to do this to us, wrong to say we're monsters! He's not our judge. If anybody's a monster, it's him!"

"But he said I was—"

"No, Victor! You're a wonderful human being, a wonderful brother! Think of our music! Oh, if only we could have been together sooner!"

He stared at her as though trying to believe. Overhead the skimpy clouds broke and let patches of moonlight glint on the river.

"You're my brother, Victor. But we have to stop the killing. Please, Victor, throw the axe away."

"It's a sacred weapon! Buried and risen again!"

"Yes. So throw it into the sacred river, where it belongs."

A good idea. The horned head turned to look out at the roaring waters. Marty waited to see what he'd do.

"The river." He hesitated, then suddenly said "Yes!" and swung the axe back to fling it away.

A man burst from the path behind Marty, screaming, "Don't hurt her!"

Marty shouted, "Stop!" but the man hurtled across the rock, grabbing the axe head at the top of the swing. For a confused instant Marty thought her backup was here at last, out of uniform and suddenly berserk.

Then Nysa cried, "Justin, no!" and Marty saw that it was Reverend Jeffries wrestling Tor for the axe.

The big eunuch struggled for a second, trying to pull the axe from Jeffries's grip. Marty shouted again, "Stop! Reverend Jeffries, get out of the way!" But Jeffries didn't let go. He gave the axe a hard twist. Victor lost his grip and fell backward into the swirling waters.

"Dammit!" Marty holstered her gun and snatched up a long broken branch. She lunged across the rock, shoving Jeffries aside with a shoulder to his sternum, not gently. He sat down with a grunt. Marty swung the leafy end of her branch into the water and shouted, "Victor! Grab the branch!"

He was splashing wildly and struggling to remove his great horned headpiece. Nysa turned and ran away along the footpath.

It could be a lot worse, Marty thought. Victor had fallen into the river downstream of the fishing rock. The water here was deep but not as fast-moving as out in the main channel. But as he clutched at the headpiece he was bobbing toward the swifter water. Already he was beyond the reach of Marty's branch. She looked at the submerged part of the fishing rock. She could get ten or fifteen feet closer, probably. The water sheeting over the rock was only three or four inches deep. As she watched a log smashed into the rock, then the river turned it, slapped it out into the main channel, and whisked it away.

Marty dragged her branch from the water and looked at Jeffries, who was getting back to his feet. "Reverend Jeffries!"

He turned to her with shocked eyes. "He was attacking her!"

"Reverend Jeffries, listen! We need a rope. Fast as you can get it. Try the Strand outbuildings, they're closest. And hurry!"

He sprinted away. Marty prayed that he'd understood. She stepped onto the submerged half of the fishing rock, hurrying but testing carefully to make sure she wasn't going over the edge into the deep channel. She skidded once and realized that she'd need more than feet for traction. Shoot, what she wouldn't give for a rope!

Victor was still wrestling with the great horned headpiece as he thrashed about. "Swim for shore!" Marty called.

"Where? Where?" he screamed in his woman's voice. Marty realized that he'd twisted the headpiece and couldn't see. He was panicking.

"Here. Grab the branch! Just to your right!" Marty lay down on the submerged rock and thrust the leafy end as far out as she could. The cool water burbled around her, occasionally splashing into her mouth. "Grab it!" she spluttered.

Her right hand was throbbing with pain now and still pretty useless, but she could use her right elbow to brace herself. She clutched the branch with her left hand at a knobby place that gave her a better grip. But when Victor finally grabbed it, it almost slipped from her grasp. "Hang on!" she gasped, as much to herself as to him.

For a moment they teetered in rough balance. Marty was on her stomach on the submerged rock, gripping the branch, and fifteen feet farther out in the deep swirling water, Victor clutched the branch with one hand and struggled with his horned crown with the other.

She wasn't strong enough to pull him in. She'd be lucky just to keep hold. They'd have to wait for Nysa's return, or Reverend Jeffries, or her long-delayed backup. And Victor was panicking, still splashing, making the branch twist painfully in her hand. She had to talk him down somehow. "Just relax," Marty called soothingly. "We're okay. Help is coming."

"Get it off! Get it off!" he shrieked, tugging at the headpiece.

"Just take it easy. Wait for—"

But he continued to thrash. The branch jerked and bucked. She gritted her teeth and held on. "Relax, Victor! Help's coming!"

The White River, pleased to have a new plaything, swirled

around Victor and nudged him gently toward the rushing current that swept past the end of the rock. Marty noticed that he was drifting to the edge of the slower water. "Victor! Kick toward shore, okay? Toward your right! Push the branch away from the current!"

He tried. There was a great panicky thrashing of long legs. The branch twisted in Marty's hand, and pain burned in her scraped palm. She held on somehow, bracing herself as best she could, spread-eagled in the water that raced over the rock.

Then the main current caught the branch and the long human legs. Victor screamed. Marty dug in toes and elbows, but was no match for the power of tons of racing water. The river yanked her from the rock and into the drunken torrent.

46

WES AND FOLEY HAD ABOUT FINISHED DISCUSSING the brown van with Kentucky plates that the state police had stopped. The dispatcher had explained that the state cops thought they had the kidnapper, but Wes wasn't convinced. For starts, Melissa hadn't been found in the van. But the driver had a record and was carrying a couple of ounces of marijuana. Wes leaned back against Dub Walters's kitchen counter and snorted. "Nothing but a drug bust unless he leads them to the Rueger girl. Okay, Foley, anything else?"

There was no answer.

"Foley?"

"Sorry, sir, emergency call just coming in. It's—wait a minute. Yeah, you're nearby already. Somebody fell in the river."

"Yeah? So the rescue squad's on it, right?"

"Yessir, but I thought you better know, because that Strand woman called it in. Happened on her farm."

"Strand!" Wes squinted out Dub's window as though he could see through the inkiness to the Strand farm across the highway. "Get Hopkins on it."

"She may be there already, sir."

"May be?"

"Can't raise her, sir."

"Damn! What's she doing?"

"Don't know, sir. Last time she called in was an hour ago."

"What'd she want?"

"Let's see. She said she found a footprint somewhere, and she was in New Concord, and—"

"What kind of footprint? The Rueger girl's?"

"She wasn't sure, sir."

"Where was she in New Concord?"

"She said she was on West Street, and she said she was going to the Strand farm."

"I'm going there now," said Wes. "Foley, get another car to meet me at West Street, and keep track of the rescue operation." He turned to Walters. "Emergency at the river, Dub. Have to finish talking later." He sprinted out to his cruiser.

There was no reason to hang on to the branch anymore, because Victor had let go. Marty, trying not to gulp muddy water, saw him splashing wildly in the moonlight downstream. She took a second to kick off her shoes and drop her gunbelt, laden with gun, flashlight, handcuffs, and other heavy items. Then she struck off in her best crawl. The river was pulling her to the middle because, after gushing past the fishing rock, the main current angled toward the far shore. The slightly slower water on the Strand side had collected a huge tangle of logs and debris. She aimed for clearer water. Even though she was being pushed downstream she could probably make shore where the river narrowed again near the highway bridge.

BLOODSTREAM

The river slammed a log into her shoulder, then sent it spinning on downstream.

That could have been your head, Hopkins.

She adjusted her crawl so she was breathing and looking upstream. When a shape appeared in the patchy moonlight she'd duck down into the water, hoping it would be gone when she resurfaced. A big one loomed suddenly and she plunged deep, then rose and took a breath, glancing downstream to see what the object was. She couldn't tell—there were beams angling up, a piece of an outbuilding maybe, or a smashed barge. She couldn't see Victor anymore. Upstream, it looked clear for the moment. She struck out again for the shore.

Her feet wouldn't move.

She kicked harder, but something held them tight.

She took a breath and dove. The water was too murky to see anything, but her fingers found the problem, a tangle of string—fishing line, that must be it. She felt with her left hand, cautiously trying to pull it from her legs, but it only seemed to get tighter. Damn. Her penknife was at the bottom of the river. She came up for air and then plunged again. Couldn't seem to find a way to loosen it. What was holding the fishing line? Her exploring fingers found heavy wire, a coil, another coil—it was a bedspring, she decided. Well, no hope of untangling the fishing line from that. She started to surface for a breath and discovered a filament of the fishing line curled tightly around her wrist. On the edge of panic, she managed to release the wrist and went up for another breath.

The river chuckled around her head, as if it found some sort of boozy amusement in tying her down this way. It was a struggle to lift her head high enough above the rollicking water to get a breath. She had a sudden image of Johnny Donato's bloated body, his L.A. Gear sneakers still bearing coils of fishing line, and she screamed.

The river splashed into her open mouth.

Get a grip, Hopkins! Use your head.

Something loomed in the water and she ducked again. Another log.

Okay, Hopkins, you've been in tight spots before. How can you make this one better?

For starters, pulling at that tangle of fishing line was useless. She was only tightening it, and endangering herself further. The worst thing that could happen would be to get her hand caught down there too. Then it would be lights out for sure.

Second, she was exhausted already, fighting to keep her head up. She knew the answer to that one: Quit fighting. She needed to breathe, but between breaths she could relax, float wherever the river chose to put her, even if it was underwater.

She relaxed and leaned on the current, still tethered by her legs, and found the rhythm of the charging waters. Relax a moment, push up and breathe. Relax, push up, breathe. Relax—

A bush spinning by raked her face. She sputtered and coughed for a moment. Okay, better add in a peek upstream. Relax, push up, peek, breathe. Relax, push up, peek, breathe. Relax, push up, peek—oops, dodge! Push up again, breathe. Relax, push up . . .

Time passed. It seemed like hours, but when she checked the moon's progress she saw it hadn't gone far. She wasn't getting any less exhausted. But rest was not an option.

The swollen, tireless river rolled on.

Wes beamed his flashlight across a rippling sea of vine leaves. Surely Hopkins wasn't in the labyrinth! Her cruiser was here on West Street by the entrance, but where was she? His light picked up the roof of a little building in the center. Beyond that he could make out nothing but more vines and eventually trees. No, wait. Something white fluttered there, across the labyrinth, over to the left.

He hurried around to the left corner. A weedy path led along the outside edge of the maze toward the fluttering object. He'd gone about twenty yards when he heard something and stopped.

A woman's voice, moaning.

Wes ran his flashlight along the vine leaves. Nothing. "Sheriff's Department!" he yelled, unsnapping his holster.

"Sheriff?" It was a youthful, tearful voice. "Oh, help, please!"

A section of the vines shimmied in his flashlight beam. Wes waded into the hedge and was bounced back by the chicken-wire support. "Just a minute!" he yelled. "Gotta get my wire cutters from the car!"

Ten minutes later he found her, curled on the sandy path below the vines. She was crying and clutching her leg.

"Hey, what's up?" he asked her. It wasn't Hopkins. This one was blond, he saw now, and injured. Filthy, dirt all over her clothes and skin. He ran his light around the area with a cop's instinctive caution, but saw no sign of anyone else. He knelt and looked at the leg. Big scrape was all he could see. She was young, hard to recognize behind the dirt. Could this ragged, filthy thing be Rueger's daughter? "What happened, honey?" he asked. "Here, lie still. I've called for an ambulance. What happened?"

"She went crazy! He—whatever—she went crazy!"

The girl was crying, rubbing her eyes. Wes, shining his light on her face, saw that she was scratched and bleeding. There were scratches on her arms too, and grime. "Honey, you're not making a lot of sense. Who went crazy?"

"Vicki Strand! She—he—took me in a boat to that little springhouse. And then he took off his clothes—"

"Who took off his clothes?"

"Vicki!" she said impatiently.

Poor kid—confused and in shock, or maybe she'd been drugged. He'd try again to get her story when he had her in the cruiser. "You're Melissa Rueger, aren't you, honey?"

"Yeah! And you've got to catch that—that—"

"Okay, we sure will," he soothed her. "The ambulance is coming. They'll get you cleaned up and I'll call your daddy. He's worried sick about you."

Melissa started to sob. "Well, this is just about the worst day of my whole life!"

"I know, honey, I know." Wes swung his flashlight once more at the fluttery white thing beyond the field of vines.

He was starting to feel real uneasy about Hopkins. But he'd have to get a deputy to check that out.

Getting Melissa to safety was his job now.

Relax, push up, peek, breathe. Relax, push up, peek—here came something barreling toward her. The bow of somebody's smashed wooden canoe. Marty started to duck, then suddenly changed her mind and reached out to grab it. The river tussled with her for it for a moment, and the fishing line around her ankles dug in painfully as she worked the canoe bow around and upstream of her. Its bottom was gone, but there was a cross-brace with a piece of the seat still attached. If she stuck her arms over the brace—yes, it gave her enough lift so that she could breathe more easily. And with a little effort she could keep it pointed upstream, parting the waters that bore down on her. The river didn't like this idea and kept muscling at it, first from one side and then from the other, but now the floating branches and boards slipped around the sides instead of running over her. Marty hung panting over the brace. Keeping the bow pointed upstream was no easier, really, than what she'd been doing before, but at least it used different muscles. At least she didn't have to have her face underwater so much.

It wasn't much later that she heard a great pounding in the air. A brilliant light was coming up the river, briefly illuminating the highway bridge and continuing toward her. A helicopter, she realized suddenly. A helicopter, searching the river! The light moved upstream toward her, sweeping back and forth across the water. A second light appeared behind it. Marty started waving her arm, struggling to keep her fragment of canoe straight. The light and the horrendous pounding came closer. Any minute now they'd illuminate her. But could they see her? She was just a wet brown speck on the wet brown river.

Suddenly the machine reversed and sped off downstream.

"Come back! Come back!" she screamed. But it didn't. It disappeared around the curve past the big bridge. There it paused. She could tell by the faint, steady drumming that it was hovering with its fellow just the other side of the bridge.

It stayed there a long time. Victor, Marty decided. She hoped they'd save him. Save him, quick, and then come back for her.

A long time passed.

The river kept tossing bushes and bottles at her, but the canoe bow deflected them.

After a while the faint beat of the helicopters went away.

They wouldn't expect her to be so close to where she'd gone in. The tangled fishing line had caught her too soon.

Maybe they wouldn't even know she was in the river at all. Reverend Jeffries and Nysa had both seen Victor fall in. Nobody had seen her go in, not even Victor, who was blinded by his monstrous mask. If he was still alive, he might tell them to look for her. But he probably wouldn't.

Whenever she closed her eyes, the dead man from her nightmares reached out for her from his black cavern.

The river, tired of playing, aimed a heavy wooden beam at her piece of canoe. It smashed into one side and the underwater tangle of lines bit viciously into Marty's legs while the river wrenched at the canoe. The crosspiece that was supporting her cracked as the overstressed bow twisted into fragments. Marty gave up. She shoved the scraps of her little shelter out into the victorious current and went back to Plan A.

Relax, push up, peek, breathe. Relax, push up, peek, breathe.

A time or two she slid into exhausted sleep and woke instantly, sputtering and coughing. Stay awake, Hopkins, you idiot! Relax! Push up, peek, breathe. Relax, push up . . .

The moon crept across the sky and began to sink toward the dark shagginess of the wooded hills.

The river roared on.

Marty concentrated on breathing.

Rueger would be more sensible than Sheldrake had been about letting him talk to Melissa. But just in case, Wes took a preliminary statement from her while they waited for the paramedics. She'd run away from Sheldrake because she felt so bad about Kenny, and she didn't want to take those pills. And she'd walked three or four hours along the riverbank, and finally found her cows. And that was where Vicki Strand had found her. They'd talked and when Melissa had said she'd be leaving with her father, Vicki had been perturbed and asked her to come with her for a boat ride. Melissa declined but Vicki'd said it was the last chance to show her an exciting secret. So Melissa got in the boat. After that it got really confused, Wes found. Something about a springhouse and Vicki really being a man, and then she mentioned bull's horns and Wes started paying attention again. "Vicki was wearing bull's horns?"

"Yeah, he kept them in that springhouse and put them on. It was so weird! And he kept saying I shouldn't go back to Arizona, I should stay with him, and he'd help me to go to vet school and stuff. Really! He didn't seem mad at me or anything, but I was so scared!" Her lower lip started trembling and Wes feared she'd dissolve into sobs.

"But you got away!" he said heartily. "How'd you do that?"

"He wanted to show me a sacred axe. But when he bent over to pick it up I rushed to the door and ran out. And he chased me into this place, and I broke my leg and hid! And then that woman came, Deputy Hopkins? She got him away from here, but I was so scared he'd come back—"

"Hopkins." How long ago had that been? Well over an hour since she'd spoken to Foley. Shit. Something had gone wrong—she wouldn't leave Melissa so long if she'd had a choice. Hopkins tried to be such a hot dog. Why the hell hadn't she called for backup? He said, "And then I found you?"

"Yeah. It hurts so much. . . ."

"Honey, I'll be right back. I gotta call dispatch." He plowed through the cuts he'd made in the vines to the cruiser and got on the radio, shouting for Foley to call off the search for Melissa and get everybody over to the Strand place. The minute the paramedics arrived he was off to join them.

Nysa Strand was downstream with the rescue people, he

was told. But Sims and Adams had found Reverend Jeffries by the fishing rock. A man wearing horns on his head had attacked Nysa Strand with an axe, Jeffries reported. When Jeffries had wrestled the axe from him, the man had fallen into the river, and Deputy Hopkins had tried to rescue him while Jeffries fetched a rope.

"But no one was here when I got back. I yelled for a few minutes, then your deputies came," said Jeffries. The preacher looked very scared and confused. He was carrying a big coil of rope looped over his shoulder.

Wes asked Sims, "Does the rescue team know there may be two?"

"Yes sir, I called them right away," said the gangly deputy. "They've already spotted the one with horns. Said they'd look for the other one too. But we don't know for sure she's in there."

Wes walked to the edge of the water and looked out at the river, inky except for occasional blotchy glints of moonlight that revealed dark shapes riding it downstream. He played his flashlight on it, but it didn't help much. "Dammit, when's she going to learn to call for backup?"

Sims cleared his throat. Wes turned to see Adams frowning at the other deputy. Wes said sharply, "What is it, Sims?"

"Uh—she did ask for backup, sir. I overheard her on my radio."

"Who did Foley send?"

"I don't know, sir. He told her everyone was busy. I got out to stop a van with Kentucky plates, but when I called in ten minutes later he didn't ask me to go."

"Dammit." Wes looked out at the water.

"Sir, she might have gone along the footpath," Sims offered. "To see if she could help the victim. You can make better time on land."

"Yeah. Let's go take a look." Wes strode off down the dark footpath.

After a long time there was another noise, a chugging. Not a helicopter, Marty thought drowsily, no need to wake up all the way. Relax, push up, peek, breathe. Not a helicopter, just somebody's outboard motor. Just a boat.

She jerked awake and looked around frantically. The last moonbeams slanted across the water and picked out a dark shape downstream. Marty shouted, "Here! Here! Help!" and hoped that her voice would carry over the sound of water and machine.

The chugging changed in pitch, grew louder. For a moment Marty feared that she'd be run over. Doc Altmann's words clanged in her mind: *Boat propellers. Chop wounds.* But the noise throttled down suddenly and a woman's voice said, "Deputy Hopkins! Thank God!"

"Nysa? Please, I—"

"Duck!" Nysa commanded. Marty bobbed under, and a shape hurtled downstream above her. She came up again, gasping.

"What's holding you there?" Nysa asked. "Are your feet caught?"

"Yeah, tangled up in fishing line."

"Okay. I'll keep the life jacket just for a minute, then, and tie a knife to this rope. Dive down and cut yourself loose. But hang on to the rope—this current is strong."

"Yeah, I've noticed." Marty concentrated on catching the rope. Her reflexes were shot, and she kept missing. Finally she succeeded, looped the rope carefully under one arm and across her back and chest to the other side of her neck, then took the knife in her left hand because it was sore but not as stiff as her right. She dove and cut four times. As she went down the fifth time, the river suddenly shoved her downstream, bowling her boisterously along. She dropped the knife and grabbed at her rope harness. She managed to keep it around herself as she kicked her way to the surface.

Nysa called, "I don't want to catch you or the rope in the propeller. I'll head for shore upstream so as to keep you well out of the way until we can land. Okay? Do you want the life jacket?"

"Just go," said Marty.

Nysa towed Marty into an eddy below a little rise on the

north side, hauled the boat ashore, and then helped Marty from the water. Marty fell gasping and panting onto the muddy bank. "Just a few more steps," Nysa urged. "It's drier on the rise here."

It was stonier too, lots of worn brick-sized rocks. But Marty managed to crawl a few feet before she collapsed.

47

WHEN SHE WOKE THERE WAS BIRDSONG AND A dark sky silvering in the east. The river still rumbled and splashed in the background, but she was dry and warm. Her arms and hands hurt. She brought them in front of her face and inspected them in the dim light. Chewed-up red palm on the left, stiff and painful fingers on the right. She pushed up her blue sleeve and saw the ugly cut swelling on her forearm. No wonder her fingers didn't work very well.

A blue sleeve. Why blue?

She sat up. Where was her uniform? She was in her underwear and somebody's blue shirt, and that was it. Twisting sideways, she looked at the river, and it all came back. In the early light the water seemed silky, almost placid, but now she knew its vicious power. Like a lion or a tiger, she thought, a great beast weighing . . . what? A pint's a pound—how many billion pints out there?

She didn't want to think about that.

A movement by the shore caught her eye, and she scrambled to her feet. "Nysa?" she called.

The blond woman turned and walked toward her up the little rise. She was in jeans, a navy tank top, and the aqua crocheted top she usually wore knotted around her waist. Nysa asked, "How are you doing?"

"Okay. How long—"

"You've only been asleep about an hour. Your biggest problem seemed to be exhaustion, so I let you rest. I didn't want to leave you alone while I went for help. But if you can move now, we'd better get you to a doctor. That's a deep wound, and the river water isn't that clean."

"Yeah. Nysa—your brother?"

"The river took him." Tears stood in Nysa's eyes.

"Oh, God. I'm sorry." Marty hugged the other woman. "I'd hoped—see, there were helicopters—"

"Do you want a drink?"

"Yeah. Thanks." Marty accepted the flask and swallowed. The wine felt good.

Nysa drank too and said, "The rescue team recovered his body. His poor ruined body, that people hated so much. Why? Why do people hate him for something that's not his fault?"

"I don't know. People are pretty weird about sex." Weird. Cruel too. Nysa's sweet little brother had grown up and lashed back, repaying cruelty with cruelty.

Nysa looked out at the river and rubbed a palm over her glistening cheek. After a moment she said, "The river is merciful in its way."

"Yeah. I was just thinking that too." Actually Marty had been thinking about prison, about hostile inmates, about the jailers themselves, guys who made Foley look like a model of kindly understanding.

"I just wish I'd found him when he was younger."

"I know." Marty squeezed Nysa's shoulders, even though it sent pains shooting up her arm. "I wish it could have been different too."

"It's Father Rueger again. Dying and rising— You know, he castrated his son Emanuel too."

"He did?"

"His only son. The boy grew up to have a beautiful castrato voice, like Victor's. And a great talent for music—you heard his arrangements of the hymns."

"Those were his? But—how come Father Rueger did that?"

310

"It was like Victor. Victor was caught with a picture of a naked woman that one of his friends had given him. The Rueger boy was caught peeking into the outhouse when a girl was using it." Nysa shook her head. "But that was a kinder time, really. They viewed Emanuel Rueger as a eunuch for the kingdom of heaven's sake. Some of them probably envied him having a decreased sex drive, and all of them valued his special musical abilities."

"But—I don't understand. He was the only son, right? And he couldn't have children. So how could Bob Rueger be descended from him?"

"He couldn't, of course. He's some other Rueger bloodline. Not ours."

"You knew that? And you went along with his historic project?"

"A music teacher doesn't make much money. I'd spent so much on those detectives who located Victor, and I hoped to save enough for hormone treatments. I wanted to give Victor a chance to be what he thought he wanted to be. But I found him too late. And then the bull calf's death, the boys taunting him again—I was too late."

Marty looked at the river. Maybe it was foolish of Nysa to think she could have changed her brother. But she liked the woman for trying, for having the courage and love and family loyalty to gamble on someone that everyone else— including Victor himself—agreed was a monster. Maybe someday all the Foleys would be gone and poor souls like Victor would have a chance . . .

Nah. Get real, Hopkins, that's a long way off. Young George Muller had already been taught that women were different, that there were topics unfit for their ears. Young Johnny Donato had already been taught that it was okay to beat up freaks, faggots, weirdos, okay to taunt them with those names. Even you, Hopkins, you called him weirdo too.

The sun wasn't up yet, but the shredded clouds in the east were beginning to turn pink. Nysa said, "I spread your clothes on the rocks there. But they're probably not dry yet."

Stepping carefully because the brick-like rocks and stickerbushes were real hard on bare feet, Marty made her way over to her uniform. "I guess damp trousers are better than none," she said, starting to pull them on. There were rips in the legs, but they'd give some protection against the thorns. "Is it okay if I keep your shirt a little longer?"

"Of course."

Marty zipped her clammy trousers and leaned over to pick up her damp brown uniform shirt. Then she paused. Was there writing on that rock? "Nysa, look," she said.

Nysa joined her and dropped to her knees. "Man—no, Hans Neu—Neufeld. Hans Neufeld," she read. "Something here—a date, I think, something-something thirty-five." She looked up at Marty. "The cemetery!"

Marty picked up another of the little brick-sized rocks. Unreadable, but clearly something had been cut into it, many rains ago. "So it was here across the river all along!"

Nysa stood and slowly turned in a full circle. "I see," she said. "No, it wasn't across the river when Father Rueger was here. Look." She swept her arm around. "This is a little hill, and all around it's lower. And straight across the water is the fishing rock. Don't you see? This hill used to go all the way across! The river used to loop around this rise!"

"I see," said Marty. "And then it cut through, where it is today."

"Rivers do that all the time. Silt up the slow curves, flood over the necks of loops and cut new channels through the weak points. It's cutting this channel wider right now. I bet those old bones were buried right here!"

Marty made her way to the edge of the water and looked down. It was true—the river was chewing away, undercutting this bank so that chunks of earth had fallen in, leaving a scalloped edge. Somewhere under here it had uncovered a coffin, rotted it open, stolen the bones. She shivered. Nysa had come to her side and touched her arm gently. "It's all right. The river is sacred too."

After last night, Marty figured she'd just as soon look somewhere else for God. But when she glanced at the other woman she stayed quiet. The rosy dawn light splashed lovingly on Nysa's face, and Marty was touched by the sorrow and strength she saw there. *Seize the joy*, Nysa had told her, *because the horrors will seize you.* If the river helped Nysa cope with the horrors that had seized her, maybe she was right, maybe it was sacred.

"I'm glad we found your cemetery," she said. "But maybe we'd better go."

"Yes, we'd better." Nysa smiled and started for the road.

Marty turned to follow, glancing upstream to the east. A red gleam behind the far hills showed where the sun would rise. It flamed the clouds with scarlet and made the river shine as bright as blood.

48

IT WAS MIDAFTERNOON ON FRIDAY. WES SAT AT HIS scarred desk, putting together the material on the White River murders. Foley buzzed him and he said, "Yeah?"

"Mr. Rueger's here, sir."

"Send him in."

"Yes sir."

The door opened, but Bob Rueger was looking back over his shoulder. "Melissa, stay out here. I'll be back in a minute." He turned to Wes as he shut the door and said ruefully, "I hate to leave her even a minute."

"She'll be safe enough with Hopkins," Wes said. "Here, have a seat."

Rueger sat in one of the visitors' chairs. His vibrance was back again, a man ready to burst from his shirt and tie with sheer vitality. Wes lounged back in his desk chair and asked, "What can I do for you?"

"Wanted to thank you," Rueger replied gruffly. "There were problems and false starts, but looking at the whole picture, you folks did some damn good police work."

"Thanks."

"Melissa admits to confusing her trail and hiding from passing cars. I'm amazed your deputy figured out where she was."

"We do our best."

"Well, I just wanted to say that, what with one thing and another, I'm pulling out my investments here. I'm turning them over to Mr. Walters to sell. I'm sure Mr. Walters will get me the best available prices on the properties, since he has a major interest in property values in that area."

"Yeah."

"And I also wanted you to know that the proposal we spoke of briefly yesterday won't be happening. My local partner turned out to be unreliable. I've spoken to the governor, and now he agrees that some of my alternative projects on the other side of the naval property are more desirable."

Alternative projects. So the guy hadn't put all his eggs in one basket. A prudent gambler. Wes tented his fingers. "You've given up on restoring your ancestors' town?"

Rueger smiled again. "Oh, that. It was never that clear that I was descended from Father Rueger directly."

"Aren't you scared, doing this kind of work? Shooting and fighting?" Melissa, her leg in a cast, was fidgeting with her blond hair, spooling it around her forefinger.

Marty looked up from the report she was trying to complete. "Yeah, sure, sometimes."

"I was so scared! I wish I could be tough."

"Being scared is part of being tough." Marty was bone-tired, and the stitches in her arm hurt, and that antibiotic they'd given her made her woozy. But Melissa needed to talk about what had happened. "Being scared gives you power and energy," Marty went on. "If you keep your head you can use that emotion for fuel."

"Really?"

"How do you think you escaped? And stood up to the pain of a broken leg? You're tough, Melissa. Smart and tough." Marty glanced over at the opening door and leaped to her feet. "Mr. Donato!"

"Uh, hello." Carl Donato looked weary, his handsome face long and sad. "Sue said I should let you know I'm here."

"Where have you been? She was so worried!"

"I know. That's why I came back." He was standing uneasily at the door, as though he might bolt again at any moment. "Uh, Mr. Brewster didn't file a complaint against me?"

"Brewster? Why would he— Oh. You're the one who beat him up?"

"He said I didn't have to admit anything."

"Okay, you're right, he didn't file a complaint. You've talked to him already?"

"Yeah, I apologized. See, I was drunk, and so was he."

"You weren't at Clyde's Bar."

"No, I was sitting in my van. See, Sue was so upset. I didn't want to break down in front of her."

"Yeah. So you went out to the van to—to drink." But really to cry. He'd lost his son, and he believed a man wasn't supposed to cry.

"Yeah. I was sitting there, minding my own business, and along comes the professor. He's tanked up too. And he says, hey man, I'm sorry, can I do anything to help? And I said, yeah, get out of this town! A man slaves his life away to keep his family safe, and look what happens! And he said, our project will help you appreciate beauty and history and blah-blah-blah, and give you a better life. Like he'd done us this big favor, moving into the neighborhood and fixing things so—so Johnny—" Carl's fist clenched.

"Yeah," said Marty. "I would've wanted to hit him too."

"I didn't mean to rough him up so bad. And when I saw what I'd done I tried to help him up. But pretty soon he passed out, and I ran. I figured he'd have me locked up, and Sue had enough trouble already."

"But instead he understood what you meant?" Marty remembered Drew in bed, commenting on how different his students' lives were, refusing to snitch on Carl Donato. There was hope for the guy.

"Yeah. When I called home I found out the guy hadn't

mentioned my name, and Sue said to come back. And when I called him he apologized too. Said he was drunk and I was right. Gotta hand it to the guy. I never expected that."

"Tell you what," said Marty. "If Professor Brewster doesn't want to press charges, we'll let it go. Your record's clean and you were under a lot of stress. So go home and hug your wife and daughter, okay?"

"Okay."

"But don't ever let us hear that you've hit anyone. Okay?"

"Yeah." He started out the door.

"And sir—it's okay to cry."

He looked back at her bleakly, and she knew that it would never be okay for Carl Donato to cry.

After Rueger and his daughter had gone Wes stuck his head out the door. "Hopkins!"

"Yessir?"

"I want you on dispatch for five minutes, and I want that report finished. And then I want you outta here for a week."

"A week, sir?"

"You've got all those bandages—"

"Sir, my fingers work okay!"

"You've got bandages, and you're tired, and you lost another gun. You look like hell. Take the week off."

"Yessir. Uh—you said dispatch?"

"Yeah. Foley, get in here a minute."

"Yessir." Foley limped across the room and into Wes's office while Hopkins moved to the dispatch desk.

Wes closed the door. "Want you to hear something." He turned on the recorder. He'd set the tape to 9:00 P.M. yesterday.

"Three twenty-one," said Hopkins's voice.

Silence.

Then her voice again. "Concord. West Street by the maze, across from the appliance store. I saw some footprints on the riverbank that could be Melissa's."

Now Foley's voice, loud and clear. "Could be. You're not sure?"

"I'm looking into it. I'm going over to the Strand farm on

foot and down the creek to the river. Get me some backup, okay?"

"Everybody's busy, b—"

"So'm I. Well, send someone as soon as you can."

And then silence. Wes said, "Foley, I got a pretty good idea of what you erased there."

Foley drew himself up stiffly. "I didn't! She's just trying to make trouble! Erased it herself so she could accuse me—"

"Shit, Don, don't make it worse by lying! The person who accused you was a citizen with a police scanner."

"A citizen, sir?" Foley gave a nervous glance at the door, then back at Wes.

"Hopkins is a team player. Hasn't said a word about it. But you oughta know you're a big star in scanner-land. Lots of people hear you. Lots of people heard the shit you erased."

Foley licked his lips. "It was just a joke, sir. Just teasing her."

"A joke?" Wes let his voice rise. "A joke? Screwing up a tape that might be needed in an investigation is a joke? Teasing a woman officer so she can sue the county for harassment is a joke? Making my department sound like a junior high school locker room is a joke?" He jabbed a stiff forefinger into Foley's flabby chest and yelled into his face. "Ignoring a deputy's request for backup is a joke? Tell me, Foley, does it look like I'm laughing?"

"No sir." Foley's round face had paled.

"One of my deputies almost drowned, Foley, because of your goddamn joke!"

"Sir, I tried to get back to her later. I didn't mean to—"

"Don't give me that." Wes glared at the dispatcher for a long moment, then said, "You're thinking I'm going to fire you, right? Do you out of your nice pension? Nah, not yet. Not unless more gaps turn up on the tapes. If they do you're dead meat. This ain't Watergate. And you're dead meat too if any ugly rumors about Hopkins turn up in this campaign. Understand?"

He licked his lips again. "Yessir."

"You've got one more chance to get back on this team, Foley. Just one. Now get back to your desk."

Foley limped out, looking shaken. Wes sighed as he sat down again. He was betting that the asshole wouldn't figure out that no matter what the rule books said, in this county the treatment of a woman deputy wasn't grounds for firing anyone, especially not a veteran officer with a limp. It'd cost Wes the election.

But hell, who said life was fair?

JayJay had the window seat, and sitting in the middle Bonnie had shown him houses and roads and the topside of clouds. Now he settled down for a moment with a game the flight attendant had given him. Bonnie sighed and closed her eyes. "So tired! I'm glad to be going home," she said.

Justin squeezed her hand. "It'll still be hard," he warned her. "So many terrible things. And some my fault."

"Justin, you believed you were doing the right thing. You were trying to help Nysa. I think you were very brave."

He shook his head. "I don't know how I went so wrong! I had no idea what was really happening!"

"Well, it was their family secret," said Bonnie reasonably. "We didn't know either one of the Strands that well."

Guilt washed over Justin again. He'd known Nysa that well. Why hadn't he known this? And trying to thank her for the help she'd given him, he'd brought more tragedy upon her. He said, "It sure was a terrible chapter in our life story."

"Yeah," said Bonnie lightly. "Or maybe we're a terrible chapter in her life story."

Justin's universe gave a little twitch as God, in Bonnie's voice, explained where he'd gone wrong. He'd seen Nysa only as part of his life story, and hadn't realized that she had a story too, a full life that went on even when he wasn't there. He'd forced himself into her life as though the fragments he knew were the entirety. He closed his eyes and thanked God for humbling him, and prayed for the wisdom to remember that other people had stories too.

God asked, what do you know about Bonnie's story?

This was going to be tougher than he'd thought.

THE THIRD SATURDAY IN JULY

49

"WHY DID THE LITTLE PISTONS THROW THEIR money into the river?" Romey, high on the scaffolding, tested the last section of the frame and pointed across at the board Marty was balancing at her end of the scaffold.

"Because they heard it had a bank." Marty grunted as she shoved the board toward him. They fitted the ends onto the support pipes and stepped on it. It was solid. Romey stretched to touch the top of the gable. He'd taken off his maroon shirt and the sun glistened on his thick-muscled shoulders. *You grew up nice,* he'd told her. So had he.

He glanced across and caught her looking. She pulled her paint scraper from her belt and started scratching at the old paint on the gable. "Romey, don't you know any *new* Little Pistons jokes?"

He picked up a scraper too. "I've got a problem with that, Marty LaForte."

"What?"

"Well, I know it's been a long time since we were in that kiddie pool together." He scraped vigorously, and paint flakes showered down like snow. "The thing is, Marty, these days my piston isn't little."

She rolled her eyes but couldn't help laughing. "Romey! You're such a goofus!"

He grinned and went on scraping.

A red Mazda pulled into the driveway next to Romey's Taurus. "Oh, they're here!" exclaimed Marty. But before she could start down her daughter was swarming up the ladder.

"Hi, Mommy!" Chrissie, fearless, flung herself at her, and Marty braced herself against the pipes to catch her. "This is really cool! Can I paint too?"

Marty squeezed her daughter. Chrissie's dark curls were held back with a yellow headband, and her earrings looked like bright yellow smiling stars. It was so good to hold her again. *Seize the joy*, Nysa said. This was joy.

"Sure, you can paint," Marty said. "But it's hard work. We have to scrape off the old stuff that doesn't work anymore before the new stuff will stick. And you can't wear your good clothes."

"Okay." Chrissie poked a finger at Marty's bandage. "What happened to your arm?"

"Run-in with a bad guy. I'll tell you about it later. I'm fine."

The girl looked at her suspiciously, then at Romey at the other end of the board. "Oh. Hi."

"Romey, this is Chrissie," Marty said. "And this is my husband Brad."

Romey waved amiably at both of them. Brad slammed the door of his car and squinted up at them. "Glad to meet you. You're painting the house, huh."

"No, he's helping with the scaffolding," Marty said. "I'm painting it."

"You're kidding!"

"Nope."

Romey pulled on his shirt and started down the ladder.

"Well," Brad said generously, "it's not a bad idea. It'll add to the value." He was in a blue-and-white shirt, jeans, and boots, and to Marty he looked like a country-western star. "But kitten, it'll take you forever! Why don't you call

Eddie Bronson like I said? He's a buddy—he'll give you a special price."

"I did, and it wasn't special enough."

"But it'll take you forever!"

Marty shrugged.

"Hey, good to meet you." Romey stuck out his hand for Brad to shake. "I hear you've got a radio show."

"Yeah, weeknights in Memphis."

"Got a story your daughter might be interested in." He squinted up at Marty and Chrissie.

"What is it?" Chrissie asked.

He tilted his head at her as though sighting on the hoop. "When I was in Greece I heard a story about the olden days. Seems a princess lived on the shore, and a prince named Theseus came sailing from far away. She fell in love with him, and since she was wiser than he was, she showed him the way to slay monsters and all the usual stuff. And he said, 'Marry me and be my queen!' "

Brad said, "Pretty old-fashioned story." But Chrissie was gazing down at Romey intently.

He went on, "Problem was, Theseus was a forgetful sort of prince, and sailed away without her. The princess was very sad, and she cried and cried. But then one of the gods appeared, and she discovered that she'd really been married to him all along."

"A god?" Marty snorted. "How'd she know he wasn't some dumb goofus with an ego?"

"Maybe he was a dumb goofus, but he reminded her of a divine truth about herself—that she was wise and strong and had important work to do. She was much more than a princess."

Oh, wow. Wow. This guy knew the stories, all right. She remembered Nysa's words about her life's work, *it's like a marriage to a god*. Marty ran her fingers through her hair, and paint chips fell out. She said thoughtfully, "Maybe she hadn't really forgotten who she was. Maybe she'd just been confused for a while because folks like Theseus kept telling her she belonged in the princess pigeonhole, but in her heart she knew all along that she didn't."

"I bet you're right."

Brad said, "You know the stories people are interested in now? Elvis sightings. Swear to God, we get more calls about those than anything."

Impatient with the grown-ups, Chrissie asked, "So anyway, did they live happily ever after?"

Romey looked at her gravely. "There were more adventures later for all of them, and adventures usually have sad times too. But yes, they were all happier after she remembered that she was much more than a princess."

"A good story." Marty stroked Chrissie's curls. "And since she was more than a princess she had important work to do, so she did that. And doing the work made her happy. She didn't have to rush into anything."

The brandy-colored eyes crinkled as Romey grinned and gave her a thumbs-up. "Hey, you know this story better than I do."

"Weird story," said Brad.

Romey smiled. "Oh, it's not over. Listen, man, you ever need a chain saw or a trailer, stop by our place. We've got a great line of party supplies too." He got into his car. "See you soon, Marty."

A goofus, maybe, but not dumb. Not at all. She looked down at Brad, handsome and puzzled, watching the Taurus back off. Shoot, life could sure be confusing.

But hey, it was interesting.

She picked up her scraper and nudged Chrissie. "Okay, kid, there's iced tea in the fridge. Then go get on your old clothes. It's time to get to work."